MacCallister:
Day of Reckoning

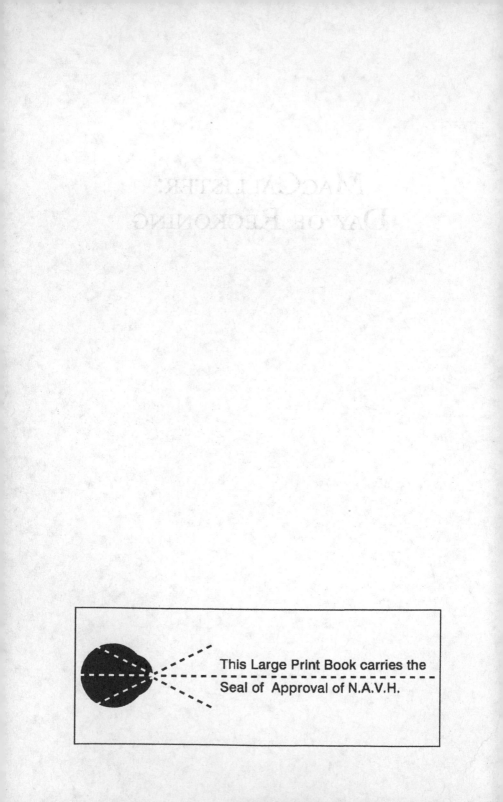

This Large Print Book carries the
Seal of Approval of N.A.V.H.

MacCallister:
Day of Reckoning

William W. Johnstone
with J. A. Johnstone

THORNDIKE PRESS
A part of Gale, a Cengage Company

A Cengage Company

Farmington Hills, Mich • San Francisco • New York • Waterville, Maine
Meriden, Conn • Mason, Ohio • Chicago

LIBRARY OF CONGRESS CATALOGING-IN-PUBLICATION DATA

Names: Johnstone, William W., author. | Johnstone, J. A., author.
Title: MacCallister : day of reckoning / by William W. Johnstone with J. A. Johnstone.
Other titles: Day of reckoning
Description: Large Print edition. | Waterville, Maine : Thorndike Press, a part of Gale, a Cengage Company, 2017. | Series: Thorndike Press Large Print Western
Identifiers: LCCN 2017027746| ISBN 9781432842918 (hardback) | ISBN 1432842919 (hardcover)
Subjects: LCSH: Large type books. | BISAC: FICTION / Men's Adventure. | GSAFD: Western stories.
Classification: LCC PS3560.O415 M32 2017 | DDC 813/.54—dc23
LC record available at https://lccn.loc.gov/2017027746

Published in 2017 by arrangement with Pinnacle Books, an imprint of Kensington Publishing Corp.

Printed in Mexico
1 2 3 4 5 6 7 21 20 19 18 17

MacCallister:
Day of Reckoning

CHAPTER ONE

Archer, Wyoming Territory

The first rider came into town from the north, stopping in front of Mrs. Steinberg's Boarding House. He tied his horse off at the hitching post, then went inside. He was a large man who had once been a prize-fighter, and that occupation had left him with two distinguishing features. His nose had been broken so that the bridge of it lay closer to his face than normal, and he had a cauliflower left ear. He signed his name, Clay Callahan, with tobacco-stained fingers.

"Will you be staying with us for an extended period of time, Mister . . ." Bella Steinberg paused to read the name, "Callahan? The reason I ask is, anyone who stays longer than a month gets a special rate."

"No," Callahan replied. "Just for a few days."

"Oh? Well don't get me wrong, I am most happy to have you, but generally people who

7

stay less than a month take their lodging at the hotel."

Callahan smiled. "I like the homey atmosphere of a boardinghouse," he said.

"Yes," Mrs. Steinberg replied. "All of our residents regard this as their home, and as you will see when you dine with us, it is as if we are one big family."

"That's exactly the way I like it."

Zeke Manning rode into town two days later, checking in to the Adam's Hotel. Manning and Callahan weren't in the same room at the same time until the next evening after Manning arrived. Manning went to the Cock o' the Walk Saloon, where Callahan, who had already been in town for three days, was joking and laughing with the new friends he had made. And though Callahan saw Manning come in, the two men maintained a separation.

In a town as small as Archer, any new visitor was noticed, and several of the saloon patrons commented on getting two new people coming to town within just a few days.

It created even more attention when two more strangers arrived later that same evening. The two men were laughing and talking loudly as they stepped up to the bar.

"Barkeep!" one of them called. "A beer

for me 'n my brother."

The bartender filled two mugs and set them before the brothers. One of the two turned away from the bar and looked out over the ten tables, all of them occupied by from one to four men. A couple of bar girls were hopping from table to table.

"Hello to all here. My name is Dan La-Farge. This is my brother, Don. Anyone here from Texas?"

"Yeah, I'm from Texas," a rather large man said.

"I'm from Texas, too. What about it?"

"We're from Texas, too. Barkeep, give our Texas friends a drink on me 'n my brother."

Dan and Don flirted outrageously with the bar girls and went from table to table, laughing and talking with the other saloon patrons.

Archer was a railroad town, five miles east of Cheyenne, and it was here that the holding and feeding pens were located for shipping cattle. Earlier that day, Duff MacCallister, Elmer Gleason, and Wang Chow had brought cattle here to be shipped out.

"Here you go, Mr. MacCallister, a receipt for the rail shipment of two hundred Black Angus cattle to the McCord Beef Processing Plant in Kansas City. Your beeves will be there in two days," Bull Blackwell said.

Blackwell was the shipping agent for the Union Pacific Railroad in Archer. He got the name "Bull" because he was a big man, with broad shoulders and a somewhat oversized head that seemed to sit directly on those shoulders, without benefit of a neck.

"Thank you, Bull," Duff replied.

"You know, Mr. MacCallister, you have become one of our largest cattle shippers. You are, by far, the largest shipper of Black Angus, and while I would have to examine all the documents to be certain, I can tell you without equivocation that you are in the top five for all of Wyoming."

"Aye, coming to Wyoming was a good thing for me," Duff replied. " 'N I can say, 'tis lucky I have been in introducing the Angus cattle to the American market."

"Luck hasn't had anything to do with it, the way I've heard it told," Blackwell said. "You come to Wyoming and started raising all these black cows that many of the other ranchers teased you about." Blackwell chuckled. "I'd be willing to bet a dollar to a cow turd that nobody is teasing you now."

Duff laughed. "Sure 'n ye meet a lot of people who are willing to bet a cow turd do ye? 'N would be for tellin' me, Bull, what you would do with the cow turd once you won it?"

"Well, I don't really want a cow turd, you understand, it's just . . ." Blackwell stopped in mid-sentence when he saw the twinkle in Duff's eye. "You're funnin' me, aren't you? 'N here I didn't think you Scotsmen had a sense of humor."

" 'Tis thankin' ye I am, Bull, for handling the shipping for me. I'll see you next time I come this way."

"You going back home today?" Blackwell asked.

"Nae, I think I'll ride over to Cheyenne before I go back. Cheyenne is only five miles, and 'tis so infrequently that I am this close that I plan to stay for a day or two 'n enjoy all the benefits of a big city."

To anyone from one of the bigger cities back east, such as St. Louis, Chicago, Philadelphia, or New York, Duff's reference to Cheyenne as a "big" city might sound laughable. But compared to where Duff called home, Cheyenne was a metropolis.

Home, for Duff, was Sky Meadow, a very large ranch that was located about eight miles south of Chugwater. He did his banking there, he shopped there, he had very good friends there, most notably Biff Johnson who owned Fiddler's Green.

11

Biff Johnson was a retired army first sergeant who had served with General Custer. Indeed, Biff had made that last scout with Custer, though he was spared the ultimate disaster because when Custer divided his regiment, Biff was with Captain Benteen.

Biff's saloon, Fiddler's Green, got its name from an old cavalry legend. The legend claimed that any trooper who had ever heard the sound of "Boots and Saddles" would, when they die, go to a broad, inviting meadow, surrounded by shade trees and bounded by a sparkling brook. Then all the old cavalrymen there gathered would have all they wanted to eat and drink, they would enjoy the music of "Garryowen" and "The Girl I Left Behind Me," and sit around telling drunken war tales until the last day.

Fiddler's Green wasn't just a saloon for men, it was more on the order of what the English called a pub, and thus was of the character that decent women did not have to feel out of place while visiting. One woman who was a patron of the saloon was Meagan Parker. Meagan owned a dress emporium in Chugwater, and she and Duff had what could be referred to as a "special" friendship.

Meagan was also Duff's business partner. She had been an early believer in his idea of introducing a new breed of cattle to the area and had loaned him money at a time when he needed it. Duff, long ago, had gathered the wherewithal to repay Meagan, but she didn't want to be repaid. She preferred, instead, to be a part owner of the cattle, and the nature of their relationship was such that Duff found her interest and participation in his ranch to be agreeable enough that he made no effort to disentangle himself for her involvement.

Though he didn't share the information with Bull Blackwell, one of the reasons Duff wanted to go to Cheyenne was because Meagan would be there on a buying trip for her store. They had already planned their rendezvous.

As Duff left the cattle holding lot, he had absolutely no idea of the drama that was occurring at this very moment just down the street in the Cattlemen's Bank and Trust of Archer. There, Callahan, Manning, and the two LaFarge brothers were about to play out the real reason they had come to Archer, for though the four men had arrived in town separately, that had been a subterfuge. They were about to come together to carry out the nefarious scheme they had planned two days earlier.

It was Callahan who went into the bank first to break a fifty-dollar bill, requesting five- and one-dollar bills. Counting out the money, kept the teller preoccupied. Because of that, he paid no attention to Manning who came into the bank shortly thereafter and stepped over to a table, where he began to fill out a bank draft.

A moment later the two LaFarge brothers stepped into the bank as well. It wasn't until then that the teller noticed, with some surprise, that there were so many people in the bank at the same time. But what was even more surprising than the number of customers was the fact that he didn't recognize any of them. And, in his position as bank teller, he knew almost everyone in town.

The two LaFarge brothers raised their guns.

"This is a holdup!" one of them shouted.

"Oh, I'll be damned!" the teller said to Callahan. "I believe they intend to rob the bank!"

"Oh, we not only *intend* to rob the bank, we are going to do it," Callahan said.

"You are a part of this?" the bank teller asked.

"We all four are," Manning said from the

14

table where he had, ostensibly, been filling out a bank draft. Manning, like the two La-Farge brothers, was holding a pistol in his hand.

Callahan handed the teller the pillowcase he had taken from his bed in the boarding-house.

"Empty the cash drawer and the safe, and put the money in this if you would, please."

"Four strangers in the bank at the same time," the teller said. "I should have realized that something strange was going on."

"Shut up and empty the cash drawer and safe like I told you to," Callahan said, his tone of voice little more than a growl.

Complying with the request, the teller filled the pillowcase with money.

"Get the money," Callahan ordered, and Manning took the money from the teller. Then, just as the four men turned to leave, a man and woman came in through the front door.

"Ernie, this is a wonderful day! The collection in church yesterday was the best we've had in a long time!" The man who called out was wearing a black suit and a low-crown, black bowler hat.

"Run, Reverend Pyle, run! The bank is being robbed!" Ernie, the teller, shouted.

"What?" the reverend replied. He was unable to get another word out, because all four robbers began shooting at them. Both the good reverend and his wife went down under a hail of bullets.

The four men ran from the bank and leaped onto their horses, followed out the door by the teller.

"Bank robbery!" the teller shouted. "These men robbed the bank!"

Callahan and one of the LaFarge brothers turned to fire at the teller, and he went down with one bullet in his heart and one in his neck.

Callahan was the mastermind of the robbery, and he had researched it quite thoroughly, including the fact that there was no city law in town, only a sheriff's deputy who didn't spend all his time here.

What he did not know, and could not have possibly anticipated, was the fact that Duff MacCallister was in town. Duff was also, at that very moment, no more than one block away from the bank, and he had both heard the teller's shout and seen the teller shot down.

The four men mounted their horses, then started galloping away from the bank. They were bearing down on Duff, who, in contrast to all the others in town who hurried to get out of the way, had stepped out into the street in front of them.

"Who is that crazy son of a bitch?" Dan LaFarge shouted.

"Shoot him!" Callahan ordered. "Shoot him!"

All four of the bank robbers turned their guns toward the man who was standing, like a statue, in front of them.

With bullets whizzing by him, Duff raised his pistol and fired. His first shot took one of the LaFarge brothers from the saddle.

"Dan!" Don LaFarge shouted.

Don LaFarge was taken down by the second shot.

"Hold it up! Hold it!" Manning shouted, pulling his horse to a halt. "Don't shoot, don't shoot! Here's the money!" Manning, who was carrying the money, threw the bag on the ground and put up his hands.

"Manning, you cowardly bastard!" Callahan shouted. Callahan aimed at Duff, but when he saw Duff's pistol being pointed unerringly at him, he had second thoughts and threw his gun down as well.

Now, with two of the robbers lying dead in the street and the other two still mounted but sitting still, with their hands up, an enraged citizenry began to appear from the buildings where they had taken shelter.

"Two of 'em is still alive," someone said.

"They kilt Reverend Pyle 'n his wife," another said.

"An' don't forget Ernie, they kilt him, too," a third added.

"String 'em up!" someone shouted. "String the bastards up!"

"I'll get a rope!" another shouted.

The shouts were interrupted by Deputy Wallace firing a pistol into the air.

"No!" Deputy Wallace shouted. "There's not goin' to be any lynching while I am here."

"What do you mean while you are here? Where was you awhile ago, when the bank was bein' robbed? Where was you when we needed you?"

"I was having lunch," Wallace said.

"Come on, Larry," one of the angry mob said. "You heard what they done! They kilt the preacher 'n his wife."

"And they'll hang for it," Wallace replied. "But I'm takin' 'em to Cheyenne where they'll get a trial, and then we'll hang 'em all legal like." He looked over at the two men who were still holding their hands in the air.

"And this way, they'll have plenty of time to think about it."

CHAPTER TWO

Deputy Wallace had company for the five-mile ride as he took the prisoners from Archer to Cheyenne. Duff was with him, and so were Elmer and Wang.

"I tell you the truth, Duff, I don't know why you didn't shoot these two the way you did the LaFarge brothers," Deputy Wallace said. "If you'd done that, these two men would be back at the undertaker's parlor with the other two."

"The difference is, the other two men were trying to shoot me," Duff said.

"Hell, the way I heard it told, all four of 'em was shootin' at you."

"Aye, but these two changed their mind and threw down their weapons. And I'm for thinking that it would nae be a good thing to shoot an unarmed man."

"You mean the way these two sons of bitches shot down Reverend Pyle 'n his wife?" Wallace asked.

19

"We didn't know they was unarmed," Manning said.

"A man wearing preacher's garb, 'n his wife standin' right beside him, 'n you didn't know he was unarmed?" Deputy Wallace asked. "Ha. Try that in court 'n see how far it'll get you."

"What are we goin' to do, Callahan?" Manning asked, his voice on the edge of panic.

"We're goin' to hang I reckon," Callahan replied.

"That's the first thing you've said that's right," Deputy Wallace said.

News of what had happened in Archer had already reached Cheyenne, and more than a hundred people lined up on both sides of the street, watching as the little parade of men rode down Central Avenue. Many of them followed the riders, so that by the time they dismounted in front of the sheriff's office, more than a dozen of the citizens of the town were there.

"Is it true they kilt Reverend Pyle?" someone shouted.

"Yeah," another answered. "Shot him 'n his wife down in cold blood they did."

"You two are goin' to hang, 'n I plan to be there to watch," another shouted.

"Hell, why wait? Let's hang the bastards now!"

"You gotta pertect us," Manning said.

"Why?" Wallace asked.

"Because you do! That's your job!" Manning said, his voice breaking with the terror he was feeling.

By now Sheriff Sharpies had come out of his office, accompanied by two more deputies.

"Don't you worry any," the sheriff said. "I'm not going to let anything happen to you two boys. If you're lynched, I won't have any hand in it. But if you're hung legal, I'm proud to say that I'm the one that'll march you two up those thirteen steps to meet the hangman."

"It's goin' to be a public hangin', ain't it, Sheriff?" someone from the crowd asked.

"Oh, yes indeed, it will be public," Sheriff Sharpies answered.

"Then hell, that's as good as us doin' it our own selves, I mean, if we get to watch it 'n all."

"Sheriff, I think you need to know that it was Duff MacCallister that caught these two, 'n he's the one that kilt the other two," Wallace said.

"Yes, I've already been told." The sheriff smiled at Duff. "There was already a two-

21

hundred-and-fifty-dollar reward on each of these men, even before they tried to rob that bank. Looks like you've got a thousand dollars comin'."

"Sheriff, if it's all the same to you, I'd like you to give that money to the orphanage."

"That's damn decent of you, Duff. I know the orphanage will be most appreciative."

When Sheriff Sharpies took the two prisoners into the jail, Duff, Elmer, and Wang rode out to the railroad depot. Elmer and Wang had helped Duff deliver the cattle to the holding pens at Archer, and even had there not been prisoners to escort to Cheyenne, Duff, Elmer, and Wang would have come anyway.

With a wave, Elmer and Wang started back toward Sky Meadow. Duff, who had arranged to meet Meagan in town, decided that he wanted to be a bit cleaner and smell somewhat better for the rendezvous, so he stopped at Mac's Barbershop for a haircut and bath.

"Is that him?"

"Yeah, that's him. That's the son of a bitch that kilt both my brothers."

Eric LaFarge and Ira York were standing just outside Nippy Jones Tavern, which was across the street from Mac's. Eric had been part of the planning of the bank robbery gone wrong in Archer. He had not gone into the bank with the others because his job was to stay back in town to see what sort of posse was put together, then to meet the others at a prearranged place and give them warning.

But there was no prearranged place for them to meet, and there was no posse. One man, Duff MacCallister, had stopped the bank robbers before they even got out of town. And Eric LaFarge had stood helplessly by as he watched MacCallister shoot down both of his brothers.

Blood was strong, and even Ira York felt the connection because he was a first cousin. And it was the blood connection that brought LaFarge and York to this place and this time.

"The son of a bitch just went into the barbershop," York said.

"Yeah, well, he won't come out alive," LaFarge said.

Drawing their guns and holding them down by their sides, LaFarge and York started across the street toward the barbershop.

Mac was just building up some lather when Duff happened to glance out the window.

He saw the two men crossing the street with what could only be described as a purpose-ful stroll. He also saw that both men had drawn their pistols and were holding them down, tight against their legs.

"Mac, get out of here, go into the back room," Duff said in a stern order.

"What?" Mac replied, confused by the unusual demand.

"Just do what I say!" Duff said, even louder. "There are two men coming in here, and there's going to be shooting." Duff drew his own gun and was holding it under the apron.

Mac didn't need any further persuasion.

"Oh, my!" he said in a worried tone as, holding the lather cup in one hand and the brush in the other, he hurried into the back of the shop.

The bell on the door tinkled as the two armed men pushed it open.

"You gentlemen might want to come back a little later," Duff said in a calm voice. "I'm afraid the barber had to step away."

"Yeah?" one of the two men said. "Good, that'll just make killin' you easier."

"Oh? And why, may I ask, would you want to kill me?"

"My name is LaFarge," one of the two men said. "Eric LaFarge."

"Oh, I see," Duff said. "And you were related to the two men I killed?"

"They was my brothers," LaFarge said.

"And do ye be a LaFarge as well?" Duff asked the second man.

"No, I'm Ira York, 'n Dan 'n Don was my cousins."

"Gentlemen, I'm sorry it came to the point where I had to kill them, but they had just robbed a bank and they were trying to kill me. I had nae choice; 'twas either them or me."

"Yeah, well, now it's down to you 'n us," LaFarge said. He brought his pistol up and pointed it at Duff. York followed suit.

"Aye, so it would appear," Duff said. " 'N that bein' the case, I would advise the two of ye to drop your guns now before this goes any further."

"Ha! You would like that, wouldn't you?" LaFarge said.

"Aye, I would like that. I plan to have a good dinner with a beautiful lady tonight, 'n it always puts me off my feed a bit when I have to kill someone. I'd just as soon not have to kill the two of ye, but if I have to, I will."

"I would tell you to say your prayers," La-Farge said. "But you didn't give my brothers time to do even that, did you?"

25

"Their choice, not mine," Duff replied.

"Now!" LaFarge said, thumbing back the hammer on his Peacemaker. York followed suit.

Duff had cocked his pistol even before the two men came into the barbershop, so when he saw them pull the hammers on their pistol, he didn't hesitate. He pulled the trigger twice, the shots so close together that to anyone who may have heard them, they would think only one shot was fired.

Both Eric LaFarge and Ira York went down with a look of surprise on their faces and a bullet in their hearts.

Duff stepped out of the chair and examined both men. They were dead.

"Mac?" Duff called. "You can come out now."

After explaining the situation to Sheriff Sharpies, with corroborating testimony from Mac the barber, the sheriff had the two bodies removed. Duff finished his shave and haircut, then topped it off with a bath. An hour later he checked in to the Mixon Hotel on Central.

"Yes, sir?" the desk clerk said, greeting him with a practiced smile.

"I'd like accommodations for the night if such be available," Duff said.

26

"Yes, sir, we can take care of that," the clerk said, turning the book around to allow Duff to register.

"I'm expecting a lady friend; if she should inquire, please tell her the number to my room," Duff said. "I hope that will nae be a problem."

"No problem at all, sir," the clerk said. "Cheyenne's ladies of the evening are quite familiar with our hotel and need fear no harassment for the practice of their avocation."

Duff looked up from the registration book with a flash of anger in his steel-blue eyes.

"She is *not* a lady of the evening," he said, coming down hard on the word "not" and using the more Americanized negative instead of his more comfortable Scottish "nae" to emphasize his response.

"Of course not, sir, and I beg your pardon for the inference," the desk clerk replied. He took a key down from a marked board on the wall behind him. "Your room is two oh five, sir."

"Very good."

Not long after Duff checked into his room, there was a light knock on his door.

"Duff?" It was Meagan Parker's voice.

Duff opened the door and Meagan stepped inside to an embrace and a kiss.

27

After dinner that evening, Duff took Meagan to the Cheyenne Theater to see Annie Mack Berlein in a production of *Oliver Twist.* There was a reception after the play, and the theater director, James Anderson, introduced the star to Duff MacCallister.

"I know you have heard of our 'wild west,' " Anderson said to the actress. "Mr. MacCallister here is a part of that wild west. Why it was just this morning that he broke up an attempted bank robbery in Archer, killing two of the perpetrators and capturing the other two. Then this afternoon, two other outlaws, seeking revenge, tried to kill him, but Mr. MacCallister bested them as well."

"My," Annie said, flashing a broad smile toward Duff. "I have certainly dealt with 'heroes' on the stage, but I'm not sure I've ever encountered such a person in the flesh."

"Sure 'n 'tis not a word I would apply to m'self," Duff said.

"The accent! Scottish born, are you?"

"Aye."

"Then we share a kinship, for I am Irish born."

"We share a connection beyond that," Duff said. "I met ye 'n your husband once before."

Meagan, who had been standing at Duff's side from the time of the introduction, smiled and breathed a bit easier when she heard that the beautiful young actress had a husband.

"We have met before?" Annie questioned.

"Aye. 'Twas working backstage at the Rex Theater I was, for the production of *The Highlander.*"

"Ah yes, *The Highlander.* It starred Andrew and Rosanna MacCallister, brother and sister, and two of the most skilled and famous actors in New York. Wait a minute. MacCallister? And would you be kin, Mr. MacCallister?"

"Aye, I would be, for 'tis my cousins they are."

"Oh, how exciting. I'll be seeing them again next month; it will give me a great pleasure to tell them that I met their handsome cousin . . . and to pass on news of your heroic exploits."

The next morning Duff and Meagan rode back to Sky Meadow and Chugwater. Chugwater was some sixty miles north of Cheyenne, but Sky Meadow was only thirty miles, so Meagan would spend the night at the ranch.

"It will give me a great pleasure to tell them that I met their handsome *cousin,"* Meagan said, mimicking the actress. However, the smile on her face gave evidence that she was teasing, and not jealous or upset.

"Here now, lass. 'N would ye be for saying that I am nae handsome?" Duff replied, his smile as broad as Meagan's.

"You'll do," Meagan said.

CHAPTER THREE

One week later Duff returned to Cheyenne and was, at the moment, standing on the depot platform with his friends Elmer Gleason and Wang Chow. Elmer and Wang were both holding railway tickets to San Francisco. Their baggage had been previously brought to the depot by stagecoach and had already been checked through.

When Wang first came to work for Duff, there had been times when travel by train had caused problems. No matter what class of ticket Wang bought, he was often relegated to the immigrant car. But over time, and with frequent train trips taken with Duff or Elmer, the Union Pacific Railroad informed Duff that they no longer had such stringent restrictions on travel for those Chinese passengers who could pay full fair.

"From what I've heard," Duff said, "there wouldn't even be a Union Pacific Railroad without all the work done by the China-

31

men." He looked at the two men. "I want ye to do me a favor 'n keep him out of trouble."

"Don't you worry none about Wang," Elmer replied. "I'll keep him on the straight 'n narrow path."

Duff laughed. "Elmer, 'tisn't Wang I'm worried about. 'Tis Wang I'm asking to keep you out of trouble, old reprobate that ye be."

"The man who does wrong is a lonely man. The man who is virtuous is surrounded by friends," Wang said.

"There he goes again," Elmer said, "making one o' them comments that I don't have no idea what he is a-sayin'."

Duff chuckled. "Think about it, Elmer. It'll come to ye."

"Yeah, well, I think what he is sayin' is, nobody likes a bad man but ever'body likes a good man," Elmer said.

"Aye, see there, ye do understand."

"Then why don't he say it like that?"

"Woo, woo, woo! Look at me, Mama, I'm a train!" a little boy shouted, and he darted around the depot platform, moving his arms as if they were the long piston rods connected to the driver wheels. "Woo, woo, woo!"

Before the railroad, the inhabitants of the

far western settlements felt totally isolated from the rest of the world. But they didn't feel that way anymore because they had the telegraph system, which kept them in instantaneous contact with the huge metropolises of the East, and even with great cities of Europe and Asia. There were also the trains, which could traverse in a matter of days vast distances that, but a few years previous, had taken months to cover. The trains meant that produce from farms and ranches could go to markets all over America, while bringing the manufactured goods from factories of the East that could be enjoyed by settlers in the West.

Because of what the railroad meant to the people in the far-flung settlements, the daily arrivals and departures of the trains, even in a town as large as Cheyenne, were cause for spontaneous celebrations. The depot platform filled with people who were neither departing nor meeting arriving passengers, but were merely meeting the trains. There was always a buzz of eager anticipation as the time drew near. And due to the miracle of the telegraph, they were able to keep abreast of the approaching trains so that at any given time they knew whether the train was running a few minutes early, on time, or a few minutes late.

"She's right on time!" someone shouted after the stationmaster made an entry of the latest update on the schedule board. "She'll be here in no more'n ten minutes!"

A few minutes later they heard the sound of a distant whistle, then the chugging of the engine.

"Here she comes!"

There was, of course, no need for the announcement. The approaching train was obvious to everyone now, not only by sound but by sight, for the huge engine arriving from the east came chugging into the station, its bell clanging. Finally it came to a halt with a squeal of brakes and a loud hiss of vented steam.

After the arriving passengers had detrained, the conductor made a big show of examining his pocket watch.

"Board!" he shouted.

"All right, Duff, if you think you can handle Sky Meadow without us, me 'n Wang will be on our way now," Elmer said.

"I'll do the best I can," Duff replied with a chuckle, and with a final round of handshakes, Elmer and Wang boarded the train.

Duff stood on the platform watching as the train pulled out of the station. Riding his horse, Sky, he then led the two horses that had been ridden by Elmer and Wang.

Before starting back he decided he would get something for Meagan. He would have done it when he was here a week earlier, but she was with him for practically the entire time and he wanted it to be a surprise. Stopping in front of a jewelry store, he tied off all three of the horses, then went in and began looking at the display.

He saw a Scottish Celtic knot worked in gold and hanging from a gold chain. It would, he thought, be a perfect gift for Meagan.

"I'll take that," he said, pointing to the pendant.

"Oh, what a wonderful selection, yes indeed," the jeweler said, smiling at the prospect of selling the valuable piece.

With the little gold piece of jewelry tucked away safely in his pocket, Duff left the store.

"Paper, mister?" a young boy said. He was standing on the corner, holding at least a dozen newspapers under his arm.

"Aye, lad, sure 'n I would be happy to buy one."

"Thanks!" the boy said.

Before starting back, Duff took the paper into the Rendezvous, a saloon that he often visited while in Cheyenne. Ordering a scotch, he found a table near the back of the room and began to read the paper.

TRIAL DATE SET
For *Murderers* and *Bank Robbers*

On Monday, the 8th, instant, Clay Callahan, Zeke Manning, and the LaFarge
brothers robbed the bank in Archer. During the robbery, the well-respected and
beloved minister of the Gospel, the Reverend Nathan L. Pyle, and his wife, Anna
Marie, happened into the bank to deposit
the collection made in church on the day
previous.

Callahan, Manning, and the two LaFarge
brothers turned their guns toward these
two innocent disciples of God's Holy Word,
energizing their pistols with deadly effect.
The Reverend and Mrs. Pyle went down
under a hail of bullets, perhaps dead
before they even realized they were in
danger.

As the evil four were leaving the bank
with money in hand, Ernest Jones, the
teller, in an act of bravery that would cost
him his life, stepped out behind them and
gave the alarm that the bank was being
robbed. The evil men then turned their attention toward him, shooting down the
husband and father of two.

But the evil men were soon to meet their
match, for Duff MacCallister, a well-known

rancher from Chugwater, stood in the road before them, as immovable as the Greeks at Thermopylae. In an exchange of gunfire he killed Don and Dan LaFarge, and brought about the surrender of Clay Callahan and Zeke Manning.

In a related story, as published last week, Duff MacCallister was accosted by Eric LaFarge and Ira York. Attempting to see revenge for the righteous shooting of their kinsmen, LaFarge and York were themselves killed. As that shooting was ruled justifiable homicide, there was no need for any further legal action.

As to Clay Callahan and Zeke Manning, however, Judge Commodore Butrum has set the date for the trial on Monday next. The trial will be held here, in Cheyenne, and it is widely expected that a public hanging will soon follow.

"Reading about yourself in the paper are you, Mr. MacCallister?" the bartender asked. He had left the bar and was running a towel across the table that was adjacent to the one where Duff was sitting.

"Hello, Mel," Duff said. "Aye, 'tis guilty I am, though I granted no interview 'n I seek no such notoriety."

"No, 'n I don't think anyone believes such

a thing, either," Mel said. "But I know for a fact that the people of Archer are beholdin' to you for stopping the bank robbers when you did. When banks are robbed, it's the people of the town who are most hurt."

" 'Tis sorry I am that three good citizens of the town lost their lives," Duff said.

"Yes, sir, well, you don't have to be worryin' none about that. Callahan 'n Manning will pay for what they done when they get their necks stretched within the next week or so."

"Aye, I expect they will."

"Will you be here for the trial?" Mel asked.

"I don't expect to be. I signed some statements as to my role. I'm hoping to avoid having to come back."

"Not even to watch the hanging?"

"I take nae pleasure from watching a man hang," Duff said. "I just came to town to see some of my friends off at the railroad depot and thought I'd stop in to have a drink to see me through the ride back home."

"Well I, for one, am glad you did. You're always welcome here, anytime you're in town."

Chugwater, Wyoming Territory
Duff rode into town the next day after he

38

returned to the ranch, to present Meagan with the gift he had bought for her.

"Oh, Duff, this is an absolutely beautiful piece of jewelry!" Meagan said, holding the gold pendant in her hand. "I know I'm supposed to say, 'you shouldn't have,' but I love it too much to say that."

" 'Tis thinking, I am, that 'twould look even prettier around the neck of a beautiful young lady. Now if I could just find such a lass, why we could hang this on her 'n see for ourselves."

"If you can find one?"

"Aye," Duff replied with a broad, teasing smile. "If I can find one."

"Perhaps Miss Willeena Pearcie would serve such a purpose," Meagan replied.

Willeena Pearcie was a matron lady in her late forties who had the misfortune to possess a countenance that was often described as "horse-faced." She was a stout woman who had a stubble of hair over her upper lip that was almost as heavy as a man's mustache.

"Och, woman, ye can be cruel," Duff teased. He hung the piece around her neck, then bent forward to kiss her.

"And now, lass, 'tis asking you I am, if ye would accompany me for a dinner being given by m' neighbors, Captain Culpepper 'n his wife."

"You're sure I would not be an unexpected guest?"

" 'Twas their suggestion that I make the invitation," Duff replied.

"Oh?"

Duff smiled. "After I put forward the idea," he said.

Two days later Duff and Meagan were the guests of Ed and Julie Culpepper, owners of the Twin Pine Ranch. Because Ed was a West Point graduate and had served for many years in the army, he was universally referred to as "Captain."

Twin Pine was adjacent to Duff's own ranch, Sky Meadow, which meant that Ed and Julie Culpepper, along with their daughter, Ina Claire, were Duff's nearest neighbors.

"Both of my parents were Scottish," Julie Culpepper was telling Meagan. "There were some who teased my mother for her brogue, but I think sometimes she just made it stand out even more in response to the teasing."

"Aye," Duff replied. "Sure 'n 'tis an accent that sets you apart from the others. But I've nae wish to lose the tongue, for seems to me that to do so would be to turn my back on all that I held dear."

"Please don't lose it," Julie said. "I love to hear you speak, for it puts me in mind of my mother."

Meagan chuckled. "I have to confess that I love to hear his brogue as well."

"Then why is it, lass, that so often ye mock me for the tongue?" Duff challenged, though the smile on his face ameliorated the words.

"Sure, 'n would ye be for tellin' us now that ye have nae heard that imitation be the sincerest form of flattery?" Meagan responded, mimicking Duff.

"Oh, how well you do that!" Julie said, clapping her hands in delight. " 'Tis like m' own mither ye sound!"

"Lord save me, I've been invaded by Scotland," Ed said with a little laugh.

"Mr. MacCallister, did you bring your pipes?" Ina Claire asked.

Ina Claire was the fifteen-, soon to be sixteen-year-old daughter of Ed and Julie Culpepper.

"Sure now, 'n would I be for coming to visit without m' pipes?" Duff asked.

"I've learned the drum to 'Scotland the Brave,' " Ina Claire said. "I want to play it with you."

"Why, 'tis proud I'd be to play the song with you," Duff replied, "but first you'll

41

have to give me a moment or two to prepare. 'Twould be a sacrilege to be playing such a song without m' kilts."

Duff disappeared into one of the other rooms of the house. When he reappeared a few minutes later, he was wearing kilts, complete with a ceremonial knife called the *sgian dubh,* and the Victoria Cross, the highest honor that could be bestowed by the British Army. He was also carrying his bagpipes.

One month shy of sixteen, Ina Claire was already a very pretty young lady, with hair the color of copper, blue eyes, high cheekbones, a small, well-formed nose, and full lips. She had a drum strapped around her shoulders and she lifted the drumsticks just over the drumhead and glanced toward Duff.

"All right, lass, jump in when you think the time is right," Duff said. He inflated the bag and then started to play. Ina Claire joined in immediately, the roll of her drums matching the keening sound of the pipes. For the next few minutes the stirring tune of "Scotland the Brave" filled the house with music.

"Ahh, lass, you were wonderful on the drum," Duff said when they finished.

"Thank you for playing the pipes with

me," Ina Claire said.

"No, lass, 'tis I who should be thanking you. 'Twas as if I were listening to the Black Watch Pipes and Drum Corps."

"I've made haggis, tatties, and neeps for our dinner tonight," Julie said. "It's my mother's recipe. I hope it's to your liking."

"Och, sure 'n 'tis as if I've gone to heaven," Duff said.

"Meagan," Julie said during dinner. "I've been admiring that beautiful pendant you are wearing. It's the Celtic knot, isn't it?"

"Yes, it is," Meagan said. She took it off and handed it to Julie. "I know that the Scottish Heritage Day celebration will be coming up soon. Would you like to wear it for a few days? Duff was so generous to buy it for me, but I'm sure he wouldn't mind me sharing it with you in this way. You can give it back to me after the celebration is over."

"Oh!" Julie said excitedly. "Are you sure you don't mind, Duff?"

"Who would I be to say that Meagan can nae be generous?" Duff said.

During dinner Duff entertained the Culpepper family with tales of Scotland.

"Oh, it sounds so wonderful," Ina Claire said. "I would sure like to go there."

"Your pa has been promising to take me

there ever since we've been married," Julie said. "One of these days I'm going to hold him to it."

Ed smiled. "How about this fall?"

"Papa! Do you mean it?" Ina Claire asked excitedly.

"Yes. As soon as I market this season's cattle, I think this would be a good time to go. I think you are old enough to enjoy it now."

"Oh, Ed! Thank you!" Julie said.

"I was wanting to save it as a surprise for you, but with the music, our Scottish guest, and this fine meal you prepared, tonight seemed the perfect time to tell you about it," Ed replied.

"Sure 'n 'tis wishing now that I was goin' with ye'," Duff said.

CHAPTER FOUR

After dinner Duff answered dozens of questions about Scotland, then bid the Culpeppers good night before he and Meagan left.

"Meagan, 'tis thinkin' I am that it being so late, 'twould probably be better for you to pass this night at Sky Meadow," Duff said.

Meagan smiled. "If you want me to spend the night with you, Duff, all you have to do is ask. You don't need an excuse."

Duff chuckled. "All right, lass, 'tis askin' I am. Would ye be for spendin' the night with this auld Scotsman?"

"Why, I'd be happy to spend the night with you, Duff MacCallister, wanton hussy that I am," Meagan replied with a laugh.

It was mid-morning of the next day when Duff took Meagan back to town, making the trip in a buckboard as he had some things he needed to pick up for the ranch.

"I should have opened two hours ago," Meagan said as they pulled to a stop in front of her dress shop.

"Och, one of the joys of working for yourself is you never have to explain to the boss why you are late," Duff said.

"That's true, isn't it?" Meagan replied with a little laugh. "I also don't have to explain why a strange man is kissing me in front of the shop." She leaned over to kiss him.

"Strange man, am I?" Duff said after the kiss. "And would you be tellin' me, lass, 'tis it your habit to be kissing strange men?"

"Yes," Meagan replied with an enigmatic smile. "That is, if I find them appealing enough." She kissed Duff again, then before he could react, or even speak, she stepped down from the buckboard.

"It has been a perfectly lovely interruption to my schedule," she said as she started for the front door of her shop.

After picking up the needed supplies, as Duff drove the buckboard back home he spoke to the team of horses.

"Sure now, 'n if I'm not the luckiest man in all of Christendom to have such a fine lady as Meagan," he said.

Dooley Cooper and Pogue Morris had just broken their last dollar to buy a beer. They were sitting at a table in the Hog Waller Saloon, drinking slowly to make the beer last.

"We got to get us some money, somewhere," Morris said. "We're so broke now, I'm thinkin' 'bout actual takin' a job."

"And do what? Punch cows for twenty dollars and found?" Cooper asked. Cooper had a large, purple scar on his face that ran like a streak of lightning from the side of his left eye down across his cheek to hook under his mouth. That was the result of a knife fight that Cooper liked to say "left me permanently scarred, 'n left the other feller permanently dead."

"Twenty dollars looks awful good to me right now."

"What about a hunnert dollars?" Cooper asked. "I'm talkin' about a hunnert dollars apiece."

"Where we goin' to get a hunnert dollars apiece?"

"From the purser on the *Lady Harlie*," Cooper said. "The boat is anchored here right now 'n is s'posed to go upriver to Fort Fetterman tomorrow, takin' some supplies to the soldier boys up there. The boats always start out with two hunnert dollars in cash. All we got to do is slip on board now while there ain't hardly nobody there payin' any attention, then go into the purser's office 'n take the money."

"What makes you think there ain't nobody on the boat payin' no attention?" Morris asked.

Almost as soon Morris asked the question, the squeal of one of the bar girls was answered by the loud laughter of a group of men. There were nine men in the group, all of them wearing blue-and-white-striped buttonless shirts and dark blue trousers. There was nothing of western attire about their clothing. At least two of the men were also wearing jackets and billed caps. One of the men had four silver stripes around the cuffs, the other had two. The remaining seven men seemed to be subordinate to those two.

Cooper pointed toward them. "All them men is from the *Lady Harlie,* 'n the ones that's wearin' the jackets is the officers. There ain't normally never no more 'n ten men on one o' them boats, 'n since they's nine of 'em here now, it's likely there ain't no more 'n one man that's been left on board. Right now would be the best time there is to go on board, take the money, then be gone."

Morris smiled. "Yeah," he said. "Yeah, let's do it."

The *Lady Harlie* lay bow first against the bank of the Platte River, connected by a two-inch-thick hawser that was attached to a forward stanchion on the boat, then wrapped around a wooden post that had been buried deep enough in the ground to be well secure. A lantern hung from a hook on the bow, and two more were at the stern. Besides those three dim lights, there was no other illumination other than the moon itself at this point on the river.

There was no actual fire in the boiler furnace, though it was kept banked so the fire could be quickly rebuilt in the morning to make steam. Because of that, a tiny rope of smoke climbed up from the twin chimneys, and a little wisp of steam curled up from the relief pipe.

Cooper and Morris stepped on board, then looked back along the deck. They saw no one.

"The purser's office is in here," Cooper said. Though Cooper had never been on board the *Lady Harlie,* he did know riverboats, having worked as a deckhand on one until he was fired.

The two men slipped into the purser's office and lit a lantern. Cooper began jerking open drawers until he found a small canvas bag. Opening the bag, he found two hundred and twelve dollars.

"What did I tell you?" Cooper asked with a broad grin.

"Yeah, that's good. That's real good."

"What are you doing back on board, Mr. Roland? I thought you were going to stay in town tonight and . . ." the sailor who was asking the question stopped as soon as he realized this wasn't the purser, or anyone he knew.

"Who are you? What are you — ?"

That was as far as he got before Morris, who, because he had stepped behind the door and stayed out of sight, stepped up behind the sailor and stabbed him in the middle of the back.

The sailor went down with a muffled groan.

"Help me move him," Cooper said. "We'll tie him on a log and set him adrift. The crew will think he ran off with the boat's money."

Cooper and Morris went back into town, where they bought themselves a late dinner before returning to the Hog Waller for more drinks, and spent the night with a couple of the bar girls.

The newspaper the next day carried the story.

DECKHAND STEALS PURSE FROM THE *Lady Harlie*

The *Lady Harlie,* which was en route from North Platt, Nebraska, to Fort Fetterman, had, as the riverboats often do, put in here at Hartville for rest and restocking of the boat's larder. Also, as often happens, the purser drew two hundred dollars on a draft drawn from the Platte River Transport Company.

During the night, while all the crew but one had come to town, the remaining crewman, a deckhand by the name of Abner Keller, took advantage of being the only one on the boat and stole the money from the purser's office. Keller has since disappeared, no doubt to visit his criminal ways on some other innocent and unsuspecting person.

"Look here," Morris said, having read the story over the supper they were enjoying at Kirby's Café. "You were right."

Cooper read the story and chuckled. He started to hand the paper back, when another story caught his attention.

"Oh, damn," he said.

"What is it?" Morris asked.

"Here's a story that was picked up from the Cheyenne newspaper. A couple of real good friends of ours is in bad trouble."

"Who are you talkin' about?"

"Clay Callahan and Zeke Manning."

Cooper showed Morris the article in the newspaper.

"We have to go get 'em out of jail," Cooper said.

"Why?"

"Why? 'Cause I think they'd do the same thing for us, iffen we was to be in the same fix," Cooper replied.

"Yeah, but we ain't in the same fix."

"We might be some day, 'n it would be good to have somebody like Callahan owin' us."

"All right," Morris agreed. "If you're a-wantin' to do somethin' like that, well, I'm willin' to go along with you."

Twin Pine Ranch

Captain Culpepper was drawing a bucket of water from the well when he saw two riders approaching. Seeing riders out on the road was not that unusual, but these two had come through the gate and were coming up the approach to his house.

He set the bucket on the edge of the well and waited until the two were close enough to engage in conversation.

"Howdy," he said. "What can I do for you?"

"We'd like to fill our canteens at your well if you don't mind," one of the riders said. The rider had a prominent purple scar on his cheek.

The other rider nodded toward a watering trough. " 'N maybe water our horses?" he added.

"Sure, climb down, help yourself to the water," Culpepper offered. He extended his hand. "I'm Captain Culpepper and this is my place."

"Captain?" one of the two men said.

Culpepper chuckled. "I'm sorry, in truth I'm no longer a captain. But I was for quite a while and many of my neighbors still refer to me in such a way."

"Well, Cap'n, I'm Dooley Cooper, this here is Pogue Morris," the taller of the two men said.

"Been traveling long?"

"Most of the day," Cooper said. "We're goin' to Cheyenne to see a couple of friends of our'n."

Morris took the two horses over to the watering trough as Cooper began filling the

53

canteens.

"You got no hands on the place?" Cooper asked.

"No need for 'em at the moment," Ed said. "We just sold off what cattle we're goin' to for the year, and I'm afraid I don't have a large enough operation to afford any full-time employees. What cows we got left can shift for themselves until roundup time next spring. Why, are you looking for work?"

"We'll probably be goin' into business with our two friends in Cheyenne," Cooper said.

"Oh? What kind of business would that be?"

"First one thing and then the other," Cooper replied.

"Ed?" Julie called from the porch. "I see that we have visitors. Dinner's about ready and there's plenty. Why don't you invite them to sit at the table with us?"

Culpepper chuckled. "My wife is big on having company. I'm sure it comes from living in such an isolated place. Would you like to eat with us? That is, if you aren't in any particular hurry."

Morris was returning at that moment, leading the two horses who had drunk their fill at the trough.

"Did you say come eat with you?" Morris asked.

"Yes. Unless you are on some schedule and have to move on."

"No, we ain't got no particular schedule," Morris said. "I don't know about Dooley here, but I'm hungry and appreciate the invite."

By the time the three went into the house, Julie, anticipating that the invitation would be accepted, had already set two extra plates at the table.

"This is my wife and this is my daughter, Ina Claire," Ed said, introducing the two men to the women of the house. "Ina Claire will be turning sixteen soon, but she'd have you to think it'll be twenty-one," he added with a little laugh.

"Well, I for one appreciate that she shows such maturity," Julie said. "Think of how many girls her age give their parents nothing but grief."

Ed smiled at Ina Claire. "I agree," he said. "And I wouldn't have it any other way."

Conversation flowed during the meal. Cooper and Morris said that they had been soldiers once, and since getting out had spent some time in the Medicine Bow Mountains looking for gold.

"We didn't find none, though," Morris said.

"I have to confess that I don't know much about the Medicine Bow Mountains," Culpepper said.

"I'll tell you this about 'em. If ever a fella was wantin' to hide out, you could stay in them mountains 'n nobody would ever find you," Morris said.

"Oh, heavens," Julie said with a little shiver. "I would hate to think that I would have to be somewhere totally devoid of civilization."

"Why would you want to do that, anyway?" Culpepper asked.

Cooper shot a reproving glance toward Morris.

"Oh, uh, no particular reason," Morris said. "What I was talkin' about was if some fella was wantin' to hide out." He smiled at Julie. "But I'm like you, Miz Culpepper. Them mountains ain't a place I'd ever want to spend any time in, to speak of. I'm just glad that I ain't someone that needs to hide out from anybody."

"Did you men like soldiering?" Ed asked.

"None too particular," Cooper replied. "That's why me 'n Pogue got out, quick as we could."

"Ed was in the army," Julie said. "We lived

56

at Fort Lincoln."

"Yes, I told them, dear," Ed said.

"I remember when we were in the army," Ina Claire said. "I don't remember it very well though."

"Well, I don't see how you could. You were only six years old when your father resigned his commission," Julie said.

"That's when you was a captain?" Cooper asked.

"Yes."

"Was you in the war?" Morris asked.

"No, I graduated from West Point in sixty-seven, after the war was over. I was with the Seventh Cavalry, but during Custer's last fight, I had been detached from the Seventh and was with General Cook. By the time General Cook arrived at the battlefield, it was all over."

"He was very lucky that he wasn't with Custer on that fateful day," Julie said. "It was after that battle, when Custer, Keogh, and so many of Ed's friends were killed, that I begged him to leave the army."

Ed chuckled. "And if you men ever get married, you will learn that the most important thing you can do is keep your wife happy."

An hour later, Dooley Cooper and Pogue Morris, with food provided by Julie so they "would have something to eat for their supper," said good-bye and rode off, headed north.

"I'm glad they're gone," Ina Claire said.

"Why?"

"They were frightening looking. Especially the one with the scar on his face. I've never seen such a scar."

"You heard them," Ed said. "They were in the army. It could be that Mr. Cooper got that scar from an Indian war club."

"I suppose so," Ina Claire said. "But still, I'm glad they're gone."

CHAPTER FIVE

Chugwater

That same day Duff was standing at the bar of Fiddler's Green Saloon, nursing a scotch whiskey that the proprietor, Biff Johnson had just poured from the private stock he kept exclusively for Duff.

"How did you find Cap'n Culpepper?" Biff asked.

"It wasn't hard, I just went a bit west from m' ranch, and there he was," Duff replied.

For a moment Biff was confused, then, seeing the smile on Duff's face, he realized that it was a joke and laughed.

" 'Twas not much of a joke, I admit," Duff said. "But to answer your question, the captain seemed to be in fine spirits, aye, 'n his wife 'n daughter, too. The wee lass 'n I played the pipes and drum together."

"I saw them when they were in town last week. The 'wee lass' as you call her isn't so wee anymore. She's growing quickly into a handsome young lady."

"Aye, 'n 'tis sixteen she'll be soon," Ed said.

"Sixteen is it? And I remember well the day she was born," Biff said. "Born at Fort Lincoln she was, and you never saw anyone any prouder than Cap'n Culpepper was that day. He gave cigars to all the NCOs in his command. He was a good officer, as fine an officer as I ever served under. I've no doubt he would've made general if he had stayed."

"As I understand, 'twas the missus who talked him into leaving," Duff said.

"Yes, when he was detached from the rest of us, and sent to be a liaison with General Cook, it was that, and that alone, that kept him from being killed. He had just taken over C Company, which was Tom Custer's company, and the general was goin' to make his brother his adjutant. But, when General Terry detached Cap'n Culpepper from the Seventh, Tom Custer kept his company for one more scout. If Cap'n Culpepper had taken the company as originally intended, he would've been killed.

"Anyway it was after that, that Mrs. Culpepper was convinced that was God telling him to get out of the army, and he listened to her."

"You left soon after as well," Duff said.

"Yes. When Cap'n Culpepper was detached to be with Cook, I was reassigned to Benteen, and when Cap'n Culpepper left the army, my assignment to Benteen became permanent. I tell you the truth, Duff, I hated that son of a bitch, and I knew that the day would come when I wouldn't be able to keep myself from knocking him on his arrogant ass. What with Benteen being a captain and me being a sergeant, well, I don't have to tell you that would not have turned out well for me. I had enough time in for my pension, so I retired."

"And 'tis happy I am that you did, for had you not, where would I go for m' Glenlivet?" He lifted his glass.

"It's always a pleasure to serve a man who has a genuine appreciation for the finer things," Biff said. He chuckled. "Now you take someone like Elmer, he'll drink anything I put in front of him."

"Aye, Elmer does have what you might call an eclectic taste," Duff replied with a grin.

"Eclectic?" Biff laughed. "Does that mean he'll drink anything?"

"Aye, within reason."

"How long do you reckon Elmer and Wang will be gone?"

"A week, maybe two."

"That's left you sort of short-handed, hasn't it?"

"Not terribly so. This is a slow time, and I have half a dozen men who are watching over things."

"Will you be calling on Miss Meagan today?" Biff asked.

Duff chuckled. "Sure now, and 'tis necessary for me to visit with the lass from time to time. After all, she is my partner, so 'tis a matter of business, as I'm sure you ken."

Biff laughed. "Don't tell me it's all business. You could buy her out as easily as snapping your fingers."

"Aye, but would ye be for telling me, First Sergeant, why I would want to buy her out?"

"Why indeed? There's not a prettier woman in town, that's for sure. But don't let my wife know I said that," he added with a smile, and holding his index finger up in warning.

"Your secret is safe with me," Duff said. Finishing his scotch, he held up the empty glass. *"Bacchus' blessings are a treasure, drinking is a soldier's pleasure."* Setting the glass on the bar, and with a good-bye nod, Duff took his leave.

Before heading back to Sky Meadow, Duff went to see Meagan.

"I saw you ride into town earlier today,

and I was hoping you would stop by to see me," she said by way of greeting.

"Meagan, m' lass, 'n did you think I would come to town 'n nae stop to see ye?"

"I've something I would like to show you," Meagan said. She took a dress down from a rack.

"I made this for Ina Claire for her birthday. I had to look through some old books that I had, but I found it," Meagan said. "Here it is. What do you think?"

The dress was white, with a plaid of small stripes of black, blue, and red. It was bound by a silver buckle just below the breasts.

"Och, you did a wonderful job with it, Meagan. I remember such dresses worn by all the ladies back home."

"What is it called?" Meagan asked.

"This is called an *arisad*. 'Tis the traditional lady's dress of Scotland."

"Do you think it's wrong of me to give her such a gift?" Meagan asked. "I wouldn't want her mother or father put out with me for imposing myself into the family with such a gift."

"Hasn't the lass learned the Scottish drum? And isn't her mother half Scot?" Duff asked.

"Of course the answer is yes, to both questions," Meagan replied.

"Then I think the lass and her parents would be most pleased for you to think of her in such a way."

"I got the idea when I heard the two of you discussing performing together at the upcoming Chugwater Festival. What a treat that will be," Meagan said with a broad smile. "Would you come with me to present it to her?"

"Nothing would please me more," Duff replied.

Night had fallen, and all in the Culpepper house had gone to bed.

"Oh, Ed, were you serious when you said that we would go to Scotland?" Julie asked.

"Quite serious," Ed replied. "I know that you have always wanted to see the land of your mother's birth, and I confess, I've always been curious about it myself. We'll visit Scotland, England, and Ireland. It will be a fine trip."

"Oh, and how wonderful it will be for Ina Claire," Julie said. "It is something she will remember for the rest of her life."

Cheyenne, Wyoming Territory
Cooper and Morris were in the Rendezvous Saloon, standing at the end of the bar and separated from many of the other custom-

ers who were at the same bar.

"We shouldn'ta told that feller we was in the army," Cooper said.

"We ain't in the army no more," Morris said.

"Yeah, we are. I mean, yeah, we ain't actual in the army, seein' as we ain't still at the post or nothin' like that. But we didn't get discharged, we deserted, 'n that means if we was to get caught, we'd more'n like be brought back to the army to be court-martialed."

"I reckon that's right, but why did you say we oughtn'ta tole that Culpepper feller that we was in the army?"

"On account of because he was a captain, 'n officers kinda all stick together. We told him our real names, 'n he might find out we was deserters."

"What difference does that make, anyhow? It ain't like we'll ever see 'im again," Morris said.

"Yeah, I reckon you're right about that."

The two were quiet for a moment, as if lost in thought, then Morris spoke again.

"Are we going to the trial?"

"Yes, we're going to the trial. Why the hell do you think we came here in the first place?"

"I was just wonderin', I mean, seein' as

what we done in Hartville 'n all. I thought maybe we ought to lay low for a while."

"Why? We spent two more days in Hartville without nobody suspectin' anything a-tall. If nobody suspected us in Hartville, what makes you think they would suspect us here?"

"I don't know. I was just thinkin', if somebody found the deckhand's body, they might start wonderin' who it was that actual done it."

"More'n likely that deckhand has done been ate up by bears or wolves or somethin'," Cooper said. "And even if they do find him, all they'll know is that he warn't the one that done it. They still won't have no idee who it really was."

"I guess you're right," Morris said.

"Damn right, I'm right. There didn't nobody see us, did they? I mean, if anybody was suspectin' us, Cap'n Culpepper would've maybe knowed about it. Only he didn't know nothin', which is why he brung us in to eat with 'em 'n all."

Morris smiled. "We did get away with it, didn't we, 'n we still got money."

"Yeah, 'n after we get Clay 'n Zeke out, we'll have even more money."

"How do you know?"

"I know because Clay is real smart about

66

things like that. He'll figure out just real quick where we'll be able to come up with some more money. 'N knowin' him, I expect it'll be a lot of money."

"Yeah, well, he didn't do all that good with the bank he tried to rob in Archer, did he?"

"More'n likely it was because of them La-Farge brothers," Cooper said. "I knowed all three o' them LaFarge brothers, 'n there warn't none of 'em was worth a tinker's damn."

Morris looked up at the clock. "Yeah, well, if we really are a-goin' to the trial, we prob'ly need to get goin'. It'll be startin' just real soon now."

Callahan saw Cooper and Morris as soon as the deputy brought him and Manning into the courtroom. Like Manning, his hands were shackled in front of him and secured to a chain that went around his waist. His ankles were shackled as well, not only to each other but also to the shackles around Manning's ankles. As a result, they were able to move only with very small and coordinated steps.

Callahan nodded at Cooper, who returned his nod, then inclined his head toward the door. Callahan correctly interpreted that as a signal that Cooper and Morris would break them out of jail. He smiled.

"What are you smilin' at?" Manning asked. Callahan realized then that Manning hadn't seen them, and he decided not to tell him. Manning was too easily excitable and might not be trusted with the secret.

"I just thought of somethin' funny is all," Callahan said.

"There ain't nothin' funny 'bout this," Manning replied in a whining tone. "There ain't nothin' funny about it a-tall."

When Circuit Judge Commodore Butrum stepped into the courtroom, the bailiff gave a loud shout, bringing an instant halt to the buzz of conversation.

"All rise!"

There was a scrape of chairs and the rustle of skirts and trousers as more than one hundred people responded to the bailiff's call.

A black judicial robe covered the judge's rather corpulent frame, and his head was bald. He took his seat behind the bench.

"You may be seated," he said.

As the defendants, counsel, and gallery sat, Judge Butrum removed his glasses and began cleaning the lens, doing so as if totally unaware that his action was being observed by so many people.

"Why the hell don't he get on with it?" Zeke Manning hissed. Their lawyer, Dan Gilmore, had tried unsuccessfully to separate the trials.

"Shh. You'll be found in contempt," Gilmore whispered.

"What's that mean? He'll give us thirty days in jail before he hangs us?" Callahan asked with a mirthless laugh.

Judge Butrum put his glasses back on, very methodically hooking them over one ear at a time. He nodded at the bailiff, and the bailiff opened the door to allow the jury to enter.

Twelve men came in, and without looking at anyone in the gallery, or either of the two defendants, they took their seats in the jury box. Judge Butrum addressed them.

"Gentlemen of the jury, have you reached a verdict?"

The jury foreman stood. "We have, Your Honor."

"What is your verdict?"

The jury foreman, who owned a wagon freight company, pointed at Callahan and Manning. "We find both of those low-assed sons of bitches guilty of murder in the first degree."

The gallery laughed, and Judge Butrum brought his gavel down hard, the loud bang-

69

ing of the gavel rising above the sound of laughter.

"This is a solemn moment," the judge said gruffly. "There will be order in my court. Counselor for the defense, please bring the two defendants before the bench."

"Let's go," Gilmore said to his two clients, and he, Callahan, and Manning moved to stand before the judge.

"Clay Callahan and Zeke Manning, you have both been represented by counsel, supplied to you by the state. Your trial was heard and your fate decided by a jury of your peers. This means that you have both been accorded all the rights provided you by the Constitution of the United States, and because of this, there can be no appeal based upon any denial of rights or court procedure. Do both of you understand that?"

"Yeah, yeah, we understand it," Callahan said. "Get on with it, you fat-assed bastard."

There was an audible gasp from the gallery.

"Oh, I will, Mr. Callahan, I will," Judge Butrum said. "Clay Callahan and Zeke Manning, you have both been found guilty of murder in the first degree. It is, therefore, the ruling of this court that you be remanded to jail, where you will remain to

70

await the construction of a gallows. Then, two weeks from this date, at the hour of ten o'clock in the morning, you will both have a hangman's noose put around your necks and be placed upon a platform that is so constructed that it can be opened under you, thus allowing the two of you to drop into eternity.

"May God have mercy on your souls, for I have none. Sheriff, return these two men to the cell." The judge brought his gavel down sharply. "Court is adjourned."

When Callahan stood, he turned to look back to where he had seen Cooper and Morris, but they were no longer there. He was glad they weren't, because he didn't want there to be a chance that Manning might see them.

Callahan began to whistle a little tune as he and Manning, coordinating their shuffle as before, left the courtroom to be returned to jail.

"What the hell you so happy about, Callahan?" the escorting deputy asked.

"You like snow?" Callahan asked.

"Snow? No, I ain't none too particular about it. Why do you ask about snow?"

" 'Cause this here is June," Callahan replied.

"What?"

"This here is June, 'n I'm about to be hung. That means I won't be here this winter, 'n I won't have to be puttin' up with all the cold and the snow like you will."

"You are as crazy as a loon," the deputy said. "Come on, get a move on it. I want to get you two back in your cell so I can go eat my lunch."

"Why don't you take these ankle shackles off, 'n maybe we can walk a little faster?"

"Ha! You are a real funny man, Callahan, you know that? Let's see how funny you are once you got that rope around your neck."

CHAPTER SIX

San Francisco

"I am most pleased to meet the esteemed relatives of my good friend Wang Chow," Elmer said to an elderly Chinese couple. The man had a white mustache that curved around his mouth, and a long, very narrow beard that hung almost like a white string from his chin. The woman had a round face and white hair that was held in place by long, ivory pins. This was Mr. and Mrs. Yo Sinh, Wang Chow's aunt and uncle.

Elmer had spoken in Chinese, and Yo, with a broad grin, responded in the same language, speaking very quickly.

"Wait, hold on there, pardner," Elmer said, holding his hand up, palm out, facing the Asian gentleman. "I can speak a little of your lingo, but it don't come easy to me."

Wang translated what his uncle had said.

"He says that he is pleased to meet the man who has befriended his nephew." Wang laughed. "And he says that you have the lines of age in your face and it is good that I have befriended an old man."

"Old man? Let me get this straight. Your uncle is calling me an old man?"

Wang laughed again. "You are old, Elmer. But you should be proud that Yo has spoken of you in this way, for my people have great respect and honor for those who are old. They believe that with age comes much wisdom and humanity, for one must have those attributes to become old."

"Wisdom, huh?" Elmer replied. He smiled, then put his hands together, prayer like, and dipped his head toward Yo. "Tell him that I appreciate his kind words and that I honor him as well."

During the ensuing visit and dinner, Elmer impressed the Chinese with his occasional remarks in Chinese and his dexterous use of chopsticks.

"Mr. Gleason was a sailor," Wang told his family and friends, explaining his use of the language as well as his expertise with the chopsticks. "He has sailed all over the world and has visited China many times."

Although Wang now knew much more about Elmer's past, including the fact that he had been a guerrilla fighter for the South during the Civil War, and that after the Civil

War he had, for a while, ridden the owl hoot trail, he didn't share any of that with his family for fear they would think less of him.

It wasn't until the dinner was completed, and after a demonstration of *wu shu* by some very young students of the martial art form, that the expression on Yo's face indicated his concern over something. The women and children left, so that only Elmer, Wang, and Yo remained in the room, all three sitting on individual rugs.

"You are troubled, Uncle," Wang said, speaking in English so Elmer didn't feel left out.

"Shi de," Yo replied. "Yes," he translated, then he continued in English, thinking it would be rude to speak in front of Wang's friend without including him in the conversation. "Our little neighborhood has been threatened, and some have been forced to pay much money to prevent evil from falling upon us."

"Who is the person doing such a thing to you?"

"It is not one person," Yo said. "It is the *Boo how doy* of the Tong."

"It's the what?" Elmer asked.

"Boo how doy," Wang said. "Killers, hired by the Tong to enforce their bidding."

"They demand that we pay money in

tribute," Yo said. "They have taken two hostages, one an old woman and one a young girl. They are both of the family of Mr. Huang. One is his mother and one is his daughter. They are asking money from Mr. Huang and all of his neighbors. If Mr. Huang, his friends, and neighbors do not pay them, they will kill Mr. Huang's mother, and if they are still not paid, they will kill the daughter the next day."

"Does Mr. Yo think they will follow through with their threat?" Elmer asked.

It was not necessary for Wang to translate the question, Yo understood and responded immediately, speaking in English.

"In the month before this one, some men of the Tong took an old man and his grandson from the family of Mr. Chang. They demanded money, and when they were not paid on the first day they killed the child, then lay his dismembered body in front of the Quang Ming Buddhist Temple. The tribute was paid, and on the next day Mr. Chang's father was released, but he is stricken with guilt because he could not save his grandson, and now he is unable to speak."

"How much money are they asking for?" Wang asked.

"They are asking for a lot of money, ten

76

thousand dollars."

Elmer let out a low whistle. "You're right," he said. "That's a hell of a lot of money."

"Does Mr. Huang have that much money?" Wang asked.

"He does not."

"What about family? Friends? Neighbors?" Wang asked.

Yo shook his head slowly. "I do not think that much money can be raised by the Huang family or all of his friends. I fear the worst for them."

"Where can we find the sons of bitches?" Elmer asked.

"He?" Yo responded.

"Where are the Tong gathered?" Wang repeated the question in Chinese, eschewing the "sons of bitches" part. "Do you know?"

"Yes, I know. They are in a building on the corner of Grant and Sutter," Yo replied, speaking in English so that Wang would not have to translate for Elmer.

"Wang, what do you say we pay those bastards a little visit?" Elmer suggested.

Wang smiled. "It would bring me great pleasure to make such a visit," he replied.

"I do not believe you can talk them into releasing their hostages," Yo said.

"Oh, honorable uncle of my friend Wang,

I do not plan to do any talkin' to those low-assed bastards," Elmer said resolutely. "I intend to kill the sons of bitches."

After staying long enough that their departure would be neither too early, which would be discourteous, nor too long, which would be an infringement upon Yo's hospitality, Elmer and Wang left. It was dark outside, though Bush Street was well illuminated by gaslights at the corners. There were few people on the streets, and those who were, were engaged in avocations that were best not pursued in the light of day.

Elmer and Wang took a trolley to an area close to, but not directly at, the address Yo had given them for the location of the Tong. There were no gas lanterns in this area of town, the only light being that which was cast in small squares from the buildings they passed. The aroma of incense hung heavily in the air, and they passed a small building that had the large front door rolled up on a track, thus disclosing the interior of the building. This was an opium den. The room was redolent with the perfume of burning incense sticks, and dimly lit by a few, flickering candles. There were in the room four Caucasian users in semiconscious stupors, lying on the couches. One of the men looked directly at Elmer as he and Wang passed by, but Elmer was certain the man wasn't seeing him.

When they reached the building that Yo had said would house the Tong, the ground floor was dark. There were lights coming from the second floor, and loud and animated conversations could be heard through the open windows.

"What are they talking about?" Elmer asked. "Are these the people we are after?"

Wang listened for a moment, then he nodded. "Yes, it is as my uncle said. They are holding an old woman and a young girl as hostage, and they expect to get ten thousand dollars for the hostages."

"The evil bastards."

Wang listened for a moment longer. "There are eight Tong in the room."

"What? How the hell do you know that? You got some secret power that lets you see through walls or something?"

Wang smiled. "I counted the voices."

"Ah, then you don't know that there are only eight, do you? What you mean to say is that there are eight who have spoken. Hell, for all we know there could be twenty in there," Elmer said.

"Yes, only eight have spoken, but there could be more."

"Well, hell, Wang, you didn't have to agree with me," Elmer said. He drew his pistol, then, because he always carried it with the firing pin resting on an empty chamber, he slid a bullet into that chamber as well. That gave him six rounds to be used when the ruckus started. If there were only eight of them, and of course he had only Wang's estimate of the number, he would still be two bullets short.

By coincidence, Wang took out two throwing stars. The throwing stars weren't Wang's only weapons. He also had two knives, but Elmer knew him well enough to know that Wang's hands and feet were as formidable as any weapon. Wang had been trained in the martial arts in a Shaolin temple and was a priest of that movement, a kung fu master.

"How do we want to play this?" Elmer asked.

"We will kill all in the room except the woman and the child," Wang said.

Elmer chuckled and nodded his head. He cocked his pistol. "Sounds like a plan to me," he said.

The ground-level door was locked, but Wang picked it as quickly as if he were using a key. Immediately inside the door was a stairway, dark except for a bit of ambient light at the base of the stairs, while at the top of the stairs a tiny sliver of light slipped under the door.

Without a word, Wang went up the stairs, climbing slowly and quietly. Elmer went up behind him.

There was no landing at the top of the stairs; the steps ended right at the door. There was a large guffaw of laughter from the other side of the door, just as they arrived.

"Are you here?" Wang asked in a low voice.

"I'm here and ready," Elmer replied.

Wang lifted his leg, then kicked the door, right next to the doorknob. The door lock gave way with a large smash, and the door swung open.

"Ya!" one of the occupants of the room shouted in surprise. If he intended to say anything else the words died with him, because with a rapid flip of his wrist, Wang buried a throwing star in his forehead. Almost as quickly a second man went down with another throwing star buried in his neck.

Elmer began shooting. He fired three times in quick succession, and three men went down.

Wang had been correct in his assessment as to how many Tong had been in the room, because five were now down and three remained standing. Elmer shot two more while Wang took out the last man with a knife to his heart.

With eight men down, Elmer walked around checking each man. All were dead.

From the moment they entered the upstairs room, neither Wang nor Elmer had spoken a word. Wang recovered his throwing stars and knife, wiping the blood from the blades on the clothing of the victims.

"Mrs. Huang, we have come to return you and the child to your family," Wang called out. When he didn't get an answer he tried again, this time adding a phrase Yo told him to use, to prove to Mrs. Huang that Wang actually did represent her son.

"The red and yellow roses honor the spirit of your husband."

"We . . . we are in here!" a woman's voice called back from beyond a second door.

Wang frowned at the response, perceiving a sense of fear. Of course, under the circumstances, some fear was obvious. But he was certain that the words Yo gave him to use would ease her fear. Unless there was still someone in there with her.

Pulling both knives and holding one in each hand, Wang stepped up to the door. This door opened outward, toward them, and he nodded toward Elmer, indicating that Elmer should open it.

Elmer put his hand on the knob, turned it, then jerked it open. Wang stepped through the open door, then with a knife in each hand threw his arms out beside him, with the blades of the knife pointing to the rear. He thrust both knives backward and felt the blades bury themselves into flesh. With an audible groan of pain and surprise, the final two Tong, who had been standing on either side of the door to surprise him when he went into the room, were themselves surprised. Wang pulled both knives free as he let the two men tumble to the floor.

Elmer, with his gun reloaded, stepped into the room just behind Wang. Learning quickly that there was no need for the gun, Elmer looked across the room to see an elderly woman and a young girl, tied back to back. The older woman's eyes grew wide in fear when she saw an armed white man coming into the room.

"It is not to worry," Wang said with a calming smile. "This man is a friend of mine, and he will help me take you home to your family."

Overcome with joy and relief, the woman began spewing an almost unbroken stream of words. Wang cut the ties that bound

83

them, and both got to their feet quickly to bow to Wang and Elmer in their thanks.

"I think we need to get these people back home, don't you?" Elmer asked.

"Yes, but first I will leave a note for the Tong."

"All right," Elmer said. "What are you going to say to them?"

"I will read it to you when I have finished," Wang promised.

Finding a pen, paper, and ink, Wang prepared the note, in beautiful Chinese calligraphy.

To the Tong
We, the Shaolin Temple of the Dragon, have put the Chinese people who live in this city under our protection. We tell you now that for every innocent person who is taken or killed, we will kill five Tong. Today we rescued two whom you had taken, and as a way of illustrating our commitment to this vow, we leave behind ten dead Tong.

We have eyes everywhere and will be watching you closely.

"What is the Shaolin Temple of the Dragon?" Elmer asked after Wang read the note to him.

Wang smiled. "You and I are the Temple of the Dragon," he said. "I hope the Tong are convinced that the message is truthful."

Elmer chuckled. "Ten bodies ought to go a long way toward convincing them," he said.

CHAPTER SEVEN

From the *Cheyenne Defender:*

CALLAHAN AND MANNING
TO BE HURLED INTO ETERNITY

On the morning of Thursday, but two days from now, the bank robbers and murderers Clay Callahan and Zeke Manning will, for the last time in their lives, be treated to the beauty of a rising sun, which, in its morning transit, will turn the mountaintops golden. For the last time in their lives, they will hear the sweet trilling of songbirds, the clarion call of roosters greeting yet another day, and the communal sound of mankind engaged in conversation, both convivial and commercial.

The two condemned souls will be offered one last chance to break the fast of the night before, after which they will be extended an opportunity to, with the help of clergy, come to peace with their Maker. Then, shortly before the hour of ten o'clock, they will be led from the cell they now occupy to a gallows recently constructed for just such a purpose, and there, before the eyes of a hundred or more witnesses, the noted hangman Mordecai Luscombe will once again ply the profession, which over the last few years has earned him a well-deserved reputation.

After the hanging, a reception will be held in the Souls of Heaven Church in the memory of its late pastor, the Reverend Nathan L. Pyle, and his wife, Anna Marie.

On the night before the scheduled hanging, Dooley Cooper and Pogue Morris found themselves nursing a beer in the Rendezvous Saloon. This time it wasn't a lack of money that caused them to nurse a beer; it was because they didn't want to get drunk.

"We're goin' to have to be sober if we plan to pull this off," Cooper said.

"Yeah, well, I don't plan on gettin' drunk, but I would like a couple more drinks just to settle my nerves."

"Your nerves are settled enough," Cooper said.

"What time do we do it?" Morris asked.

"Not 'til after midnight," Cooper said, glancing at the large grandfather's clock that stood against the back wall.

Two blocks down the street from the Rendezvous, Zeke Manning stood at the barred window in the cell he was sharing with Clay Callahan.

"They've finally got the gallows done," Manning said.

"Well, they should have. They been workin' on the damn thing ever since the judge sentenced us to hang." Callahan was lying on one of the two beds with his hands laced behind his head.

"Is that all you got to say about it?"

"What else do you want me to say?"

Manning put his hand to his neck and grimaced. "Ain't you worried none 'bout the hangin' tomorrow mornin'?"

"No, I ain't none particular worried."

"How can you not be worried about it?"

"Hell, what good does it do to worry about it? You didn't eat your biscuit 'n bacon. Do you mind if I eat it?"

"What? Are you crazy? How can you eat now?"

"I can eat now 'cause I'm hungry. And the bacon was good."

"Go ahead, eat it," Manning said. "I don't

want it."

"You'll get hungry later on 'n you'll wish you had eaten," Callahan said as he reached for the bacon. He made a low, guttural sound that might have been a laugh. "Though, come to think of it, I don't think you can get hungry in hell," he said.

"That ain't funny!" Manning said. "That ain't funny a-tall!"

"You worry too much," Callahan said, making a sandwich of the bacon and biscuit.

A few minutes later, Moe Dinkins, the deputy sheriff, stepped into the back of the jail. He was accompanied by a tall, very slender man. The sallow skin was so tightly drawn across his face that it looked almost as if it were an animated skull. The man was wearing a dark suit and carrying a bowler hat.

"Callahan, Manning, I need you two boys to step up here," Dinkins called out to them. "I've got someone who wants to meet you."

Callahan looked over toward Dinkins and the man with him, then went back to eating his biscuit and bacon. "I ain't interested in meetin' no preacher man," he said. "I ain't been inside church since I was nine years old, 'n I don't intend to start now."

Dinkins laughed. "Oh, this ain't a

89

preacher," he said. "This is Mordecai Luscombe. He's the fella that's goin' to hang you."

"You?" Manning asked with a gasp. "You're the one that's goin' to hang us?"

"I am indeed, sir," Luscombe replied.

"Oh! Oh!" Reacting in panic, Manning put his hand to his neck.

"Why you gettin' so worked up over it, Manning?" the deputy asked. "You've knowed ever' since the trial now that this was a-comin'."

"I . . . I hadn't thought about the hangman," Manning said.

"Somebody's got to do it, lessen' you want to save the county some trouble and do it yourself," Dinkins said with a chuckle. "But we'd heap rather you don't kill yourselves, seein' as we got just a whole lot of people that's come into town now just to see the hangin'. You have to admit, it sure would be a shame if the two of you did it yourself 'n cheated all those people out of a good show." Again, Dinkins laughed at his own joke.

"Would you gentlemen please step up here?" Luscombe asked.

"What for? You'll be seein' us in the mornin', won't you?" Callahan asked. "I mean when you hang us?"

90

"Yes, but I do want to do a good job. Why, if I don't get everything just right, the rope could jerk your head right off your shoulders. That's always so messy when that happens, to say nothing of it being terribly upsetting to all the ladies."

"What the hell?" Manning asked, his face growing ashen. "You mean that has actually happened?"

"Oh, yes, from time to time," Luscombe replied. He chuckled. "I have to confess that I've done it on purpose a few times when my subjects don't show me the proper respect. Now, if you two don't want your heads jerked off your bodies, you'll step up here and let me examine you."

"It don't hurt no more to have your head pulled off your body than it does to just hang, does it?" Callahan asked.

"Oh, my, you are a particularly large one, aren't you?" the hangman said to Callahan. "I'll have to make allowances for that. But to answer your question, I expect it actually doesn't hurt as much, because when your head comes off like that, why you die right away. However, it sort of upsets the ladies when they see somethin' like that. On the other hand, I've seen some men take several minutes to die by hanging, 'n it's almost as awful to watch, the way they just sort of dangle there 'n twitch around so. Of course, if I do my job right, your neck will be broken as soon as you make the fall and you'll die quite quickly. I pride myself on being able to manipulate the outcome in any way I want."

"I'll be damned. You actually enjoy doing this, don't you?" Callahan asked.

"I confess that I do enjoy it. I have always believed that a body needs to enjoy the work that they do, don't you agree? Otherwise you need be looking for some other form of employment. I not only enjoy my work, I am quite good at it, and to that end your survivors will proudly proclaim that you were hanged by Mordecai Luscombe. I would think you would take some pride in that. It is said that I am the best hangman in all of Wyoming Territory."

"Yeah, well, we can't be proud for very long now, can we?" Callahan asked. "I mean, seein' as we're goin' to be hung at ten o'clock tomorrow mornin'."

Luscombe laughed. "I suppose you do have a point there," he said. "Turn around please so I can get a good look at you."

"You ever have bad dreams 'bout people you've hung?" Manning asked.

"No, why should I? When men such as you live a life of crime, you reap your own rewards."

"Turn around, like Mr. Luscombe told you to," Dinkins ordered.

As Callahan and Manning turned in the cell, Luscombe examined them closely. "Let's see, I'd make you to be about a hundred and fifty-five, maybe a hundred sixty pounds," he said to Manning. "And you, sir, must run at least two hundred, to two hundred and ten pounds. Am I about right?"

"How the hell do I know how much I weigh?" Callahan replied in a growl.

"Well then, you are just going to have to trust my talent at guessing weights. And I have developed quite a talent in that particular skill, so I think I can promise you both a fine hanging."

"Is that all you need, Mr. Luscombe?" Dinkins asked.

"Yes, thank you, sir, that is all I need. By the way, Deputy, do you have any idea how many people will be here for the hanging tomorrow?"

"I'd say three, maybe four hundred," Dinkins replied.

"Oh, my, that is quite a crowd, isn't it? Well, good, I'm glad you are expecting so many. You see, what I normally do after each hanging is I cut the rope into foot-long lengths, then I sell those pieces of rope as keepsakes to those who have come to the hanging. They will make marvelous souvenirs that can be passed on to grandchildren."

"How much do you sell them for?" Dinkins asked.

"Oh, it quite depends upon how famous my subject is. Why, when I hung Lucien Pardo, I got five dollars apiece for each of the rope segments."

"What about these two?"

"Ha! A bungled bank job by a couple of unknowns? No, the only value these rope segments will have is that I was the hangman. And of course, there is some value there. I suppose I will be able to get two dollars each for them. You, of course, will get a piece of the rope gratis."

"Gratis? What does that mean?"

"That means I'll give you a piece of the rope and you won't have to pay for it."

"Gee thanks, Mr. Luscombe," Dinkins said.

"Well, it's off to the Del Rey Hotel and bed for me. I do always like to get a good night's sleep before I do a job."

CHAPTER EIGHT

Cheyenne jailhouse

The clock struck two, but because Deputy Dinkins was asleep he didn't hear it. He was sitting in his chair with it leaning against the wall behind the desk. His head was tilted back, his mouth was slightly open, and his lips were quivering as he snored. He wasn't supposed to be sleeping; it was his job to stay awake all night to make certain there was no problem that would interfere with the hanging the next day.

Two men came into the office then; both were dressed in black and both carrying pistols.

One of the two men, noticing the sleeping jailer, held his finger to his lips, then put his pistol away and drew his knife.

Dinkins was awakened by a sharp pain in his neck, and, reflexively, he put his hands to the pain, surprised to feel a wetness. Opening his eyes, he saw two men standing

95

there looking down at him. One of the men was holding a knife.

"I'll bet that really hurts, don't it?" the man asked, his face twisted by a malevolent smile.

Dinkins tried to speak, but his windpipe had been severed by the blade and he was unable to make a sound.

"Get the keys, Morris," the man holding the knife said.

"I got 'em," Morris replied, holding up a key ring.

As life drained out of him, Dinkins watched the two men step into the back of the jail.

"Here, you can't go back there!" Dinkins shouted.

But though his lips formed the words there was no sound; the shout was in his mind only and it was his last, conscious thought. Dinkins closed his eyes and had the strangest sensation of collapsing in on himself, falling . . . falling . . .

"Callahan! You back here?" Morris shouted, and though his shout was loud enough to reverberate through the entire jail, Dinkins heard nothing, because he was dead.

"Cooper! Morris! What are you two doin'

here?" Manning asked, surprised to see them.

"They come to get us out of jail," Callahan said with a broad smile.

"Damn! You knowed all along they was a-comin', didn't you?"

"Yeah, I knew."

"Why didn't you tell me?"

" 'Cause I wanted to eat your biscuit and bacon," Callahan said with a little laugh.

"Let's go, we got the horses out back in the alley," Morris said.

"Uh-uh, we ain't goin' nowhere 'til we stop by the Del Rey Hotel," Callahan said.

"What the hell do we want to do that for?" Cooper asked. "We need to get the hell outta here!"

"We will. But first I want to pay a visit to someone."

"Yeah," Manning said when he realized what Callahan was saying. "Me too."

Five minutes later the four men were moving quietly down the upstairs hall of the Del Rey Hotel. "The guest register said he is in this room," Callahan said.

"What if someone comes in and sees the desk clerk?" Manning asked.

"They'll just think he's sleeping," Callahan said.

Unlocking the door with the key taken

from the front desk, the four men went into Mordecai Luscombe's room. He was snoring loudly.

"Gag the son of a bitch so he can't call out," Callahan said.

"Uhhmmm!" Luscombe mumbled as he awakened with his socks pushed down into his mouth.

"Lookie here," Manning said, holding up a rope. "These are the ropes he was going to use to hang us with."

"Ha! I got me a good idea," Callahan said.

With their prisoner bound and gagged, Callahan and the others left the hotel by the back door. Moving down the alley, their nostrils were assailed by the smells of the many outhouses that were set against the alley.

"Damn, that smells like shit," Manning complained.

"What else is it supposed to smell like?" Cooper asked with a little laugh.

Leaving the alley, the four men and their prisoner walked up between Blum's Mercantile and White's Apothecary. When they emerged in the street, they could see the scaffold dimly illuminated by the corner streetlamp.

"Let's get 'im up there," Callahan said.

"Uhmmm! Uhmmm!" Luscombe said, his

eyes open wide as he realized what the men had in store for him.

"Well now, you was tellin' us how much you loved your job," Callahan said, " 'n here you are, about to be hung, just like all them people you hung before. Now ain't that somethin'?"

With his eyes open in terror and his attempt to call out stifled by the socks stuffed down in his throat, Luscombe struggled against his captors, but to no avail. He was pulled up the thirteen steps to the scaffold, then dragged over to the trap door.

Callahan tossed the rope over the hanging frame, then looped the rope around Luscombe's neck.

"That ain't the right kind of noose," Cooper said. "There ain't no knots in it to break his neck."

Callahan smiled. "I don't want to break his neck," he said. "I want the son of a bitch to just dangle there until he chokes to death."

"Yeah," Manning said with an evil giggle. "Yeah, that's a good idea."

When the sun came up the next morning, Mrs. Emma Rittenhouse was just opening the front door of Emma's Kitchen, the restaurant she owned. She was getting an early start on the day because she needed to get the biscuits in the oven in time for breakfast. She hated that the gallows had been erected right in front of her restaurant, but on the other hand, there would be a lot of people coming in town today to see the hanging. That would mean more business for her.

She glanced toward the gallows, then, shocked by what she saw, let out a blood-curdling scream that woke much of the town.

From the *Cheyenne Defender:*

TERRIBLE TRAGEDY

Zeke Manning and Clay Callahan, having been duly tried, convicted, and sentenced to hang for the horrendous crime of murdering three innocent souls, have escaped their punishment. In so doing, they have added even more despicable deeds to their evil resume.

It is not known how the two men were able to leave their jail cell, but the tracks of four horses were found behind the jail, so it is reasonable to assume that at least two men provided assistance on the night before they were to hang. After gaining their freedom, Manning and Callahan, and the men who freed them, killed Moe Dinkins, the jailer. Mr. Dinkins, a fine county servant, leaves behind a wife and two small children.

Not content with killing Moe Dinkins, the two escaped prisoners visited the Del Rey Hotel, where they killed the night clerk Abner Martin, then they managed to take from his bed the hangman Mordecai Luscombe, who had come to the city to carry out the dictates of the court, scheduled for ten o'clock this morning.

Instead of hanging Manning and Callahan, it was Mr. Luscombe himself who faced that fate, his body discovered hanging from the gallows by Mrs. Emma Rittenhouse as she was opening her restaurant for business this morning.

Chugwater

In addition to Duff, who was actually from Scotland, there were several people of Scottish descent who lived in or around Chugwater. Biff Johnson, who was the proprietor of Fiddler's Green, was married to a Scottish woman, and her parents lived in town. Julie Culpepper, whose maiden name had been McClain, was a first-generation American, the daughter of native Scots. There were also several others in and around Chugwater who could claim some connection to Scotland.

It was because of this shared background that, every year, Chugwater celebrated Scottish Heritage Day.

Earlier in the day there had been a pipe and drum band, its members drawn from as far away as Oregon and California to the west, Texas and New Mexico to the south, Illinois and Ohio to the east, and from Montana and Alberta to the north. The air was redolent with the aroma of traditional Scottish food, and the event was so festive that even those who weren't Scottish seemed to be enjoying themselves.

Duff had already won the shooting games, coming in first with both the pistol and the rifle. After the marksmanship contest, Duff and Ina Claire Culpepper played a duet, she on the drum and he with the pipes. They played the traditional Scottish song "The Green Hills of Tyrol," and Ina Claire's mother wiped a few tears away as she listened to the music.

One of the games was "throwing the caber," which was such a severe test of muscle and skill that only the strongest could compete. Duff and the three other contestants removed their shirts as they prepared to play the game.

"Och," a man named MacDavish said. "Sure now, MacCallister, ye've nae wish to hurt your hands so's that ye can nae longer play the pipes, do ye, lad? 'Twould be a shame for 'tis a valuable thing ye do, keeping the music of dear Scotland alive so that native sons and heathens alike can enjoy it."

MacDavish owned a bar in Cheyenne, but that wasn't too far for him to come to enjoy the games.

"Here 'n would ye be for listenin' to MacDavish now?" Murchison, another who would be competing in the game, said. "Would it be to try 'n make Mr. MacCallister drop out so that ye might win with the caber?"

"Sure 'n how is it that someone like MacDavish could win the game when his muscles be so wee?" another asked.

There was a great deal of laughter in response to that comment, for MacDavish was a big man with broad shoulders and rippling muscles.

The good-natured, but spirited, arguments continued among the contestants until the judge called for the game to begin. The entire town had shown up to watch, for there was no game that anyone had ever played that required more strength than the heaving of the caber.

The game, which had been played by the hardy Scots since the earliest times was, because of the strength required, one of the most featured events on the programs of all athletic contests. The game centered around a long section of tree trunk, which had been tapered so that one end was considerably smaller than at the other.

"All right, MacDavish, by the luck of the draw, you have the first toss," Biff Johnson said. Biff had been selected by all contestants to be the judge of the caber.

MacDavish reached down to grab the tree trunk, then he raised it to a vertical position with the smaller end down, and with a mighty yell he threw it into the air and away from him.

The object of the game was to throw the caber in such a way that the large end of the pole would hit the ground and the pole fall so that the small end would wind up pointing away from the thrower. MacDavish made a perfect throw.

The prize would go to the man whose caber lands on the ground with its small end farthest away from the throwing point. It was a feat that required as much finesse as strength to make the throw. That was because, if not handled exactly right, the caber would be just as likely to fall over sideways instead of straight forward when the large end hits the ground, or likely to fall at an angle or even fall back the way it came.

After all the contestants completed their throws, the prize went to Angus MacDavish.

There were several other games and demonstrations spread up and down Swan Avenue until nightfall. That night a wooden floor had been laid in the middle of the street. The floor, which was brightly illuminated by kerosene lanterns, was turned into a dance floor. For the dance the Scottish theme was temporarily put aside in favor of the more familiar band of fiddles, guitars, and a dance caller.

The dance didn't break up until nearly midnight, then Duff walked Meagan back to her home, an apartment over her dress shop.

"You could stay, you know," she said suggestively.

Duff smiled. "I am grateful for the invitation, but there are too many in town who saw me walkin' ye back to yer house, and 'twould be a shame to sully your reputation now."

Meagan laughed. "Leave it to you to be

my Sir Galahad."

"Och, woman, do you nae ken that Galahad is an Englishman? Why would I want to be an Englishman?"

"Knight or not, you're not so cautious that you won't kiss me, are you?"

"I'm nae too cautious for a kiss," Duff replied, his smile growing even broader.

CHAPTER NINE

Medicine Bow Mountains

Clay Callahan lay flat on his stomach just below the crest of the hill and looked down into the narrow canyon below. Sheriff Sharpies was riding in front of a posse of twelve men. Although Callahan was a safe distance from them, they were below him in a natural bowl, which had the acoustical effect of gathering the sound waves and projecting their voices upward so that he could overhear the conversation of those who were in pursuit.

"If you ask me, we're barkin' up the wrong tree," someone said. "We ain't seen hide nor hair of 'em, 'n we ain't seen no tracks for more 'n ten, maybe twelve miles by now."

"I think they came this way," Sheriff Sharpies said.

"Then how come we ain't seen no sign of 'em?"

"We've been following a creek for the better part of two miles. If they kept in the creek bed, they wouldn't be leaving any sign."

"You know they didn't do that. Hell, you can't hardly get a horse to walk through a creek, let alone get 'im to stay in the middle of the damn thing for a couple of miles or so."

"Gibbons, bein' part of a posse is a volunteer thing," the sheriff replied. "If you don't want to stay with us, I've got no authority to make you do so. You can turn around right now and go back to town."

"No, thank you," Gibbons said. "What if I start back and they're somewhere along the trail, just a-waitin' on me. Why, bein' as I'd be all by myself, 'n I'd be a sittin' duck for 'em. If you don't mind, I'll just stay with the posse."

"All right then, if you can keep up with us you're welcome to stay. But quit your bitchin' about ever'thing you can think to complain about."

One of the posse members who had gone ahead of the others returned. The staccato sound of the hooves echoed back from the surrounding walls of the canyon.

"See anything, Dobbs?" Sheriff Sharpies called to the returning rider.

"I didn't see a damn thing," Dobbs said. "I can guarantee you that if they were ridin' down through the middle of this creek, they didn't leave. And that means they weren't in it, 'cause the creek kind of disappears up ahead. The canyon does, too."

"You know what I'm beginnin' to think?" Kelly asked. Kelly owned the leather goods store back in town.

When nobody asked what he thought, Kelly volunteered the answer anyway. "I'm thinkin' that they ain't up here in this canyon at all. I'm thinkin' they led us into the crick, then most likely instead of comin' this way like we've all done, they doubled back 'n went the other way."

"Why would they go the other way?" Dobbs asked. "That don't make no sense; it leads back down into the flatlands. There ain't no place they can hide out in the flatlands."

"It's on account of it don't make sense that it does make sense," Kelly said.

Sheriff Sharpies laughed. "You know what? I don't know why, but I think I'm agreein' with Kelly."

Up on the ridgeline, Callahan continued his observation.

"Do you see anything, Callahan?" Manning asked.

"Shh!" Callahan said, waving his hand sharply. "They're just real close now!" Callahan didn't realize that the acoustic conditions that so clearly broadcast the conversations of the posse to him did not work in reverse. Manning's words couldn't be heard down on the canyon floor.

"Listen."

The others grew quiet and strained their ears to hear what was being said by those who were chasing them.

"All right," Sheriff Sharpies said, his voice as clear as if he were standing next to Callahan and the others. "Let's get on back to town. We ain't doin' any good out here."

"What are we goin' to do, Sheriff? We ain't goin' to let the sons of bitches get away clean, are we?" one of the riders asked.

"I can't see as we have much choice in it now," the sheriff replied. "About the only thing we got left to do, I suppose, is to send out telegrams to all the other towns in Wyoming Territory, Colorado, Nebraska, 'n maybe Idaho, sayin' that the men escaped."

"What about reward posters?" Gibbons asked. "We goin' to put out rewards on them?"

"I reckon I'll be able to get permission to

do that," Sheriff Sharpies replied.

From his observation post, Callahan watched as Sheriff Sharpies gathered his entire crew together, spoke to them quietly for a moment or two, then started back out of the canyon, retracing the path over which they had come.

"Posse's pullin' out," Callahan said.

"What'll we do now?" Cooper asked.

"We'll camp here the rest of the night, then get under way again in the morning."

"Damn!" Manning said with a broad smile spread across his face. "Boys, looks to me like we got away as clean as a whistle!"

Sky Meadow Ranch

Duff was standing on the back porch of the house, watching as the two riders approached. Even before they were close enough to see their faces, Duff knew who they were. He could tell by the way they were sitting their horses that it was Elmer Gleason and Wang Chow.

As he watched the two men, he couldn't help but think of the strange circumstances that had sent him halfway around the world to find two such unlikely men to be his best friends.

Duff had left everything behind him when

111

he came to America, and Elmer Gleason was the first non-kinsman friend he had made. Elmer had been working an old gold mine, having found a producing vein in a mine that had been abandoned. He was living there as well, an almost skeletal apparition that had the people of Chugwater thinking the mine was haunted. The mine was on Duff's property, and because he also had mineral rights as well, legally, all the gold in the mine belonged to Duff. Instead of running Elmer off, Duff offered him half the mine, and as a result, Elmer had become his best friend.

Duff had saved Wang Chow from a lynching, then took him on as one of his hired hands. The result was a lifetime of fealty. Wang brought more than loyalty to the relationship. Wang was forced to leave China after he effected a terrible revenge upon those who had murdered people that were very close to him. He brought to America the same disciplines, both mental and physical, he had exhibited while a Shaolin priest.

Both Elmer and Wang had saved Duff's life, and he theirs, more times than any of them could count.

Duff stepped down from the porch, greeting his friends with a welcoming smile.

"What did ye do, rent those horses? If ye

had sent me a wire, tellin' me ye would be comin' back, I woulda had your horses in town waiting for you."

"We wasn't all that sure we was comin' back so soon," Elmer said.

"The people of San Francisco could nae put up with the two of you 'n so they threw you out, did they?"

"Here now, you heathen Scotsman," Elmer replied, "I'll have you know there was much wailing and gnashing of the teeth when we left, them wantin' us to stay as bad as they did."

"Well, 'tis glad I am that ye didn't give in to the siren song, but instead came back to your true friends. Get down, come in, have a drink, 'n tell me all about your trip."

"Hello, the house!" someone shouted shortly after Duff had invited his two friends to come inside.

Recognizing Meagan's voice, Duff got up and walked to the kitchen door. "Meagan," he called. "Come on in. Guess who is back?"

Meagan was warmly greeted by Elmer and Wang. What followed was a discussion of their trip to San Francisco, though without mention of their run-in with the Tong.

"What brings ye here?" Duff asked Meagan. "Though I dinnae want ye to think that by the question that I'm nae happy to see ye."

"I've brought the finished dress for you to see," Meagan said.

"Finished dress? What dress?"

"What dress? Why, the dress I made for Ina Claire, of course. Have you forgotten that today is her birthday? I'm to deliver it to her today, and you said you would go with me to give it to her."

"Oh, aye, I did say that," Duff replied. "Well, 'tis good of ye to come 'n remind me."

"You ain't got nothin' to give 'er?" Elmer asked.

"Oh, I got something for her, all right," Duff replied. "Captain Culpepper has already picked it up."

"We'll be takin' these rented nags back into town while you 'n Miss Meagan are deliverin' your gifts to the young girl," Elmer said. "Tell her that me 'n Wang wish her a happy birthday."

"We'll do that," Duff promised.

Twin Pine Ranch

"Oh, it is beautiful!" Ina Claire said, looking at the dress Meagan gave her.

"It is lovely," Julie agreed. "Ina Claire, when I was your age I had one just like it. It

114

is called an *arisad.* Meagan, it is so sweet of you to give her this. I know I'm going to enjoy seeing her in it, quite as much as she will enjoy wearing it."

"I must try it on," Ina Claire said.

"Wait," Ed said, holding out his hand. "You can wear it for dinner tonight. For now you might want to come out to the barn. I have something I want to show you," Ed said.

"The barn?"

"Yes, the barn. It is your birthday, isn't it?"

"Thunder!" Ina Claire said.

"What?"

"Papa, you bought Thunder for me, didn't you? For my birthday!"

"Are you talking about that worthless horse Heckemeyer was trying to sell me?"

"Oh, Papa, he isn't worthless! He is a marvelous horse."

"Well now you're beginning to make me feel bad," Ed Culpepper said. "You're so set on that horse that I reckon you're going to be plumb dissatisfied with anything else I might have gotten you for your birthday."

"I'm sorry, Papa," Ina Claire said. "It's just that I wanted Thunder so bad. But I know he must cost way too much, and the truth is, I'll be satisfied with whatever you got for me."

"That's my girl," Ed said. He looked at the others. "You might all come; I think you will appreciate this as well."

Ed and Ina Claire led the way to the barn with Julie, Duff, and Meagan following. Julie, Duff, and Meagan were all smiling because they were in on the secret.

"Go ahead and look inside," Ed said when they reached the barn.

"What am I looking for?"

"I think you'll see."

Ina Claire stepped into the barn, and for a moment she had to let her eyes adjust to the dark. Then she heard a horse whicker, and looking in the direction of the sound, she saw a coal-black horse in the first stall, looking back at her.

"Thunder!" she shouted at the top of her voice. "Oh, Papa, you *did* get him for me!" She ran back to embrace her father.

"Your mama and I got him for you," Ed said.

"Can I ride him now?"

"Well, he's your horse," Ed said with a little wave of his hand. "I reckon you can do just about anything you want with your horse."

"Papa, Mama, thank you so much!" Ina Claire said.

"Before you ride, you might want to saddle him," Ed suggested. "That is, unless you plan to ride him bareback."

Ina Claire started for a table where lay some of the saddles used for the ranch horses.

"Wouldn't you rather have this saddle?" Ed suggested, stepping over to another table and removing a blanket to disclose a saddle. Unlike the worn, dark work saddles, this saddle was made of thick leather, with an all-over hand-carved floral tooling, accented with silver conchos and a rawhide trim cantle.

"Oh, what a beautiful saddle! It is perfect for a horse like Thunder."

"It is, isn't it? You can thank Mr. MacCallister for that one."

Spontaneously, she threw her arms around Duff's neck to give him a hug. Then, self-consciously, she stepped back and looked at Meagan. "I, uh, hope you didn't mind that I gave him a hug. I mean, how must it look to you, when you see another woman embracing your man?"

Meagan laughed. "I didn't mind at all," she said.

"I'm going to saddle my horse now," Ina Claire said, grabbing the saddle and stepping into the stall where Thunder waited.

Thunder was a big, muscular, black horse that stood eighteen hands at the withers. All the time she was saddling him, he kept moving his head and lifting first one hoof and then another. He looked like a ball of potential energy.

Once she had him saddled, she led him out into the corral.

"You need me to help you into the saddle?" Ed asked.

Ina Claire laughed. "Papa, you haven't had to help me into the saddle since I was seven years old."

She put one foot into the stirrup and then swung up into the saddle. Her dress pulled back so that she showed more leg than she intended to, and as soon as she was seated, she pulled the skirt down as far as she could.

"I should be wearing trousers for this," she said.

"Trousers aren't ladylike," Ed replied.

"Neither is showing so much of my legs."

Ed laughed. "I guess you've got a point. I'll go open the corral gate for you."

"Neither Thunder nor I need you to do that," Ina Claire replied. She slapped her legs against the side of the horse and he started forward at a gallop. As the horse approached the fence, she lifted herself slightly from the saddle and leaned forward.

118

"Come on, Thunder," she said encouragingly. "Let's show everyone what you can do." Even as she spoke to the horse though, she realized that she was more interested in showing the others what she could do than what the horse could do.

Thunder galloped toward the fence, then sailed over it as gracefully as a leaping deer. Coming down on the other side Ina Claire saw a ditch about twenty yards beyond the fence, and Thunder took that as well. Horse and rider went through their paces, jumping, making sudden turns, running at a full gallop, then stopping on a dime. After a few minutes she brought Thunder back, returning the same way he left, over the ditch, then over the fence. She slowed him down to a trot once they were back inside the corral, and the horse was at a walk by the time she rode up to dismount in front of her father and the others. She was smiling broadly.

"What do you think?" she asked.

"I think you and Thunder belong together," Ed said. He chuckled. "If we were still at Fort Lincoln, I could use you to give riding demonstrations to the troopers who are just learning to ride."

"Oh, yes, I'm sure they would like that," Julie said. "You remember how the old-timers always teased the new men. Doing something like letting a sixteen-year-old girl show them up would be devastating."

"Yes," Ed said. "But it would sure be good for my ego."

"Ina Claire is going to be such a beautiful young lady," Meagan said as she and Duff left Twin Pine. "She'll be a great catch for some young man."

"Assuming he can keep up with her," Duff said. "Ina Claire is quite the tomboy."

Meagan laughed. "I can't argue with you there. I thought I was a tomboy when I was a young girl, but I wouldn't dare attempt to do some of the things Ina Claire has done."

Duff and Meagan were met by Elmer when they returned to Sky Meadow. Duff invited Meagan to spend the night, but she declined.

"I need to open on time tomorrow," she said. "And if I start back now, I'll be back in town before it grows dark."

CHAPTER TEN

When Ina Claire went to bed that night, it was with happy memories of the Scottish games in town and eager anticipation of the days to come with her new horse, Thunder.

"Papa?" she called.

"Yes?"

"Thank you for Thunder. You are the best papa in the whole world."

Ed chuckled. "You remember that next time I ask you to do something you don't want to do."

"I'll remember," Ina Claire promised.

Ina Claire got out of bed and walked over to the window. She could see the barn glimmering dimly in the light of the moon. Thunder was in there tonight, in a place that was new for him. She hoped he wasn't homesick for where he was before he was brought here.

"I'm going to love you so much that you'll never give a second thought to where you were before," Ina Claire said, speaking quietly. The leaf of a nearby tree moved slightly in a gentle breeze and, catching a beam of moonlight, sent a sliver of silver through the night.

"Good night, Thunder."

Turning away from the window, it was a happy Ina Claire who climbed back into her bed.

"Papa?" she called out into the night.

"Yes, darlin'?" Her father's voice drifted down the hall to her.

"Didn't Mr. MacCallister and Miss Parker give me some wonderful birthday gifts?"

"Yes, they did."

"I hope they know how much I appreciated them."

"I'm sure they do."

"Ina Claire, sweetheart, I know you are excited," her mother called back to her. "But you need to settle down and go to sleep now."

"I will, Mama," Ina Claire promised. "It's just that this is the most wonderful day of my whole life, and I'll never forget it."

"It was a wonderful day," her mother replied. "And I'm sure you will remember it forever."

"Mama, I love you," Ina Claire said.

"I love you, too, darlin'."

"Papa, I love you."

"And I love you back, sweetheart. Now, you aren't going to yell out the window that you love Thunder, are you?"

Ina Claire chuckled. "I love you, Thunder!"

Horse Creek

"We been eatin' nothin' but rabbit for four days, 'n with no salt 'n no coffee to wash it down," Manning complained.

"You got nothin' to complain about," Callahan said. "Me 'n you could both be lyin' in a coffin under the ground by now."

It had been four days since Callahan and Manning had escaped jail, and in so doing evaded the hangman's noose. They had also managed to avoid the posse that had come for them. But neither Morris nor Cooper, who had arranged the escape, had had the foresight to bring any rations to sustain them while they were on the run.

"That's true, but ain't you gettin' a little hungry for somethin' beside rabbit cooked on a stick without nothin' with it, not even no salt?" Manning asked, continuing his complaining.

"I know where we can get some vittles," Cooper said.

"Where?" Callahan asked. "It ain't like we

can go into a general store and buy what we need. In the first place, we might get recognized, 'n in the second place, just in case you ain't thought about it, we ain't got no money. So just where do you plan to get this food you're talkin' about?"

"I know the place, 'n it ain't far from here. It ain't very far at all. You remember it, don't you, Morris?"

"It ain't far from here, you say?"

"It prob'ly ain't no more 'n four, maybe five miles from here."

For just a moment Morris was confused by the comment, then he realized what Cooper was talking about and a big smile spread across his face.

"Oh, wait a minute, yeah, I do know," Morris said. "Yeah, I know exactly where we can go. You're talkin' about the cap'n, ain't you?"

"Yeah."

"Who, or what is this cap'n you two are talkin' about?" Callahan asked.

"It's a feller me 'n Morris met," Cooper said. "We can get some food there, 'n maybe a little money. We can be there in a couple of hours, real easy."

"That'll be after midnight," Manning said.

Cooper smiled. "Yeah, midnight is prob'ly about the best time to visit him."

"He must be an awful good friend if he's goin' to be willin' to give us food in the middle of the night," Manning said.

Now it was Callahan who smiled. "You don't understand, Manning. I don't think this cap'n is a friend, and I don't think he plans to give us anything."

"Then how . . ." Manning started, but he interrupted his question in mid-sentence. "Oh, I see what you're talkin' about. We ain't goin' there for him to give us anything. We're goin' there to take it."

"See there, Cooper, I told you Manning warn't all that dumb. He's done figured this out all by his own self," Callahan declared.

"Yeah, I seen it right off," Manning said, smiling as he mistook the sarcasm for a genuine compliment.

A little over two hours later the four men reined up on top of a ridge and looked down onto Little Bear Creek below them. The narrow stream of water glistened silver from the full moon overhead. Just on the other side of the creek, they saw a cluster of buildings, a barn, a bunkhouse, and a larger, white house.

"I see a bunkhouse. Are you sure there ain't no hands here?" Manning asked.

"I'm sure," Cooper answered. "Me 'n

Morris stopped here for water just the other day. There warn't nobody here but a man 'n woman, 'n a young girl."

"They was real nice folks, too," Morris said. "They not only let us have water for the horses, they also brung us into the house 'n give us dinner."

"It don't matter none whether they was nice or not," Callahan said, his voice a snarl. "We got business to take care of, 'n them bein' nice don't have nothin' to do with it. We need some food, and this is where we can get it. Tell me, do you think they got 'ny money here?"

"Hell, I'm sure of it," Cooper said. "They ain't got no hands on the place right now, 'n the reason they ain't got nobody here is 'cause they ain't got no cows. 'N they ain't got no cows 'cause they just sold 'em."

"Yeah, and I know men like him," Morris added. "They'd rather keep the money themselves than put it in a bank. Most special when he'd either have to go all the way to Chugwater or Cheyenne in order to get to a bank."

"Besides which, we know they got food," Cooper said. " 'N we're goin' to be needin' some food if we're goin' to stay out on the trail for a while."

"All right," Callahan said. "Let's get this done."

"What the hell?" Cooper said. "There's a light comin' from one o' the winders."

"Maybe they left a lantern burning," Manning suggested.

"No, they wouldn't leave a lantern burnin' all night."

"What'll we do?" Morris asked.

"I've got an idea," Cooper said.

Ed couldn't sleep. He had been promising to take Julie to Scotland ever since they had gotten married. He had gotten the idea while he was still in the army when, one night, a group of soldiers came by to serenade the officers and their ladies with the song "I'll Take You Home Again Kathleen." That didn't particularly refer to Julie, she hadn't been born in Scotland, but she had always wanted to see the homeland of her parents.

Now he had enough money saved that he could do that, and with the cattle sold, there was no reason they couldn't leave the ranch for a period of time.

Ed began putting some figures on a piece of paper. It would take a week to go by train to New York, then ten days by steamship to England. To go there and back, they would be traveling for thirty-four days. He would buy first-class passage on the ship so that even the trip would be enjoyable. The question was, how long could they stay in Scotland?

Ed smiled. He saw no reason why they couldn't stay for a month, which meant he would be gone from the ranch for two months. But he knew that he could arrange to put the few remaining cattle with Duff's over on Sky Meadow. He knew, also, that he could count on Duff to keep an eye on his place while they were gone.

With the logistics of the trip figured out, his next step would be to determine just where they would go and what they would do while there. He had bought a book about Scotland, doing so in secret because when he first began contemplating the trip he wasn't sure he would be able to do it, and he didn't want to get Julie's hopes up if they couldn't. Now that he knew he could, he would find some things in the book to share with Julie and Ina Claire.

Ed was looking through the book when he thought he heard something on the front porch. He started toward the door to have a look, when he was surprised to hear a light knock. *Who in the world would be paying a visit at this hour of the night?*

"Yes? Who is it?" he called through the door.

"Cap'n? Cap'n Culpepper, it's me, Dooley Cooper. Me 'n my pard stopped by a few days ago, remember?"

Ed opened the door. "Yeah, I remember. What are you doing here in the middle of the night?"

"It's my pard, Pogue. He's been hurt real bad, Cap'n. Could you step out here and take a look at 'im?"

"Why'd you bring him here instead of taking him to a doctor?"

" 'Cause this here was the closest place. Please, just take a look at 'im, tell me what you think."

Ed paused for a moment. He didn't have a good feeling about this. On the other hand, if someone was hurt and he could be of some help, it wouldn't be right for him to refuse.

"All right, I'll take a look at him," he said. "Where is he?"

"He's out front here."

As soon as Ed stepped out onto the front porch, Manning, who was waiting on one side of the door, moved up behind the rancher and wrapped his arms around him, effectively pinning Ed's arms to his side.

"Here, what the . . ." Ed said, startled by

the act. That was as far as he got before Callahan stepped up behind him from the other side of the door. Callahan grabbed a handful of Ed's hair and jerked his head back. Then he drew his knife across Ed's throat. Ed's struggles ceased, and he fell to the floor.

From her bed Ina Claire heard a horse whinny, and it sounded much closer than the barn. Going to the window and raising it, she looked outside but saw nothing.

"Oh, Thunder, don't tell me you got out," she said quietly. "I know this all seems unfamiliar to you, but this is where you live now."

She put on a pair of jeans and a flannel shirt, and was just pulling on her boots when she heard footsteps in the hallway. She opened the door of her bedroom.

"Papa, if it's Thunder I'll take care of . . ." She stopped in mid-sentence when she saw not her father but four men illuminated by the lamp one of them was carrying. By the light of the lantern, she could see the purple scar on the face of one of the men.

"Mr. Cooper!" Ina Claire called out in panic. "What are you doing in our house at this time of night?"

"Cooper, get her!" one of them shouted,

pointing toward Ina Claire. The man who shouted was a big man, and in the flickering light of the candle, Claire saw that his nose was flat against his face. Because of his size, and the shape of his nose, he reminded her of an ape.

Ina Claire screamed, then slammed the door. There was no lock on the bedroom door and no way to keep anyone out. She thought of crawling under the bed but knew that would be the first place someone would look. She started toward the open window but heard the doorknob being turned. She had just gotten her jeans from the clothes hamper and quickly she climbed into it and pulled the lid down. Once inside, she pulled the clothes over her. She heard her mother's voice.

"Who are you? Ed! Ed, where are you?"

Her mother's words were followed by a gunshot.

"That takes care of both of them," Ina Claire heard a gruff voice say. "What about the girl?"

Both of them? Ina Claire wasn't sure what they were talking about, but to say both of them had an ominous sound to it. Where was her father? She stuffed a shirt into her mouth to muffle her cry.

"She slammed the door and went back

inside," another voice said.

"Morris, go in there and take care of her."

"What the hell, Callahan? She ain't nothin' but a young girl; she ain't goin' to be a-givin' us no trouble."

"I'll check on her," another voice said, and Ina Claire held her breath as she heard someone come into her room. "Cooper, bring the lantern in here, I cain't see nothin'."

"Manning, look under the bed," Cooper said. "That's where kids always hide."

Ina Claire heard the scruffing sound of someone getting down on the floor. "She ain't under here."

"Well, hell, you can see there where she went. She crawled out through the winder," Cooper said.

Having just heard him speak a moment earlier, Ina Claire knew that this was Cooper's voice. She knew also who at least two of the men were. They were Dooley Cooper and Pogue Morris, the same men who had stopped by the ranch a few days ago. She had also picked out two more names during their conversation, though the names meant nothing to her.

She intended to remember these names so she could tell the sheriff. That is, if she lived through the night.

"Come on, leave the girl be. Let's look for some money 'n food."

Ina Claire heard the footsteps of the men leaving her room, then she stayed quietly in the clothes hamper until she was sure that everyone was gone. Quietly she lifted the top of the hamper just high enough to have a good look around. She could see nothing because the room was too dark. She could, however, hear voices coming from the kitchen, and as she listened, she realized that she was hearing all four voices.

"Get the cap'n," one of the voices said. "Take 'im back into the bedroom, then put him 'n the woman in the bed."

"What for?"

"When they find the bodies, they'll think that the both of 'em died in the fire."

"What fire?"

"The fire we're goin' to set afore we leave here."

Again, Ina Claire stuffed a shirt into her mouth to muffle a sob. She had expected it before, but now she was almost certain that both of her parents were dead.

Dooley Cooper, Pogue Morris, Callahan, and Manning. These were names she didn't want to forget.

"Ten dollars?" someone said. "He ain't got nothin' but ten dollars?"

"Wait a minute," another voice said. "Lookie here."

"What've you got, Manning?"

"This here is a note from the bank sayin' he just put in fifteen hundred dollars," the one called Manning replied. "Damn, Morris, I thought you said folks like him didn't put their money in banks."

"Most of 'em don't," Morris replied. "Come on, let's get some food 'n get outta here."

134

CHAPTER ELEVEN

Positive now that there was nobody left in her bedroom, Ina Claire crawled out of the clothes hamper, walked as quietly as she could over to the window, then climbed through it. Once outside she ran across the lawn and down to the creek. She knew of an old abandoned fox den in the bank that couldn't be seen even in the daytime, if one didn't know where to look.

She felt tears streaming down her face, and she bit down on her shirtsleeve to keep from crying out loud. She worried about her mama and papa, and felt guilty about having run out on them. But reason told her that if she stayed in the house she might have been discovered, and if discovered, the men would no doubt kill her.

She reached the old fox den but didn't climb into it yet. She could see the four horses of the men who had killed her parents, and she knew they hadn't left yet.

She would keep her eyes on the horses until the men appeared, then she would crawl into the hole until she was sure they were gone.

"I will remember you, Dooley Cooper, Pogue Morris, Callahan, and Manning." She said the words aloud to embed them in her memory. "I will not forget Dooley Cooper, Pogue Morris, Callahan, and Manning," she said again.

Cooper, Morris, Callahan, and Manning were still in the house, still searching, unsuccessfully, for money.

"You know what?" Callahan said. "We'd better grab what food we can and get out of here. What if the girl comes back?"

"Ha, what if she does? Are we supposed to be afraid of her?" Morris asked.

"We don't know where she went. She could be comin' back with a dozen men," Callahan suggested.

"Callahan's right," Cooper said. "We need to get out of here."

"Yeah," Callahan agreed. "But not until we've set the house on fire."

From her hiding place on the bank of Little Bear Creek, Ina Claire saw the four men approaching their horses, so she climbed down into the fox den. There, she waited until she heard the sound of horses as the men left. As carefully as she could, she crawled up the side of the bank. She lay down so that even if they looked toward her they wouldn't be able to see her, and she watched as the four men rode away.

Then she saw something else that caused her heart to leap into her throat. Flames were licking out of the kitchen window!

"Mama! Papa!" she yelled.

Getting up then, and without regard as to whether she could be seen or not, she ran back to the house and in through the front door. So far the flames were confined to the kitchen, which was in the back of the house, and none of the rest of the structure was involved. She looked into the kitchen to see if she could extinguish the fire but saw that it was too advanced, and putting it out was not an option. She had to get her parents out of the house.

Running into their bedroom, she saw both of them lying in bed.

"Mama! Papa!" she called out in the forlorn hope that they might still be alive. But she realized as soon as she reached them that both were dead.

Grabbing her mother by her feet, Ina Claire was able to pull her out of the house.

Dead or not, she didn't intend to let them stay in the burning house. But it was a struggle to move her mother, and, with a sinking heart, she realized she wouldn't be able to get her father out.

"Oh, Papa, I'm sorry," she said. "I can't get you out."

She closed her eyes, trying to erase the image in her mind of her father's body, not only dead but burned and blackened beyond recognition.

She heard the excited whinny of the horses. Made uneasy by the nearness of the flames, they were beginning to get restless. That was when she got the idea.

"Thunder!" she shouted, knowing then how she would extract her father.

Running into the barn she grabbed a rope, tied it around Thunder's neck, and led him back to the house. She tried to get him to go into the house, but he was too frightened by the flames. Then she took off her shirt and wrapped it around Thunder's head and over his eyes. That done, she was able to lead him into the house, where she tied the rope around her father's ankles.

By now the fire had broken out of the kitchen and into the dining room. The smoke was growing heavy, too, but with her urging, Thunder pulled her father out of the house and into the front yard, far enough away from the house so as not to be caught up in the flames.

She looked down at both of them for a long moment.

"Mama, Papa," she said. "I know who did this. And I will see that they pay for this, no matter how long it takes."

Ina Claire was still holding on to the rope that was around Thunder's neck, and she led him back into the barn, where, by the light of the burning house, she saddled him.

There were four other horses in the barn, and she turned them out to pasture as a safety precaution in case the barn should catch fire.

Then, mounting Thunder, she rode him to her nearest neighbor.

Behind her, the house continued to burn.

"Mr. MacCallister! Mr. MacCallister!"

Duff was awakened by the call from outside the house. It sounded like a young woman was calling him, but who would it be? And what was she doing here at this hour?

"Mr. MacCallister, it's me, Ina Claire Culpepper. Please, come out!"

Startled by the announcement, Duff sat up in the bed. "I'll be right out, Ina Claire!"

he called.

Dressing as quickly as he could, Duff lit a lantern and started toward the front door. As he passed by the wall clock he saw that it was a little after four thirty in the morning.

When he reached the front porch, he saw Ina Claire sitting on the steps, holding the reins of her horse.

"Ina Claire, what is it? What's wrong, lass?"

"They're dead."

"Who's dead?" Duff asked, though he feared that he knew the answer.

"Mama and Papa. They're both dead. The men who did it burned the house."

Duff looked in the direction of Twin Pine and saw an orange glow on the horizon.

"Your mother and father? Are they . . . ?"

Ina Claire answered the question before Duff had to ask it.

"They didn't burn up. I got them out of the house and now they're both lying in the front yard."

By now Elmer and Wang had joined them.

"Who would do such a thing?" Elmer asked.

"I know who it was, Mr. Gleason. I know all their names, and I'm going to find them and make them pay for it."

■ ■ ■ ■

From the *Chugwater Newspaper:*

A DEED MOST FOUL

In the dead of night four scoundrels, who by their action could scarcely be called men, entered by stealth the house of Captain Edward Andrew Culpepper. Captain Culpepper, known and respected by all in Chugwater and by most in the country, was a West Point graduate, who after his service in the army became a rancher, a pillar of the community, and a vestryman in St. Paul's Episcopal Church.

Of his wife, Julie Ann McClain Culpepper, there are insufficient accolades to do her justice. Loved by all who knew her, she was a devoted wife and a caring mother. Beyond that, she was a woman who could be found participating in any charitable event and, like her husband, was a member of St. Paul's Episcopal Church.

This article speaks of these two fine citizens in the past tense, for it was four evil men who cut short the lives of Captain and Mrs. Culpepper. Their daughter, Miss

Ina Claire, survived the carnage by slipping away from the house before the foul deed could be visited upon her as well.

Funeral services will be held at St. Paul's on Friday at two o'clock.

Almost all of the businesses in Chugwater, including even the saloons, were closed for the funeral of Ed and Julie Culpepper. The cemetery was so crowded with mourners that the Nunnelee Funeral Home hearse, bearing both coffins, had a difficult time getting through the crowd to the burial site, where there were two open graves, side by side.

Two sets of pallbearers removed the coffins from the hearse and carried them over to rope cradles that were stretched across the excavated graves. Then, from another part of the cemetery came the sound of a muffled drum, joined quickly by the bagpipe playing of "Amazing Grace." Those gathered around the graves separated to provide a path for the pipes and drum. The drummer came first, the drum draped in black.

"Who's that playing the drum?"

"Why, that's Captain Culpepper's daughter, young Ina Claire."

"I had no idea she could play the drum. What's that she's a-wearin'?"

"I'm not sure."

Ina Claire was wearing the *arisad,* the traditional Scottish lady's dress that Meagan had given her for a much more joyous occasion than this.

Duff followed behind, wearing the kilts of the Black Watch, the music of the pipes filling the cemetery like the wailing of a thousand mourners.

Meagan had helped Ina Claire get dressed this morning and had supplied the black bunting for the drum. Meagan stood at the graveside watching as Ina Claire and Duff approached. Her own eyes welled with tears but she saw no tears in Ina Claire's eyes. She saw, instead, an expression that was difficult to ascertain. It was somewhere between anger and determination.

"It's all right to cry, dear, nobody will think the less of you for it," Meagan had told her while she was helping her prepare for the funeral.

"I don't have time to cry right now," Ina Claire had replied.

Meagan wasn't sure what that meant, but she didn't press the girl for an explanation.

Ina Claire and Duff marched to the edge of the grave and then stopped. The music ended and the priest nodded toward the pallbearers, who lowered the coffins into the open graves. Father Ericson then dropped a handful of dirt on each of the coffins as he read from the prayer book. *"Unto Almighty God we commend the souls of our brother Ed Culpepper, and our sister Julie Culpepper, departed, and we commit their bodies to the ground; earth to earth, ashes to ashes, dust to dust; in sure and certain hope of the Resurrection unto eternal life, through our Lord Jesus Christ, at whose coming in glorious majesty to judge the world, the earth, and the sea shall give up their dead; and the corruptible bodies of those who sleep in him shall be changed, and made like unto his own glorious body; according to the mighty working whereby he is able to subdue all things unto himself."* Several of the mourners had tears streaming down their cheeks, but Ina Claire did not. She was still dry eyed and stone faced.

The priest concluded the burial ceremony. *"Oh, Lord Jesus Christ, who by thy death didst take away the sting of death; Grant unto us thy servants so to follow in faith where thou hast led the way, that we may at length fall asleep peacefully in thee, and awake up after thy likeness; through thy mercy, who livest with the Father and the Holy Ghost, one God, world without end. Amen."*

"Amen," the mourners repeated, many of

whom, including Ina Claire, crossed themselves.

The mourners were surprised, then, to see Biff Johnson, the man they all knew as the proprietor of Fiddler's Green, step up to the side of the grave. Biff was wearing the dress uniform of an army first sergeant, complete with a gold *aiguillette* hanging from his shoulder and looping around the bright yellow chevrons on his sleeve. On his left breast he wore the Medal of Honor, having won the prestigious award at Saylor's Creek during the Civil War.

Biff lifted a bugle to his lips and held it for a long, silent moment, then began to play "Taps."

Starting with two short notes in G, it moved to a middle C, which Biff held much longer than the dotted half-note called for. Then several quick notes, ending with a high E again, the note held long.

Echoes of the music returned from a near-by rock face, almost as if the very hills were crying.

There were many old soldiers among the mourners who had a personal connection to this solemn music, which not only put soldiers to bed but lay them down for that long, final sleep. Even Ina Claire could remember back to her time as a young girl listening to the lone bugler, standing out in the quadrangle beneath the flag pole, lifting the doleful notes to reach into every barracks, BOQ, and married officers and NCO quarters.

Some might think Biff was playing "Taps" only for her father, but she knew better. She knew that her mother had also listened to that most sacred of all bugle calls, and she knew that this was for her as well.

Biff finally reached the last note, a middle C, which he held for a very long time . . . as if reluctant to say good-bye to Captain Edward Andrew Culpepper and his wife, Julie Ann McClain Culpepper. Then, that long, final note just drifted away, and the last tenuous connection between Ed, Julie, and those who were still among the living was severed. Their souls were answering muster on the other side of that great divide, and they were gone forever.

CHAPTER TWELVE

With the graveside service completed, the mourners left the cemetery, many to reopen their place of business. Meagan did not return to her dress emporium but went instead to Fiddler's Green, where she joined Duff and Biff at the "owner's" table. Duff was no longer wearing his kilts, having changed in a room that Biff had made available for him. Biff had stopped by his house on the way back to change out of his uniform, so that once again he, too, was in mufti.

Together again at Fiddler's Green, Biff and Duff were drinking scotch, while Meagan had wine.

"The girl seems to be taking it well," Biff said.

"No, she's taking it very hard," Meagan said.

"I didn't see her crying," Biff said.

"That's just it. Her grief is well beyond

crying. I studied her face during the funeral. I don't think I've ever seen such a face. It was a combination of grief, anger, retribution, and resolution."

"Where is she now?" Biff asked.

"The lass is still in the cemetery," Duff said. "I started to ask her to come with me but decided against it. 'Tis sometimes best to give a body time for some private grief. I know," he added.

At the cemetery

Except for the gravediggers, Ina Claire was the last one remaining in the cemetery, and she stood there looking down into the two open graves.

"Miss, you just take your time," one of the gravediggers said. "We'll close the graves after you're gone."

"You can do it now," Ina Claire said.

"No, ma'am, it wouldn't be proper for us to do it now. Not with you standin' here."

"If you won't do it, I will," Ina Claire said, and, grabbing a nearby shovel, filled the spade from the pile of dirt and tossed it into the nearest grave. She could hear the loud thumps of dirt as they fell on her mother's casket.

"No need for you to be doin' that, missy. We'll take care of it."

Ina Claire surrendered the shovel and stepped aside to watch. She remained until the men finished covering the two graves, then pounded down the mounds of soil so that they were smooth, with no large dirt clods left. Then, tossing the shovels into a wagon, the four men drove out of the graveyard, leaving Ina Claire behind.

A dust devil developed on the far side of the cemetery and moved across the ground until it reached her parents' graves. There, benefiting from the new dirt, it grew twice as large before finally moving on.

A ray of sun, split by the limbs of a nearby aspen tree, fell in two distinct spears, one on each of the two graves.

A dog came trotting through the cemetery and stopped to sniff the two mounds of dirt. The dog looked up at her with soulful eyes, holding his gaze for a long moment as if he could share her sorrow, then he moved on. A crow called, then all sound and movement stilled, and Ina Claire felt suspended in time and place.

"Mama, Papa, I will see to it that the men who did this terrible thing are found and punished. I know you may think I'm just a girl, and have no place making such promises, but it is a promise I intend to keep.

"Mr. MacCallister is a very good friend of

149

yours, and I have heard the stories, some of which you have told, Papa, of the many brave and wonderful things he has done in the past. I will see him because I know he will help me. And if he doesn't help me, I'll do it myself."

At Fiddler's Green

"Duff, what do you think is going to happen to Ina Claire?" Meagan asked. "I'm worried about her, so young and now all alone."

"I don't know. The lass has lots of sand, I can tell you that. I expect that she'll wind up with her grandparents."

"They are where now? In Ohio?"

"Aye."

"Do you think they'll come out to live on Twin Pine?"

"I hope so," Duff said. " 'Tis a fine ranch, I would nae like to see the girl lose it."

Elmer and Wang came into the saloon then. Elmer was uncharacteristically wearing a suit including a shirt and tie. He stuck his finger down in the collar to pull it away from his neck.

Wang was wearing a black *changshan,* the traditional dress for Chinese of station and, as a Shaolin priest, Wang qualified.

"That was a real nice funeral, and it was

150

some particular nice when you played 'Taps' like that," Elmer said as he joined the others at the table. "I knowed all about Duff bein' able to play the bagpipes, 'cause I've done seen him do it enough times. But I have to admit that you surprised me, Biff. I had no idee you could blow the bugle like you done."

"When I first came into the army, I was a bugler," Biff said. "As I moved up in rank, I was no longer a bugler but I didn't put it away. I still play it enough to maintain the embouchure."

"The what?" Elmer asked.

"To keep my lips in shape," Biff said.

"Well, why didn't you say so?"

"I believe that your music comforted the souls of Mr. and Mrs. Culpepper as they lay there, awaiting the change," Wang said.

"Thank you, Wang, this was my hope," Biff replied.

"Oh, Duff, I just thought I'd tell you, we've got all of Cap'n Culpepper's livestock took care of now. All his cattle 'n horses is in with our'n, so it'll be easy to look after 'em 'til the girl decides what she wants to do with 'em."

"Oh, there's Ina Claire now," Meagan said, nodding toward the front door. They saw Ina Claire, still wearing the plaid dress,

151

and still carrying the black draped drum, standing just inside the batwing doors.

"Miss Culpepper, you don't want to come in here," the bartender called to her.

"Oh, Lord," Meagan said quietly. "Biff, please, you can't send her away."

"It's all right, Tony, the young lady is welcome here," Biff called over to his bartender. Then to Meagan, "Miss Meagan, bring her into the meeting room in back. Have Tony draw a sarsaparilla for the young lady."

"Good idea and I'll have one as well," Meagan said as she hurried to the front door to meet the young girl.

Duff, Biff, Elmer, and Wang moved from the barroom into a smaller room at the back of the saloon . . . a room that was often used for civic meetings. Meagan and Ina Claire came into the room a moment later, each of them carrying a glass of sarsaparilla. All four men were standing, and they remained standing until the two ladies were seated.

"Ina Claire, darlin', I'm so sorry about your mama and papa," Elmer said. "They was both people to ride to the river with."

"Papa thought the world of you, Mr. Gleason. And you, too, Mr. Wang," she added, nodding toward Wang.

"I knew both of them very well, and they

were two of the finest people I have ever known," Biff said.

"Thank you, Mr. Johnson."

"Honey, when we leave here, I want you to come on down to my store with me," Meagan said. "I know that you lost all your clothes when your house burned, so I'm going to make you an entirely new wardrobe, free of charge."

"Thank you, Miss Parker, I appreciate that. But as soon as I'm able to get some money from Papa's bank account, I'm going to be making some other purchases from Chugwater Mercantile."

"I know, you're going to have to start all over with cooking utensils, lanterns, furniture, and the like," Meagan said. "But you won't need to be wasting your money on that. I've already heard several of the men and ladies talking. The men plan to rebuild your house, and the ladies are making a collection of everything you'll need to get started again or to sell your house if you decide to leave."

"Oh, I have no intention of leaving, and I think it is wonderful of everyone to do something like that for me. But some of the things I'll need I'm sure they won't be collecting."

"What would that be?"

"A hat, jeans, shirts, boots, a bedroll, canteen, camp skillet, pistol, rifle, hunting knife, and a couple of boxes of pistol ammunition, as well as a box of rifle bullets."

Ina Claire issued her shopping list quietly, resolutely, and without expression.

"Heavens, child, why would you need all of that?" Biff asked.

"Because I'm going with Mr. MacCallister when he goes after the men who murdered my mama and papa. And I expect I'll be needing such things."

"Ina Claire, I —" Duff started to say, but Ina Claire interrupted him.

"And if you are about to tell me that you aren't going after them, then I expect I'll be going after them myself," the girl said.

Duff shook his head slowly. "I wasn't about to say I wasn't going after them. I fully intend to do that. I was about to say I wouldn't want you to be going with me."

"Mr. MacCallister, I'll either be going with you . . . or I'll be trailing along behind you. And disabuse yourself of any idea that I won't be able to keep up with you. Thunder is a very good horse, I am a very good rider, and I'm at least eighty pounds lighter than you are. There is absolutely no way you could lose me."

Biff laughed out loud. "Are you *disabused*

of that idea, Duff?"

"Please, Mr. MacCallister, let me go with you." Much of the defiance was gone both from Ina Claire's words and facial expression. "I won't get in your way, I promise. And I might be able to help you."

"How are you going to be able to help him, honey?" Meagan asked.

"Well to begin with, I know the names of all the men who did it." She stopped, then counted out the names on her fingers as she recalled the names she had heard spoken by the men: "Callahan, Manning, Dooley Cooper, and Pogue Morris."

"What? How could you possibly know that?" Biff asked.

"About a week ago, Dooley Cooper and Pogue Morris were traveling through, and when they stopped for water, Papa invited them to have dinner with us. That's how I know their names. I heard the other two names spoken while I was hiding from them, but I don't know their whole names. Please, Mr. MacCallister, let me go with you. Those evil men set at our table with us, ate food that Mama had cooked, and then broke into our house in the middle of the night, killed Mama and Papa, and set the house on fire."

"That would be Clay Callahan and Zeke

Manning," Duff said.

"How do you . . ." Meagan started, then she stopped in mid-sentence. "Those are the two men who tried to rob the bank in Archer, aren't they?"

"Yes, I didn't know they weren't in jail. Last I heard they had been tried, convicted, and sentenced to hang."

"They musta broke out of jail," Elmer suggested.

"Which means there's nothing holding them back," Biff said.

"Oh, Duff. And if you're the one who put them in jail, they'll be coming after you."

"Unless I go after them first," Duff said.

"Good!" Ina Claire said. "I knew you would be going with me."

"Let me ask you this, Ina Claire. How did you get your mother and father out of the house?" Duff asked.

"I was able to drag Mama out, but Papa was too heavy. So I brought Thunder into the house, tied a rope around Papa's ankles, and had Thunder pull him out."

"You took your horse into the house while it was on fire?" Meagan asked.

"Yes, ma'am."

"How in the world did you do that?"

"I have to admit that Thunder wasn't any too happy about it, but I covered his eyes

156

and he went along with it."

"That's amazing," Meagan said.

"Come to the bank with me," Duff said.

"I beg your pardon?"

"Come to the bank with me. I'll help you get the money to buy the things you need. You won't have to worry about the food, I'll take care of that."

Ina Claire's eyes grew wide. "You mean I *can* go with you?"

"Aye, lass, you can go with me."

"Duff, you aren't serious?" Meagan said.

"Sure 'n anyone who can take a horse into a burning house has earned the right. You did say that two of the men had taken sup at your house, didn't you?" Duff asked Ina Claire. "Do you think you'll be able to recognize them if you see them again?"

"Yes, sir, I know I will recognize them. Remember, they sat at the table with us and ate our food. One of them has an ugly scar on his cheek. I would recognize one of the others, too. He's a big man, as big as you are, Mr. MacCallister. He's an ugly man, too, his nose," she paused and put her hand to her own nose. "His nose is real flat right here."

"Aye, ye've just described Callahan, all right. His features are just as ugly as his soul."

157

Ina Claire was quiet for a moment, then her eyes welled with tears. "They ate with us, then repaid us by killing Mama and Papa."

"Anybody who would repay a kindness like that by doin' what these men did are nothin' but low-down sons of bitches," Elmer said. Then, realizing what he said, he apologized. "Sorry 'bout usin' words like that in front of you two ladies."

"That's quite all right, Elmer," Meagan said. "There are times when 'son of a bitch' is the only appropriate sobriquet."

"Do you want me 'n Wang to go with you?" Elmer asked.

"No, I don't think so. Somebody needs to watch over Sky Meadow, and I'd feel better if it were you."

"All right," Elmer agreed. "I reckon we'll just go on out there now. If you need us for any reason, send us a telegram 'n we'll be there quicker 'n . . ."

Duff held up his finger and shook his head. "Nae, Elmer, I'll not be for hearing another one of your quaint aphorisms. Remember, there be ladies present."

Elmer smiled. "Why, Duff, I was only goin' to say 'quicker 'n you can stop me from cussin'.' "

The others around the table laughed.

"Come, lass, I'll go to the bank with you and see that you get your pa's money," Duff said to Ina Claire.

CHAPTER THIRTEEN

"Oh, my, it appears that Captain Culpepper died intestate," the president of the Bank of Chugwater said as he examined the late rancher's account.

"What does that mean?" Ina Claire asked.

"It means your father left no will, so I have no authority to grant you access to his account until the estate is adjudicated."

"But, Mr. Montgomery, Papa wasn't an old man. He didn't have a will yet because he wasn't expecting to die so young. You knew him, and you know he intended to leave the money to Mama, or if Mama wasn't around, to me."

"Oh, I have no doubt but that you will be the beneficiary of your father's account," Montgomery agreed. "But legally, before I can release any of his money to you, Judge Thorndike will have to sign off on it, and more than likely, that will take a week or two."

"No, I don't have a week or two."

"I was afraid that you might run into something like this," Duff said. "Dinnae you be worrying about it. I'll make a loan to you of all the money you'll need until ye have access to your own money."

"Oh, would you? How wonderful of you to do such a thing," Ina Claire said. "Thank you. Thank you so much."

Fifteen minutes later Duff and Ina Claire were at Sikes Gun Shop, with Ina Claire holding the pistol Duff had picked out for her. "This is an Army Colt, .45 caliber, single action. 'Tis a good, dependable weapon," he explained. "And because it is a .45 caliber, it has a lot of stopping power. You'll be needin' a holster as well."

"What about a rifle?" Ina Claire asked.

Duff shook his head. "Nae, 'tis better off you would be with a shotgun." He handed her a double-barrel gun from the display rack.

"Oh, this is pretty heavy," Ina Claire observed.

Duff smiled. "It won't be all that heavy after we saw off the barrel."

"You're going to saw off the barrel?"

"Not all of it," Duff said. "I'm going to leave you about six inches. That way it'll be lighter and easier for you to carry. It will

161

also be for giving you a wider spread o' the shot, 'n woe betide anyone who would try 'n come after you when such a weapon is in your hand."

Ina Claire smiled. "I hope it's one of the men who came to the house."

"Steve, m' lad, have ye any ammunition for my pistol?"

"An Enfield Mark 1 Revolver," Sikes replied. "Forty-seven caliber. You're the only one in town with such a weapon and probably the only one in the county. Why do you carry such a gun?"

"I carry it because 'twas the side-arm of all the officers in Her Majesty's army. It served me well then, 'n it has served me well since."

"Yeah, as long as you can get ammunition for it," Sikes replied. Then he smiled. "But as it so happens, I just got in a new order for you." He opened a cabinet drawer and took out five boxes. "Here are two hundred and fifty rounds. That ought to hold you for a while, unless you're plannin' on startin' your own private war."

"I may not be too far removed from that very thing," Duff replied with a little chuckle. "Ina Claire, lass, suppose you go down to the mercantile and take care of the rest of the things? You'll not be needing me for that." Duff hefted the double-barrel shotgun they had just purchased. "I'll be for taking care of this for you."

"All right, Mr. MacCallister, and thank you," Ina Claire said.

Duff turned back toward the storeowner to pay for all the purchases.

"Tell me, Duff," Sikes said as he counted out the change. "Why such things for a little girl? And when I said you may be startin' your own private war, why is it you said that you weren't that far removed from it?"

"Here now, Steve, 'n you're nae for tellin' me that you're unaware of what happened to the girl's family, are you?"

"No, no, of course not. I know about it, ever'one in town knows about it. I couldn't make it to the funeral but I did close the store down. Oh, wait, I see now. That's in case the men decide to come back, so she'll have some protection."

"Nae," Duff replied with a broad smile. "This is because the young lass is goin' after the brigands. She intends to see that justice is served."

"Lord no! Here now, she's just a young slip of a girl, not even a woman yet. Surely you can stop her from doing such a foolish thing."

"Stop her? Steve, m' boy, I expect to be

163

right there by her side the whole while."

"Well, if she is bound 'n determined to do such a thing, I'm glad you'll be with her."

With his purchases securely packaged, Duff stepped outside and saw his friend Bob Guthrie just opening the door to his lumber and building supply store, which was next door to Sikes Gun Shop.

"Duff," Guthrie greeted with a large smile. "It's good to see you this morning. Is that old coot with you?"

"If it's Elmer ye be inquiring after, he and Wang left for Sky Meadow a short while ago. I expect they may be there by now."

The smile left Guthrie's face to be replaced by an expression of extreme sadness.

"I want to say that was a good thing you did, playing the bagpipes for the funeral of Captain Culpepper 'n his wife. And the old first sergeant, playing 'Taps'? It brought back memories, I'm tellin' you. By the way, who was the young lady who played the drum with you?"

"Sure 'n you're not for tellin' me that ye didn't recognize the captain's own daughter, Ina Claire?"

"Lord, how grown up she has become. Why, I can remember when she was barely walkin'. Her pa would come in here for things he needed out at the ranch."

"Did ye not see her at the Scottish Heritage Day?"

"That was the same young lady, wasn't it? Yes, I do remember seeing her there, but I didn't realize who she was at the time." Guthrie unlocked the door and then glanced back at Duff. "Will you be seeing her again?"

"Aye, I'll be seeing her," Duff said without being too specific.

"Then, please give her my personal condolences."

"I'll do that," Duff replied.

After she left the gun store, Ina Claire walked three buildings down the street to Falkoff's Men's Clothing Store. She was surprised to see Meagan coming toward the store.

"Miss Mcagan, what are you doing here?"

"Same thing you are doing, I expect," Meagan replied. "I'll be buying the things I'll need for traveling."

"Oh? Where are you going?"

"I don't know, that depends," Meagan replied mysteriously.

"Depends on what?"

"It depends on where Duff takes us."

"Where he takes *us*?" Ina Claire asked, still not sure she was following Meagan's explanation.

"Yes, where he takes us, you and me, during our quest to find the men who killed your parents."

"Oh! Does Mr. MacCallister know you're going?"

"He doesn't know yet."

"What if he says no?"

"He said no to you," Meagan replied.

"Yes, but —"

"But what?" Meagan asked, interrupting Ina Claire in mid-sentence. "When he said no to you, that didn't stop you, did it?"

"No," Ina Claire said with a little laugh. "No, it didn't stop me."

"Besides, I know Duff, quite well actually. And I know what a pigheaded man he can be. If we are ever going to have anything to say about what's going on, we two girls are going to have to stick together." Meagan stuck her hand out. "Is it a deal?"

A broad smile spread across Ina Claire's face, and she reached out to take Meagan's hand. "It's a deal," she said with a little laugh.

"You understand, I've no trousers for young ladies," David Friedman said, coming back from another part of the store. "These are men's trousers, boys actually, as there are no men's trousers small enough to fit you."

"That will be fine," Ina Claire said.

"Miss Parker," Friedman said, having just noticed her and surprised to see her in his store. He got a guilty expression on his face and gestured toward Ina Claire. "I'm not trying to steal any of your customers," he said quickly. "I don't sell ladies clothes as you know. This young lady —"

"I know why she is here," Meagan said, interrupting him in mid-sentence. "I'm here for the same reason."

"I beg your pardon?"

"I want to buy some trousers."

"Yes, ma'am, I'll be happy to take care of you," Friedman said with a relieved smile.

On the road between Fort Laramie and
  Bordeaux,
Wyoming Territory
The peddler's wagon was making a great deal of noise as the pots and pans banged, clanged, and rattled. The peddler was singing aloud, his off-key rendition of "Buffalo Gals" adding to the cacophony.

"Tell me again why we're robbin' a peddler?" Pogue Morris asked. The two men rode a good distance behind the oblivious peddler. "It ain't like we're a-needin' any pots 'n pans. Or any of his notions."

"How much money do you have?" Calla-han asked.

"Countin' the money I got left over from when me 'n Cooper robbed the boat, I got near seventy dollars."

"What about you, Cooper?"

"I got seventy-two dollars."

"And on account of Manning 'n me was in jail, we got five dollars apiece from the ten dollars we took from the rancher's house. And unlessen you two is willin' to divide up what you got, that means that me 'n Manning don't have any more than to say, nothin' a-tall. But now, that peddler has been out sellin' to farmers 'n ranchers 'n such. It ain't more'n likely he'll have over fifty or sixty dollars on 'im. But it ain't more'n likely he'll have less than twenty dollars, neither, 'n right now to me 'n Manning, twenty dollars is a lot."

"Yeah, I see what you mean," Cooper replied.

By now the peddler was close enough that his singing could be heard even over the clanging of the pots and pans, and the squeak and rattle of the wagon on the move.

". . . come out tonight, come out tonight,
Buffalo gals, won't you come out tonight,
'N dance by the light of the moon."

168

"Here 'e comes," Callahan said. "Get ready."

Cooper and Morris moved to one side of the road and got behind a high growing mesquite tree . . . . Callahan and Manning waited on the opposite side of the road behind an outcropping of rocks.

"As I was walking down the street,
Down the street, down the street,
A pretty little gal I chanced to meet,
Chanced to meet, chanced to meet."

"Hold it up there, peddler!" Callahan shouted as the four of them moved quickly around in front of the road.

Startled by their sudden appearance, the peddler's team of horses whinnied and reared up. That caused the horses the outlaws were riding to twist around, and the peddler, seeing that, tried to take advantage of the situation by picking his pistol up from the seat beside him and firing at the men who had accosted him.

His shot was hurried and inaccurate. Callahan fired back, and the peddler fell from his seat.

"I'll search the wagon," Cooper said.

"Yeah, do that, but more'n likely, any money he has is on him," Callahan said, dismounting.

As Cooper and Morris banged the pots and pans around, looking through the wagon, Callahan searched the peddler. He saw a small pouch hanging from the peddler's belt. Opening it, he saw a roll of bills. He removed the bills and counted the money.

"Whooee, boys, we done hit the jackpot," Callahan called to the others. "There's two hundred and thirteen dollars here!"

"How we goin' to divide it up?" Manning asked.

Callahan did some figuring. "The way I figure it, we'll all have ninety dollars apiece."

"Wait a minute, I ain't all that good at cipherin'," Cooper said, "but even I know that if we divide two hunnert 'n thirteen dollars up into four equal parts, you ain't goin' to come up with no ninety dollars apiece."

"Sure we will," Callahan said. "Countin' the money you 'n Morris already got, we can come up with ninety dollars apiece, easy."

"You ain't got no right to take any of our money," Morris said angrily.

"I'm not taking any of your money."

"The hell you ain't. You just said you was goin' to."

"How much money do you have now?"

Callahan asked.

"I told you before, I got seventy dollars."

"By the time we get this all divided out, you'll have ninety dollars, 'n that's twenty dollars more'n you got now. So how is that takin' any of your money?"

"Well, all right," Morris said. "I guess I didn't look at it like that."

A few minutes later the four men rode away, leaving behind them a team of mules, a wagon loaded with pots, pans, and notions, and a dead peddler.

CHAPTER FOURTEEN

Chugwater

"What do you mean you're going with us?" Duff asked when he came back to Meagan's dress emporium and saw that both Meagan and Ina Claire were wearing jeans, flannel shirts, wide brim hats, and, significantly, holstered pistols.

"I thought I spoke my words pretty clearly," Meagan said.

Duff was carrying two canvas bags, and he lay them down on one of the dress tables.

"Meagan, no, I'm going to have enough trouble looking out for Ina Claire. Having to look out for both of you is going to make my job even more difficult."

"Ina Claire and I will look out for each other, and you look out for yourself."

"Meagan . . ."

Meagan held up her hand. "Suppose I give you a good reason for taking us along with you. If I can give you such a reason . . . and

172

if you will consider it honestly, will you change your mind about taking us?"

"All right, what is the reason?"

"You're the one who stopped Callahan and Manning and put them in jail in the first place, aren't you?"

"Aye, that I am."

"Don't you think he might be looking for you?"

"Aye, he might be. But he'll nae be looking for me as hard as I'll be looking for him."

"Do you think he'll be looking for a man traveling through the countryside with his wife and his sister-in-law beside him? Or would, perhaps, that just be another family out on the road? That wouldn't arouse any interest at all, let alone suspicion."

"Wife and sister-in-law?"

Meagan smiled, then reached over to put her hand on Duff's cheek. "My darling husband, I think it is just wonderful of you to take in my sister like you have done." She put her arm around Ina Claire's shoulder. Smiling, and getting into the idea, Ina Claire leaned against Meagan.

"Yes," Ina Claire said. "After all, you are my favorite brother-in-law."

Duff stared at the two of them for a moment as if they had lost their minds, then he laughed. "Suppose I take my little family down to Mountain View Café for dinner?"

When the three of them stepped into the Mountain View Café, Meagan and Ina Claire drew curious stares. Because Meagan owned the dress shop, she hardly ever allowed herself to be seen in public dressed in anything but the latest fashion. Meagan was a very pretty woman, and wearing such attire was a very good method of advertising her dresses. But this was a total change from how she was normally seen.

After they took their table, Meagan glanced at those who were staring. "I may have cost myself a lot of business coming in here like this," she said quietly.

"That's why I wanted us to come here," Duff said with a sly smile.

"What?" Meagan asked, clearly shocked by his comment.

"If you are going to force me into doing something I would rather not do, like taking you with me, then I want you to have to suffer the consequences for it."

"I can't believe that you, of all people, would say something like that to me," Meagan replied, though the smile on her face proved that she wasn't really angry with him.

"Maybe you should begin selling denim

trousers for women," Ina Claire suggested. "Who knows, you might start a whole new fashion."

"Ha! Can you see women wearing waist overalls? No, my dear, not in one hundred years will we ever see women wearing Mr. Levi's trousers as a fashion," Meagan replied.

"I wish it would become something that women would wear. You can do ever so much more wearing trousers than you can wearing a dress."

"Well, that is true," Meagan admitted. "I have to admit that when I accompanied Duff in the delivery of some cattle to Fort Laramie, I wore such garb as I find myself in today. And I'm sure I would not have been able to make the drive had I been wearing a dress."

"Aye, 'n 'twas a fine cowboy ye made, too," Duff said.

"Cowboy? Cowboy? Duff MacCallister, I might have been dressed like a cowboy, but I'll have you know, I was no cowboy!"

Duff laughed. "Right you are, Meagan, 'twas not a cowboy I stole a kiss from in the moonlight."

"Duff MacCallister!" Meagan gasped. "How can you say such a thing in front of this child?"

Ina Claire laughed. "Well, if you are going to pretend to be Mr. MacCallister's wife, don't you think he might have to kiss you from time to time? Even in front of me?"

"That is true," Meagan said, joining Ina Claire in laughter.

"Ina Claire, m' lass, 'tis good to see you laughing," Duff said. "But, I've a suggestion for you."

"What is that?"

"If you are to be my sister-in-law, dinnae ye think 'twould be better if ye'd be for calling me Duff?"

"All right, Duff," Ina Claire replied.

When the diners at the adjacent table finished their meal and departed, Duff glanced over and saw that they had left a newspaper behind. He stood up.

"Where are you going, Duff?" Ina Claire asked.

"It would be my guess that he's going to retrieve a free newspaper," Meagan said. "Since I've become quite familiar with this . . . 'character' . . . I can tell you from firsthand experience that anything you may have heard as to how frugal a Scotsman might be is all true."

"I heard ye talking to the lass, but because I am careful with money doesn't mean I'm parsimonious. 'Tis a reasonable man I be, and if chance grants me the opportunity to take advantage of a free newspaper, then 'twould be foolish of me . . ." Duff glanced at the newspaper, then stopped in mid-sentence. Something had caught his attention.

Meagan and Ina Claire exchanged a glance, as if questioning each other about Duff's interrupted dialogue.

"There is a story in the paper of Zeke Manning and Clay Callahan," Duff said after a moment of reading.

"What is the story?" Meagan asked.

" 'Twas to hang, they were, but they escaped jail on the night before, murdering the jailer and the hangman as they did so. The story says 'tis believed that two unknown men helped them escape, but 'twould be my thinking that those men would be none other than Dooley Cooper and Pogue Morris."

"It was Ina Claire who put all the names together," Meagan said.

"Aye, 'tis thanks to Ina Claire."

"Then see? I've already been of help to you, and we haven't even started yet," Ina Claire said with a triumphant smile. "Aren't you glad you're taking me?"

The dirt streets were covered with layer upon layer of horse droppings that, over time, had broken down into an emulsified muck. The result was a stench so strong it overpowered everything. To an Easterner, the smell may have been unbearable, but to men like Callahan, Manning, Cooper, and Morris, it was so much a part of their personal history that they barely noticed it.

Picking their way through the malodorous ooze, they crossed the street and stepped up onto the boardwalk in front of the Wrangler Saloon, where they made use of a brush shoe-scraper that was nailed to the boardwalk just for that purpose. Callahan stood for a moment outside looking over the batwing doors into the shadowed interior of the saloon.

"Any law in there?" Cooper asked.

"None that I can see," Callahan replied. " 'N if there was, I don't think they'd know anything about us."

When the four rough-looking and unkempt men stepped into the saloon, all the patrons looked at them pointedly. Most of the saloon customers were working cowboys, and they could tell in one quick glance that the four armed men who had just come in rode for no brand.

Callahan knew that everyone in the bar was eyeing them with curiosity, but he also was aware that there would be no one in here who would challenge any of them, especially since none of the saloon patrons were wearing pistols on their hips.

Unlike the polished bar of some of the better saloons Callahan had seen, this one was made of unpainted, rip-sawed lumber. Its only concession to decorum was to place towels in rings spaced about five feet apart on the customer side of the bar. But the towels looked as if they had not been changed in months, if ever, so their very filth negated the effect of having them there.

When the four men stepped up to the bar, the bartender, with a dirty towel thrown across one shoulder, moved down to him.

"Yeah?" he said.

"Whiskey," Callahan said.

The bartender took a bottle from the shelf behind the bar and poured four glasses, passing the bottle across them without spilling a drop. Each man paid for his own drink, plopping down ten cents apiece, and then, taking the shot glasses with them, left the bar and found an empty table.

"You said you had an idee as to how we could get some more money," Cooper said.

"Yeah, I do."

"I hope it ain't another peddler," Manning said.

"What are you complainin' about?" Callahan asked. "If we hadn't pulled that little job, you wouldn't even be able to afford the whiskey you're a-drinkin' now."

"Callahan's right," Morris said. He chuckled. " 'Cause I damn sure wouldn'ta bought nothin' for you."

"What do you have in mind?" Cooper asked.

"One of the places I checked out before we tried that place in Archer was in Bordeaux," Callahan said.

"The one in Archer didn't work out all that well for you, did it?"

"No."

"Why'd you wind up choosin' that one?"

"The LaFarge brothers said they knew it well, and knew it had a lot of money. And things were going well until MacCallister come along."

"MacCallister?" Morris said.

"Yeah. Duff MacCallister. He's the one that stopped ever'thing."

"Wait a minute. Are you talkin' about just one man?"

"He ain't like no normal man," Manning said. "That son of a bitch stood right in the middle of the street 'n kilt both the LaFarge brothers, 'n woulda kilt us iffen we hadn't give up when we did."

"Is he a deputy sheriff or a bounty hunter or some such?"

Callahan shook his head. "I don't know who the hell the son of a bitch is. But if I ever find out who he is, I'll damn well make 'im pay for what he done to us that day."

"Yeah, well, we'll just have to keep on the lookout for him. Right now I'm more interested in getting some money," Cooper said. "You say you checked out Bordeaux?"

"Yeah, they got a nice little bank and it should be just right for us. And unlike Archer, it ain't close to no big town. There ain't no railroad or even a telegraph that comes to it, so it would take a long time before any word could get out as to what happened. It's more'n likely that there ain't nobody there that's even heard of what happened down in Archer, let alone heard of us."

"What about the *Lady Harlie*?" Manning asked. "Bordeaux ain't all that far from Hartville. It could be that they heard about that job."

"Hell, they still think it was one o' the deckhands that took the money," Cooper said with a little chuckle. "We don't have to worry none about that."

"And we didn't leave no witness back at the peddler's wagon," Morris said. He smiled. "I think Callahan is right. This may be just the job for us."

Callahan held his glass out. "Drink up, boys. We're about to come in to some money. If we're lucky, a lot of money."

Twin Pine Ranch

There were three wagons filled with building material. Half a dozen men pulled away the charred timbers and the blackened contents of what had been the main house at the ranch. Ina Claire was staying at Sky Meadow now, but she, Duff, and Meagan had ridden over this morning just to see what was going on.

This was the first time Ina Claire had been back since the night of the fire, and at the sight of what had been her house, her eyes welled with tears. Meagan put her arm around Ina Claire, drawing the girl close to her.

R. W. Guthrie, who owned the company in Chugwater from which all the building material came, walked over to greet them.

"Hello, Duff, Miss Parker," he said. Then he turned his attention to Ina Claire.

"Miss Culpepper, I want to tell you again how sorry I am for what happened to your mama and papa." He pointed to the pile of blackened timbers. "And I want you to know that we are going to build this house back, exactly the way it was, and it will be fully furnished and ready for you whenever you are ready to come back."

"Thank you, Mr. Guthrie," she said. Then she called out to the men who were working.

"Thank you, all of you," she said.

"You're mighty welcome, Miss Culpepper," one of the men called back, and the others seconded his comment.

Ina Claire saw something familiar lying in the middle of the blackened residue, and she went over to pick it up. It was a bisque, porcelain doll, and though its dress had been partly burned away, the doll itself had survived the fire. Ina Clair brushed away the soot and ash.

"I remember when I got this doll," she said with a wistful smile. "Papa was still in the army then. We were at Fort Lincoln, and Mrs. Custer gave me this for my sixth birthday."

Meagan took the doll and examined it. "It's an exquisite doll," she said. "I'm glad it survived the fire, and I promise you that when this is all over, we, you and I, will make the most beautiful dress any doll has ever worn."

"Delight will like that," Ina Claire said. "She's very vain you know, and she enjoys pretty clothes and people making over her."

"Delight?"

"The doll's name. I named her," Ina Claire said, smiling for the first time since they arrived at the burned-out house. "Her full name is Delightful Charm Culpepper. But I always called her Delight."

Meagan laughed. "I must say, Ina Claire, that is the most inventive and 'delightful' name I have ever heard for a doll."

"Now you've done it," Ina Claire said. "You've given her a big head."

Meagan laughed again, and then Ina Claire walked over to Thunder and put the doll into the saddlebag.

After their visit as they set out toward Sky Meadow, Ina Claire looked back at the men, still busily working. It had been sad, seeing the house like this. But she held close to her heart R. W. Guthrie's promise that the next time she came back to Twin Pine, the house would be just as she remembered. It was, she thought, a testament to the esteem in which her mother and father were held in the community.

CHAPTER FIFTEEN

Bordeaux, Wyoming Territory

Before they reached the town of Bordeaux, Callahan, Manning, Cooper, and Morris split up. Cooper and Morris gave the town a wide berth so they could approach it from the north, and Callahan and Manning rode in from the south.

"You sure this is the bank we want, Callahan? It don't seem to me like there's many folks goin' in 'n out of it," Manning said as they approached the bank.

"We don't care how many people are in the bank, we only care about the money that's in the bank," Callahan replied.

"Yeah, well, that's what I'm talkin' about. If there ain't many people, then there ain't goin' to be much money."

"Ha! The ranchers 'n farmers around here got plenty of money, don't you worry none about that."

"Here comes Cooper 'n Morris," Manning said.

The two men Manning pointed out were approaching the town, riding in from the north. As soon as all four met in the middle of the street, Callahan gave the others a nod, then they cut their horses toward the Brown Dirt Cowboy Saloon. There, they dismounted in front of the establishment, looped their reins over the hitching rail, and went inside.

Because the sun had been so bright, it took a few seconds for their eyes to adjust to the dimness. Their noses were assailed by the smell of beer, tobacco smoke, and unwashed bodies. As it had been some time since any of the four of them had had a bath, the odor of unwashed bodies was lost on them.

"Find us a table where we can talk," Callahan said. "I'll get us a bottle."

When Callahan stepped up to the bar, a young woman approached him. She was dressed in a way that was designed to best display her assets, and those assets were worthy of such display.

"Hello, cowboy. I haven't seen you in here before. Would you like to buy me a drink?" She put her hand on his arm.

"No," Callahan replied gruffly. He pushed her hand away from his arm. "Get the hell away from me."

Hurt by the hateful response to her friendly greeting, the girl turned away.

"There was no need for you to treat Suzie like that," the bartender said.

"Shut up 'n give me a bottle 'n four glasses," Callahan said.

"That'll be two dollars," the bartender replied, making no move to get a bottle.

Callahan put the two dollars on the bar; the bartender took the money, then gave him a bottle and four glasses.

When Callahan returned to the table, he saw that Manning and the others were enthusiastically responding to the flirtatious attention of a couple of the bar girls.

"Get," Callahan said in a growling voice as he put the bottle and glasses on the table. He made a dismissive sweep with his hand.

"Honey, are you sure you don't want company?" one of the two women asked.

"I said get!" Callahan replied, raising his voice.

With expressions that mirrored that of the young lady Callahan had turned away at the bar, the two young women hurried from the table.

"Now what the hell did you do that for?" Morris asked.

"You plannin' on settlin' down in this

town after we take care of our business, are you?" Callahan asked.

"Well, no, but . . ." Morris started to say, but Callahan interrupted.

"There ain't no buts to it," Callahan said. "We plan to do our job, then get the hell out of town. We don't need nobody cozyin' to us a'fore we get around to takin' care of business. If they know us, they can tell the law all about us."

"What law?" Manning asked. "I ain't seen no law."

"That don't mean there ain't no deputy here."

"Yeah, all right," Morris said. "We won't talk to none of the girls."

"Not just the whores. You don't talk to nobody."

Callahan filled the four glasses and then grabbed one. "Drink up," he said.

The men tossed the drinks down, and there was enough left in the bottle for one more round.

"What did it look like, comin' in from the north?" Callahan asked Cooper. "Any reason why we can't go that way when we leave town?"

"There warn't no reason that we seen as to why we couldn't go that way," Cooper said. "I figure we could follow the north fork

188

o' the Little Laramie River, they'd be plenty of water for us, 'n it wouldn't be easy for nobody to be a-trackin' us."

The three saloon girls were standing in a small group at the bar.

"Now there is one ugly man," one of the girls said. "That flat nose, and that scrunched-up ear."

"He isn't just ugly in looks. He acts ugly, too. That's a man only his mama could love."

"What makes you think someone like him ever even had a mama?" the third girl asked, and the three laughed.

The object of their conversation was sitting at the table with Cooper, Manning, and Morris, unaware that he was the subject of their teasing.

"When are we a-goin' to do it?" Manning asked. "I don't feel good, hangin' around in this town for so long."

Callahan finished his second drink, wiped his mouth with the back of his hand, and grinned at the other three. "All right, if you're all ready then, why don't we do it now?"

"You're in charge," Cooper said. "How are we goin' to do it?"

"Cooper, you 'n Morris will go into the bank with me. Manning, you'll be outside already mounted and holding the leads of the other three horses," Callahan said in response to the question. "When we come out, I don't want to take the time to untie 'em. I think that's where we made our big mistake in Archer . . . we didn't leave nobody with the horses, 'n the time it took to untie 'em and get mounted was all the time MacCallister needed. I don't plan to give nobody that much time today."

"I'll have 'em ready," Manning promised.

With a scrape of chairs, the four men stood up and walked, purposefully, from the saloon.

"Hey, how come you girls aren't working the floor?" the bartender asked, coming down to where the three girls were standing.

"Come on, Mel, there ain't but three men out there," one of the girls said. "And one of 'em is so old that I bet he ain't had it up in more'n ten years."

"Well then, that leaves one apiece for the two of you."

The two girls Mel was talking to put on practiced smiles and started out onto the floor in response to the bartender's nudge.

"What about you, Suzie?" Mel asked.

"You want me to take the old man, do you?" Suzie replied.

"Why not? If anyone can do it for him, you can."

"It would probably give him a heart attack. You don't want to kill him, do you, honey?"

Mel laughed. "Why not? If that's what kills him, he'll at least die a happy man."

"Listen, Mel, before I go give the old gent a heart attack, did you pay much attention to those four men that just left?"

"Not particularly. Why?"

"I think there's somethin' awfully peculiar about them," Suzie said.

"You mean 'cause that big pig-faced bastard pushed you away?"

"No, not just that. Betty and Annie were over at the table with the other three men, and when he went over to join them he ran them away, too. Then, all the time the men were in here, they were talkin' so low that nobody could hear what they were saying."

"It wasn't anybody's business what they were saying, was it?"

"I don't know, it depends on what they were talking about. What if they were planning something evil?"

The bartender laughed again. "You know

what, Suzie, you missed your calling. Maybe you should have been a detective for Pinkerton instead of wastin' your time as a bar girl."

"Maybe I should have," Suzie agreed. She pointed to the door as if in doing so she was pointing toward the men who had just left.

"But you mark my words, there's something awfully peculiar about those men."

Suzie walked up to the batwing doors and looked outside.

"Do you see any of them out there?" the bartender called.

"No," Suzie replied. "They must have ridden on."

"Well, good riddance, I say," the bartender replied.

Pasting a practiced grin on her face, Suzie started over to the table where an old man, with a full white beard and long white hair, stood staring into his glass of beer.

"No need for you to be staring at the beer, honey, it's not goin' to get up 'n run away on you," she said.

"I sure hope it don't, little lady, 'cause I'm pretty sure these ole legs wouldn't let me run it down."

"Would you like to buy me a drink?" Suzie asked.

"As long as you don't expect anythin' else from me," the old man said. " 'Cause I tell you the truth, if you was lyin' naked on the bed in front of me, all I could do is say, 'Damn, ain't you purty.' "

Suzie laughed and lay her hand on his cheek. "Well now, comin' from you, I'd just take that as a big compliment," she said. "Let me get my drink, then you can tell me stories about the old days."

In front of the bank

When Callahan, Manning, Cooper and Morris stopped in front of the bank, nobody paid any particular attention to the fact that only three dismounted, or that rather than tying their horses off at the hitching rail, they handed the reins to a fourth man who remained sitting in his saddle. The three who did dismount went into the bank. There were three men inside, but it appeared as if all three were bank employees. Two were behind the counter, and one was at a desk on the side of the room. One of the tellers greeted the three men with a practiced smile.

"Yes, sir, what can I do for you gent— ?"

Before the teller could finish his question, Callahan and the other two men with him pulled their guns.

"What is this?" the teller asked, the smile leaving his face.

"We're robbing this bank. Don't any of you shout out!"

Cooper and Morris jumped over the counter.

Callahan, who remained out front, looked toward the man who had been sitting at the desk.

"You the president of this here bank?" Callahan asked.

"No, sir, I'm just a bookkeeper. I'm afraid that the president of the bank isn't here." The quaver in his voice displayed his fear.

The two bank tellers had looked expectantly toward the man sitting behind the desk, as if awaiting instructions from him. When he denied his actual position with the bank, the two tellers looked away from him.

Callahan smiled. "Well now, it 'pears to me like maybe you're lyin'. I think you're the man I'm lookin' for," Callahan said. He made a motion with his gun toward the safe. "Open the safe for me, Mr. Bank President. And be damned quick about it. The sooner this is done and we get out of here, the safer it will be for you."

"I can't open the safe," the man said.

"Why not?"

"It's on a time lock."

"Then when can you open it?"

"It'll be at least ten minutes before I can open it."

"We goin' to wait, Callahan?" Morris asked.

"Morris, you dumb son of a bitch! You said my name."

"Sorry," Morris replied nervously.

Callahan turned back to the man who had been sitting at the desk. "You know what, mister? I just don't believe that a bank this small would actually have a time lock," he said.

"Yes, sir, we just put it in," the man replied.

"What's your name?"

"Mister . . . uh . . . that is Dempster. My name is Dempster."

"Mister, huh? You mean like in Mister Bank President?" Callahan asked.

"All right, I am the bank president, but it is on a time lock."

"Ten minutes, huh?"

"Yes, sir, ten minutes."

"Mr. Dempster, here's what I want you to do," Callahan said in a deceptively calm voice. "I want you to put your hand here on the counter."

"I beg your pardon? Why on earth would I do that?"

Callahan cocked his pistol, the hammer making a deadly sounding click as it rotated the cylinder. He pointed the gun at the man's head.

"Because I will blow your brains out if you don't."

Hesitantly, Dempster put his hand on the desk. To his utter horror, Callahan drew his knife, then brought it down sharply. Before Dempster even knew what had happened, Callahan had chopped off his little finger.

"Ahhhh!" Dempster called out in pain, drawing back a hand with blood oozing from the wound. "Why did you do that?"

"Well, you said we had ten minutes to wait before the time lock would let us open the safe, didn't you? You've got ten fingers . . . well, nine now," he amended with a little laugh. "And that works out just real good, because I figure we'll just cut off one finger a minute from now until we can open the safe, you know, just to kill the time?" Callahan laughed demonically.

"No, no! I . . . I just remembered . . . I forgot to set the time lock last night. I can open the safe now!" Dempster said. "Please, don't hurt me anymore!"

"Well, now, ain't it just real lucky for you that I won't have to be cuttin' off no more fingers."

"Open it, Carl. For God's sake, open it," Dempster said. As the teller, Carl, hurried over to open the safe, Dempster took off his shirt with difficulty and pressed it against the bleeding stub of his little finger.

Carl opened the door to the vault, and Morris, carrying an empty sack, stepped inside.

"You see any money?" Callahan called.

"Yeah, there's paper money and coins," Morris said.

"Forget the coins and grab all the paper you can. Carl, you get back over here with the others," Callahan ordered. "And you jaspers — put your hands up. I don't want to see any of you reachin' for anything. If you do, I'm goin' to be real nervous, 'n when I get nervous, I shoot."

CHAPTER SIXTEEN

As Morris was taking money from the safe, Callahan and Cooper continued to hold their guns on the tellers. Carl and the other teller had their hands raised. Dempster didn't raise his hands, but was still holding his shirt over his finger. At that moment a customer came into the bank and realized at once what was going on.

"Help!" he shouted at the top of his voice. "Bank robbery!"

Even as the customer was giving the alarm, he was drawing his pistol. Callahan swung his gun toward the armed customer. The customer fired first, his bullet hitting an inkwell on one of the tables and sending up a spray of ink. Callahan returned fire and his bullet found its mark; the customer went down.

Another citizen of the town came running into the bank and fired as soon as he stepped inside. His bullet shattered the shaded glass around the teller cages. Cooper returned fire, killing him.

"Morris, grab what you can 'n let's get the hell out of here!" Callahan shouted.

"But there's a lot more money I ain't grabbed up yet!" Morris replied.

"Now! Get out of here now or we'll leave you behind!" Callahan yelled.

Callahan's suggestion that they might leave him had its effect, and Morris came back out, clutching the bag that was no longer empty.

Outside the bank the townspeople, hearing the shots, realized at once what was going on.

"The bank!" someone shouted. "They're robbin' the bank!"

"Callahan! Cooper! Morris!" Manning shouted. "Get out of there! Fast!"

One of the armed townspeople started running toward the bank with his pistol drawn. Manning shot him, dropping him in the middle of the street. Until that moment not everyone realized that the man sitting on a horse in front of the bank was one of the robbers, though if they had seen that he was holding the reins to three other horses, they probably would have known. Seeing now that he was one of them, the townspeople began screaming and running for cover.

With Morris clutching the bag in his left hand, he, Callahan, and Cooper backed out of the bank, with Callahan firing back inside.

"Hurry up and get mounted!" Manning called, holding the reins down to the other three.

Across the street a young store clerk, who couldn't have been more than sixteen, came running out of the store, wearing his apron and carrying a .22 rifle. Raising the rifle, he fired at the four robbers but missed. Cooper returned fire, and the boy fell back to lie spread out in the street.

"You son of a bitch! That was my boy!" a man yelled, running out of the same store the boy had exited. He was carrying a shotgun, and he fired both barrels, but his gun was loaded with light birdshot and the shooter was too far away to be effective. The pellets peppered and stung, but none of them penetrated the skin.

Still another citizen fired at the bank robbers, and Manning's horse went down under him. Manning leaped from the struck animal before he could be pinned beneath it, then ran to the nearest hitching rail where several horses had been left by their owners. Spooked by all the gunfire, they reared and pulled against their restraints, but Manning was able to untie the first horse, then swing into the saddle.

"That's my horse!" someone shouted, stepping through the front door of the leather goods store. Manning shot at him. He didn't hit the angry owner, but the shot did have the effect of driving him back inside.

The town marshal, an older man, was just now reaching the scene, having run the entire length of the street from the sheriff's office. Puffing and wheezing loudly from the unaccustomed effort of the long run, he raised his pistol toward them. "You fellas stop right there!" he called.

Callahan shot at the sheriff and the man went down, a dark hole appearing right in the middle of his forehead.

The four robbers rode toward the north end of town only to see a dozen or more of the townspeople rolling a wagon into the street. The townspeople then tipped the wagon over as a barricade and gathered behind it, all of them armed and ready.

"Callahan, we can't go that way!" Cooper shouted.

"This way!" Callahan replied, turning off the street and leading them through a churchyard. Only a few moments before all the shooting started, a funeral had been conducted in the church. At the moment, the body was just being carried out to the cemetery for the committal. Having heard all the shouting, the mourners stared in terrified fascination at the four armed and mounted men who were bearing down on them.

Screams and shouts of fear and terror greeted the bank robbers as the mourners split, then ran to either side of the churchyard to allow the robbers to pass. The pallbearers dropped the coffin, which turned on its side, causing the remains of a young woman, dressed in white, to spill out.

"Jolene!" one of the mourners shouted out in the horror of seeing his loved one so unceremoniously dumped onto the ground.

Once the robbers were through the churchyard, they headed south.

As the horses pounded by, they kicked up dirt to soil the white burial gown Jolene was wearing.

"You bastards!" cried the mourner who had called out Jolene's name.

The retreating riders did not react to the shouted epithet.

"Grab a gun and get mounted!" someone shouted back in the town. "Those sons of bitches held up the bank!"

Responding to the call, several men armed

themselves, saddled their horses, and got mounted. But they were without a leader.

"All right, men, let's go!" John Ray Dumas shouted, assuming the role of leader when no one else stepped up. John Ray was the owner of the hardware store, and he was the one whose earlier shouts had rallied the townsmen into forming a posse.

It was almost fifteen minutes before they were ready to go and they galloped out of town full of resolve and confidence. Several had seen the robbers turn south after they passed through the churchyard, so south the posse went.

The posse stopped when they reached the Laramie River.

"What now?" one of the men asked. "Which way do we go?"

"Yeah, John Ray, you're in charge. Which way do we go?"

"I don't know," John Ray admitted.

"I think we should get back to town," one of the others said. "We've left it completely unguarded."

"Yeah," another said. "And we need to bury our dead."

"Who the hell were they? Does anyone know?"

"I don't have any idea," another said. "But I'd sure as hell like to know."

"Yeah, me too. I got money in that bank. I wonder how much they got?"

"Six hundred and twenty-nine dollars," Callahan said after he counted the money at their encampment that night. "Damn, I woulda thought we got more than that."

"Yeah, well, that's sure more'n we had, 'n I'd like to find us some place where we can spend the money," Manning said. "I want some good whiskey and a bad woman."

The others laughed. "Yeah, what do you say, Callahan? Let's find us a place where we can spend some of the money."

"All right," Callahan agreed. He smiled. "The way I look at it, there ain't no sense in havin' money if you can't spend it."

"It was them," Suzie said to the bartender. The Brown Dirt Cowboy was filled with customers now, many of them the men who had gone out in the posse. Others were there also to find out how the posse had fared, as well as to talk about the robbery and murder. "The ones that robbed the bank are the same four men who were in here."

"You're kinda puttin' the cart before the horse, ain't you?" the bartender asked. "We don't know it was them."

"Well, think about it, Roy. Four men came in here, wouldn't have anything to do with any of the girls. They stayed less than fifteen minutes, talked real low so's that nobody could hear 'em, then left. Five minutes later the bank was robbed by four men. Who were those men? None of us had ever seen 'em before, 'n it's for sure we haven't seen 'em since."

Roy nodded. "You might have a point there," he said. "But I'd be careful about sayin' anything to anyone else about it. If word gets back to them that you've figured out they're the ones who robbed the bank, they may wind up comin' back for you."

Suzie's suspicions were well confirmed when several of the townspeople filled the saloon that evening, talking about the bank robbery.

"Four of 'em, they was, 'n one of 'em was a big man with a real flat pug nose, like as if it had been real bad broke."

Suzie glanced over at Roy, and the bartender nodded. It was the same four men who had been in there, who robbed the bank, all right. But what good did it do for her to know that now? Nobody had ever seen them before, so she didn't have any idea as to their names, and they had certainly left town as quickly as they could.

And enough people had seen them and described them, that even if she did share her thoughts about the men with others, she wouldn't be adding anything to the information, so there was no way the men would come back on her, as Roy had suggested.

"Here's the thing though. They left before they got most of the bank's money. Turns out they didn't get no more'n five or six hundred dollars, or so."

CHAPTER SEVENTEEN

Sky Meadow Ranch

Because there was no railroad or telegraph service for Bordeaux, nobody at Sky Meadow Ranch, or even in Chugwater, had heard about the bank holdup. As a result, Duff and the others were unaware that the men they were searching for were the same men who had held up the bank in Bordeaux.

After buying the things they would need for the pursuit of the men who had killed Ina Claire's parents, Duff had invited Ina Claire out to the ranch to prepare for the upcoming mission. He had invited Meagan as well, because he thought her presence would make Ina Claire more comfortable.

"If you're going to come with me, I need to teach you to shoot," Duff said to Ina Claire.

"You don't need to teach me. I've already learned to shoot."

"Is that right?"

"Yes, do you think that just because I'm a girl, I can't shoot?"

"All right, let me see what you can do." Duff walked over to the fence and put an empty can on each of four posts.

"Take a shot at that first can for me," he said when he got back to her.

Ina Claire raised the pistol to eye level, extended her arm, took very careful aim, and pulled the trigger. She was rewarded with a clinking sound as the bullet from her pistol swept the can from the post. She looked at Duff with a satisfied smile of accomplishment.

"What do you think of that?" she asked. "Papa taught me how to shoot."

"That's pretty good," Duff said.

"*Pretty* good? What do you mean that's pretty good? I hit the can, didn't I? How could it have been any better?"

"It could have been better if you hadn't aimed at the can."

"What do you mean if I hadn't aimed at the can? Isn't that what you told me to aim at?"

"No, I told you to shoot it. I didn't tell you to aim at it."

"Mr. MacCallister . . . ."

"Duff," Duff corrected. "You're my sister-in-law, remember."

208

"Duff, you aren't making sense. You said shoot the can but don't aim at it. How do you expect me to shoot the can if I don't aim at it?"

"Like this," Duff said. He pulled his gun and, without raising it to aim, shot two times and knocked two of the cans off the posts.

"How did you do that?"

"I did that by thinking where I wanted the bullets to go."

Ina Claire laughed. "You *think* where you want them to go?"

"Aye, lass, I think them to the target. There is one can remaining. Shoot at it again, but don't aim this time."

"I believe I see what you mean. If you draw your pistol fast, you won't have time to aim it."

"That's partly it," Duff agreed. "But the truth is, I've never been proficient in what the Western Americans call the fast draw."

"But Papa said you had been in many gunfights," Ina Claire said. "How did you survive them if you aren't fast on the draw?"

"Being the first one to draw your pistol isn't as important as being the first one to hit what you are shooting at. Most fast-draw gunmen depend upon their speed to intimidate the adversary. If you are able to with-

209

draw your pistol in a reasonable amount of time, and put the first shot on target, ninety-nine and nine-tenths of a percent of the time, you will emerge victorious."

"Ninety-nine point nine percent of the time?" Ina Claire asked. She chuckled. "That still leaves one-tenth of one percent of the time where you would lose. And you only have to lose once."

"That is true, lass. That is also why you must be accurate one hundred percent of the time. Now, draw your gun and shoot at that can. Don't aim at it, just feel where it is."

Ina Claire pulled the pistol and started to raise it, but stopped, then fired from the hip. The can was unscathed.

"I missed," she said sheepishly.

"You missed, did you?" Duff laughed. "No doubt now you'll tell me that your hair is red."

"You needn't make fun of me," Ina Claire said, stung by his reply.

"You're right, lass, and 'tis sorry I am for doing such a thing. Here, let me help you out. Don't forget, someone may be shooting at you as well, so don't give them much of a target. Turn yourself so that you are showing only your side." He moved Ina Claire into position. "Now don't turn your body, but look at the target by turning your head back toward it."

Ina Claire did as she was instructed.

"Bring the pistol up to eye level and aim at the target, just as you did before, but don't shoot. Good. Now close your eyes and lower your pistol so that it is pointing straight down. With your eyes closed, aim at it again."

"How am I going to do that if my eyes are closed?"

"Just listen to me. Close your eyes, then bring your arm back up, thinking about where the target is. When you think you have it lined up, tell me."

With her eyes still closed, Ina Claire brought her arm up until she thought it was aligned with the target. "All right, I think I have it lined up."

"Pull the trigger, but don't open your eyes."

Ina Claire pulled the trigger.

"Now open your eyes and look."

Ina Claire opened her eyes and saw a nick in the post just below the can.

"I almost hit it!" she said excitedly. "I had my eyes closed, and I almost hit it!"

"Aye, lass, indeed you did. Now spread your feet apart about the width of your shoulders. Keep your legs straight but not stiff. Think you can do that?"

"Yes, of course I can."

"Now let me ask you something," Duff said. "What are you going to do with your other arm?"

"I don't know, I hadn't thought about it."

"Good."

"Good?"

"It's good that you hadn't thought about it. As far as you're concerned, the other arm isn't even there. None o' the rest of your body is there, not your other arm, not your legs, not your back. There is only your right arm, your hand, and your mind."

"And the gun," Ina Claire said.

"Nae, lass, the gun is nae there, either."

"What do you mean, the gun isn't there? That's the whole point of it, isn't it?"

"The gun has become a part of your hand, you see. So when 'tis your hand you're thinkin' of, 'tis actually your gun."

Ina Claire nodded. "All right," she said. "All right, I think I can do that."

"Good. Now put your pistol back in the holster, then look at your target by turning your head and eyes slightly without moving from the neck down. When you know exactly where the target is, pull the pistol from the holster, but don't raise the gun to eye level and sight down it. Shoot it as soon as your arm comes level."

"Should I try and draw the gun very fast?"

"No. Remember, it's more important to hit the target than it is to get the gun out fast. Just pull the pistol at a normal pace, raise your arm just far enough to extend your gun, and shoot."

Ina Claire followed his instructions and was rewarded for her effort by seeing the can fly off the fence post.

"I did it!" she cried in delight.

"Good. I'm going back to the house now. I want you to stay out here and continue to practice your shooting. And I want you to keep practicing until you can hit twenty cans in a row without a miss."

"What if it gets to be lunchtime and I still haven't hit twenty cans in a row?"

Duff laughed. "Oh, now, lass, I dinnae expect you to be able to do that in one day. Nae, it'll take you several days I think, maybe a week before you'll be able to do that."

"A week? A whole week? That's too long."

"You're young, Ina Claire. What's time to you?" Duff asked.

"But they'll get away."

"They've already gotten away, and they'll nae be any farther away for the wait. We'll find them, all right. And when we do find them, I want to make certain that you can defend yourself.

"I'm giving you eight boxes of shells. That will give you forty shots a day for ten days. If, at the end of ten days, you can't get twenty in a row, then you're never going to be able to do it."

"I'll do it," Ina Claire said. "And it won't take me any ten days to do it, either."

Duff smiled. "I have every confidence in you, lass."

As Duff started toward the house, Elmer and Wang came over to stand by Ina Claire.

"Have you come to spy on me, to make sure I don't cheat?" Ina Claire asked.

"Those who cheat do not succeed. Those who succeed do not cheat," Wang said.

"What?"

Elmer laughed. "Wang is always sayin' stuff like that. At first I just passed it off as bein' somethin' a crazy Chinaman is sayin'. But then I got to listenin' to him, 'n damn if from time to time, the words didn't start makin' some sense."

"Yes," Ina Claire said. "Like now, he's telling me not to cheat, isn't he?"

Elmer shook his head. "No, darlin', he's tellin' you that it won't do you no good to cheat."

"That's easy for him to say," Ina Claire said. "He doesn't have to hit the can without looking at it."

Wang was looking directly at Ina Claire. Without turning his head he pulled a throwing star from a little leather pouch that hung from his belt, then, with his back to the can, he threw it with a side-arm motion and a little flip of his wrist. The star flew through the air, flashing in the sun as it did so. It sliced entirely through the can so that the top of the can fell to one side of the post, and the bottom of the can fell to the other.

"Wow! How did you do that?" Ina Claire asked, shocked at what she had just seen.

"Darlin', don't ask Wang to fly," Elmer said. "I ain't seen 'im do it yet, but I wouldn' pass out in total surprise if he up 'n done it one day."

"To think is to do," Wang said with an enigmatic smile.

"To think is to do? That's sort of what Mr. MacCallister, I mean Duff, he told me to call him Duff, that's sort of what he said when he told me to think the bullet to the target."

Elmer walked over to the fence post and put another can in position. "Now try it," he said when he rejoined Ina Claire and Wang.

215

Ina Claire drew her pistol and, extending her arm, but not specifically aiming, she fired.

The can flew off the post.

"To think is to do," Wang said, turning away to start back toward the bunkhouse.

Elmer didn't say anything, but he did smile and nod at her.

Uva, Wyoming Territory
When Clay Callahan and the others stepped into the Red Sky Saloon in Uva, Callahan put a nickel on the bar, then took a newspaper from the stack. The four of them bought a bottle between then and took it and four glasses to a table that sat under the painting of a ship in full sail.

"Ha!" he said. "Listen to this." He cleared his throat then began to read: *"Bank of Bordeaux held up by gunmen, robbers unidentified."*

"Son of a bitch!" Manning said with a broad smile. "Boys, we got away, slicker'n a whistle."

"Hey," Callahan said as he continued to read. "Did you know they got Bates, Donner, and Pardeen in jail up in Millersburg? Says they're goin' to be tried for murder next week."

"That's too bad," Morris said. "They're

216

good boys."

"Yeah, I rode with 'em for a while my own self," Cooper said.

Callahan looked up with a smile. "You know what I'm a-thinkin'?"

"What's that?"

"I'm thinkin' that if we had them three boys, that would make seven of us, 'n we could put together a gang that would be strong enough there wouldn't be no posse in all of the Territory of Wyoming that could handle us."

"That'd just be more men to split our take with, though," Morris said.

"The bigger the gang, the bigger the take," Callahan said. "And the bigger the take, the bigger the split. I don't know about you three, but the two hundred 'n thirteen dollars we got from the peddler, 'n the six hundred and twenty-nine dollars we got in Bordeaux ain't hardly worth the effort. We need to do a job that'll give us a lot more money'n that, 'n with seven of us, why, there wouldn't be a bank or a train in the whole territory we couldn't take. Yes, and in Colorado as well. I ain't talkin' about hundreds of dollars here, boys. I'm talkin' thousands. No, tens of thousands."

"Damn, that's a lot of money," Manning said.

"That's the size of jobs we would go after, if we had a gang big enough," Callahan insisted.

"All right, let's get 'em out," Cooper suggested.

"We've got a week to come up with an idea," Callahan said.

CHAPTER EIGHTEEN

Sky Meadow

Duff and Meagan were sitting in the parlor of his house, while the sound of gunfire could be heard outside.

"Did you tell her how to think the bullets to the target?" Meagan asked with a little chuckle.

"Aye."

"And did you make her close her eyes and take a shot?"

"Aye, that, too."

"Well, it worked for me, so I see no reason why it wouldn't work for Ina Claire."

"Oh, 'twas much easier with Ina Claire because I had more to start with. Unlike you, the lass was already a very good shot. All I had to do is change her technique a bit."

"I know you are teasing me, just trying to see if you can get my dander up. But I have no doubt but that she was much better than

I was. Remember, until you taught me to shoot, I had never even fired a gun."

"You were a good learner," Duff said.

Meagan smiled, then leaned over and planted a gentle kiss on Duff's lips. "You were a good teacher," she said.

Outside, the steady barrage of shots continued.

"Bless her heart, she's been doing that for three days now," Meagan said a few days later.

"Aye, but according to Elmer, twice she's gotten as many as seventeen in a row, and once she got eighteen. I expect it won't be much longer before she does it."

"When are you going to tell her?" Meagan asked.

"Tell her what?"

"You know what. When are you going to tell her the most important thing about learning to shoot?"

"I'll tell her as soon as she hits twenty cans in a row. What's for dinner?" he asked.

"Ham, fried potatoes, biscuits, and gravy," Meagan replied.

Duff chuckled. "You can't get much more American than that."

"You could always go back to Scotland, you know," Meagan teased.

"Nae thank ye, lass, but I'll be for stayin' here."

"Sure 'n 'tis hopin' I was for a favorable response from himself," Meagan said.

"Och, woman, 'tis a foul mouth ye have when ye try 'n mimic the sound o' Scotland," Duff replied, his laughter ameliorating the harsh meaning of his words.

Millersburg, Wyoming Territory

It was eleven o'clock at night and the entire town was closed, except for the North Star Saloon. Even here, at the last bastion of people who were reluctant to let the night pass, there were only a few patrons remaining. At the moment, Callahan, Manning, Cooper, and Morris were in the Uva Corral. The air was heavy with the smell of horse droppings and hay. A full moon cast a bar of light a few feet through the large opening of the front door. Beyond that silver splash of moonlight, though, the barn was pitch-dark.

"You got that candle with you, Cooper?" Callahan asked.

"Yeah."

"Light it."

Cooper struck a match and held it to the candlewick. A little golden bubble of light disclosed a row of stalls on each side. The

221

horses, curious by the midnight entry, had come to the edge of the stalls and were peering over the gates, their eyes reflecting the orange glow of light.

"Here, you men, what are you doing?" an angry voice called out to them. Looking toward the speaker, they saw someone dressed only in his long johns underwear and boots.

"We didn't mean to wake you, sir," Callahan said. "We're just looking for my horse. Oh, I see him. How much do I owe you?"

"I ain't seen you before. Which horse is yours?" the stable attendant asked.

"It's that one down at the far end," Callahan said. When the liveryman looked away, Callahan pulled his pistol and brought it down hard over the man's head.

Ten minutes later the stableman was bound and gagged, and left in an empty stall. With the three horses they had selected now saddled, the four men left the stable, then retrieved their own horses that were tied outside. Leading the three just acquired horses, they rode down to the city marshal's office, also the jail, which was at the far end of the street from the stable.

"Cooper, you come with me," Callahan said. "Manning, you and Morris wait here. If you see anything you think we should know about, give us a whistle."

"We will," Manning said.

"All right, Cooper, you know what to do."

Dismounting, Callahan and Cooper stepped into the marshal's office. Cooper had Callahan by his collar, and he was jamming the barrel of his pistol into Callahan's back. Their abrupt entry awakened the deputy.

"Here!" the deputy demanded. "What's goin' on? What do you mean bargin' in here like this?"

"I mean to collect me some reward money," Cooper said. "In case you don't know it, Deputy, this here feller is Clay Callahan. Him 'n another feller escaped from jail down in Cheyenne a week or so ago, 'n I caught this one. I want you to keep 'im in jail here 'til I can send off for the reward."

"How am I supposed to know this is who you say it is?" the deputy asked.

"Well, hell, Deputy, look at 'im," Cooper said. "You know anybody who looks like this?"

The deputy studied Callahan. In the lamp light of his office, Callahan's deformed nose and scrunched-up ear were clearly visible.

"Now that I look at 'im, he does look like the descriptions I've heard," the deputy

223

said. "Uh, how much money you reckon you're goin' to be a-gettin' for 'im? The reason I ask is, if I'm goin' to keep 'im here for you, seems like you might be willin' to share a little of the reward with me 'n Marshal Williams."

"Yeah, I will. Just get the keys, 'n let's get this man in jail."

The deputy got the ring of keys down from the wall, then started toward the back. "Just bring 'im along and we'll take real good care of 'im for you."

The deputy marshal turned his back on Callahan and Cooper as he led them to the cell area. Callahan waited until they reached the cell block, then Cooper handed him a knife and Callahan reached around to cut the deputy's throat.

Five minutes later with the deputy lying dead in a pool of his blood, the seven fugitives rode out of town.

Near Cummins City, Wyoming Territory
Founded in 1879, Cummins City was a Wyoming Territory gold rush town. There were thirty-one houses, four stores, and four saloons, with a population that was very close to three hundred. That figure wasn't entirely representative of the town, though, because neighboring ranches, farms, and

mines brought the number of people who actually did business in the town to nearly double that of the posted population.

The town wasn't served by railroad or telegraph, and as a result it was isolated from the rest of the country, except for the daily stagecoach run between Cummins City and the considerably larger railroad town of Laramie, which was twenty miles north.

Because of its isolation, Callahan and the six men who were now riding with him were able to move through the town with little danger of being recognized as wanted men, even given Callahan's unusual looks. They were in the Lucky Nugget Saloon when they heard the conversation from an adjacent table.

"They say it's five thousand dollars' worth," one of the conversationalists at the other table said. "It's all the gold that's been took out of North Star Mine this month."

"Yeah, I heard that, too. They shipped it up to the assay office on the stage yesterday."

"That's funny, I didn't see no extra guard when the coach left yesterday," one of the others said. "All I seen was just the regular shotgun guard."

"No, 'n you wouldn't have, not for the

shippin' up. The gold ain't even been extracted from the ore yet, 'n there ain't no bandit worth his salt would want anything to do with it. But now ever'time a shipment goes up, they's always from five hundred to as much as twenty-five hundred dollars that comes back down the next day so's there is enough money that ole John Cummins can keep workin' the mine."

"How much money you think'll be comin' down today?"

"I'd say at least two thousand, seein' as they was five thousand dollars' worth of ore that went up. But they ain't likely to have no extra guard this time, either, 'ceptin' for the regular shotgun guard. They ain't goin' to have no extra guard lessen they's at least ten thousand dollars bein' shipped."

Callahan finished his beer. "Let's go," he said to the others.

"Damn, I was waitin' to see Velma," Cooper said. "She's busy right now, but she said I would be next."

"You can see her later," Callahan said. "We got business to take care of."

"How much money you reckon this coach will be a-carryin'?" Pardeen asked when Callahan proposed that they hold up the stagecoach.

"Accordin' to what them men was sayin' in the saloon, the coach tomorrow is more'n likely to be carryin' two thousand dollars."

"What if it ain't carryin' no money at all?"

"Then we'll take whatever money the passengers has," Callahan answered.

"That ain't likely to be much."

"Well, let me ask you this, Pardeen. How much money do you 'n Bates 'n Donner have now?"

"We ain't got nothin' at all now, 'n you know that. We wouldn't even be able to stay here without you payin' for it."

"Then no matter how much we get, it'll be more'n you got now, won't it?"

"Yeah, well, you already know that. Uh, look, seein' as me 'n Bates 'n Donner ain't got no money at all, you reckon you could see clear to lend us a little 'til tomorrow? I mean, just enough to maybe buy a drink or two 'n sit-down supper in a restaurant, 'n maybe even get a woman? I ain't had me no woman in a month o' Sundays."

"Yeah, all right," Callahan agreed. "I'll give you boys twenty dollars apiece. That ought to hold you 'til tomorrow when we take the stage, then you can pay me back."

The place where they were staying was a large room filled with sleeping cots.

Gent's Lodging
Cot — *15 cents*
Pillow — *5 cents*
Blanket — *5 cents*

After supper that night at Audrey's Beanery, Callahan, Manning, Morris, Bates, and Donner gathered around a table at the Lucky Nugget Saloon. Cooper had been with them until Velma was available, and with a big grin on his face, he followed her up the stairs to her room.

Only Pardeen wasn't with them, choosing to check out the Cow Palace, which was a saloon at the opposite end of town from the Lucky Nugget. Cummins City was too small to have streetlights, so except for a square of light cast through a window now and then, the street was totally dark. As Pardeen rode through the darkness, a dog came running from the space between two of the buildings yapping and snapping at the heels of his horse. The horse grew skittish and began kicking at the dog, prancing away from it, and since the horse was relatively new to Pardeen because it had been stolen on the night he escaped from jail, he had a difficult time calming the animal.

After he regained control, he stopped in

front of the Cow Palace and tied his horse off at the rail. From inside he heard a woman's short, sharp exclamation, followed by loud boisterous laughter from several men.

"That wasn't funny!" a woman's voice said. Her protest was met with more laughter.

Pardeen went into the saloon and stepped up to the bar. The most important thing he had on his mind right now was getting a woman. But even before that, he decided he would have a drink.

Not one drink, several drinks. He would buy a whole bottle.

Pardeen was so often broke that he had developed a look that bespoke a man without money. The bartender noticed that look right away.

"Mister, if you've come lookin' for a handout, you've come to the wrong place," the bartender said. "We don't give away drinks, 'n we don't allow bums to cadge drinks for our customers, neither."

"Well, it just so happens that I got money," Pardeen said.

"What do you want?"

"Whiskey." Pardeen put two dollars on the bar. "And leave the bottle."

"This is good whiskey," the bartender

said. "It's going to cost you more than two dollars."

"It's rotgut, colored with rusty nails and flavored with iodine," Pardeen said. "I've tended some bar in my day, so I'm pretty sure you ain't goin' to walk away from the two dollars."

The bartender thought about it for a moment and, with a shrug, picked up the two dollars and left the bottle sitting on the bar.

Pardeen poured himself a drink, then turned to have a look around the room. When he caught the eye of one of the bargirls, he nodded. She smiled at him, and he wished that she hadn't, because the smile exposed at least four missing teeth. When she approached him he saw that she might have actually been pretty at one time, but the dissipation of her profession had taken its toll.

"What can I do for you, honey?" she asked, smiling again.

"Don't smile," he said. "With them missin' teeth, your mouth looks like an open barn door."

"Well, I'm sorry about that, honey, but last year a mean man beat me up and knocked out five of my teeth."

"Yeah, I thought you was prob'ly missin' about that many," Pardeen said. "What will it cost me to go up to your room with you?"

"Two dollars," she said, again smiling at him.

Pardeen corked the bottle and pushed it down into his pocket. "I'll give you two fifty if you'll promise to keep your mouth shut so I don't have to look at them teeth."

The girl used her hand to block his view of her mouth.

"You got it, honey, anything you say," she said.

Pardeen stood at the window of the second-floor room, looking down onto the street below. The whore was lying on the bed behind him.

"Do you want to spend the night, honey?" she asked. "It will only cost you two dollars and fifty cents more."

Pardeen looked back toward her. It had been awhile since he had a woman, and the thought of spending an entire night with one wasn't a bad idea. He thought about taking the woman up on her offer, but Callahan had said that he wanted all of them tonight.

"No, I'd like to, but I got some business to attend," he said.

Turning back to the window, he looked down toward the stage depot at the far end of the street. An empty coach sat there, its tongue lying on the ground free of horses.

Would this be the coach they would be robbing tomorrow?

CHAPTER NINETEEN

It was a Concord stagecoach, tough and sturdy from its seasoned white ash spokes to the leather boot. It had no springs but was suspended on layers of leather straps, called through braces, and those through braces helped, somewhat, to soften the ride. The body of the coach was red and the lettering on the doors was yellow, although the paint was tired and the colors faded because the coach was at least ten years old and had seen a great deal of use during its lifetime. For all its wear, it was well maintained.

The coach belonged to the Calloway Express Service, a stage line that connected outlying settlements throughout Wyoming with the railroads that passed through the territory. As the stagecoach came down out of the high country and began rolling across the flats, the six-horse team broke into a lope. The wheels of the swiftly moving stage kicked up a billowing trail of dust to roll and swirl on the road behind them, though a goodly amount of dust also managed to find its way into the passenger compartment.

"Oh, this dust," a woman, one of the two passengers in the coach, complained. "It is intolerable. I don't know how anyone can live out here. Why, I can't even get my breath. George, do something."

"Now just exactly what do you expect me to do, Millicent?" George replied.

"You could tell the driver to slow down. Perhaps if we wouldn't go so fast the dust wouldn't be so bad."

"I am certain that he would not slow down, and there is no way of knowing just what his response would be. You know how these Westerners are," George replied. "Lord knows we have encountered enough of them since we left New York."

"I don't know why we had to come out here in the first place."

"I have explained it to you. Our bank wants to look into buying the gold mine in Cummins City, and I am to inspect it for them."

"It is the absolute end of the world," Millicent said.

"You didn't have to come with me, you

234

know. You could have stayed in New York."

"Nonsense. You did say we are going on to San Francisco, didn't you? I don't intend to miss that opportunity. Please, just tell him to slow down a little."

"I told you, that would do no good. You'll just have to find some way to tolerate it."

On that same road being traversed by the stagecoach carrying the passengers, which was the road between Tie Siding and Cummins City, Clay Callahan and his men were waiting. At this particular location they were in the shadows of the Medicine Bow Mountains.

Callahan walked over to a cholla cactus and began relieving himself.

"Ha, you better watch out there, Callahan," Morris said. "You're pissin' on one o' them jumpin' cactuses, 'n one o' them needles is liable to jump up 'n stick you right in your pecker."

The others laughed.

Finishing, Callahan buttoned his pants and turned toward the others. "Seems to me like you boys could think of somethin' a little more serious to be concerned about than me takin' a piss," he grumbled.

"Like what?"

"Like, keepin' a lookout for the stage-coach."

"What if it don't come?"

Callahan spit a stream of tobacco into the dirt, then wiped his mouth with the back of his hand. "If the stage comes every other time, just what the hell makes you think it won't be comin' this time?" he asked.

"I don't know. It coulda broke down or somethin'."

"It ain't broke down. Anyhow, even if it is, they'd just bring another'n along."

"How long are we goin' to wait?" Bates asked.

"We'll wait as long as it takes," Callahan said. "What else do we have to do?"

At that moment, the stage was less than a mile away from where the seven men were waiting. It squeaked and rattled as it made its way along a road that had grown rutted and rough from use. The driver and shotgun guard were in a constant cloud of dust, thrown up by the team of horses, which were traveling at rapid trot. The run from Tie Siding was twenty-five miles, and though the distance between stage stops was normally twenty miles, it didn't seem prudent to put a stop between Tie Siding and Cummins City. As a result, the horses were always on the edge of exhaustion by the time the run was completed.

They had already come twenty miles, and the horses' bodies were covered with foam and sweat, but still they trotted on.

"I don't want to tell you how to do your job, Adam, but seems to me like you should give them horses a bit of a breather," the shotgun guard said.

"I tell you what, Ray. You don't tell me how to drive, 'n I won't tell you how to shoot that scattergun of yours."

"All right, like I said, you're the driver."

"You're right though," Adam admitted. "Problem is, the train was late comin' into the depot, 'n we had to wait for the passengers. I was just tryin' to make up for the time. I'll slow 'em down to a walk for a while."

"Oh, thank goodness," Millicent said from inside the stage as she fanned away the last of the dust. "Finally, he has slowed down."

"All right, here it comes," Callahan said. "Donner, you know what to do. Lay down there in the middle of the road."

"What if it runs over me?"

"He ain't goin' to run over a body that's lyin' in the road."

"How 'bout I lie on the edge of the road?"

237

"No, we have to make certain they see you, 'n the only way we can do that is for you to be lyin' right in the middle of the road. Hell, even if he don't see you the horses will. And they ain't goin' to run over you."

"All right," Donner said as, rather reluctantly, he walked out into the middle of the road and lay down.

"What the hell, Ray? Is that a man lyin' in the middle of the road?" the driver asked.

"Yeah, I think so. You reckon he's dead?"

"I don't know," Adam said. "But we can't just leave 'im there. Whoa!" Adam called, pulling back on the reins.

The coach lumbered to a stop.

"George, we're stopping," Millicent said. "Why are we stopping?"

"Maybe it's to give the horses a rest," George suggested. "I know he has kept them at a pretty rapid pace ever since we left the railroad."

"Now!" Callahan shouted, and three men suddenly appeared from either side of the road.

"Here, what are you men —" That was as far as the driver got with his question before all six of the men opened fire. By prearrangement, the three men on the left side of the road shot at the driver, and the three men on the right side of the road shot at the guard. Both driver and shotgun were killed in the fusillade of bullets.

Inside the coach, George and Millicent heard the sudden and unexpected outbreak of gunfire.

"What is it?" Millicent asked in fear. "George, what's going on?"

"I don't know," George answered.

At that moment someone jerked open the door of the stagecoach. Millicent stifled a scream, not only because of the gunfire but also because of the appearance of the man who had jerked the door open. He was a big man, with a deformed nose and ear.

"You folks in the coach," the man said in a loud, gruff voice. "Come on out of there!"

Millicent stared at him, too frightened to move.

"Come on, get out of there, I said. I ain't goin' to tell you again." His voice was little more than a low, evil growl.

Cautiously, George stepped out onto the ground, then he turned and helped his wife down. In addition to the man who had ordered them out of the coach, George counted five more. Six men. George intended to remember that.

"What is this?" George demanded. "What's going on here? How dare you to stop this coach! I'm a very busy man."

"Yeah? Well your business is going to have to wait," the big man said.

Millicent looked up toward the front of the coach, where she saw the driver and the messenger guard both slumped forward.

"George!" Millicent gasped. "The driver . . ."

"Is most likely dead," George said, completing the sentence.

"You found the bank bag yet?" the big man called to one of the men who had climbed up onto the driver's seat.

"Not yet," the man called down. The man up on the stage had a purple scar on his cheek.

George amended his count to seven.

"I got it!" the scar-faced man shouted a few seconds later.

"All right, come on down, let's go." It was obvious by the reaction of the others to the big man's orders that he was in charge.

George watched the man climb down over the wheel, studying him as if transfixed.

"George?" the big man said.

George was startled that the highwayman addressed him by name.

"That is your name, ain't it? That's what I

heard the woman call you."

"Uh, yes," George replied.

"Are you heeled?"

"I beg your pardon?"

"I don't see you wearin' no gun. You ain't carryin' a holdout, are you?"

"No, most assuredly not. Why should I have a gun? My wife and I are from New York. The people there are quite civilized, and there is no need for anyone to be in possession of a firearm."

The big man studied the two of them for a long moment, and Millicent was certain he was going to kill them both. Then he turned away from them and mounted his horse.

"Let's go," he said to the others, and the seven men rode away.

George and Millicent stood on the ground beside the coach for a long moment until the highwaymen were completely out of sight.

"George?" Millicent said in a pained voice. "Do you really think that the driver, and the man with him . . . ?"

"Are dead?" George asked, completing the question for her. "I don't know for sure, but I expect they are. I'll climb up there and take a look at them," George put a foot on one of the spokes of the front wheel and, grabbing the edge of the front box, pulled himself up to examine the two men. Their status was quickly determined.

"They are both dead," George said.

"Oh, my goodness!" she gasped. "George! We are stranded out here! What are we going to do?"

"We're not stranded. We have a coach and six horses. I'm going to drive them on into town."

"Don't be silly! You can't drive a stage-coach."

"You forget, Millicent, I was in the war, and during the war, I drove an artillery caisson," George said. "It's been almost twenty years, but I expect I can drive this coach, at least well enough to get us on to Cummins City."

"But, the driver and the guard . . . what will we do with them?"

"I'll put them inside the coach."

"Not with me in there, you won't!" Millicent insisted.

"Then, Millicent, you can just ride up here on the driver's seat with me."

Less than one hour later George and Millicent saw some riders coming toward them.

"Oh! George! They're back!"

George stopped the coach. For a moment

he, like Millicent, thought that the stage-coach holdup men were back. But as they drew closer, he saw that these weren't the same men.

The approaching riders stopped, right in front of the coach. "Who are you, mister?" one of the riders asked. "Where's Drake 'n Carter?"

"If you are talking about the driver and the man who was with him, they are back in the coach," George replied. "We were held up, and they were both killed."

The questioner stroked his chin and nodded. "Yeah," he finally said. "When you was as late as you was, we was sort of afraid it mighta been somethin' like that. Come on, we'll ride alongside you for the rest of the way in."

"Thank you, I very much appreciate that," George said.

As the riders accompanied the coach on into town, Millicent reached out to grasp George by the arm.

"George?" she said.

"Yes?"

"I'm very proud of you."

"Nothing!" Callahan said, throwing the canvas bag down in disgust. "Not a damn thing in this bag but a bunch of letters 'n a

243

couple of newspapers!"

"I thought it was supposed to have two thousand dollars," Cooper said.

"Yeah, well, you heard them men talkin' in the saloon, same as I did," Pardeen said. "They was talkin' just real big about how the stagecoach would be carryin' two thousand dollars when it come back."

"Only there warn't nothin' there," Manning said.

"Hell, we all know there warn't nothin' there," Morris said. He pointed to the canvas mailbag. "All you got to do is look into that bag to see that there ain't nothin' there."

"Damn," Pardeen said. "And the three of us," he took in Donner and Bates with a wave of his hand, "still ain't got a pot to piss in, 'ceptin' what you loant us."

"Speakin' o' which, maybe you could lend us another twenty dollars," Donner asked.

"Get it from one o' them," Callahan replied. "I done give you the loan of twenty dollars."

"I'll lend you boys twenty dollars apiece," Cooper said.

"Thanks, Cooper," Pardeen said.

"Onliest thing is, when you do get some money, you'll have to pay me back thirty dollars."

"Thirty dollars?" Bates said. "Hell no, I ain't goin' to give you thirty dollars for the loan o' twenty."

"I will," Donner said. "I'm tired o' bein' out of money."

CHAPTER TWENTY

Sky Meadow Ranch

"I did it!" Ina Claire said excitedly, coming into the house where Duff and Meagan were sitting in the parlor listening to the music box. "I hit twenty cans in a row, and it didn't take me ten days to do it, either."

"Good for you!" Meagan said.

"What about you?" Ina Claire asked Duff. "Aren't you going to say good for me, too?"

"Aye, but I knew ye could do it, or I would have nae asked ye to try it in the first place."

A while later as they sat at the table eating lunch, Duff stared across the table toward Ina Claire. He said nothing, but he held his stare until she either saw, felt, or sensed it, and she looked toward him.

"Have I suddenly gone green?" she asked with the hint of a laugh in her question.

"I beg your pardon?" Duff replied, surprised by the question.

Meagan laughed. "I think that must be a

young person's expression," she said.

"But, whatever does it mean?" Duff asked.

"It means you are staring at me," Ina Claire said. "Why are you staring at me?"

"Oh. Well, I suppose I was staring at you. It's just that now comes the most important, and the most difficult, part of your training," Duff said.

"You mean you want me to shoot some more?"

"Nae, lass, this has nothing to do with the accuracy of your shooting. This has to do with your willingness to set aside the natural, human reluctance to do something that violates all nature and decent behavior."

"I still don't know what you are talking about."

"I'm talking about your willingness to kill."

"My willingness to kill?"

"Aye. I'm not saying that you have to be eager to kill, but I am saying that you must be willing to do it. I'm going to let you in on a little secret. Successful gunfighters aren't good because they are fast, or because they can shoot straight. Obviously that is important. But the most important thing is the ability to recognize and act upon the pivot point, that is to say the point of no return."

"The point of no return?" Ina Claire asked, still not certain that she understood what Duff was talking about.

"Yes, the point of no return, and by that I mean a situation where you know you must kill or be killed. Taking another person's life from them is an awesome thing. And the average person, when they reach that point of no return, will hesitate. The task we have set for ourselves almost guarantees that you will reach that point, and when you do, there will be no time for hesitation. You must be willing to kill a human being with as little thought as in slapping a mosquito. Can you do that?"

"If I answer truthfully, would you change your mind about taking me?" Ina Claire asked.

"I want a truthful answer."

"All right, the truth is, I don't know if I could do that or not. Killing a human being is not like swatting a mosquito. If that means you won't take me with you, then I suppose I'll just have to accept that."

Duff didn't respond for a long moment, then he smiled at her. "If you had answered any other way, I wouldn't have taken you. You're right, killing a human being isn't like swatting a mosquito. But you can use the time between now and when you will have

248

to face that possibility to prepare yourself. You can go with me."

"Us," Meagan corrected. "She can go with us."

"Us," Duff agreed.

"When will we go?" Ina Claire asked.

"Is tomorrow too soon for you?"

"No, it isn't too soon at all," Ina Claire replied. "I am ready to go."

"You're sure you don't want me 'n Wang to come with you?" Elmer asked the next day. It was mid-afternoon before Duff, Meagan, and Ina Claire were finally ready to get away.

"I've given it some thought," Duff replied, "but I think for now that 'twould be best for the two of you to stay here 'n keep an eye on the ranch."

"All right, whatever you say, you're the boss," Elmer said.

"Elmer ye ken that ye be my partner now, 'n ye have been from the time we built this ranch. If we are partners, then that means I am nae your boss."

"You was in the army, same as I was," Elmer replied. "All right, yeah, you was an officer in the British Army, 'n I rode as a guerrilla for the Confederates. But they was both the same in that they needed to be someone that's in charge. 'N you bein' a heap smarter'n I am, I figger that makes you the boss."

Duff laughed. "All right, I suppose you're right, someone does have to be in charge. But I wouldn't be for makin' a bet that I'm smarter than you. Maybe you don't have a formal education, but I've seen few people who have a higher innate intelligence than you."

"Innate? See there you go using one o' them words that I don't have no idee what means."

"Intuitive acumen," Duff said.

The expression on Elmer's face indicated that he was still in the dark.

"It means you were born smart," Meagan said with a little chuckle.

"Well, hell, why didn't you say that?" Elmer asked. "Besides which, I already knowed that I was born smart. I just said you was smarter, that's all."

Duff shook his head and laughed. "Meagan, Ina Claire, let's go before Elmer gets me totally discomposed."

"Well, at least we can see you off," Elmer said as he and Wang followed Duff, Meagan, and Ina Claire out to the three saddled horses that waited for them.

Elmer watched them ride through the gate.

"Since it is so late now, they'll more'n likely be campin' out tonight so's that they can be in Cheyenne tomorrow mornin'."

"When will we go?" Wang asked.

Elmer chuckled. "You knew damn well I didn't intend to stay out of this, didn't you? I'd say we give 'em a week, or maybe ten days, 'n if they ain't back by then, we'll go hunt 'em up."

That night, Ina Claire lay near the fire, watching as the red sparks rode the heat waves up to join with the blue stars in the black velvet sky. As she lay out under the stars, she couldn't help but think of her mother and father, and her eyes filled with tears. Those evil men had taken them from her far too early. When Ina Claire got married, her children would never know their grandmother and grandfather.

The sadness was replaced by anger, and the anger by determination.

She would find the men who did this to her parents, and she would see that justice was done. Even as she was thinking this, though, she knew that justice might well mean that she would have to kill one or more of the men.

She recalled Duff's challenge to her.

"Taking another person's life from them is

an awesome thing. And the average person, when they reach that point of no return, will hesitate. The task we have set for ourselves almost guarantees that you will reach that point, and when you do, there will be no time for hesitation. You must be willing to kill a human being with as little thought as in slapping a mosquito. Can you do that?"

Ina Claire thought about pulling the bodies of her mother and father from a burning house, and the anger grew more intense.

"Yes," she said aloud, though speaking very quietly. "I can kill those men with as little thought as slapping a mosquito."

With the knowledge that she was physically involved in locating the men who did this, and in seeing to it that they received justice, a grim peace came over her, and Ina Claire's active mind stilled enough for her to fall asleep.

Although Ina Claire had said the words so quietly that she didn't think she would be heard, Duff did hear them. Duff not only heard them, he well understood the anger that was driving her now. All he had to do was think back to the tragedy that had caused him to leave Scotland.

■ ■ ■ ■

Skye McGregor, his fiancée, had been murdered by Sheriff Somerled and his deputies. Duff killed two of the deputies but the others got away. Because he had killed officers of the law, Duff was forced to flee the country, and he wound up in New York working as a stage manager for the theater production company of his American cousins, Andrew and Rosanna MacCallister.

But the Somerled brothers came to America after him, catching up with him backstage one night just after the curtain had closed on his cousins' production. He was working on one of the stage flats when he realized that he wasn't alone.

"Duff MacCallister, we have come for ye," a familiar voice said from the darkness.

The voice was familiar, because it was the voice of Alexander Somerled.

Startled at hearing Alexander's voice here, in America, Duff turned toward the sound but saw nothing in the darkness. He was at a disadvantage because while Alexander was cloaked by the darkness, he was well lighted.

"Alexander Somerled," Duff said. *"Have you come alone?"* Duff moved away from

the flat to the properties locker. Alongside the properties locker was the light control panel.

"I am with him," Roderick said.

"And so am I, Deputy Malcolm," a third voice said.

"Deputy Malcolm is it?" Duff replied. *"Well you have wasted a trip, Deputy Malcolm, for you have no jurisdiction here. You can nae arrest me."*

"Och, but 'tis not for to arrest you we have come, Duff MacCallister, but 'tis to kill you," Alexander said.

Reaching his hand up to the light control panel, Duff turned off the backstage lights. As soon as the theater went dark, he grabbed the claymore sword, the same sword Andrew and Rosanna had handled on stage. And though it was used as a prop, it was a real claymore sword, fifty-five inches in overall length, with a thirteen-inch grip and a forty-two-inch blade.

"What the hell, where did he go?" Malcolm asked.

"Where is he?" Roderick asked.

"Shoot him!" Alexander shouted. *"Shoot him!"*

"Shoot where?" Roderick asked.

Duff picked up a vase and tossed it through the darkness to the opposite side of the room. When it hit the floor, it broke with a great crash.

"Over there! He's trying to get away! Shoot him! Shoot him!" Alexander yelled at the top of his voice.

All three men began to shoot in the direction of the sound of the crashing vase, the flame patterns of the muzzles illuminating the room in periodic flashes like streaks of lightning.

The flashes of light enabled Duff to come up behind them.

"Here I am, boys," he said.

The three men turned toward him, but with a mighty swing of the great claymore sword, Duff decapitated the two Somerled brothers.

Malcolm got away from him that night, but Duff encountered him again, in the streets of Chugwater, bested him in a gunfight, and his revenge was complete. Now, as Duff lay in the darkness, recalling the blood-boiling anger he had felt that night in partially avenging the murder of Skye, he could understand what was driving Ina Claire.

"We'll find them, lass, and we'll avenge the murder of your parents." Like Ina Claire, Duff spoke the words aloud, but unlike Ina Claire's words, his were not heard.

Duff lay on his bedroll long after the other two had gone to sleep. Sleeping out under the stars had become second nature for Duff, especially since arriving in America. To the west he could see Laramie Mountains, their snow-capped peaks gleaming under the bright moonlight. Much higher than the mountains in his homeland, these mountains seemed majestic and imposing. One of the things that had most impressed him about this country was its vastness. And it was the wild beauty of his adopted country that he loved most.

He heard the hoot of an owl from somewhere close by while overhead, bats, their wings gray against the dark sky, darted about in search of insects. A night breeze came up, and while it was brisk enough to rustle through branches of a nearby poplar tree, Duff smelled no rain on its breath.

At breakfast the next morning, Ina Claire seemed just a little nervous and she kept looking around. At first, Duff thought that she might be frightened that someone was close by. But as he read the expression in her face he realized that it might be one of discomfort, more than worry, and he realized what her problem was.

"Meagan, while I'm cleaning up the camp,

why don't you and Ina Claire take a little walk to explore the foliage. 'Tis thinkin' I am that you might find some relief in that little exercise."

Meagan caught on immediately, and she smiled. "I was just about to make that suggestion myself," she said. "Come along, Ina Claire."

"You want to explore the foliage?"

Meagan laughed. "Look, child, if the three of us are going to be traveling so close together over the next few weeks or so, there are going to be times when one of us will have to step away to find a moment of privacy, don't you think?"

"What?" Then, with an embarrassed smile, Ina Claire realized exactly what Meagan was talking about.

"Yes," she said. "Yes, I think you are right."

"So in the future, don't be too embarrassed to say so. It's going to happen to all of us."

"You're right. I won't be embarrassed anymore, and, uh, I'm relieved to know that anytime I want to uh, be relieved, all I have to do is ask."

The two ladies walked away from the encampment together, laughing and talking until they disappeared behind a little copse of trees. Duff smiled and whistled a little tune as he cleaned up the camp, then saddled the three horses so they could ride out as soon as Meagan and Ina Claire returned.

CHAPTER TWENTY-ONE

Whitworth General Store

The store sat on the bank of the Little Laramie River, exactly halfway between the towns of Farrel and Howell. It did a very good business because of, rather than despite, its isolation. And because it had no immediate competition, Art Whitworth could, and did, charge a premium price for all his goods.

The store had started in a one-room building, but it had grown with success, adding at a rate of one new room per year for the last four years. Now the store spread out with the add-on rooms, their position in the chronology apparent by the different degree of weathering in the unpainted one-by-six planks that made up its walls.

WHITWORTH GENERAL STORE
~ Goods for all Mankind ~
Eats & Cots
Groceries, Guns, Ammunition, Whiskey

Callahan and the others with him were on top of a ridge, looking down onto the store. From here, they not only had a good view of the store itself but also the road approaching the store. For more than a mile in either direction, the road was empty. That meant they could conduct their business without fear of being interrupted. And the business they had in mind was robbery.

"How much money you reckon he's got in that place?" Cooper asked.

"More'n that damn stagecoach had, that's for sure," Morris replied.

"All right, boys, what do you say we do a little early-morning business?" Callahan suggested as he sloped his horse down the ridge toward the store.

Art Whitworth saw the seven riders approaching his store, and his first thought was that they were here to conduct business. If he could count on five dollars of business from each of them, that would be thirty-five dollars earned in no longer than the time they would spend here.

But as he stepped toward the door to watch their approach, something about them disturbed him. They weren't coming by way of the road as most customers did. They were coming down from the Medicine

Bow Mountains. Whitworth knew for a fact that there were no settlements for many miles in that direction, even though he sometimes got customers from mountain men, trappers, or hunters, or just a hermit. But to see seven men coming from such a direction was a little unsettling.

"Mary Lou, I want you to go back into the storeroom and lock yourself in. Don't come back out until I tell you."

"What is it, Whitworth? What's wrong?" Mary Lou asked. "You're frightening me."

"Just do what I say. There's no time to argue. Please, just go now before they get in here!" he said with a sense of urgency.

This time Mary Lou reacted without further questioning, pulling the door to the storeroom shut but a moment before the front door opened.

Mary Lou wished there was a crack so she could look out to see what was going on, but there was no such crack available. She could hear, though, and she put her ear to the door to listen to the conversation.

"Yes, sir, gentlemen, what can I do for you today?" Whitworth asked, forcing a smile.

"Your sign out front says you have goods for all mankind," one of the men said. He was a large man, clearly the largest of the entire group. His nose was pressed flat against his face, and one of his ears was deformed. "Is that true? Do you really have goods for all mankind?"

"Yes, sir, that certainly is true," Whitworth said. "You setting up a house, and you need furniture, lanterns, wood-burning stoves, I've got 'em. You want to farm? I've got plows, harrows, potato diggers. For ranchers I've got saddles, tack, and . . ."

The big man waved him off. "Yeah, yeah, I believe you," he said.

"Ah, but you men didn't come here to set up a house, or farm, or ranch, did you?"

The big man chuckled and looked at one of the others. "Well, what do you think about that, Cooper? Mr. Whitworth here is just real smart to figure that out."

"I tell you what, Callahan. I'll just bet he ain't smart enough to figure out what we're really here for, though," Pardeen said with a little laugh that sent shivers of fright up Whitworth's spine.

Whitworth cleared his throat nervously. "Yes, well, you gentlemen just look around the store. If you see something you'd like, I'll be glad to get it for you."

"Yeah, we'll just do that," Callahan said.

As Whitworth stood behind the counter, watching the seven men move through the store, he began to be somewhat less nervous. They were, after all, just shopping. And how they were shopping . . . by Whitworth's most conservative estimate, they had gathered at least three hundred dollars' worth, from guns and ammunition, to knives, blankets, bacon, and cans of peaches.

"I see that you have only the seven horses you rode in on," Whitworth said. "You might have already bought more than you can carry away, but I have a suggestion."

"Yeah? What suggestion is that?" Callahan asked.

"I could sell you a pack mule," Whitworth said.

"That's a good idea. Yeah, we'll take the mule."

Several minutes later, with all their purchases piled up on the counter, Whitworth, no longer nervous now, was adding everything up. He was about to call Mary Lou out of the storeroom so she could help him but decided against it. She had been in there this long; she could stay a little longer.

"You gentlemen didn't separate your purchases as you brought them to the counter, so I'm going to charge just one price for all of it, and you can settle it up among yourselves later."

"Oh, we've already settled it up among ourselves," Callahan said again with a broad smile. Perhaps it was Callahan's smiles that were making Whitworth nervous. As far as Whitworth could tell, there was no humor in any of them.

"Have you?" Whitworth asked.

"Yes, it was very easy." Callahan made a little waving motion of his hand over the pile of merchandise. "You see, the thing is, there ain't none of us goin' to be payin' nothing at all for any of this."

"Whatever do you mean? Are you saying that after gathering all this together, that now you won't be taking it?"

"Oh, we'll be takin' it all right," Callahan said. "We just won't be payin' for it."

"I don't understand," Whitworth said.

Callahan pulled his pistol and pointed it at Whitworth. "Oh, I think you understand all right. And we'll also be a-takin' any money that you've got in your cash box there. I expect it's a right smart amount of money, too . . . seein' as you sell goods for all mankind," he added with a chuckle. Now, all seven men had their guns out, and all of them were pointing at the storeowner.

"Sure, I've got the cash box right under here," Whitworth said. He reached under the counter, but instead of coming up with the cash box, he had a double-barrel shotgun in his hand.

As soon as he lifted the shotgun, all seven men fired at him. Whitworth pulled the trigger on the shotgun as well, but it was a reflexive action and the shotgun did no more than tear out a huge chunk of the counter.

"Pardeen, you, Bates, 'n Donner get this stuff loaded on the pack mule. Manning, you 'n Morris grab us some whiskey, one bottle, no, make it two bottles apiece. Cooper, you help me load the cash box."

Inside the storeroom, Mary Lou was biting down hard on some washcloths to keep from crying out loud. As soon as she heard the gunfire, she knew what had happened. Somehow, her husband had known beforehand. How could he have possibly known? And why didn't he use that knowledge to save his own life?

Mary Lou wanted to run outside to check on Art, but from the number of gunshots, she was positive he would be dead. Killed by these men . . . she stopped in mid-thought. She had heard the names as one of them had called out to the others. She tried to recall them, but, for now, only three of the names had stuck with her. She could recall the name Manning, because a family by the name of Manning had a farm next to her parents' farm back in Mississippi. She could remember the names Cooper and Callahan, too. The other name that stuck with her was Pardeen and it only because she thought it was a rather peculiar name.

"All right, Mr. Manning, Mr. Cooper, Mr. Callahan, and Mr. Pardeen," she whispered. "I'll remember your names, and if they find you, I don't expect they'll have that much trouble finding the others."

Howell, Wyoming Territory

It was nearly noon when the wagon, with the gold-outlined red letters reading WHITWORTH GENERAL STORE, rolled into town. Most of the people of the town paid little attention to its arrival. It was a pretty routine occurrence; Whitworth brought the wagon into town at least twice a month to pick up railroad shipments that were being held for him at the Howell depot.

The only thing that did draw everyone's attention was the driver. Generally when Whitworth came to town he was the driver and his wife was on the seat beside him. More than just business trips, they became social occasions, as Mary Lou Whitworth would take the opportunity to visit with her

266

friends. Because of that, she was always very animated when she rode into town, smiling and waving at everyone.

That was not the case today. Mary Lou sat very stiffly on the driver's seat, looking neither left nor right as she drove down Railroad Street.

"That's odd," Jo Ellen Rice said. Jo Ellen was standing at the front window of her ladies' goods store.

"What is odd?" Kate Mullins asked. Kate was the blacksmith's wife, and she had come to the store to buy a new hat.

"Mary Lou just came into town and she didn't return my wave."

"Maybe she didn't see it," Kate suggested.

"How could she not have seen it? I was standing right here. She's always seen me before. I wonder where Art is?"

"You mean he's not with her?"

"I didn't see him. Mary Lou is driving by herself."

"Well, that's probably why Mary Lou didn't see you. If she's all by herself, more than likely she is having to concentrate on her driving."

Jo Ellen chuckled. "I'm sure you're right. Now do you plan to buy that hat or just hold it until it goes out of style?" she teased.

■ ■ ■ ■

Mary Lou stopped the wagon in front of the sheriff's office, set the brake, and climbed down. It was called the sheriff's office even though its occupant was a deputy sheriff.

Deputy Sheriff Thurman Burns was no stranger to Mary Lou. They had grown up as neighbors, and their parents had even entertained the idea that one day they might be married. Such a relationship never developed between them, though they had remained friends. Thurman was playing a game of solitaire, and he looked up and smiled when Mary Lou stepped in through the door.

"Mary Lou," he said. "You and Art in town to pick up a shipment, are you? Will we be able to have lunch together?"

Mary Lou broke down crying, the first time she had allowed herself to do so.

"Mary Lou, what is it?" Thurman asked, getting up and moving to her quickly.

"He's dead," Mary Lou said.

"Who is dead? Good Lord, you don't mean Art, do you?"

"He's in the wagon," Mary Lou said. "Some men came, they robbed the store, and they killed Art."

"Oh, my God, that's awful!" Thurman said, putting his arms around Mary Lou to comfort her.

"Deputy, have you seen what's in this wagon?" one of the townspeople said, stepping into the office then. He saw a weeping Mary Lou in Thurman's arms.

"Oh, I . . . I'm sorry," the intruder said.

"It's all right, Hal," Thurman replied. "Mary Lou just told me."

With Mary Lou somewhat able to regain control, Thurman stepped out front. By now at least thirty people had gathered around the wagon to gawk at Whitworth's bullet-ridden body.

"Cecil, would you drive Mrs. Whitworth's wagon down to Prufrock's?" Thurman asked. Andrew Prufrock was the town mortician.

"Sure thing, Deputy," Cecil, one of the men who had gathered to gawk at the body, replied.

"Then have the wagon cleaned of his blood. You can send the bill to my office."

"Damn," Thurman said after Mary Lou told him everything she knew, including repeating the names she had heard. "I know exactly who it was that did this."

Thurman pulled some wanted posters from his pile and looked through them. "Yeah," he said, thumping his finger against them. "Callahan and Manning were broke out of jail by Cooper and Morris. Then, a few days ago, Pardeen, Bates, and Donner was also broke out of jail. From the names you can remember, it looks as if they've all joined up together. I'll get a telegram off to Sheriff Sharpies right away. Don't you worry none at all, Mary Lou. We're goin' to get the men who killed Art, you can take my word on that."

"I'm glad, but . . ."

"But what?"

"It won't bring Art back."

Deputy Burns nodded, then, in a comforting way, put his arms around her again.

"You're right," he said softly. "It won't bring Art back. But to those of us who considered Art to be a good friend, it will at least give us some sense of satisfaction that justice will be served."

CHAPTER TWENTY-TWO

Cheyenne

When Duff, Meagan, and Ina Claire stepped into the governor's office that morning, they were greeted by a clerk.

"What can I do for you gents?" he asked.

"We're not all gents," Meagan replied with a smile.

"Oh, I beg your pardon, ma'am. But the way you are dressed, I didn't, uh, that is . . ." the deputy let his sentence run down without completing it.

"That's all right. The reason my sister and I are dressed like this is because it makes riding easier."

"Yes, ma'am, I reckon it does. Now, what is it I can do for you folks?"

"We would like to speak with the governor," Duff said.

"Do you have an appointment?"

"We dinnae have an appointment, but we would like to speak to him."

"Governor Hoyt is a very busy man, too busy to speak to just anyone who gets it in mind to come in off the street for a visit." The clerk was a very thin man with a prominent Adam's apple that bobbed up and down as he talked.

"Oh, I don't think we'll be needing an appointment," Meagan said with a broad smile. "Just tell Uncle John that Meagan Parker would like to visit with him."

"Uncle John?" the clerk replied.

"I suppose I should say Governor Hoyt, but he has been Uncle John to me for a long time. Please be a good man and tell him that I'm here, would you? I think he would be very upset with you if you don't."

The clerk studied Meagan for a long moment, then he lifted his finger. "I will tell him, miss. But if this is some ploy, I will have you escorted out of the capitol building."

"Oh, I assure you, mister" — she paused to read the nameplate on his desk — "Fitzhugh, that the governor will thank you."

"Wait here," Fitzhugh said.

When the clerk stepped into the governor's private office, Duff looked at her in surprise.

"Lass, I've never heard you say that you

know the governor. 'Tis hoping I am that there be some substance behind your words."

Meagan laughed. "Duff, don't you know that a woman always has to keep some secrets?" She glanced over at Ina Claire. "Keep that in mind, Ina Claire. You're a beautiful young lady and the time will come, and soon, when you'll have men paying attention to you."

While they were waiting, Duff picked up a newspaper that was in the chair beside him and began reading from the *Cheyenne Defender.*

STAGECOACH ROBBERY

On two days previous, the Cummins City stagecoach was held up. The driver, Adam Drake, and his shotgun guard, Ray Carter, were both killed in the robbery. The robbers, seven of them, stole the mailbag, thinking, perhaps, that the bag would contain sufficient money to make their effort worthwhile.

However, this newspaper has received information from the express company, which states that there was no money transfer on the day of the robbery. Mr. Drake and Mr. Carter were both killed for

naught, as the robbers left the event unre-
warded for their evil deeds.

It was one of the passengers, a Mr.
George Jeffries of New York, New York,
who drove the coach from the point where
it was robbed on into Cummins City. Mr.
Jeffries also gave a description of the apparent leader of seven robbers, describing
him as a big man, over six feet tall, with a
deformed nose and ear. It should be noted
that such a description is a perfect fit for
Clay Callahan, who so recently escaped
from the Cheyenne jail, leaving two dead
innocent victims behind.

"Look at this," Duff said, showing the
newspaper to Meagan and Ina Claire.

"That's them!" Ina Claire said excitedly.
"Oh, but this says there were seven men
who robbed the stagecoach. It was only four
men who killed Mama and Papa."

"Aye, but the description does fit Callahan, so 'tis obvious they have found three
more men to join them. And this is how
we're going to find them," Duff said. "Men
such as these can never stop their evil deeds.
It's like putting a bell on a cat . . . we'll be
able to follow them by their transgressions."

The door to the governor's office opened,
and Fitzhugh appeared with a stern expres-

sion on his face.

"Uh-oh," Ina Claire said quietly.

Fitzhugh stepped aside, and a man with a full head of white hair and a sweeping mustache appeared in the door behind him. In contrast to the clerk's stark visage, the governor wore a broad smile.

"Meagan!" he said, opening his arms and coming toward her.

"Hello, Uncle John." They embraced.

"Come in, child, do come in!" he invited. "Bring your friends with you."

Meagan looked at Duff and Ina Claire, both of whom were wearing expressions of surprise if not total shock.

"What do you hear from your father?"

"He and Mama are doing well," Meagan said.

"When next you write to them, please give them my best," Governor Hoyt said. Then, to Duff, he added, "This young lady's father, Caleb Parker, is the best friend I ever had, and the brother I never had."

"Then you and the governor are nae actually . . ." Duff started, directing his question to Meagan.

"Related? No. But the governor and my father were so often together that, long ago, I began calling him uncle."

"And at my urging, I hasten to add,"

Governor Hoyt said. "Now, Meagan, to what do I owe the pleasure of your visit? And why would a beautiful woman like you dress in such a manner?"

The governor took in Meagan's attire with a sweep of his hand.

"This is my very good friend, Duff Mac-Callister," Meagan said. "He owns a rather substantial ranch up by Chugwater. I'm going to let him tell you why we have come to see you."

"Mr. MacCallister, I do believe I have heard of you, sir," the governor said with an extended hand.

"Sure 'n 'tis my pleasure to be making the acquaintance o' an honorable gentleman such as yerself, Governor," Duff replied.

"A Scotsman are you?"

"Aye, 'tis Scottish he be, from the wee bairn he was to the foine mon who before ye stands today," Meagan said, perfectly mimicking Duff's accent.

Governor Hoyt laughed. "I'd say your friendship is more than casual," he said. "You sure didn't grow up with that accent."

"The lass enjoys a bit o' fun with m' brogue I fear," Duff said. He smiled. "But mimicry be the sincerest form of flattery, I've always heard."

"Yes, I've heard the same thing. Now,

what can I do for you?"

"Governor, would you be for remembering some days past, when two brigands b' the name of Clay Callahan and Zeke Manning escaped from jail, here in Cheyenne?"

"Indeed I do, sir, indeed I do. I remember, also, that they were to have gone to the gallows on the very next day. I remember this, because I had turned down the petition for a commutation of their sentence. They not only escaped, they left behind them a couple of their foul deeds, the murders of the jailer and Mordecai Luscombe, who was to have been their hangman. The poor fellow wound up being hanged by his own rope."

"Two men it was that helped them, Governor." Duff glanced toward Ina Claire. "Tell the governor who they were."

"Their names were Dooley Cooper and Pogue Morris," Ina Claire said.

"Cooper and Morris? And tell me, young lady, how would you be knowing that they were the ones who helped Callahan and Manning?"

"I know, because while they were on their way to Cheyenne, Cooper and Morris took a meal at my parents' house." Ina Claire paused in mid-sentence, during which time tears began to stream down her face. "And I know because when Dooley Cooper and

277

Pogue Morris came back to . . . to kill my parents, Callahan and Manning were with them."

"Oh," Governor Hoyt said quietly. "Oh, my dear, I'm so sorry."

"That's why we're here, Governor," Duff said. "We are going after the brigands who murdered Ina Claire's family. And we want you to commission us as special law officers with jurisdiction all over the territory."

"I don't know. I'd have to get legislative approval to finance such a thing."

Duff waved his hand. "I'm sorry, Governor. I should have been more clear. You dinnae need to seek approval for compensation, for 'tis nae money I'm asking for. What we seek now is only the authority the commission will give us."

"All right, I see no problem in appointing you a special officer answerable only to the governor."

"Us," Meagan said.

"I beg your pardon?"

"We're asking for us, Uncle John. We want commissions for all three of us," Meagan said.

"Oh, well now, I don't know about that," the governor said.

"Governor, the ladies will be traveling with me," Duff said. "There may be times

278

when having the authority of the law will be beneficial to them."

Governor Hoyt stroked his mustache. "Meagan, girl, if something were to happen to you, how would I ever explain my role in it to your father?"

"Uncle John, you heard what Duff said. We are going with him, with or without the authority of the law. I just feel that we would be better served if we did have your authorization."

The governor let out a long sigh. "All right," he said. "I'll have the commissioning documents drawn up and filed. You can pick them up tomorrow."

"Thank you, Uncle John!" Meagan said, giving the governor a big hug.

"What will we do until tomorrow?" Meagan asked after they left the capitol building.

"We'll just wander around town, keeping our eyes and our ears open," Duff said. "We might hear something that will be of some value."

"Where would we have to go to overhear something like that?"

"A saloon," Duff said.

"A saloon?"

"I suppose we could get a couple of rooms at the hotel and you and Ina Claire could wait there."

"No, in for a penny, in for a pound," Meagan said. "Ina Claire and I will go with you."

"Meagan, I —"

"Duff, you can't be worrying about protecting our virtue. My goodness, the way we are dressed now, the average person would think we have no virtue to protect. If we are going to be partners in this adventure, we are going to be full partners. Besides, I've been to Fiddler's Green, often as your guest I might add."

Duff thought of the White Horse Pub in Dunoon, owned by Ian McGregor. The White Horse had an island bar, Jacobean-style ceiling, beautiful stained glass windows, and etched mirrors. Despite its elegant décor and clientele of nobles, it was primarily a place for drinking and most who came behaved with decorum, enjoying the ambience and convivial conversation with friends. McGregor's daughter, Skye, had worked in the pub. He thought about her now, and realized that if he had no problem with Skye being a regular part of the White Horse Pub, then he had no right to be critical of Meagan if she chose to visit a saloon. And as she stated, Meagan was often a patron of Fiddler's Green, and what was it, if not a saloon?

"All right," he said. "You can come if you feel you must."

Meagan laughed.

"Why are you laughing?"

"You don't understand, do you? I wasn't asking for your permission, I was merely providing you with the information that Ina Claire and I would be with you."

Duff laughed. "And 'tis glad I would be for the company."

CHAPTER TWENTY-THREE

Office of J. P. Sharpies, sheriff of Cheyenne
"Sheriff, I just got this telegram from Deputy Burns out in Howell," Phil Barkett, the telegrapher, said, stepping in to the sheriff's office. "I figured I should bring it to you right away."

"What is it about?"

"It's about a murder, Sheriff. Some outlaws robbed Art Whitworth's store and shot him dead."

Sheriff Sharpies read the telegram.

TO SHERIFF SHARPIES CHEYENNE FROM DEPUTY BURNS HOWELL STATION STOP SEVEN MEN HELD UP WHITWORTH STORE KILLED WHITWORTH STOP NAMES SUPPLIED BY MRS WHITWORTH ARE MANNING CALLAHAN COOPER AND PARDEEN STOP THOSE NAMES SUGGEST THAT THE SEVEN MEN MIGHT BE CALLAHAN

Sheriff Sharpies wondered if Mrs. Whitworth had actually given Burns all the names, or if she had only given him a few names, and Burns, extrapolating, put the rest of them together. Burns was a former Texas Ranger and a very intelligent man. Sharpies had used him before when he wanted some detective work done.

Though Burns didn't point it out in the telegram, Sharpies was able to do a little deduction on his own. Like Callahan and Manning, Pardeen, Bates, and Donner had managed to escape from jail shortly before they were to go to the gallows. That was three men, added to Callahan, Manning, Cooper, and Morris, who were already known to be riding together. Seven men robbed the stagecoach, killing the driver and the shotgun guard. The description of one of the men matched that of Clay Callahan.

Seven men also robbed the Whitworth General Store, killing Art Whitworth. Callahan was also with that group. It took little deduction now to know that it was the same seven men who had robbed the stagecoach, and now all the names were known.

"Good job, Thurman," Sheriff Sharpies

said quietly, as a broad smile spread across his lips.

Then, as he thought of how he came by the names, the smile faded. Art Whitworth, a good man, was killed by these outlaws. Sharpies vowed he would do all he could to see to it that they paid for their evil deed.

Even as the sheriff was contemplating the information he had just received, Duff, Meagan, and Ina Claire were walking toward the Rendezvous. Duff knew from his previous visits that this was Cheyenne's finest drinking establishment.

It had been Duff's observation that the Westerners, whose society he had joined, were a gregarious lot. They didn't like to drink alone; they preferred the company of friends, and even strangers. They congregated in saloons where conversation flowed. The customers ranged from prospectors to gamblers, cowboys, stockmen, coal miners, railroaders, drummers, lawmen, honest workmen, and, of course, occasional desperadoes.

The interior of the Rendezvous was a long, low room, illuminated only by the sunshine that spilled in through front windows. There were several men standing along the bar, many with their feet propped up on the brass rail. Chairs and tables were scattered along the walls, as well as in the center of the room, and the place was filled with customers smoking, playing poker, and engaged in loud and animated conversation. Painted women moved from table to table like bees darting from flower to flower.

Four men abandoned a table just as Duff, Meagan, and Ina Claire arrived.

"There," Duff said, pointing to the empty table. "Sit there and I'll get our drinks."

"I want a beer," Ina Claire said.

"You'll drink a sarsaparilla," Duff said.

"Duff, a beer will draw less attention," Meagan said.

Duff looked at Ina Claire for a moment, then nodded. "All right, a beer it is."

As Duff stepped up to the bar, Meagan and Ina Claire hurried to claim the table that had been vacated. As soon as they sat down, a woman approached them. Her eyes were darkly outlined, her cheeks heavily rouged, and her lips bright red with paint. The top of her dress was cut so low that her breasts were about to spill out.

"Well now," she said with a practiced smile. "If you two aren't the most hand-some critters in here. You're a young one, ain't you, honey?" she said to Ina Claire.

"I'm old enough," Ina Claire replied.

The bar girl blinked a couple of times, then got a surprised expression on her face. She leaned back, then straightened up.

"What the devil? You're a girl!"

"See there, Ina Claire, I told you we were girls," Meagan said with a little laugh.

"Why are you dressed like that?" the bar girl asked.

"Why are *you* dressed like *that*?" Meagan asked.

Duff came to the table then, carrying three beers. "Hello," he said, greeting the bar girl with a smile.

The bar girl returned the smile. "At least *you* are a man," she said.

"Aye, that I am," Duff said. He took in Meagan and Ina Claire with a wave of his hand. "And as you can see, I've come to this place with m' wife 'n sister-in-law, so we'll nae be needin' yer services. But I'll be thanking you for coming over to offer your company."

Duff gave the woman a dollar. "And to show you my appreciation, here, buy yourself a drink for being so nice to the womenfolk while I was getting our beers."

The girl smiled at getting the dollar. "I thank you, sir." She looked at Meagan and Ina Claire. "You two have a fine man here. But take some advice from Sadie. If you want to keep him, you need to change the way you're dressed. Why, at first glance, nobody would even know that you aren't a man. You should wear something more lady-like."

"Thank you, we will consider that," Meagan replied.

Meagan and Ina Claire laughed as the bar girl walked away.

"Have you ever had a beer before?" Duff asked as he set the mug in front of Ina Claire.

"Not a whole beer. I've taken a few swallows from Papa's glass, from time to time."

"Just take a few sips and when my glass is low enough, I'll be for pouring some of your beer into my glass."

"Thank you," Ina Claire said.

"Now, you take Callahan. Him 'n Manning was s'posed to hang, you know. They'd done built the gallows, but ole Callahan, he was too smart for 'em, 'n he 'n Manning escaped."

That bit of conversation came from a man who was sitting with three others at an adjacent table. He punctuated his sentence by spitting a tobacco quid toward a brass spittoon. At least half of it made its mark.

" 'N here's the thing. The gallows wasn't

only built, when them two left town, hell they left the hangman hisself, ole' Mordecai Luscombe, danglin' from the same contraption he aimed to use for the execution of Callahan 'n Manning," another man said.

"You two ain't tellin' me nothin' I don't already know. Hell, I was plannin' on watchin' the hangin', 'n when I come out into the street to get me a spot, why they was already twenty or thirty folks or so. They was all standin' aroun' just a-starin' at the gallows, 'n I didn't have no idea what they was all lookin' at 'til I looked my own self 'n seen that hangman feller just a danglin' there. That was a'fore they cut 'im down, you see."

"Wonder where them two boys is now?" a third asked.

"Ain't you read the story in the newspaper? They just held up the Cummins City stagecoach the other day."

"I didn't read it. You mean they's a story in the paper that says Callahan and Manning robbed a stagecoach?"

"Well, it don't say Manning, but it does say Callahan."

"How do they know it was Callahan?"

"What do you mean, how do they know? Ain't you never seen 'im? It ain't somebody you might mistake for someone else. He's a big man, 'n he was a prize-fighter once, so his nose is kinda flat, 'n one o' his ears is all scrunched up."

"Yeah, I seen 'im at the trial that was held for him 'n Manning," one of the other men at the table added. " 'N it's like Charley said, once you've seed the son of a bitch, it ain't likely that you'll forget 'im."

Charley jumped back into the conversation. "Callahan was one of 'em all right, 'n if he was there, you can believe Manning was along, too. Seven of 'em, they was."

"Seven? Who was the rest of 'em?"

"I don't think there's nobody that knows that. All the paper said was they was seven of 'em what held up the stagecoach."

"Laraby, you been awful quiet here," Charley said. "You rode with 'em two boys once, didn't you?"

"I ain't never rid with Callahan," Laraby replied. "But me 'n Manning rid together some. We never did no killin' when I was with 'im, though. 'Bout the onliest thing we ever done was we throwed a long rope now 'n then. I spent two years in prison for it, 'n I tell you true, that ain't no place I ever want to go back to, which is why I'm satisfied now to be a cowboy for forty 'n found."

"Hell, who ain't throwed a long rope now 'n then? It's just that some of us ain't dumb enough to have ever been caught," one of the others replied in a joking manner, and the others laughed.

"You know what I think?" Laraby asked.

"What's that?"

"I'm a-thinkin' that I wouldn't be none surprised if they wasn't the same ones that held up that bank up in Bordeaux. They said it was four men that done it, 'n it went off slick as a whistle. 'N folks is sayin' one of 'em was Callahan."

"Four men?"

"That's what they're tellin'. Four men it was that robbed the bank, 'n one of 'em was a big man with a broke nose."

"Yeah, but it was seven men what held up the stagecoach."

"And Callahan was one of 'em," Charley said. "It's just real plain to me that Callahan rounded up some more people, is all. Don't know who the others are, though."

"Yeah, well, how do you think Callahan 'n Manning escaped? Had to be someone that helped 'em do that, 'n more'n likely, that's who the other men is."

"Have either of you ever been to Cummins City?" Duff asked quietly.

"I haven't," Ina Claire said.

"I have. I sold some dresses to a Mrs.

Allen who lives there. Her husband, Tom, is a big farmer in the area."

"Good, then you can show us around."

At that moment a big brute of a man, with long, stringy hair and an unkempt beard, stepped through the batwing doors. He stood just inside the doors for a moment, scratching his crotch and looking around the saloon floor.

"Oh, hell, there's Pete Pollard," one of the men who was sitting at the other table said.

"What's he doing here?" Charley asked. "I thought that son of a bitch was in jail."

"Yeah, for beatin' up a store clerk. But he only got thirty days for it, 'n here he is, out again."

"Don't nobody look over toward 'im," Laraby said. "Otherwise he might come over to our table, 'n I'd just as soon he don't."

The big bearded man the other table had identified as Pollard happened to walk by where Duff, Meagan, and Ina Claire were sitting. He gave them a casual glance, looked away, then stopped and did a double take.

"By damn, you are women, ain't ya?" he asked.

"Yes," Meagan replied. "We are women."

"Sir, 'tis a convivial conversation that we are having, 'n your intrusion is unwelcome,"

291

Duff said.

"Yeah? Well it don't seem fair to me that you'd be sittin' in here with two women, and I don't have none."

"Who would want anything to do with you? You are ugly," Ina Claire said.

Meagan and Duff laughed.

"You think that's funny, do you?" the big man said to Duff. He pulled his pistol and pointed it at Duff's head. "Now, I tell you what I'm goin' to do. I'm goin' to take one of these women upstairs with me, 'n I'm goin' to let you decide which one it's goin' to be."

Pollard's voice was loud and challenging, and it got the attention of everyone in the saloon, especially after he drew his pistol.

"Oh, I don't think I would want you to have either one of them," Duff replied in a voice that was as calm if he were engaged in a friendly conversation. "Actually, I doubt if any o' the ladies in here would be amenable to such a request. Ye' might be better off taking your proposition to a pub that caters to a lower class of patrons."

"Mister, you talk so damn fancy that I don't understand half o' what it is you're a-sayin'. But I'm tellin' you now that you had better make up your mind just real quick which one of these women I'll be

292

takin' or else I'm goin' to blow your head off . . . uhh!" the big man's blustering challenge was interrupted by a grunt of pain.

"Here now, 'n would you be for feelin' a wee bit of a pin prick in your belly?" Duff asked, the tone and tenor of his voice unchanged. "That would be the point of my knife. I've stuck it no more than, oh, I'd say half an inch into you, just enough so that you would know that it's there. And if I see your thumb draw the hammer back, I'll gut ye like a fish, 'n ye'll be for bleedin' to death on the floor."

"Be . . . be careful with that knife." The bravado in the man's voice was gone, replaced by fear.

"Turn your gun around, then give it butt-first to my wife."

"It's your wife, is it? Well, mister, I didn't mean no harm here, I sure didn't know that it was your wife."

"Hand her the pistol, please."

Turning the gun around as he had been ordered, the big man handed the pistol to Meagan.

"Now, I'll be for asking you to be leaving the table. Oh, and if I were you, I'd do something about that wound in your stomach. 'Tis a small wound, that's true, but as filthy as you keep your person, 'tis likely to get infected. And an infection there could go to your inner organs, and it would be a very painful death."

"What about my gun?"

"I'll leave it at the sheriff's office for you."

"Wait a minute . . ."

"You'd better do what the man says, Pollard," Charley, from the adjacent table, said, stepping up then. "You'd better get yourself cleaned up. I seen a feller die once from a wound that warn't no bigger'n that'n you got, but it up and putrefied on 'im, 'n he died hard."

Duff watched as the big man left the saloon, then he turned back to Meagan and Ina Claire.

"I expect we had better leave as well," he said. "I doubt we'll get any more information here today. We'll drop the gentleman's gun off at the sheriff's office, then check into a hotel for the night."

CHAPTER TWENTY-FOUR

"You stabbed him, you say?" a deputy at the sheriff's office said.

"Aye, but only a wee bit," Duff replied. "Just enough to discourage him it was."

The deputy laughed. "I would like to have seen that. Pollard is a big man full of swagger, and more often than not people back down to him. He just got out of jail this very morning for beating up a man. I'm glad to see that he got his comeuppance."

"I'll get us three rooms for the night," Duff said as they walked from the sheriff's office to the hotel.

"There's no need for you to be getting three rooms," Meagan said. "Two rooms will do."

"Aye, the two of you can stay in the same room."

"Now how is that going to look?" Meagan asked. "We're supposed to be married, but you'll be in a room by yourself and I'll be sharing a room with my sister?"

"Meagan, I . . ."

Meagan smiled and held out her hand. "Sure 'n if 'tis your virtue ye be worryin' about, Duff MacCallister, ye can put such fears to rest, for m' motive be as pure as the driven snow."

Duff laughed. "Meagan Parker, so perfectly does the brogue o' Scotland roll from your tongue, are you sure ye nae be from Edinburgh?"

Meagan dropped the brogue. "You are trying to avoid the subject. You know that if we are to maintain this façade, that what I'm saying is correct. We must share the same room."

"Aye, woman, there is truth in what ye say. It's just that I'm a wee bit concerned about the lass here."

"Oh, Ina Claire, I wasn't thinking about you. Of course, if you're too frightened to stay in a room by yourself, I'll stay with you."

"No, I'm not too frightened," Ina Claire replied. "I'll be fine."

Meagan smiled and put her arm through Duff's. "Good," she said. "Good for you."

Pete Pollard, with the small wound in his

stomach patched up, returned to the Rendezvous Saloon. That big galoot had caught him by surprise when he was here before, and he took his gun away from him.

Well, sir, I got me another gun, Pete thought to himself. *'N that funny-talkin' son of a bitch is goin' to play hell gettin' this one from me.*

He stood just inside the saloon door for a while, perusing the main room, but the man, and the two women who were dressed as men, weren't here. He stepped up to the bar and ordered a whiskey.

"Hello, Pollard, I didn't think you'd be back in here tonight, not after you had your little run-in with Mr. MacCallister," the bartender said.

"After my run-in with who?"

"MacCallister. Duff MacCallister," the bartender said. "That's the name of the man who took your gun away from you."

"Yeah, well, he sorta surprised me, stickin' that knife in my belly like he done. How come it is that you know him? I been comin' here off and on for most of two years now, 'n I don't think I ever seen him before."

"Well, if you had seen him before it would've been what they call a coincidence, I mean, you just happenin' to be here at the same time he was. He owns a ranch up near Chugwater you see, 'n when he's come to

Cheyenne on business, he drops in here from time to time. Most often when he's here, though, you'll see him with an older fella by the name Gleason."

"What's he doin' in town now?" Pete asked.

"Oh, hell, I don't have no idea why he's here, but generally when he's here it's 'cause he's shippin' cattle somewhere."

"Do you know them two women that was with 'im?"

"Women? I didn't see no women with him."

"No, Mel, he's right, there were some women with him," a bar girl said.

"What are you talkin' about, Sadie? Mac-Callister had two men with him when he came in here tonight. I know, on account of he bought three beers 'n took 'em over to the table where they were sitting."

"They were dressed like men, and from a distance they may have looked like men, but when you got close to 'em, they were women," Sadie said. She laughed. "I ought to know, I near 'bout made a fool of myself tonight, tryin' to pick one of 'em up."

"This man, what did you say his name was? MacCallister? He told me that one of the women was his wife, 'n the other was her sister," Pete said.

298

"Yes, he told me the same thing," Sadie said. "His sister-in-law was very young, so young that you might say she was more of a girl than a woman."

"His wife, you say? Well, well, so MacCallister got hisself married, did he? Well it must have just happened, and I'll tell you this, whoever the woman is who caught 'im, she did all right for herself. From all that I have heard about that ranch of his, it's the biggest one around Chugwater, 'n maybe one of the biggest in all of Wyoming," Mel said.

"Wait a minute. Are you tellin' me this MacCallister feller is rich?" Pollard asked.

"Oh, he's rich all right. Why, I wouldn't be surprised if he wasn't one of the richest men in the whole territory," Mel said.

"I'll be damn. Who woulda thought that?" Pollard replied.

"They didn't stay very long," Sadie said.

"He don't never stay too long," Mel replied. "Most of the time when he comes in, he'll have no more'n one or two drinks, then he goes back to the hotel. He's a quiet sort. To tell the truth, Pollard, that's why I was a little surprised to see that you had got on his bad side. He ain't riled all that easy, and somehow you got 'im riled up."

"It was just a misunderstandin' is all," Pollard said. "I didn't know the woman was his wife 'n I mighta said something that I shouldn'ta said. The reason I come in here lookin' for 'im is 'cause I was plannin' on tellin' 'im I'm sorry 'bout anythin' I mighta said that was out of line. I mean, bein' that the woman was his wife 'n all."

"I'm sure Mr. MacCallister would appreciate that," Mel said. "It's like I told you, Mr. MacCallister is a decent sort of man, only he ain't the kind you'd ever want to get on his wrong side."

"You said he generally just had a couple o' drinks, then went to the hotel," Pollard said. "Would that be the Del Rey or the Milner?"

"I'm sure it's the Del Rey. It's a lot nicer than the Milner, 'n I can't see a rich man like Mr. MacCallister stayin' at the Milner."

Another customer stepped up to the bar then, and Mel moved down to take care of him. Sadie went back to working the floor, and that left Pollard alone to stare into his glass of whiskey.

Initially, Pollard's plan had been to find the man who had humiliated him and kill him. After all, he had proof that the man had attacked him with a knife, and he had a reasonable expectation that MacCallister represented a threat. And if that was the case, he had every right to defend himself.

But the bartender said that MacCallister was a rich man, and that gave Pollard an idea. The young girl was his sister-in-law, and if they were staying at the hotel, what with MacCallister just getting married and all, he sure wouldn't want that young girl in the same room with him and his new wife. That means the girl would be in a room all by herself, and if he was able to grab her, and hold on to her, he was pretty sure that MacCallister would pay a pretty penny to get her back. After all, he wouldn't want anything to happen to his new wife's sister now would he?

He'd have to wait until late tonight in order to carry out his plan, because he would need to be certain that everyone was asleep.

Looking around the room, Pollard saw a chair open up at a table where a poker game was in progress, so taking his beer with him, he walked over to join them. He needed to kill some time, and playing poker seemed the best way to do it.

"I didn't expect to see you back here tonight, Pollard," one of the cardplayers said.

"Why not?"

"I mean, after what MacCallister done to

you 'n all."

"Yeah, well, Mel just told me that one o' them women was his wife, 'n I might of got a little out o' line. I just come back here to apologize is all."

"I'm sure he would have appreciated that," the cardplayer said.

"Look here, Mel told me that feller was rich. Is that true?"

"He's as rich as Croesus," one of the other players said.

"Yeah? Who is this Croesus feller?" Pollard asked.

"Someone who is as rich as MacCallister," the player replied, and the others laughed.

"Why would we want to go somewhere else to eat when there is a perfectly nice dining room right here in the hotel?" Meagan asked.

"Oh, but you must eat at Hogjaw's, at least once while we are here," Duff said.

"Hogjaw's? The place is called Hogjaw's?"

"Aye, 'twas Elmer who found it."

Meagan chuckled. "Now why am I not surprised that Elmer would find a place called Hogjaw's?"

"Dinnae be puttin' the place down until ye've had supper," Duff said. "Ye may find it to your liking."

"Hello, Mr. MacCallister," someone said, greeting Duff, Meagan, and Ina Claire when the three of them stepped into the restaurant. He was a rather large man wearing blue denim trousers, a white shirt, and red gallus.

"Hello, Hogjaw."

"What brings you to town? Cattle business?"

"Nae, 'tis but a visit, but I dinnae want to go back without having a meal in your foine establishment."

"It's welcome you and your friends are," Hogjaw said. "Find a table somewhere, and we'll start the pass-arounds."

"Pass-arounds?" Meagan asked as they were seated.

"Aye, 'tis a thing Hogjaw does. As soon as you are seated, someone will bring you such things as fried potatoes, fried squash, hot bread, and the like."

"Hogjaw? That's his name?" Ina Claire asked. She laughed. "What a funny name."

"His real name, as I understand it, is Norman. And who would want a name that reminds one of the Normans, one of history's most beastly lot?"

"Duff, how are we going to find these people?" Meagan asked.

"By perseverance," Duff replied without

303

further explanation.

"Perseverance?"

"Aye."

"If you will excuse me for saying so, that doesn't sound like a plan that is all that likely to succeed."

"Let me ask you this, Meagan. Do you think men such as the scoundrels we seek will, to quote Shakespeare, 'go gently into the good night'? I think not. I think they will continue with their nefarious deeds and that will leave a trail for us to follow. Remember the conversation in the saloon tonight brought up the suggestion that the men we seek may have held up a bank in Bordeaux. And 'tis most likely the same ones held up the stagecoach. But the article in the newspaper says they got no money from the stagecoach, so they'll be trying another scheme soon. All we have to do is follow the trail they will be leaving for us."

Meagan smiled. "Sometimes, Duff, I forget how smart you really are."

The night clerk at the Del Rey Hotel was sitting behind the check-in desk. The chair was tipped back against the wall, and the clerk had his ankles hooked around the front two legs of the chair. His head was buried in a newspaper, so he didn't see Pollard come in.

"Hey!" Pollard bellowed out.

The shout startled the night clerk and he came forward with a jerk, the front two legs of the chair popping loudly on the floor.

"What?" he called out, startled by the intrusion. "What is it?"

"What room is MacCallister in?"

"Good heavens, man, it's" — the clerk looked around at the clock that stood against the wall — "after eleven o'clock."

"I don't care what time it is, I want to know what room MacCallister is in."

"Why do you want to know?"

"He's my brother-in-law."

"It's my job to protect our guests from any unwanted intrusions, but seeing as he is your brother-in-law, I suppose it will be all right. But it's much too late to be disturbing Mr. MacCallister now."

"Oh, I'm not going to disturb him now. But I plan to have breakfast with him 'n my two sisters tomorrow, 'n he asked me to come up to his room first thing in the mornin'."

"Why didn't he give you his room number?"

"On account of when he told me that, he hadn't yet checked into the hotel, so he didn't know the room number."

"All right, I suppose, under those circumstances, that I can give you the information," the clerk replied. He glanced down at the registration book. "Well, let's see here, it looks like he has two rooms. Yes, one for him and his wife, and one for his wife's sister."

"Yeah, well both them women is my sisters."

"Mr. and Mrs. MacCallister are in room two oh five, and the young lady is in two oh seven."

"Thank you. I'll see you in the mornin'."

"Not unless you are here before six o'clock. I get off then," the night clerk replied.

"Then I reckon I won't see you again. It's more'n likely, I won't be comin' up to his room anytime a'fore seven o'clock."

"I should think not," the clerk replied. He picked up the newspaper and resumed reading as Pollard walked away from the front desk.

Pollard glanced up the stairs as he left the hotel.

It was nearly two in the morning and Pollard, driving a buckboard, turned up the alley between Pioneer and Thomas Avenue. He had chosen a buckboard so he could

306

haul the girl away, once he had her. The alley was lined with outhouses on both sides, so the smell was strong, but it wasn't anything Pollard wasn't used to. He passed by Dunnigan's Meat Market, Chip's Shoe Alley, and Buckner-Ragsdale's Mercantile, then stopped behind the Del Rey Hotel. This way he could enter through the back door, avoiding the lobby. This would also give him a way of bringing the girl out without being seen.

A few minutes earlier he had broken into Dr. Urban's office where he stole a bottle of chloroform. It was his intention to use the chloroform to knock the girl out so she would be easy to handle.

Tying his horse off to the railing on the stoop, he stepped up to the back door.

Damn! It was locked.

Pollard pulled his knife and worked with the lock for a moment, then, with a smile of accomplishment, managed to get the door open.

Opening the door quietly, he stepped into the hotel, finding himself in the hotel kitchen. That was good, the kitchen was sure to be deserted at this hour, which meant he would be able to do his business without fear of being discovered.

CHAPTER TWENTY-FIVE

Ina Claire had spoken bravely about having no fear of staying alone, but the truth was this was the first time she had ever been in a hotel, and the whole experience was somewhat disquieting to her. Shortly after going to bed she had been assailed by noises: loud voices from the street, an occasional woman's screech from the saloon, and even more disturbing, conversation, footsteps, and the sounds of doors being opened and closed in the hotel, right here on this very floor.

The noises and the unfamiliar situation made her a little nervous, so she dealt with the nervousness by keeping the bedside lantern burning, not too brightly, but with enough light to push away even the corner shadows of the room. She also put the sawed-off shotgun on the bedside table, within easy reach. Comforted by that, she was finally able to go to sleep.

She had no idea how long she had been asleep when she was awakened by the sound of someone at the door to her room. Was it Meagan? No, it wouldn't be Meagan, she didn't have a key to the room and if she had wanted in, she would have knocked or called out to her.

Maybe it was someone who had the wrong room, and as soon as whoever it was figured out that the key wouldn't work, they would leave.

But the key must've worked because suddenly the door swung open and a man came in. In the subdued light, she saw that it was the same man who had accosted them in the saloon. She sat up, and the man pulled a knife and held it in front of him.

"You make one sound, girly, and I'll slit your throat," he said menacingly. His face gleamed in the light of the lantern and he looked like a demon from hell. His other hand held a handkerchief, and, even from here, she could smell a strong, medicinal odor, though she had no idea what it might be. The big man held the handkerchief out toward her.

"What? What is that?" she asked.

"You're goin' to be comin' with me, little lady. But don't you be worryin' none about it. This here will make you go to sleep 'n you won't know nothin' about it," the man said.

He pressed the handkerchief over her face and Ina Claire's head began to spin with the cloying odor. Dizzily, she reached out to grab the shotgun, brought it up, shoved the barrel into his stomach, then, just before she passed out, she pulled the trigger.

"What was that?" Duff shouted, sitting up in bed at the sound of the shot.

"It came from Ina Claire's room!" Meagan said, her voice filled with dread.

Duff grabbed his pistol and, still wearing his long johns underwear, raced out into the hall. He saw that Ina Claire's door was open, and stepping inside, he saw a man lying on top of Ina Claire.

"Get off her, ye whore's son!" Duff shouted, grabbing the man by his shoulder and jerking him away. He fell onto the floor, on his back, and Duff saw then that his belly had been opened up. He saw, too, what had caused the wound, for Ina Claire still held the shotgun in her hands.

"Oh, Duff, is she . . . is she dead?" Meagan asked, clutching her dressing gown about her.

"I don't know," Duff replied. Ina Claire's eyes were closed, and she, and the bed, were

310

covered with blood.

"What is it? What happened in here?" another patron who had come to the door asked.

"What's going on?" a second patron inquired.

Duff put his fingers to Ina Claire's neck and was rewarded with a strong pulse.

"She's still alive," Duff said. He began checking her for wounds and, seeing nothing, realized that all of the blood had come from the man who was lying dead on the floor.

Ina Claire's eyes fluttered open.

"Oh!" she said. "What is it? Why is everyone in my room?"

"Ina Claire, don't you remember anything?" Meagan asked.

"Yes, he . . . he had a knife, and he put something over my face that made me . . . oh! Did I shoot him?"

"You sure as hell did, little lady," one of the uninvited men said. "The son of a bitch is lyin' on the floor now, deader'n a drowned rat."

Duff looked back down at the man and saw a knife in one hand and a handkerchief in the other. Picking up the handkerchief, he gave it a whiff, then jerked it away.

"Chloroform," he said.

"What?" Ina Claire asked.

"Chloroform. It's what doctors use when they want to put someone out."

"Duff, look who that is. That's the same man who accosted us in the saloon," Meagan said.

"You mean he isn't your brother?" The question came from the only fully dressed person in the room, and Duff recognized him as the clerk who had checked them in.

"And would ye be for tellin' me why ye think this miserable wretch would be m' brother?"

"Not your brother," the clerk replied. "The brother of the two ladies. At least that's what he told me when he asked me for your room number."

"And you gave it to him?" Meagan asked sharply.

"Please, miss, I thought he was your brother, and he said he wouldn't be calling on you until seven in the morning."

"Tell me, Wilbur," one of others said. "Didn't you think it a little suspicious, him inquiring about room numbers in the middle of the night like this?"

"It was last night that he asked," Wilbur replied. "And like I said, he told me that he wouldn't be calling until seven o'clock in the morning. Who would think that he

312

would do such a thing as this?"

"Oh, I'm all covered in blood!" Ina Claire said, as if just noticing it.

"Innkeeper, have you an accommodation with two adjoining rooms?" Duff asked.

"Yes."

"Then we shall require such a lodgment. And please bring a bathtub and enough hot water up to our rooms so the young lady can take a bath."

"I'm afraid that none of our porters are on hand tonight," Wilbur replied.

"Then you do it yourself," Duff ordered.

"But I . . ." Wilbur started. He stopped in mid-sentence when he saw the expression on Duff's face.

"Yes, sir, I'll get it done," he said.

An hour later, Duff sat in one of the rooms of the two-room suite they had been given. For some time, Meagan had been in the other room with Ina Claire. He heard a light knock on the door that separated the two rooms.

"Aye, come in," he called.

Meagan let herself in.

"She's in bed now," Meagan said.

"How is she doing?"

"I think she is all right. The incident frightened her of course, and, to wake up covered in blood had to be most disconcerting."

"I expect it was. What I can't understand is what he was doing in her room. One would think 'twas me he would be angry with. If he was going to be slipping into a room to kill someone, why didn't he come into my room?"

"He didn't intend to kill her."

"How do ye ken that?"

"Ina Claire said he told her that he intended for her to go with him."

"Och! He meant to steal her away?"

"Yes. I have no idea why, but the fact that he was using chloroform would support that, I think."

"Aye, I think ye be right. And for whatever the purpose, 'tis for sure it was evil."

"I think it might be best if I spend the rest of the night, at least what little is left of it, with her," Meagan said.

"Aye, 'tis probably best."

"Oh, and she wanted me to tell you something."

"What is that?"

"She wanted me to tell you that when the time came, she didn't hesitate."

"Aye, and 'tis a good thing she did not. Tell the lass that 'tis proud of her that I be."

Meagan smiled. "I already told her that."

■ ■ ■ ■

"Here are your letters of commission and your badges," Governor Hoyt said when they returned to his office the next morning.

"Thank you, Governor," Duff replied.

"I heard about the . . . trouble in the hotel last night," the governor said to Ina Claire. "I am so glad that you weren't hurt. I'm sure it was quite traumatic for you."

"Yes, sir, it was," Ina Claire said. "But it was a whole lot less disturbing than seeing both of my parents killed."

"Indeed, I'm sure it was. And I admire you for having the gumption to protect yourself. Sheriff Sharpies said the evidence against Peter Pollard was sufficiently incriminating that there would be no need for further inquiry."

"I'm glad he sees it that way," Duff said. "Nevertheless, I think we will call on the sheriff this morning to see if we can get any ken on the men we are after. I assume he would be willing to share with us."

"Get any ken?" the governor replied, the expression on his face indicating his confusion.

Meagan laughed. "You'll have to excuse

my Scottish friend, Uncle John. He's been here for some time now, but he hasn't entirely learned the English language. By ken, he means knowledge."

Governor Hoyt laughed as well. "Oh, I see. Well, I'm sure you'll have no problem with the good sheriff sharing any information with you. In the first place, the positions that you hold supersede his authority, or for that matter, the authority of any other law officer in the entire Wyoming Territory, with the exception of United States Marshals. But even so, Sheriff Sharpies is so anxious to bring Callahan and Manning, as well as anyone who might be with them, to justice, he will gladly do all that he can to help."

"Yes, sir," Sheriff Sharpies said when Duff showed him their documents of commission. "The governor has already told me about you three." He smiled. "I was concerned, at first, when I learned that he was giving such a commission to a couple of women, but after what happened in the hotel last night, I see that you can take care of yourself. By the way, miss, I was doing some research this morning, and it turns out that Peter Pollard was wanted for murder down in Colorado. And there's a reward of a thousand dollars out for him. I'm not sure, being as you are a law officer now, that you can collect it."

"I'm sure she can," Meagan said. "In the first place, she wasn't yet a law officer when the incident happened. And in the second place, she, in fact all three of us, are non-compensated law officers, and that exempts us from any prohibition of collecting rewards for wanted fugitives."

"I'll be damned," the sheriff said with a broad smile. "You may be right."

"Sheriff, I suppose the governor told you why he was willing to swear us in as territorial marshals, didn't he?" Duff asked.

"Yes. And, miss, you have my sympathies with regard to your parents. That was a terrible thing for you to have to go through. And I'll do all I can to help you find the evil men who did this."

"And 'tis thankful we are for your assistance," Duff said. "Ye can start by telling us anything you know about crimes that have been committed since they escaped. We already know about the bank robbery in Bordeaux and the stagecoach holdup."

"The bank was held up by four men, the stagecoach by seven," the sheriff said.

"Aye," Duff said. "Clay Callahan, Zeke Manning, Dooley Cooper, and Pogue Morris. Cooper and Morris are the ones who broke Callahan and Manning out of jail. I've no knowledge of the three additional men."

"This may help," Sheriff Sharpies said. "Here's a telegram we got from the city marshal in Uva. I don't know for sure, but based upon recent information, I believe these may be the three men who joined up with Callahan and the others."

Duff took the telegram from the sheriff, then held it in a way that allowed Meagan and Ina Claire to read it.

EMIL BATES LUCAS DONNER AND GABE PARDEEN ESCAPED FROM THE UVA JAIL ON WEDNESDAY LAST STOP THE OUTLAWS LEFT BEHIND THE BODY OF DEPUTY GOSNELL WHOSE THROAT HAD BEEN CUT STOP

"Like Papa!" Ina Claire said with a little gasp.

"I beg your pardon, miss?"

"The men we are looking for like to use a knife," Ina Claire said. "Papa's throat was cut, just as this deputy's was."

"Ye said ye had recent information to make ye suspect these three men are with Callahan?" Duff asked.

"Yes. A respectable businessman, Art Whitworth, owned a quite successful store on the Little Laramie River between Farrel and Howell. He was robbed and killed yesterday morning by seven men. Enough of the men were identified to make it seem certain that all seven men are now known. Those names are Callahan, Manning, Cooper, Morris, Pardeen, Bates, and Donner."

"Thank you for the information," Duff said.

"Yes, sir, well, given this information, Mr. MacCallister, you might want to give it some thought before you charge into them, being as there would be seven of them and only one of you."

"There are three of us, Sheriff. Or didn't you notice?" Meagan said.

Sheriff Sharpies frowned. "Surely, Miss Parker, you aren't suggesting that you and the young lady actually intend to be a part of any actual confrontation with Callahan and his gang?"

"Why not?" Meagan replied. "It should be obvious to you that, after the incident in the hotel last night, Ina Claire is perfectly capable of holding her own. And I assure you, I am no less capable."

The sheriff studied the two women for a long moment, then he smiled and nodded.

"No, ma'am, I don't think I can argue with you there," he said.

"Sheriff Sharpies, we'll be taking our leave now, 'n 'tis our thanks we give ye for providing us such information as ye have."

"I wish I could be more helpful," the sheriff said.

"Ye did all ye could, 'n we could ask for no more."

When Duff, Meagan, and Ina Claire left the sheriff's office, they started toward their horses, but Duff stopped them.

"What is it?" Meagan asked.

Duff smiled. "I have an idea that may cause Callahan 'n the others to have a wee bit o' worry," he said. "If we are lucky, it may cause them to make a mistake that we can pounce on. 'N even if it doesn't push them into a mistake, well 'tis thinkin' I am that it will at least cause them some discomfort. 'N right now, I'd be for causin' the brigands all the discomfort we be able to give them."

"All right, I'd be for that," Meagan said. "Where do we start?"

"At the newspaper office."

Chapter Twenty-Six

"Are you sure that you want to put this story in the newspaper?" Charles Denham, editor of the *Cheyenne Defender,* asked.

"Aye, I'm sure," Duff said.

"But won't this warn them that you are coming for them? It seems to me like you would want to maintain the element of surprise."

"Would ye be for running the story as I've written here, or would ye prefer that I go to the *Wyoming Territory Tribune?*"

"No, no, there'll be no need for that. I'll be glad to run the story, just as you have written it. And I thank you for giving the *Defender* the opportunity to do it."

"When will the story run?"

"I'll run it tomorrow, and I'll put it on the front page, above the fold," Denham promised.

"Thank you," Duff said.

"No, Mister MacCallister. Thank you, sir.

I'm sure this story will be picked up in newspapers throughout Wyoming Territory, Colorado, 'n the Dakota Territory."

Rock Creek, Wyoming Territory

Callahan, Manning, Cooper, Morris, Pardeen, Bates, and Donner were in the town of Rock Creek, a small railroad town some seventy miles west of Cheyenne. They were in the Railroad Saloon, and at the moment, the seven of them made up fully half of the customers.

The seven men had managed to take four hundred and sixty dollars in cash from the holdup of Whitworth's store. With that money, and the money they had taken from the bank in Bordeaux, Callahan and the three who had been with him from the beginning had managed to accumulate a few dollars. Not a lot of money but enough to keep them from being destitute. The sixty-five dollars apiece that Pardeen, Bates, and Donner got as their share of the robbery constituted their entire fortune, and that money was greatly reduced now in gambling and whoring.

"We've got to come up with somethin' else to make some money," Pardeen complained. "I ain't got but twenty-two dollars left."

"That's your own fault," Callahan said.

Callahan had taken a newspaper from the bar when they came in and saw a story that caught his interest. The newspaper was a special edition to the *Rock Creek Gazette* from the *Cheyenne Defender.*

LEADING CITIZEN VOWS
TO SEE JUSTICE DONE

Captain Duff MacCallister, one of the leading citizens of Laramie County, if not, indeed, one of the leading citizens of the entire Wyoming Territory, has stated his intention to search for and bring to justice seven men. The object of his quest are the outlaws: Clay Callahan, Zeke Manning, Dooley Cooper, Pogue Morris, Emil Bates, Lucas Donner, and Gabe Pardeen.

Our readers in Cheyenne will quickly recognize the names Clay Callahan and Zeke Manning, as those two ne'er-do-wells were but recently tried, convicted, and sentenced to hang for the vile murders they had committed but a month earlier. The scheduled hanging did not take place, however, for the villains were rescued by two of their former confederates, Dooley Cooper and Pogue Morris.

Not content with merely escaping prison, the four despicable wastrels murdered

Deputy Dinkins, as well as the noted hangman, Mordecai Luscombe. Shortly thereafter Callahan, Manning, Cooper, and Morris stopped, in the middle of the night, at the Twin Pine Ranch, belonging to Captain Edward Culpepper and his wife, Julie Ann. But a short time previous to this uninvited visit, the Culpeppers had most generously opened their home to Cooper and Morris, inviting them to sit at their table and take sup with them. And how were they repaid? They were repaid in the most brutal way possible, for both Captain and Mrs. Culpepper were killed, and their house was burned.

Emil Bates, Lucas Donner, and Gabe Pardeen were, like Callahan and Manning, about to be hung when they, too, were broken out of jail, now known to have been orchestrated by Callahan and his gang.

Duff MacCallister, whose ranch Sky Meadow is adjacent to the Culpepper ranch of Twin Pine, was a neighbor and good friend to the murdered rancher and his wife. He has vowed to seek out the outlaws and bring them to justice.

"I shall ride alone," MacCallister told this newspaper. "But I am girded with the armor of righteousness and armed with the sword of virtue. I will find these men, and justice will prevail."

"Son of a bitch! How do they know so much about us?" Manning asked.

"It's the girl," Callahan said. "She recognized Cooper and Morris from when they were there, and you let her get away."

"We didn't let her get away, she got away on her own," Cooper said.

"Maybe it is the girl that knows you four," Donner said. "But how the hell did they know we're ridin' together now? Hell, we wasn't even with you when you kilt Culpepper."

"I'll be honest with you, I don't know how the hell they figured that out," Callahan said.

"What I want to know is, who is this Duff MacCallister person?" Pardeen asked. "I mean that's big talk for some clod-hopping rancher."

"He's a lot more than some clod-hopping rancher," Manning said. "Hell, if it warn't for that son of a bitch, we woulda got away with the bank robbery in Archer, 'n Don 'n Dan LaFarge would still be alive. He's the one that stopped us."

"Wait a minute. Are you sayin' that one man stopped four of you?" Pardeen asked.

"Yeah."

"That ain't the first time this MacCallister feller has done somethin' like that," Cooper said.

"What are you talkin' about? Cooper, do you know this MacCallister person?" Callahan asked.

"I don't know him personal like," Cooper replied. "But I sure as hell know who he is. He's the one that took down Johnny Taylor, sometime back. Me 'n Johnny 'n his brother Emile rode together some. It was just a good thing that I wasn't with them when Duff MacCallister found 'em, 'cause he done 'em in."

"Ha!" Pardeen said. "To hear you two talk, this MacCallister person is Wild Bill Hickok, Wes Hardin, 'n Tom Horn, all rolled into one."

"He just might be," Cooper said.

"Hey, Callahan, how much would it be worth to you, if someone was to kill Mac-Callister?" Pardeen asked.

"How much would it be worth to me? Why are you asking that?"

"You four are the ones he's really a-lookin' for. It warn't us that kilt Culpepper. I'll bet the three of us could ride up to his ranch 'n he wouldn't think nothin' about it, 'cause he wouldn't recognize us."

"You mean three strangers would just show up, 'n he wouldn't be none curious at all?" Callahan replied.

"Not iffen we was to tell 'im that we seen this story in the paper, 'n we could tell 'im where he could find you," Bates said, now getting into the idea.

"Yeah," Pardeen said quickly. "The way we would play it is, we'd tell 'im we was in it for the reward. Then, when we got him trustin' us, we'll kill 'im. Would that be worth a hunnert dollars apiece for each of us?"

"You want a hundred dollars?"

"Apiece," Pardeen said. "You four still got some money from the bank that you robbed, but we didn't get nothin' at all from the stagecoach, 'n we didn't get practically nothin' from that store, neither, except for two hunnert dollars, which our share come to only twenty-six."

"Callahan, I'm willin' to put in my share," Cooper said. "If there's anything we don't need now, it's someone like MacCallister huntin' us 'cause of some personal revenge. I'm tellin' you, he ain't someone we want to be messin' around with. And it's enough that we have to look out for the law."

"Yeah," Manning said. "You 'member back in Archer how he was just standin' there in front of us, like he knowed he couldn't get shot or nothin'.'"

"Yeah, I remember," Callahan said, his voice nearly a growl. "What about you, Morris? You willin' to come up with your share to pay these men to kill MacCallister for us?"

"We have to come up with a hunnert dollars apiece?" Morris asked.

"Not a hundred dollars from each of us. We have to come with a hundred dollars for each of them. That would be seventy-five dollars from each of us," Callahan said.

"Come on, Morris," Cooper said. "It'll be worth it to get this son of a bitch off our backs. I'm tellin' you, I know who this son of a bitch is, 'n I don't want to run up ag'in 'im."

"There's seven of us 'n one of him," Morris said.

"Suppose he only gets two of us before we get him. Are you willin' to be one of those two?"

"All right," Morris finally agreed. "I'll go along with it."

"There you go, Pardeen," Callahan said. "The four of us will come up with a hundred dollars apiece for the three of you. But we ain't goin' to pay you nothin' 'til after you've done kilt 'im."

"All right, you got yourselves a deal," Pardeen said.

Sky Meadow Ranch

An arch stretched over the road with the words SKY MEADOW worked into it with wrought iron. A painted sign was on the fence post.

SKY MEADOW
DUFF MACCALLISTER, *Proprietor*
Fine Angus Cattle

"It's just real nice of 'im to put the sign up here so's that we know we got the right place," Pardeen said. "Let's ride on up to the house just real casual like, 'n when this MacCallister feller comes out we'll kill 'im."

"It might not be all that easy," Bates said. "Remember what Cooper told us about him killin' Johnny Taylor 'n them that was with 'im. And Cooper said they was some pretty good boys. We're goin' to have to get 'im to trust us first, then when he ain't suspectin' nothin', we'll kill 'im."

"Would you know 'im if you seen 'im?" Donner asked.

"No, but Callahan said that he was a big Scotsman, so it prob'ly won't be all that hard to pick 'im out," Bates said. "I mean if

329

a big man starts speakin' in Scottish to us, who else could it be?"

"What does Scottish sound like?" Donner asked.

"I don't know, but I reckon we'll know it if we hear it spoke."

"Well, we ain't goin' to get the job done just by jawin' about it," Pardeen said. "Let's go."

The three riders started up the long road that led from the arched sign to the cluster of well-maintained buildings.

"Have you found what the problem is up there?" Elmer called. Elmer was standing on the ground beneath the windmill and Wang had climbed to the top. The windmill had stopped working . . . the blades still, even in a brisk wind.

Wang examined the mechanism, then smiled as he saw that the gears had been jammed up by a piece of tree limb somewhat larger than a man's thumb. Reaching down into the gearbox he withdrew the offending branch, then, giving the blades a turn, they caught the wind and began spinning.

"You done it!" Elmer said. "What was the problem?"

"This," Wang called back down to him.

He dropped the three-inch-long chunk of wood.

"I'll be damn," Elmer said, picking it up for a closer examination. "We had us a pretty good wind last night. It musta blowed this right into the gears."

"Three men come," Wang called down.

"Duff?"

"I do not know these men," Wang said.

"Wonder what they want," Elmer said. "Damn, I wish I'd wore my gun. Too late now to get it."

Wang climbed down from the windmill and was standing beside Elmer as the three men approached.

"I don't know none of 'em, neither," Elmer said. "I wonder what it is that they are a-wantin'?"

"That's an old man and a Chinaman," Donner said as the three of them rode toward the two men they saw standing before them. "You don't reckon one of them is MacCallister, do you?"

"I don't know," Bates said. "I ain't never heard how old MacCallister is."

"There ain't neither one of 'em wearin' a gun," Pardeen said. "Wait 'til we get real close, then when I say so, draw your guns 'n keep 'em covered. I'll do the talkin'."

Elmer and Wang stood their ground watching as the three men approached them.

"I don't have me a good feelin' 'bout this," Elmer said. He waited until the men were within talking distance.

"What can I do for you fellers?" Elmer asked.

"Are you MacCallister?" Pardeen inquired.

"Why do you want to know?" Elmer replied.

"Now!" Pardeen said, drawing his gun. The other two men drew their guns as well.

"Now, I'm goin' to ask you again, mister. Are you MacCallister?"

"No, I ain't MacCallister," Elmer replied. "What do you want 'im for?"

"We want to kill 'im," Pardeen replied with a little laugh.

"I think you'll find he ain't goin' to be very easy to kill," Elmer said.

"You, Chinaman, go get 'im. 'N tell 'im if he don't come out here unarmed, I'm goin' to shoot this old man."

"Who the hell are you callin' an old man?" Elmer retorted.

"I'm callin' you an old man, you old goat," Pardeen said. "You, Chinaman, don't you speak English?"

"I speak English," Wang replied.

"Then what for are you still standin' there? I told you to go get MacCallister."

"He is not here," Wang replied.

"What do you mean, he ain't here? This is his ranch, ain't it?"

"Yeah, this is his ranch, all right, but Wang told you the truth. MacCallister's not here."

"Where is he?"

"I don't have no notion at all where he might be now. He's off somewhere takin' care of business," Elmer said.

"All right, Chinaman, here's what I want you to do. I want you to go into the house 'n bring anyone that's in there outside," Pardeen said.

"There is no one inside," Wang replied.

"You tellin' me that on a big ranch like this, 'n there ain't no one inside? How 'bout his wife and kids."

"He ain't married," Elmer said. "Wang's tellin' the truth, there ain't nobody inside."

"Hey, Pardeen, I'll bet there's some good food inside," Donner said. "Why don't we go in 'n get us somethin' to eat?"

"I don't believe we've given you any invite to go inside," Elmer said.

"This here is all the invite we need," Bates said, holding up the pistol.

"Donner's right, we may as well go in 'n

get us somethin' to eat," Pardeen said. "Tie them two fellers up to the windmill."

"How are we goin' to tie 'em up? We ain't got no rope," Donner said.

"Use this," Pardeen said, holding up two strips of rawhide that he took from one of his saddlebags. "Tie 'em up with their thumbs." He smiled. "I seen some injuns do that once."

Under gunpoint, Elmer and Wang were forced to stretch their arms behind them, one arm on either side of the upright shaft of the windmill. Then the rawhide strips were used to tie their thumbs together. The result was an effective restraint of the two.

"Now, you fellers don't go nowhere whilst we're inside havin' our meal," Pardeen said with a triumphant grin.

Elmer watched as the three men went into the house, the house that he, personally, had helped Duff build. Because they had been secured to the upright shaft of the windmill, and it was round, there was no edge that they could use to cut through the rawhide.

"Damn, we're as caught up here as a beaver in a trap," Elmer said. "You know they'll prob'ly shoot us when they come back outside, don't you?"

"We will not be tied up when they come

back," Wang said.

"Yeah? Well there ain't much you can do that'll ever surprise me, but if you can cut through these here thongs on a round pump shaft, then I purely will be surprised."

"Hold your hands still," Wang said.

"What do you mean hold 'em still? Hell they're tied up, how 'm I goin' to hold 'em any other . . ." Elmer stopped in mid-sentence. "I'll be damn. How the hell are you doin' that?"

Elmer's question was the result of feeling Wang's fingers working on the little pieces of leather by which his thumbs were secured. His astonishment was in how he was able to do anything seeing as Wang's thumbs were also tied.

Within less than a minute, Elmer was free. It took him a little longer to free Wang, even though he was facing him and with the full use of both hands.

"Now, let's take care of them sons of bitches," Elmer said.

The two men hurried into the bunkhouse where Elmer retrieved his pistol and Wang a knife. So armed, they returned to the windmill, then put their arms back around the pump shaft so that, by all appearances, they were still tied up.

A while later the three men left the house.

"Now, that there was some good bacon," Pardeen said.

"The cheese was good, too," Donner said.

"What do you say we kill these two sons of bitches just to leave a sign for MacCallister?" Bates suggested.

"Sounds good to me," Pardeen said. Pulling their guns the three men walked toward the windmill.

"Get ready, Wang," Elmer said quietly.

"The tiger crouches," Wang replied.

Elmer laughed. "I knew damn well you would come up with somethin' like that."

"I don't know what you're laughin' about, you old coot," Pardeen said. "Seein' as you and the Chinaman is both about to die."

"I don't think so," Elmer said, bringing his gun around.

"What the hell?" Bates shouted in surprise.

Elmer fired twice, and Pardeen and Donner went down. Bates went down as well, with a knife sticking out of his neck.

"How did you . . . ?" Pardeen gasped as he was drawing his last breaths.

"Maybe you can figure it out in hell," Elmer said as he stood over the three men. Pardeen drew two more gasps, then he died, the last to do so.

CHAPTER TWENTY-SEVEN

Chugwater

"Marshal Craig," a young man said, stepping into the marshal's office. "You might want to come out here."

The young man was breathing hard, having run a couple of blocks to deliver the information.

"My word, Tommy, what's got you all out of breath?"

"It's them two men that work for Mr. MacCallister," Tommy said. "Mr. Gleason and the Chinaman?"

"Yes, that would be Wang. What about them?"

Tommy drew another couple of deep breaths before he could blurt out the rest of the information.

"They're comin' into town now with a buckboard full o' dead men!"

As Elmer and Wang drove into town their

arrival was drawing a lot of attention, and not just from the young man who had run down to the marshal's office but from many others. The reason so many were taking notice was the three, obviously dead, men lying in the back of the buckboard.

Elmer stopped in front of the marshal's office, but it wasn't necessary to go inside. Tommy McCord's report had already brought the marshal out to meet them.

"What have you got there in the back of your buckboard, Elmer?" Marshal Craig asked.

"Dead folks," Elmer replied. Setting the brake, he and Wang climbed down to stand alongside the marshal as he examined the bodies.

"I can see that. Did you find 'em that way?"

"No, I made 'em that way, by damn," Elmer said. "That is, me 'n Wang here."

"I expect you got a good reason for havin' killed 'em, or else you wouldn't have brought 'em into town," Craig said.

"Damn right we had a good reason. These three galoots here come out to the ranch to kill Duff," Elmer replied.

"I didn't know Duff was back," Marshal Craig said.

"He ain't back. But these three wouldn't

338

take that for an answer. One thing led to another, 'n the next thing you know, they was about to kill us."

"So you killed them," Marshal Craig said. It was a declarative statement, not a question.

"It was self-defense, Russel," Elmer said, holding up his hand. "I swear it was."

"I have no doubt but that it was, Elmer. Do you have any idea who they are?"

"I ain't never seen none of 'em before, but I did hear two of the names spoke. One of the names was Pardeen, 'n the other was Donner. Never did hear the name of the third man."

"It was Bates," Marshal Craig said.

"What? Wait a minute, are you tellin' me you know these men?"

"Not by sight," Marshal Craig said. "But I got notice that three men escaped jail in Millersburg. Their names were Pardeen, Donner, and Bates. If two of these men were Donner and Pardeen, I'd lay money that the third one is Bates. There's a reward out for them, by the way, five hundred dollars apiece. I would say that you and Mr. Wang would be due that money."

"Well, I'll be damn," Elmer said, smiling broadly. "What do you think about that, Wang? We're goin' to have us some money to spend."

"I'm a little curious, though. I got word just this morning that these three men robbed a store along with Callahan, Manning, Cooper, and Morris. Aren't those the men that Duff is after?"

"Yeah," Elmer said. "Those are the men he's after." Elmer glanced back toward the three bodies. "And you say that these here men was ridin' with Callahan 'n the others?"

"That's what the report says."

"Then that, more'n likely, explains why these here galoots come a-gunnin' for Duff. They was wantin' to get 'im off their backs."

Elmer and Wang took advantage of having come to town to buy a few things they needed for the ranch. They also stepped into Fiddler's Green. Just as he kept a special Scotch for Duff, Biff Johnson kept a supply of *Baijiu,* a special Chinese drink, for Wang. He served both men.

"Hey, what the hell is a Chinaman doin' in here?" someone shouted. The complaining customer was not a resident of Chugwater and didn't know that Wang was not only accepted but liked by all.

"It looks to me like he's havin' a drink," one of the other customers said.

"Yeah? Well, he sure as hell ain't goin' to have a drink in here while I'm in here."

"What's your name?" the regular customer asked.

"The name is Foster."

"Foster is it? Well, sir, my name is Malcolm. Tell you what, Foster. Why don't you throw him out?"

Foster took another swallow of his beer, set it on the bar, then wiped his mouth with his sleeve. "You think I won't?"

Foster pulled his pistol, and when he did, at least half a dozen other customers drew their pistols as well, and they were all pointing toward Foster. Foster looked around in some surprise.

"Here, what is this?" Foster asked.

"If you want to throw Mr. Wang out, feel free to try," the man who had been having a conversation with him said. "But you ain't goin' to do it with no gun."

"You ain't all a-goin' to shoot me," Foster said.

"You're right, it won't take all of us. Two or three of us should be enough," his partner in conversation replied. "Now, put your gun back in its holster a'fore you go over there 'n throw the Chinaman out. That is, if you actually plan to do this. Go ahead, we'll watch."

By now the entire gathering of Fiddler's Green had stopped all other activity to watch the drama that appeared to be developing in front of them. Card games stopped in mid-deal. Everyone grew tense except for Elmer and Wang, who continued their conversation as if they were totally alone.

"Hey you, Chinaman!" Foster called.

Wang didn't respond.

"You, Chinaman, I'm talking to you."

Wang turned toward him. "I am called Wang. I am not called Chinaman."

"Is that a fact? Well, I'll tell you what, Chinaman. I'll call you anything I like."

"That's enough, Foster," Biff said. "I'm going to have to ask you to leave my place now."

"Wait a minute," Foster said. "Are you telling me that you are going to kick me out and let the Chinaman stay?"

"Mr. Wang is a good customer and a friend," Biff said.

"Ha! A friend is he? Well, all I can say is, you got a piss poor choice of friends."

Biff reached under the bar and came up with a sawed-off double-barrel twelve-gauge shotgun.

"Leave," he said.

Foster put his hands up. "I'm goin', I'm goin'," he said. "There ain't no need for you to be gettin' all hostile about it. I can't say as how I would want to be a-drinkin' in a place that would be willin' to let a Chinaman come in here 'n drink with white men anyway."

Foster started toward the batwing doors.

"Good riddance to you, Foster!" someone shouted, and the other patrons of the saloon followed the belligerent customer out with loud laughter.

Elmer chuckled. "You know what the funny thing is, Biff? I don't believe that Foster feller has any idea what a favor you done 'im by runnin' him out like that afore he actually tried somethin' with Wang."

Biff laughed as well. "I think you're right. He has no idea."

"I would have been gentle with him," Wang said with a broad smile.

"Yeah, about as gentle as a bucking horse," Elmer said. "Oh, hey! I near 'bout forgot. Me 'n Wang just come into a little money. Here, Biff, how 'bout you set up ever'one in here with a drink on the two of us? As sort of a thank-you for takin' up for us like they done."

"Ha!" one of the patrons said. "What the hell makes you think we was takin' up for you, old man? Far as we're concerned, Foster coulda throwed you out 'n we wouldn'ta done nothin'. It's Wang we was takin' up for," he teased.

The others laughed.

"If you take up for Wang, it's most the same as you takin' up for me, bein' as me 'n him is just real tight," Elmer said.

"All right, we'll go along with that," the patron said. "Most especial since you're buyin' the drinks." Every customer in Fiddler's Green stepped up to the bar to place their order.

Cheyenne

"What about the wagon?" Duff asked.

"It's being painted," Meagan answered.

"And Ina Claire?"

"She's back in the hotel, taking care of the medicine bottles."

"What about the costumes?"

"I've got them all picked out."

"For both of you?"

Meagan smiled. "What do you mean for both of us?"

"I mean for you and Ina Claire. Have you picked out the costumes you will be wearing?"

"Duff, I've picked them out for all three of us," Meagan replied.

"What?" Duff held out his hand in protest. "Now, wait just a minute, let's hold on here.

There is nae need for you to be getting a costume for me."

"Sure there is. If we are going to make this work, we will all have to be in costume. Trust me, I've lived here a lot longer than you have. Besides, I think you will look very handsome in what I have picked out for you," she added with a broad smile.

"I'm beginning to have second thoughts about this whole idea," Duff said.

Meagan laughed, then put her hand on his shoulder. "Nonsense, traveling through the countryside as a medicine show is a great idea. And if you are going to do that, you have to play the part, too, not just Ina Claire and me."

"All right, all right, you win," Duff said with a yielding grin. "I guess I can't expect you and Ina Claire to dress up if I refuse to. By the way, how is Ina Claire doing?"

"It was quite a shock for her to have to kill someone, so as I'm sure you can imagine she is still a little disturbed by it."

"But she isn't questioning whether or not it was something she had to do, though, is she?"

"No, she's not questioning that. She understands, fully, that she didn't have any choice."

Duff nodded. "Good. She's a strong

345

young lady, as strong as I've ever seen. I've no doubt that she'll come through this in fine fettle."

Outlaw encampment, just outside Laramie City,
Wyoming Territory

Just before they bedded down last night, Manning put a pot of beans, water, and bacon in a hole over a bed of hot coals. Covering the pot with dirt, he built a fire over the top and let it burn all night long. The result was a pot of beans for the next day.

"Damn, Manning, this is good," Cooper said as he spooned some of the beans to his mouth. "Where'd you learn to cook like this?"

"I was a belly cheater on a couple of trail drives," Manning said. "Then one day I come up on the bad side of a trail boss 'n wound up killin' 'im. On account of that, I been on the dodge ever since."

"Hey, Callahan, you think Pardeen 'n them boys will be back to collect their hunnert dollars?" Morris asked.

Callahan took a spoonful of beans before he answered.

"I think they're more'n likely dead," Callahan replied easily.

"Why do you say that?"

"If they wasn't dead, they woulda been back by now, askin' for their money."

"Son of a bitch! You mean you think this MacCallister feller kilt all three of 'em?" Morris asked.

"He damn well could have," Cooper said. "I told you, I've heard of this feller before."

"Yeah, 'n me 'n Callahan seen 'im in action when he kilt the LaFarge boys," Manning said.

"If they don't come back, what will that mean for our next job?" Morris asked.

Callahan took another spoonful of beans. "It don't mean nothin'," he said. "We'll pull the job without 'em. Cooper, you 'n Morris need to go on into town 'n get ever'thing set up for us."

"All right," Cooper replied. "But it's liable to take us a day or two."

"We'll be here," Callahan said, returning to the pot to fill his pan again.

"Hey, Callahan, have you ever robbed a train before?" Manning asked.

"No, I ain't never done it, but it can't be all that hard to do, 'cause they's sure been a heap o' folks that has done it."

"What bothers me is how we goin' to stop it," Morris said. "It ain't like the stagecoach that we stopped just by a-lyin' down in front

347

of it. You lie down in front of a train, he more'n likely couldn't get it stopped in time even if he was of a mind to."

"I'll figure out a way for us to stop it," Callahan promised. "Cooper, you just get the information we need."

"You don't need to worry none about that. I'll get the information, all right," Cooper replied.

CHAPTER TWENTY-EIGHT

Laramie City

"I don't know 'bout you, Pogue," Dooley Cooper said when he and Morris arrived in Laramie City. "But it's been a month o' Sundays since I've had me a woman, 'n now that we got us a little bit of money, I aim to have me one."

"Hell, all the girls in the bar make you buy 'em a whole bunch o' drinks before they'll let you take 'em upstairs," Morris said.

"Yeah, well, I ain't plannin' on goin' to no saloon. I aim to get me a regular whore-house woman."

"They cost more."

"Not if you count all them drinks you gotta buy the saloon whores first," Cooper said.

"Yeah," Morris said, agreeing with a smile. "Yeah, that's true, ain't it? Where at do you think we should go?"

"I been in this town before and I know exactly where to go. I ain't never had enough money to go before, but I got enough now."

Cooper led Morris to Wilma's House of Pleasure, where, getting a woman apiece, they took them to the rooms where the soiled doves did their business.

Morris was finished within less than three minutes.

"Oh, honey, that was nice," the woman said. She had told Morris her name was Louella. Louella sat up in bed, allowing the cover to fall.

"Where you goin'?" Morris asked.

"Well, we're all finished here, honey. I'm going to get dressed," Louella said.

"No you ain't. How much will it cost me to stay here 'til nightfall?"

"Oh, I could have four more visits in by that time," Louella said. "So it will cost you at least eight more dollars."

"You ain't goin' to get that much business in the afternoon," Morris insisted. "Maybe tonight, but I'll be finished with you by then. I'll give you five more dollars."

"All right, honey, if you've got it in you to do it that many more times, you can stay for five dollars."

"I don't want to do it no more at all,"

Morris said. "What I want to do is sleep here in your bed."

"Why would you want to do that?" Louella asked, surprised by the response. "You can get a room at the hotel for two dollars."

" 'Cause, even though I don't want to do nothin' more, I like the idea of havin' a nek-kid woman a-lyin' alongside me," Morris said with a broad grin.

"All right. If that's what you want."

Otto, Wyoming Territory

The town of Otto was named for Otto Franc, a local cattle baron who ranched in the nearby vicinity. Eight miles west of Cheyenne, it was the next stop for the westbound trains on the Union Pacific Railroad. Duff, with Meagan and Ina Claire sitting on the seat beside him, drove into town in a wagon that, by design, was painted to attract as much attention as possible.

The wagon was different from the normal freight or working wagons. Whereas the working wagons typically had a canvas-bowed top, this wagon had sides and a wood roof. It was smaller than the freight wagons and was painted bright red with large cursive letters, in gold, on either side.

When Duff drove the medicine wagon into town, with Meagan and Ina Claire sitting on the seat beside him, they were met by a couple of young boys.

"Mister, will you be a-givin' us a medicine show?" one of the young boys asked.

"Aye, that we will, lads, that we will," Duff said.

"Can kids come 'n watch, even iffen we don't buy nothin'?"

"Aye, 'tis no reason the wee bairns can't come."

The boy got a confused look on his face. "You sure do talk funny."

"That's 'cause he's a furriner," the other boy said. "That's right, ain't it, mister? You're a furriner, ain't ya?"

"Aye, lad, 'tis Scottish born and bred I be," Duff said.

The two boys followed the medicine wagon down to the far end of the street. Then, as Duff disconnected the team and led them to water, Meagan and Ina Claire handed a fistful of flyers to each of the boys.

"Would you two boys like to make a quarter apiece by going up and down the street, passing out these flyers?" she asked.

"Yes, ma'am! We'll be glad to," one of the boys said. "Come on, Neil!"

"We'd better get in costume," Meagan said, and she and Ina Claire stepped back into the wagon to change.

Laramie City
When Morris woke up much later, he saw that, though it wasn't totally dark outside, the room had grown much dimmer. He felt in the bed beside him, but the woman was gone.

"Hey! Where the hell are you?" he asked.

"I'm right here, honey, I haven't gone anywhere," Louella replied.

Looking around, he saw her sitting in a chair. She was knitting something.

"Hey, my mama used to do that," he said.

"It's a good way to pass the time."

"What time is it?"

"I think it's a little after five," Louella said. "It's time for me to go back out into the parlor. My evening fellas will be coming around soon," she added with a smile.

"Hell, I can tell you the exact time. I've got myself a new pocket watch," Morris said proudly. The money for the new watch, as the money he spent with the whore and intended to spend in the saloon tonight, came from his share of the bank robbery in

Bordeaux and the robbery of Whitworth's store. He hadn't brought all his money with him, Callahan had cautioned them against that, but he had brought enough to have a good time.

"It lacks ten minutes of six," Morris said, examining his watch.

"Oh, my goodness, I had no idea it was that late. I ought to charge you another two dollars."

"The hell you say. You coulda woke me anytime you wanted," Morris said as he pulled on his pants. "But I'll give you another . . ." he stopped in mid-sentence. "Where is it?"

"Where is what?"

"Where is my wallet?"

"I don't know where your wallet is."

"You stole it! What did you do with it?" Morris was growing angrier.

"I did not take your wallet," the woman insisted.

"I want my wallet, you damn whore!" Morris shouted. He slapped her.

"Please, I didn't take your wallet!"

Morris hit her again and she screamed and tried to cover up, whimpering in fear and pain as he continued to hit her.

Cooper, who had been with his own woman in the adjacent room, came in then.

"Morris come on, it's time to go." He saw the woman, sitting on the floor whimpering, her lips and nose bleeding, one eye swollen shut.

"Damn, did you do that?" Cooper asked.

"Yeah, I did it."

"What for?"

" 'Cause the bitch stole my wallet," Morris said.

Cooper laughed.

"What are you laughin' about?"

"She didn't steal your wallet. After you took out the money you was goin' to give her, you gave the wallet to me to keep, 'cause you don't have no button on your back pocket 'n you was afraid it would fall out."

"Ha!" Morris said. "Yeah, I did do that, didn't I? I forgot all about that." He looked at the prostitute. "Sorry 'bout hittin' you 'n all."

"You had no call to do that," she replied.

"Yeah, well, I told you I was sorry. What else do you want?" He took a dollar from the billfold Cooper had given him. "Here," he said. He took another dollar. "Hell, here's two dollars."

The woman managed a smile at the prospect of an extra two dollars.

The sun was low in the west when Cooper and Morris stepped outside. Wilma's House of Pleasure was just that, a two-story house in the middle of a residential area. Because of that, it was no more than a hundred yards from the house to the nearest saloon. Despite the relatively short distance, the two men rode their horses because, as Cooper liked to say, "If we was meant to walk, we'd woulda been given four legs when we was born."

They had come to Laramie City to meet with Dan Jeeter. Cooper, who had served some prison time with Jeeter, had convinced Callahan that Jeeter could help them. Jeeter worked for the Union Pacific Railroad.

"That's him, back there," Cooper said when the two stepped into the Bear Tracks Saloon. He pointed to a table where three men sat nursing drinks.

"Which one is him?" Morris asked.

"The one with the red shirt and black vest."

Cooper started toward the table with Morris trailing behind. When Jeeter looked up there was a moment of confusion, then recognition.

"Hello, Cooper," Jeeter said. "I haven't seen you in a while."

"You two fellas, find yourselves another table. I want to visit with my old pard here, and me 'n my friend need these seats."

"Find your own seat," one of the two men said.

Cooper pulled his pistol and pushed it into the mouth of the man who had talked back to him. The gunsight cut the man's lip.

"I said go away," Cooper repeated ominously.

"All right, all right," the man said, though the words came out "ag rag, ag rag."

Cooper smiled at the man and gave him a five-dollar bill. "Here, I don't want you to have no hard feelin's or nothin', so why don't you and your friend have some drinks on me?" he said.

When he saw the five-dollar bill, the angry look on the man's face was replaced by a broad smile. "Well, hell, why didn't you say so in the first place?" he said. "Sure, you can have our seats. Go ahead 'n have a nice visit."

"It's been awhile," Jeeter said after the other men left and Cooper and Morris had taken their seats at the table. "How did you find me?"

"I always like to keep up with old friends," Cooper replied.

Jeeter laughed. "Only reason we was friends was 'cause we was cell mates. We sure didn't have nothin' else in common."

"We do now."

"What's that?"

"We both make money off the railroad."

"You workin' for the U.P.?"

"No."

"Then how you goin' to make money off the railroad?"

"With your help."

"Look, I ain't in all that good with the railroad that I can talk up for you. You want a job with the railroad, you'd do just as good askin' for it your own self."

"I said I was goin' to make some money from the railroad. I didn't say I was goin' to be workin' for it."

"If you ain't goin' to be workin' for it, then how do you plan to . . . ?" Jeeter started, then he stopped and shook his head. "Uh-uh. I think I know what you got in mind, but I ain't interested. I done served my time in prison, 'n I don't plan on doin' nothin' that will send me back."

"You won't be takin' no chances at all," Cooper said. "You'll be completely out of it."

"Then I don't understand. What is it you're a-wantin' me to do?"

"All you got to do is tell us when there's goin' to be a lot of money being shipped."

"What's my share?"

"Five percent."

"That ain't much."

"It's plenty, when you figure you ain't goin' to be takin' no risk at all; not from bein' shot on the job 'n not from the law, neither, 'cause you won't even be connected to it."

"Sixty thousand dollars," Jeeter said.

"What? You're crazy, askin' for sixty thousand dollars!"

"No, I ain't askin' for sixty thousand dollars," Jeeter said. "I'm tellin' you that there'll be a shipment of sixty thousand dollars comin' through tomorrow."

"When? Where?"

"I don't have all the information yet. Meet me behind the depot corral at nine o'clock tomorrow mornin'," Jeeter said. "I should have the information by then."

Otto

With the show over, the townspeople drifted away. Ina Claire was making a count of their "product," which was little more than a commercial cough syrup to which had been added sugar and cinnamon.

"We sold fifteen bottles tonight," she said excitedly.

Meagan laughed. "There's nothing like showing enthusiasm for your job," she said.

"Oh, well, Papa always said if you're going to do something, you should do the best you can."

"Your papa was absolutely right," Duff said. "And, if we are going to use this medicine show as a means of disguising our actual intent in traveling around, then it will only work if we do it right."

"And you were wonderful on the drums," Meagan said.

"Aye, lass, that you were."

"The only thing . . ." Ina Claire started, but paused.

"What is it?"

"I can't help but feel like we are cheating the folks," Ina Claire said. "I mean we're selling them this miracle cure, and it isn't a miracle cure at all. It's just a cough syrup with sugar and cinnamon."

Meagan laughed. "Honey, there isn't one in twenty who might actually believe that they are buying some sort of miracle cure. People come to medicine shows for the show, and you and Duff certainly provided them with that."

Meagan smiled. "Good. I'm glad we aren't cheating them."

CHAPTER TWENTY-NINE

Laramie City

As per the arrangement, the next morning Cooper went to the depot corral to meet with Jeeter. He brought Callahan with him. Although empty now because this wasn't the shipping season, the grounds of the corral were still covered with the results of thousands of cattle that had been brought through this railhead over the years, and the air reeked with the odor.

"Damn, couldn't we have met somewhere else?" Callahan complained. "It stinks here."

"Yeah, well, cattle turds don't smell no worse nor no better'n any other turd," Cooper replied. "Anyhow, I figure that's why he chose to meet us here. There ain't likely to be no one around, on account of no one likes the stink."

Callahan took a handkerchief from his pocket and blew his nose. "Phew!" he said afterward, shaking his head. "I wish to hell I hadn't done that. That just made it worse."

"You ain't never cowboyed none have you?" Cooper asked with a little chuckle.

"No. I've always managed to find other ways to earn my money."

"Here comes Jeeter," Cooper said.

Cooper and Callahan watched as the short, bearded man approached, limping from an old broken leg that had not been properly set. When Jeeter saw the two men who were waiting for him, he stopped.

Cooper and Callahan approached him.

"Who is this?" Jeeter asked when the distance between them had been closed.

"His name is Callahan," Cooper said.

"Yeah? Well I don't like too many people knowin' my business, do you know what I mean?"

"Callahan is part of this business," Cooper said. "You might even say he's the head of it, bein' as me 'n the others ride for him, so to speak."

Although Callahan had assumed the leadership role in the group, this was the first time he had ever heard any of the others actually acknowledge that fact, and the words pleased him. He turned his attention to Jeeter.

"Cooper said you was sayin' somethin' about a shipment of sixty thousand dollars,"

363

Callahan said.

Jeeter looked at both Cooper and Callahan, as if uncertain as to whether or not he should trust them. Finally, taking a deep breath, he plunged on.

"All right, the money will be on train number five twenty-five. It'll be in Laramie City at eight thirty-five tomorrow morning."

"Eastbound or westbound?" Callahan asked.

"Eastbound. It's takin' the money to Cheyenne."

"How much money?"

"It's like I told Cooper. Sixty thousand dollars. How are you going to get the three thousand dollars to me?"

"We'll figure that out later," Callahan said.

"I warn you not to try and double-cross me," Jeeter said.

"Oh, you warn me, do you?"

"Yes. I will know if you have succeeded. And if I haven't received my share within one week after the robbery, I will go to the sheriff with everything that I know."

"That wouldn't be a very good idea," Callahan said flatly.

Jeeter chuckled. "No, I wouldn't think you would appreciate it." With a triumphant smile, Jeeter turned to walk away from Callahan and Cooper.

That was where he made his mistake because Callahan stepped up behind him, put his hand to Jeeter's head, and pulled it back. With the knife in his other hand, Callahan slit Jeeter's throat.

Jeeter lay on his back, looking up at the two men as he felt his life slipping away from him.

"Ahh, what would you have done with three thousand dollars anyway?" Callahan asked the dying man.

Howell

When Duff stepped into the sheriff's office, Deputy Thurman Burns looked up from his almost constant game of solitaire.

"Yes, sir, what can I do for you?" Burns asked.

"The name is Malcolm Campbell, 'n I've come to see if a permit be needed to put on my medicine show," Duff replied.

Burns smiled. "Medicine show, is it? Well, I'll be glad to give you a permit to perform. 'N after the tragic event that happened here not too long ago, why I think the folks would be more'n glad to have some entertainin'. You do some entertainin', don't you? I mean more'n just spout off your medicine."

"Aye, 'tis quite a good show we perform if

I may say so myself," Duff replied.

"Then you're more than welcome."

"Ye mentioned a tragic event," Duff said. " 'N would you mind for be tellin' me what that tragic event may be?"

Duff was well aware of what Deputy Burns was talking about, but he thought he might be able to ascertain more information by playing ignorant of the fact.

"Well, sir, a man, 'n a real good man I might add by the name of Whitworth, run him a store that's about halfway between here 'n Farrel. He was robbed by a bunch of outlaws, 'n he warn't only robbed, he was murdered, too. His poor wife, who's just a real nice lady, hid out in back of the store. She brought her husband's body in, in the back of the wagon, poor thing."

Duff had heard about the murder and robbery, but he decided to let the deputy continue on with dispensing his information.

"There's one good thing that's come from it, though," Deputy Burns said.

"What's that?"

"Three of them sons of bitches that done the murderin' has got their own selves kilt."

This was new information for Duff. "What? Who? And how is it that ye would be knowing such a thing?"

Burns chuckled, then picked up a telegram. "You ever heard of the town of Chugwater?"

"Chugwater?" Now Duff grew even more interested in what the deputy sheriff had to say. "Aye, I've heard of Chugwater."

"Well, sir, I got word from a fella by the name of Craig, he's the marshal back in Chugwater. It seems that three of them" — he read the names from the telegram, *Pardeen, Bates, and Donner* — "went out to a ranch that's near Chugwater to kill a feller by the name of Duff MacCallister. Don't know if you ever heard of him, he's supposed to be some big rancher up in that area. Anyhow, he put a story in the paper that he was comin' after them seven men, and that must be why it is that these three decided to kill him. Only the thing is, they got kilt instead."

"Who killed them?" Duff asked, though even as he was asking the question, he was reasonably certain that he knew the answer.

"I don't rightly know, the telegram don't say nothin' 'bout that," Deputy Burns replied. "But I reckon it was this feller MacCallister, since it was his ranch they went to."

"Aye," Duff said. "Aye, I suppose that's true. So, what about the other four men?"

"What other four?"

"Ye said there were seven who murdered Mr. Whitworth 'n that three of them have now been killed. That leaves four. Where are they now?"

"Oh, heavens, I don't have no idea where they might be."

"Ye dinnae go after them?"

"Well, yeah, I took a posse out to Whitworth's store 'n we had a look around, but the thing is that store is on a road 'n they was just too many tracks to follow. There warn't actually nothin' I could do about it, so I brung the posse back home. I couldn't take a chance on leavin' the town unguarded you know."

"Aye, I suppose that's true," Duff agreed. "And 'tis thanking ye again for the permit that will let me do the medicine show."

"Oh, think nothin' of it. Like I said, a bit of entertainment is just what this town needs right now."

When Duff left the deputy sheriff's office, he went straight to the telegraph office to send a telegram to Elmer.

ELMER TELL ME ABOUT YOUR RECENT ADVENTURE STOP YOU CAN REACH ME AT HOWELL ATTENTION MEDICINE SHOW STOP DUFF

"We are hot on their trail," Duff said when he returned to the wagon. He told about the robbery and murder of Mr. Whitworth at his store.

"Mr. Whitworth's wife hid in the back of the store and overheard them talking. From the names she picked up, I know this is the same bunch we have been after."

"Oh," Meagan replied in a sympathetic tone of voice. "But what a terrible way to learn it, at the expense of that poor woman's husband."

"Now that you put it that way, 'tis the thought of such a tragedy that makes me feel guilty for having celebrated being on their trail a moment ago."

"Nonsense, Duff, you don't have a thing to feel guilty about. We know what these men have done, are doing, and will continue to do so unless we stop them."

Duff nodded, then lay his hand gently on Meagan's shoulder. "Aye, lass," he said. "And we will stop them."

Sky Meadow Ranch, one hour and thirty minutes later

A leak had developed in the bunkhouse, and Elmer and Wang were making the repair. Elmer had just stepped down from the ladder to get some more shingles while Wang waited on the roof.

"Someone is coming," Wang said.

Elmer's pistol was in the holster, hanging from a nearby fence.

"Who is it?" he asked.

"He is of no danger," Wang said. "It is the boy who delivers telegrams."

"You say it is the boy who delivers telegrams? Damn, what could that be about?" Elmer mused. "Wang, you don't reckon Duff or one o' them two girls has got hurt, do you?"

Rubbing his hands together, Elmer started toward the delivery boy, who was riding a pinto.

"Now, a'fore you even hand me that thing, I want to know if it is bad news," Elmer said.

"I haven't read it," the boy replied. He looked to be no older than fourteen. "But I wasn't told it was bad news, 'n most of the time if it is bad news I get told in advance so I'll know how to react around the folks when they read it."

"It better not be bad news then," Elmer said as he reached for the document. "On account of if it is bad news after you tellin' me it ain't, why, I'm just liable to jerk you down offen o' that horse 'n tan your hide good."

That was one of the longest sentences Elmer had ever uttered, and he was still gasping for breath as he ripped open the envelope to read the message.

"I'll be damn. It's from Duff," Elmer said.

"What does *Xiānshēng* MacCallister say?" Wang asked.

"He wants us to tell him about what happened out here with them three galoots who come a-lookin' for 'im. Only, this part I don't understand."

"What is it that you do not understand?"

"He wants me to send the telegram to Medicine Show in Howell."

"Medicine Show?"

"That's what it says. Send it to Medicine Show in Howell."

Howell

Duff had made arrangements for their horses to go on ahead of them by train to Rock Creek, which wasn't the next stop on the railroad but far enough down to keep the horses always ahead of them. He also arranged to board the mules, and now he was back at the medicine wagon, getting it well set up for the show. The brake was set, the wheels were chocked, and Duff had tied it down. Meagan and Ina Claire were inside the wagon changing into their costumes for

371

tonight's show, and Duff finished with all the chores he needed to accomplish before tonight's presentation. He saw someone coming toward him and recognized him as the same telegrapher who had handled the message for him this morning. Grinning, he started toward him.

"Would that message be for me?" Duff asked, though he knew full well that it would have to be for him, or the telegrapher would have sent his copy boy.

THREE MEN CAME TO RANCH LOOKING FOR YOU STOP WHEN YOU WERE NOT THERE THEY WERE GOING TO KILL WANG AND ME STOP WE KILLED THEM STOP

"Damn," Duff said after he showed the telegram to Meagan and Ina Claire. "I dinnae think about Elmer and Wang when I started this crusade. I just figured they would be safe at the ranch."

"Apparently they are safe enough," Meagan said. "They handled these three men, didn't they?"

Duff laughed. "Aye, lass, that they did."

"You need to get into costume soon," Meagan suggested.

"I'll do so now."

Meagan breathed a sigh of relief, knowing that she would not have to fight him to get him into costume.

CHAPTER THIRTY

The medicine wagon was parked at the end of the main street and was the object of attention to some forty or fifty people. Those who were assembled represented at least one-fourth of the small town's population. They were gathered for the show more than any "miracle elixir" because entertainment in any fashion was scarce. At this particular moment, Duff and Ina Claire were performing a number on the pipes and drum.

Duff was not wearing kilts as he performed, thinking that to be so uniformed for what was essentially a medicine show would be degrading to the attire of the Black Watch. Instead, he was wearing the costume that Meagan had made for him, red and white, vertical-striped pants, and a blue jacket with stars across the shoulders. For their part, Meagan and Ina Claire were wearing dresses that wouldn't be out of place on those women who plied their profession to tease men into buying drinks in the saloons, and because both were particularly appealing, their costumes added to the overall attraction of the show.

When Duff and Ina Claire finished their number to the applause of those gathered, Duff put his pipes down and turned to address the crowd.

"Ladies and gentlemen, 'n would ye be for castin' yer eyes toward m' beautiful assistant," Duff began his spiel, exaggerating his brogue and pointing to Meagan. "Sure 'n this bonny lass will be moving amongst ye, selling these marvelous bottles of Malcolm Campbell's Heather Extract. 'Tis brewed on the moors of Scotland from a secret formula, known only to m' kinsmen. And 'tis absolutely guaranteed to cure you of sore throat, rheumatism, sciatica, lumbago, contracted muscles, and toothaches. For the men, it will restore the vim and vigor of youth. For women it will ease those bearing-down feelings, rejuvenate the spirit, and give you the energy you need to face every day. And it will do all this m' friends for the price of one quarter."

"Why hell, mister, I'd pay more'n that just to see you 'n that pretty young girl of your'n play music together," someone from the crowd called.

"Thank you, sir. We'll be playing more music for you in just a few minutes, but first, we must take the time to allow my assistant to make this miracle cure available to all of you," Duff replied.

"What the hell, Jonesy, you ain't sayin' you actually enjoyed that caterwaulin', are you? Hell the squealin' of a stuck pig sounds better," another said, responding to Jonesy's remark.

"I'll be for grantin' ye that the bagpipe isn't for everyone," Duff said. " 'Tis true that to appreciate the music o' the pipes, one must have a certain degree of sophisticated taste."

"Sophisticated taste? What does that mean?"

"I'll tell you what it means, Deekus. It means you're too dumb to appreciate it," Jonesy said, and all the others laughed at the expense of the wise guy.

"Look at that feller up there," Deekus said, pointing toward Duff. "He looks like a damn clown, all dressed up like that."

"Oh, for cryin' out loud, Deekus. Shut up, 'n let the rest of us enjoy the show these folks are puttin' on, will you? There didn't nobody force you to come here today." This comment came from one of the other men who had gathered for the medicine show.

Meagan, carrying a tray filled with bottles of Campbell's Heather Extract, began moving through the crowd then, dispensing smiles and friendly conversation.

"Hey, lady, do I get anything extry iffen I buy two o' them bottles of medicine?" Deekus asked.

"Of course you do, sir," Meagan replied.

"I do? Well then, I'll just have me a couple of bottles of that snake oil you're a-sellin'."

"Here you go, sir. That'll be fifty cents, a quarter apiece," Meagan said sweetly. She took the money, then turned away.

"Wait a minute!" Deekus called. "I thought you said I'd get something extry iffen I bought two bottles."

"Why, you did, sir. You got an extra bottle of the elixir," Meagan said, her smile masking any irritation she was experiencing from the man's complaint.

"Yeah, well what I actual expected was somethin' like this." Deekus reached down and grabbed a handful of flesh on Meagan's well-shaped derriere. Meagan whirled around and slapped him hard.

"There you go, Deekus," Jonesy said, laughing. "You got your extry."

The others laughed as well.

Suddenly Deekus had a knife in his hand, and he began waving it around. "Now," he said. "I aim to cut the top off this here girlie's dress so's we can all get us a good look at her —"

"Deekus, put that knife away! You got no call to go actin' or even talkin' like that. We got ladies and children in this crowd," Jonesy said.

"What are you doin' with that knife anyway?" another asked.

"I aim to do just what I said I was goin' to do. I aim to get me a good look. Now, ever'one back out o' my way."

Deekus turned toward the others and made several, wide sweeping motions with his hand. The women in the crowd let out little squeals of alarm, and everyone backed away, opening up a wide circle occupied only by Deekus and Meagan.

"Now, girly," Deekus said, turning back toward Meagan. "Me 'n you got some —"

Whatever Deekus intended to say was left unsaid because it was interrupted by the loud bark of a gunshot. The knife Deekus was holding flew away, and Deekus let out a sharp sound of shock and gave a look of surprise as he grabbed his hand.

"What the hell!" he said, and looked back toward the stage, which was actually just the braced tailgate of the medicine show wagon. There he saw Duff holding a smoking pistol.

"Would you be for goin' about your business, sir, 'n leavin' m' assistant alone so she can tend to hers?" Duff said.

"I'd listen to the medicine man if I was you, Deekus," Jonesy said. "He coulda just as easy put that bullet in your head as shoot that knife outta your hand. And by damn there wouldn't be nobody here that would blame 'im if he did do that."

"Go ahead," Deekus replied quietly, the tone of his voice showing contrition. "I was just foolin' aroun'; I wasn't really goin' to do nothin'."

The crowd returned, and once again, Meagan began moving through them, selling the bottles of "medicine." After selling thirty-three bottles of the medicine, Duff and Ina Claire played one more number for the crowd. Afterward, Duff closed both the awning and tailgate to his wagon just as he heard footsteps approach.

"I heard what happened here today with Deekus McCoy," someone said.

Turning, Duff saw that it Deputy Thurman Burns.

"If the young lady wishes to press charges, I'll take care of it."

"There's nae need for that," Duff said. "The lad got just a bit rambunctious is all.

No one was hurt."

"Except McCoy's pride," Burns replied. "They tell me you made quite a shot, shooting the knife from his hand as you did."

"The shot was nae that difficult," Duff said. "Twenty feet, maybe."

"Still, to be able to shoot a knife from someone's hand at twenty feet, or even ten feet, is very good shooting. How is it that a medicine peddler can shoot that good?"

"I've been thinking about putting some trick shooting into my show," Duff explained.

Burns nodded. "Yeah," he said. "Yeah, I can see how that might be. Well, if the lady don't want me to do nothin' about Deekus McCoy, I'll just let it be. It was good to have you stop by today. From what I've heard you folks gave the town a good show, 'n like I said, after Art Whitworth gettin' kilt like he done, this was just what was needed to cheer 'em again."

" 'Tis a good town ye have here, Deputy, 'n except for that one man, 'twas a foine crowd who came to see us."

"And you handled him well," Burns said. The deputy extended his hand. "You folks have a good journey to wherever you go from here, 'n if you come back through, you'll be more than welcome."

"Thank you, Deputy."

Less than an hour later they were driving out of town, no longer in costume but wearing the jeans and shirts that had become their everyday clothing. The three of them were sitting together on the front seat, and the gaudily painted wagon was heading west paralleling the railroad tracks.

Ninety percent of the towns and settlements of the territory of Wyoming were on or within less than a day's ride from the railroad, which meant if they were able to find Callahan and the others, they would most likely do so by following the railroad. To that end, Duff arranged for their horses to always be waiting for them in a stable in the next town just ahead of them. He did that by paying passage for the horses and shipping them ahead by train.

They were southeast of the town of Lookout, and adjacent to the Union Pacific Railroad line, when Duff called the mule team to a halt.

"This looks like as good a place as any for our bivouac," Duff said.

"We're sort of on a hill," Meagan said. "I think we would be more comfortable down there on the flat."

"Aye, 'twould be more comfortable, until

the rain comes," Duff said.

"Rain? What rain?"

"Give it time, lass, 'twill be raining before midnight, ye can mark my words on that."

"You want to sleep in the wagon with us tonight?" Meagan invited.

" 'Twould be too crowded for comfort, and there is nae need. I've enough canvas t' make m'self a wee hoose under the wagon, 'n come the rain, I'll be as snug as a bug."

"Do you think we're ever going to find those men this way?" Ina Claire asked.

"Aye, lass, we'll find them, because they will be visible and we will be invisible."

"Invisible?" Ina Claire laughed. "We're riding around in a bright red and gold wagon, and we stand in the street wearing red, white, and blue costumes, playing the pipes and drum, and you say we are invisible?"

"Let me ask ye this, lass. If those four blaggards rode by us while we were set up in town, would you recognize them?" Duff asked.

"Yes, I would absolutely recognize them," Ina Claire said.

"Aye, I expect you would. But now tell me this. If you 'n I were doing our pipes 'n drum, do you think they would recognize you?"

"Well, if they were out in the audience watching they . . ." Ina Claire stopped in mid-sentence and smiled, broadly. "I would be invisible because they wouldn't expect me to be part of a medicine show."

"What about the man who had a story posted in the newspaper, vowing to find them and bring them to justice?" Duff asked. "Would they for believing that such a man would be dressed in red, white, and blue, and selling snake oil?"

Ina Claire laughed out loud. "They wouldn't even see you, because you would be invisible."

"Tell me," Meagan said. "Do invisible people eat? Because this invisible person is hungry."

"Aye, 'twould be a good idea to eat our supper now, then get set in for the night," Duff said. "I want to be in a dry place before the rain starts."

"What makes you think it's going to rain?" Meagan asked. "There wasn't a cloud in the sky when the sun went down."

"I can smell it," Duff said, laying his finger alongside his nose.

"You can smell when rain is coming?" Ina Claire asked, surprised at his comment.

"Honey, you have to understand," Meagan said. "Duff is a Scotsman, and they would have us believe that a Scotsman is possessed of marvelous talents, far beyond that of we mere mortals."

"It will rain," Duff said.

Duff's prediction of rain came true shortly after all three had gone to bed, Meagan and Ina Claire in the wagon and Duff under the wagon. He had stretched a rather large canvas out from the top of the wagon and tied the mules to the back so that when the rain started, they would be sheltered as much as possible. He had also dug a drainage canal around the wagon, and he hung canvas from the two long sides of the wagon as well as a sheet behind the front wheels, and another sheet just forward of the back wheels. Those four "walls" he tucked under the canvas ground cover, and as a result of all his preparation, even when the rain started he stayed dry.

CHAPTER THIRTY-ONE

A few miles farther north and west
on the Union Pacific Railroad

Callahan had decided that the best place to hold up the train would be exactly halfway between the towns of Miser and Rock Creek. There were several advantages to this location. Both Miser and Rock Creek were so small that the only law was a single marshal in either town, and neither would have the authority nor the inclination to put together a posse, especially to recover someone else's money. And the money the train would be carrying was a shipment between two large banks, having nothing to do with the tiny railroad towns of Miser or Rock Creek.

Still another advantage of this location, and no small advantage, was the proximity of not only mountains but a stream that would cover their tracks as they withdrew. They didn't plan on staying in the mountains long. Sixty thousand dollars was an enormous amount of money, enough that they could leave Wyoming Territory and go anywhere they wanted.

"St. Louis," Morris insisted. "I'm goin' to St. Louis 'n become a riverboat gambler. After this, I'll have enough money to do that."

All the others put in their choice as to where they would go, and Callahan wanted to go to San Francisco.

"I want to go to Ozark, Alabama," Cooper said.

"I've never heard of that place. Where is it?" Manning asked.

"It's in Alabama."

"Oh."

The four men had been caught in the rain during the night and were made miserable by it, as the water ran in sheets down their ponchos, and even with the slickers, the men were soaked to the bone. The rain had stopped, but they were still wet and uncomfortable.

They had come in the middle of the night because they didn't want to take a chance on anyone seeing what they were doing. What they did during the night was remove one of the lengths of rail from the track.

"It'll be goin' lickety-split when it comes

through here, won't it?" Manning asked.

"Yeah, that's why we need to be as far away from the track as we can get, because when it hits that missing rail, there's going to be one hell of a crash," Callahan said.

"How many you think are liable to get kilt in the wreck?" Morris asked.

"What the hell do you care? Grown tender hearted, have you?" Callahan asked.

"No, I was just wonderin' is all."

"I tell you what, Morris, if you're all that curious, you can stay back 'n count the dead, while me 'n the rest of the boys will ride off 'n count the money," Cooper said with a laugh.

"Hah!" Morris replied. "I ain't that curious. Fact is, I ain't curious at all. I was just curious about it, is all."

Callahan and the others laughed at Morris's convoluted statement.

"Tell me how much one-fourth of sixty thousand dollars is again?" Manning asked.

"Fifteen thousand dollars," Callahan replied.

"Whooeee, I never knowed there was that much money in the whole world. Hey, Callahan, you can cipher real good, how long would we have to cowboy to get that much money?"

"Oh, I'd say about thirty years," Callahan said.

The other three laughed out loud.

"We're goin' to make as much money in one hour as them dumb cowboys will make in thirty years!" Cooper said. "Ain't that somethin' now?"

With the medicine wagon

The rain had stopped sometime after midnight, but the ground was still wet the next morning. Duff had taken the precaution the night before of gathering some wood and bringing it into the shelter with him. Because of that, he had dry wood for the breakfast fire, so even before Meagan and Ina Claire were awake, he lay the wood and started the fire. He had a sack of preground coffee beans he dropped into the pot of water to start the coffee brewing. Next he rolled out biscuits, then, putting them in a Dutch oven, set them on the fire to bake. The coffee was already done, the biscuits were rising in the Dutch oven, and bacon was twitching in the frying pan by the time the two ladies climbed out of the wagon.

"Oh," Ina Claire said. "That smells so good to wake up to." She held her arms up over her body for a long stretch.

"Well, 'tis good to see you this morning.

'Twas thinking, I was, that ye'd be sleeping 'til noon," Duff said with a teasing smile.

"Duff MacCallister, it is barely seven o'clock," Meagan replied resolutely.

"Besides, who could sleep with those heavenly smells coming from your cooking?" Ina Claire asked.

"We'll have biscuits soon," he said.

"Meagan, you should marry him," Ina Claire said. "You'd have a full-time cook."

"And a full-time nuisance," Meagan replied with a chuckle.

Duff fried the eggs hard, so they breakfasted on sandwiches made from the biscuits, bacon, and eggs. They were eating heartily when they heard the whistle of an approaching train.

"You think there are folks on that train, eating in the dining car?" Ina Claire asked.

"I expect there are," Meagan replied.

"I've never been on a train," Ina Claire said. "I sure wish I could eat in a dining car."

"You think it would be any better than this?" Meagan asked, holding out her biscuit sandwich.

Ina Claire chuckled. "I don't see how it could possibly be."

"Here's the train," Meagan said, though no declaration was necessary as the train was even with them now and going very fast. The engineer was standing at the window of the cab, and he returned Ina Claire's wave. Small, gleaming coals were spilling from the engine's firebox, leaving a gleaming path beneath the train, indicative of the size of the fire that was necessary to maintain such a speed.

As Duff watched the train roar by, he saw the passengers inside, some reading the newspaper, some engaged in conversation, some merely looking through the window at the passing countryside. He couldn't help but marvel at a technology that would allow people to be whisked across such great distances while in the cozy and dry comfort of the cars. It was as if an entire small town was on the move.

Onboard train number Five Twenty-Five
"Hey, Ernie, did you see that medicine wagon back there?" the engineer asked his fireman.

"What medicine wagon?"

"The one we just passed that was parked along the side of the track. It was a red wagon with yellow writin' on it, some kind of elixir, I suppose. Anyhow, there were three people with it, sittin' near a fire, and it looked like they were havin' their breakfast. A man it was, 'n he had two women with 'im."

"Damn, you musta paid a lot of attention to it."

"Yeah, I did. You mean you didn't even see it a-tall?"

"No, I didn't see it."

"Too bad you didn't. I wish you had seen it, so we could talk about it some," the engineer said.

The fireman laughed. "Hell, Doodle, seems to me we are talkin' about it. I don't know what about it that's got you so interested, though."

"Oh, I just wonder what it would be like to be livin' like that is all. It seems to me like that would be the life."

"What would be the life?"

"Going around from town to town in a medicine wagon like that with a couple of good-looking women traveling with you."

"You want to travel around in a brightly colored wagon selling snake oil, do you?" Ernie laughed and shook his head. "You're crazy, Doodle. Do you know that? You are flat-out crazy."

"No, I'm not, I mean, when you consider there'd be no railroad schedules to keep, no station managers to deal with, no division chiefs. Why, you'd be your own boss, going

391

wherever you want at whatever schedule you want to set for yourself."

"Doodle, do you have 'ny idea how many kids there is all over the country that want to grow up to do just what me 'n you are doin' now?" Ernie asked. He picked up a shovel full of coal, then grinned. "Well maybe what you do more'n what I do," he added as he tossed the coal into the furnace. "Think about it. Drivin' a locomotive at thirty miles an hour and goin' from place to place. Why, this is the best damn job in the whole country."

"Yeah, I guess you're right," Doodle admitted. He smiled. "I know it's the only thing I ever wanted to do."

"And here you are, carryin' on 'bout some medicine wagon."

"Maybe it's the romantic streak in me," Doodle suggested.

Ernie laughed out loud. "Yeah, you're romantic all right. Virgie just tells ever'one how romantic you are."

"I ain't talkin' about that kind of romantic."

"By the way, you're sure keeping the throttle open this morning."

"I'm goin' to try 'n keep 'er as close to forty miles an hour as I can, in order to make up for the time we lost back in Cheyenne."

"I'll keep the fire goin' hot as I can for as long as I can, but we're goin' to have to take on more coal when we get to Rock Creek."

"Yeah, I was plannin' on that. But I figure even with the time we'll use up takin' on more coal, we'll still be all caught up by the time we get to Rawlins. Then I can back off a little so's you won't have to be workin' so hard to keep the fire up."

"Hah! Now that's just real nice of you, Doodle, I mean, a-worryin' about me havin' to work so hard 'n all." Ernie chuckled as he tossed another shovel full of coal into the fire.

"We're comin' up on Deadman's Curve now, 'n we've already made up a lot of it," Doodle said.

Ernie stood up straight and leaned on his shovel for a moment.

"You ever wonder why they call this 'Deadman's Curve'? I mean, yeah, they was a wreck here a couple of years ago, but this ain't the only curve where there's ever been a wreck. How come they don't call the other curves, Deadman's Curve?"

With Callahan, Manning, Cooper, and Morris
"This ain't much of a breakfast," Manning

complained as he took a bite of his beef jerky.

"You didn't have to come with us," Cooper said. "You could be eatin' ham 'n eggs 'n grits if you was in town someplace. 'N that would just be more money for the three of us."

"I didn't say nothin' 'bout not wantin' to be here. All I said was this warn't no breakfast."

"Pay attention! Here it comes," Callahan said as the train drew into sight. "Ever'body, get where you're s'posed to be but remember to stay back away from the track."

Callahan and the three men with him got back into the tree line, well away from the track.

As the train got closer it grew louder and louder until, in addition to the chugging of the engine, they could also hear the sound of steel wheels rolling on the tracks and the couplings of the cars as they took up and then gave back the minute bits of space between the connections.

Callahan glanced toward the section of track where the rail had been removed. It was just beyond a long curve in the track so that it would be unlikely that the engineer would see it in time to react to the danger. It seemed to Callahan as if this would be the best solution to the problem of stopping the train. It would for sure stop it, and the wreck would no doubt immobilize any possible security men, as well as any would-be heroes from among the passengers.

The train drew closer and closer, and Callahan involuntarily held his breath.

Onboard the train
"What the hell?" Doodle shouted out. "Ernie, brace yourself! Some of the track is out!"

Doodle didn't even bother to reach for the brakes or the Johnson bar, because he knew he wouldn't have time. His stomach was in his throat as he braced himself on the window frame and the front of the cab and watched the missing track section come closer. For some strange reason he didn't even feel fear. What he felt could better be described as the acceptance of something he could do nothing to change.

He thought of Virgie and his two kids.

Callahan stood well back from the track, watching the approaching train in utter fascination. When the train hit the open section where the rail had been removed, it continued on for a long moment, the piston rods causing the huge driver wheels to spin over thin air, as if the train would actually be able to defy gravity. Then, almost as if being set down slowly by some giant, the driver wheels that were over the removed track dropped three inches. As they came into contact with the cross ties, they began chewing them up and spitting out huge chunks of timber. They continued for a short distance on the ties but then dropped even farther into the dirt. This had the effect of not only creating an imbalance but of having a disproportionate thrust, with more drive on one side of the engine than the other.

The result of this loss of equilibrium in both drive and angle caused the engine to tumble over on its side, and when it did so, the boiler exploded with a thunderous noise and a tremendous gush of steam. The next three cars behind the engine — the tender, the express car, and the baggage car — turned over as well. The fifth car telescoped into the fourth car, and the sixth and seventh car, while neither telescoping nor overturning, did leave the track. Only the final car, which wasn't a passenger car but was a stock car, remained relatively unscathed, though even it subjected the livestock to a rather sudden stop.

After the sound of the exploding boiler,

the screech of steel on steel, and the crash of tumbling and colliding cars, there was a silence, though that silence was filled almost immediately with screams, shouts of fear, anger, and the weeping of the injured and shocked passengers.

"Damn! I ain't never seed nothin' like that in m' whole life!" Manning said excitedly. "That was better'n any rodeo or show I ever been to."

"I'm glad you enjoyed it," Callahan said. "Now come on, Manning, let's you 'n me get the money and get out of there before any of the passengers figure out what's happened and come out shootin'! Cooper, you 'n Morris keep a eye open in case any of the passengers takes a notion to be a hero."

With guns drawn, Callahan and Manning approached the wrecked train.

"Help us, mister," someone called from the engine cab. "The engineer is hurt bad." Steam was still drifting from the ruptured engine boiler.

Callahan fired a shot toward the fireman, though his shot missed. "You get back in there and stay there," he demanded.

The fireman, responding to the order, slipped back into a corner of the overturned cab, out of sight.

"Damn, Callahan, lookie here! We ain't

goin' to be able to get into this thing!" Manning said. "This here car's only got one door 'n it's on the side that's a-lyin' on the ground!"

"It's got doors on the each end, don't it?" Callahan replied.

"Oh, yeah, I didn't think about that."

"We'll get into the car that way."

"No, that ain't goin' to work, neither," Manning said after a moment. "The cars is all jammed up agin one another 'n we can't get to the doors."

"You mean to tell me there's sixty thousand dollars in that car 'n we can't get to it?" Callahan asked angrily.

"I don't see how we're a-goin' to do it," Manning replied.

Because he was unwilling to accept Manning's appraisal of the situation, Callahan made a personal inspection of the wrecked express car.

"Damn it!" he shouted angrily when he saw that entry to the car was, indeed, denied.

"Here, you men!" someone called from back in the train. "We've got some injured passengers here. How about comin' back 'n givin' us a hand?"

Callahan saw that the man who had called out was wearing the uniform of a conductor. Callahan took a shot at him but missed.

"My God! You're the ones who did this, aren't you?" the conductor called.

Callahan fired a second shot, again missing, and the conductor hurried back into the train.

"Help!" they heard the conductor's voice shout. "Any of you men who have a gun, turn to! The train is being robbed!"

"Morris, Cooper, Manning, let's go!" Callahan shouted. "We got to get out of here!"

"We ain't figured out a way to get into the express car yet!" Manning called back.

"It don't matter whether we have or not, we got to get out of here now!"

Almost on top of Callahan's shout came gunfire from the rear of the train.

"Wait! We can't go yet! We didn't get none of the money!" Cooper yelled.

"You can stay if you want, we're gettin' the hell out of here!" Callahan shouted.

Cooper took one look back toward the passengers who were gathering alongside the wrecked train, then he spurred his horse on to catch up with the others.

They had not gotten one cent from the aborted robbery.

CHAPTER THIRTY-TWO

"I always love the smell of things on the morning after a rain," Meagan said after they had eaten their breakfast and were under way later that morning.

"I liked listening to it against the wagon," Ina Claire said. "It helped me sleep. Though I worried about Duff being out in the rain."

"Nae need for you to have been worryin' about me, lass. Sure 'n I had a good dry place last night. There was nae a drop of rain got in."

"I'm glad you made a place for the mules. I wouldn't want to think of them standing out in the rain, either," Ina Claire said.

They heard a distant, rumbling noise.

"Oh, it's thundering," Ina Claire said. "I hope we don't get more rain."

"That wasn't thunder, lass," Duff said.

"I heard it, too. If it wasn't thunder, what was it?" Meagan asked.

"It sounded like distant artillery, but it

could nae be that."

"Perhaps it is someone blasting in the mine," Meagan said.

"Aye, could be," Duff replied, but the worried expression didn't leave his face.

It was less than half an hour later that they approached the train wreckage. They could see the engine and the first few cars on the side, as well as several more off the track. There were also several people moving around, many of them bleeding, nearly all of them in various stages of shock.

"Oh, my! That sound we heard wasn't thunder, it was a train wreck!" Ina Claire said.

"Aye, that it was," Duff said, and he hurried the mules into a lumbering run.

As they reached the train they saw a stock car attached to the rear, and it was one of only two cars that hadn't overturned.

"Thunder!" Ina Claire called out. "Thunder is in that car!"

"Duff, Sky, and Shadow are there as well!" Meagan added. Shadow was Meagan's horse, a purebred stallion she had only recently acquired.

This was the train that had been selected to transport the horses on to Laramie, which was the next town of any considerable size.

Stopping alongside the stock car, Duff opened the door and went inside. Sky recognized him immediately and came over to nuzzle him.

"Och, 'tis good to see that neither you nor your traveling companions are hurt," Duff said, rubbing Sky behind the ear.

"You! Get out of there!" someone shouted. "Just because the train was wrecked doesn't give you the right to take the horses."

"They are our horses!" Ina Claire said resolutely.

"What do you mean they're your horses?" The questioner was wearing the uniform of a conductor. "You weren't even on the train."

"We were nae on the train, but these are our horses," Duff called back from the stock car. He stepped down, then showed the conductor the shipping documents.

"Oh," the conductor said after he examined the papers. "I'm sorry."

"There is nae need to be sorry. Ye were but doing your job." Duff held his hand out toward the train. "What happened?"

"I'll tell you what happened. A bunch of bastards removed a rail to purposely wreck the train, intending to rob it."

"Four men?" Duff asked.

"Four? Yes, I think so. At least, that's all

402

that I saw."

"And would one of the four have been a large man with a rather flat nose?"

The conductor looked surprised by Duff's question. "Yes, now that one I did see," he answered. "How did you know?"

Duff started to tell the conductor that he had been looking for them, but he had a second thought.

"I've been reading about him. His name would be Callahan," was Duff's only response. "Have ye any fatalities?" Duff asked.

"Five, so far, including the engineer. And we still haven't gotten everyone from the cars. By the way, do you suppose we could use your wagon to haul some of the injured to the next town?"

"Aye, we would be glad to let you use the wagon."

One of the porters came running up to the conductor then. "Mister Decker, sir, Mr. Poindexter is still alive, we've heard him pecking on the side of the express car."

"I don't know how we're goin' to get Poindexter out," Decker said. "The car is lying door-side down, and it's jammed up against the adjacent cars at either end."

"I'll be glad to lend a hand," Duff said. "Meagan, would ye be for making the wagon available?" Duff asked.

"Yes," Meagan replied, and she hurried over to a place where many of the injured lay, as Duff followed the conductor to the front of the train and the overturned express car. There were two porters and a third man, standing on the topside of the overturned car. They had begun to cut through.

"Nae," Duff called, holding out his hand toward the men on the car. "That is nae good. If he is injured, you will have to lift him out. Ye should be on the ground and go in through the roof of the car. It will be easier to get him out that way."

"Yes," the conductor said, nodding his head. "Yes, that's a good idea."

The men who were standing on the car came down, then started using their axes on the roof. It took but a couple of minutes, and they had a hole big enough for Duff and one of the porters to climb through.

"Mr. Poindexter? Mr. Poindexter, it's me, Jackson. Are you here?"

"Yes, Jackson, I'm here," a weak voice replied.

It was dark in the car, the only light coming through the hole that had been chopped through the roof.

"There he is," Duff said, pointing toward the sound of the voice.

Poindexter was trapped under some of the

shelving, and Jackson reached for him.

"I'll pull you out from under all that," Jackson said.

"Wait, dinnae be so fast to move him," Duff said. "Sometimes if ye aren't careful, ye can make things worse."

"I think I have a broken arm, but if you can get everything off, I'm pretty sure I can move myself," Poindexter said.

For the next couple of minutes, Duff and Jackson worked, moving shelves and crates, until Poindexter was freed. Then, as he had said, he was able to move on his own.

By the time Duff crawled back out of the express car, the wagon had already left, filled with the most seriously injured.

"How far is it to the next town?" Duff asked.

"It's only four more miles to Rock Creek. The wagon left ten minutes ago. I expect it will be there within another few minutes."

"The money is safe," Poindexter said. Poindexter was cradling his arm. "The train robbers didn't accomplish a damn thing."

"I cannae agree with you, Mr. Poindexter," Duff said. "They killed five, wounded several more, 'n they wrecked a train."

"Five were killed?" Poindexter asked.

"Five so far," the conductor replied. "We're still pulling people from the wreck-

405

age, and there may be more. I hate to tell you this, Andy, but one of the ones who was killed was Doodle."

"Doodle? Oh, damn," Poindexter said. "Someone's goin' to have to tell Virgie. And they have two kids."

"Doodle?" Duff asked.

"The engineer. His real name was Cephus. Cephus Prouty," Decker said. "But I've never heard him called anything but Doodle."

"What I don't understand, though, is how they knew we were carrying the money," Poindexter said. "None of the money shipments are ever publicly announced."

"Maybe it was just a coincidence. Maybe they just intended to take their chances on whatever the train was carrying," Decker suggested.

"No, sir, I clearly heard one of 'em say, 'we ain't got the sixty thousand dollars yet.' And since that is exactly the amount of money we were carrying, then that tells me that they knew all about it," Poindexter said.

"We need some help back here!" someone shouted, and Duff, Decker, and one of the two porters answered the call. The other porter stayed with Poindexter, leading him to a spot where the less seriously injured were gathering.

It took almost an hour to get everyone free from the wreckage. The fatality count went up by two when they found a mother and her little girl dead in the twisted wreckage of one of the cars. Shortly after they performed the sad duty of laying those two bodies beside the engineer and the other passengers who were killed, they heard the whistle of an approaching train.

"Is that the westbound?" Poindexter asked.

Decker pulled his watch from his pocket and examined it. "No," he said with a shake of his head. "That's not due for another two hours." He smiled, then looked at Duff. "I'd say the wagon reached Rock Creek, and they must've wired back to Laramie to send a special train for us."

Decker was right, and shortly after the relief train arrived, every passenger and crewman, including the injured and the dead, had been evacuated from the site of the wreck. The conductor of the relief train said that telegrams had been sent out, halting all traffic in both directions until lifting cranes could be brought onto the scene so the track could be cleared for further traffic.

Duff, Meagan, and Ina Claire did not go with the train. Instead they saddled their horses and rode into Rock Creek.

Rochelle, Wyoming Territory

When Callahan and the others left the wrecked train, they rode southwest until they reached the town of Rochelle. Rochelle was a small, off the track town at the edge of the Medicine Bow Mountains. The town existed primarily as a result of the nearby coal mines. And like Cummins City, it had a bunk room where cots could be had for fifteen cents.

Passing themselves off as cowboys who were "returning to Texas," they stayed in Rochelle for a few days, confident that there would be little chance of their being connected with the attempted train robbery.

"Nothing!" Cooper said a few days later. "We didn't get one dime from the stagecoach holdup and nothing from this, either. Hell, if it warn't for that peddler 'n the store, we wouldn't have no money a-tall, which is damn near what we don't have already."

"You forgot about the bank in Bordeaux," Callahan said.

"Oh, yeah, I did forget. But we didn't get no more'n a few hunnert dollars there, neither. I mean a bank, a whole bank, 'n we didn' even get a thousand dollars. I thought robbin' the train was goin' to make us rich. Sixty thousand dollars rich. But we come away from it without a damn cent."

"The money was there," Callahan said. He held up a copy of the *Rochelle Standard*. "It says right here that the sixty-thousand-dollar shipment was untouched."

"So, what are we going to do next?" Cooper asked.

"How much money do we have now?" Callahan asked.

"What do you need to know how much money we have for?" Morris asked.

"If I'm goin' to make any plans, I need to know where we're startin' from. If you remember, we got two hundred and thirteen dollars from that peddler, that give us fifty-three dollars apiece, six hundred and twenty-nine dollars from the bank in Bordeaux, 'n that give us a hundred 'n fifty dollars apiece, 'n another hundred and eighty-three dollars from the store."

"Which broke down to only twenty-six dollars, seein' as we divided it up seven ways 'cause Pardeen, Bates, 'n Donner took their cut, remember?" Cooper said.

"And don't forget, when we first broke 'em out of jail, why we give them boys twenty dollars apiece outta the money we took from the bank," Morris said.

"I'm just damn glad we didn't give 'em a hundred dollars apiece before they went to kill MacCallister," Cooper said.

"Which they didn't do, or they woulda done been back here askin' for their money," Manning said.

"So, how much do we have now?" Callahan asked, repeating his question.

The four men emptied their pockets and came up with a total of five hundred and sixteen dollars between the four of them.

Callahan did some figuring. "All right, that comes up to one hundred and twenty-nine dollars apiece," he said.

"Hey, wait a minute, that ain't fair!" Manning said. "I put in a hunnert 'n forty-two dollars. What do you mean it comes up to a hunnert 'n twenty-nine? That's less money than I put in."

"We're goin' to divide it equal," Callahan said resolutely.

"No we ain't. That ain't right," Manning said. "There ain't nothin' at all right about that."

"Come on, Manning, you're in this like the rest of us," Cooper said.

Grumbling, Manning assented to the division of the money.

"All right, we've got the money all divided up," Morris said. "But I can tell you now, it ain't goin' to last long. We're goin' to have to get us some more money, some'eres, 'n we're goin' to have to get it soon."

"Well, seein' as the only time we've been able to make any money is when we've held up a bank, I think we should hit another bank," Callahan suggested.

"You got somethin' in mind?" Cooper asked.

"Yeah, I got somethin' in mind," Callahan said. "The First Federal Bank in Cheyenne."

"What?" Cooper replied incredulously. "Are you out of your mind? That bank is like a fort."

"Yeah, it is," Callahan said. "And you know why it's a fort? It's where the Union Pacific Railroad keeps all their money. There ain't never less than a hundred thousand dollars there, and more'n likely it would be closer to two hundred thousand dollars." Callahan smiled. "And, boys, two hundred thousand dollars, divided four ways, would be fifty thousand for each of us."

"Fifty thousand?" Manning said. He smiled, put his hand to his forehead. "Wow, just thinkin' about that much money makes my head spin."

"Ha!" Morris said. "With that much money, forget about me gamblin' on a Mississippi riverboat, I'll buy the damn thing."

Cooper shook his head. "Don't you all go spendin' money we don't have now. Hell, it wouldn't make no difference if it was a million dollars. I don't see no way that the four us could rob that bank 'n get away with it. Don't forget, Pardeen 'n the others didn't come back. 'N if you ask me, they didn't come back 'cause they got themselves kilt by MacCallister."

"Yeah, that's what I'm thinkin', too," Callahan said. "But that means if MacCallister killed Pardeen and the others, then he's still at his ranch. 'N if he's at his ranch, he isn't looking for us."

"A hundred thousand dollars, huh?" Cooper asked.

"At least. And it's like I say chances are there will be two, maybe three times as much money there."

"Damn! Divided by four, huh?"

"Five," Callahan said.

"Five?"

"Yeah, five. There's one man in particular I want, seein' as he is the one who first come up with the idea of robbin' this particular bank. He's also done a lot of studyin' on it."

"What would be our cut if they was five of us, 'n we got a hunnert thousand dollars?" Manning wanted to know.

"Twenty thousand," Callahan said.

"Twenty thousand? Hell, just a minute ago we was talkin' about fifty thousand apiece, 'n now it's dropped down to no more'n twenty thousand?" Manning said.

"What the hell, Manning? You plannin' on turnin' your back on twenty thousand dollars?" Cooper asked.

"When I was talkin' fifty thousand, that was if the bank had two hundred thousand dollars 'n they was only four of us. But I say better to take a smaller cut and get the money, than not have enough men to do the job and get nothin' at all. Anyway, it's like I said, there could be twice as much money in that bank," Callahan said.

"Yeah, well, we was goin' to get fifteen thousand apiece from the train robbery, too, wasn't we? Only we didn't wind up with nothin'," Manning said.

"The bank ain't likely to turn over on its side with the door side down, neither, is it?" Callahan replied.

" 'N we don't have to stop it, neither, on account of 'cause it ain't goin' nowhere. The bank just sits there," Cooper said.

"Are you for this, Cooper?" Morris asked.

"You're damn right I'm for it."

"All right," Morris said with a nod of his head. "I'm in."

"Me too," Manning said.

"Who is this other feller you're a-wantin'?" Morris asked.

"His name is Red O'Leary, 'n I know just where to find 'im," Callahan replied.

CHAPTER THIRTY-THREE

Duff, Meagan, and Ina Claire had taken two adjoining rooms in the Dorsett Hotel in Rock Creek. At the moment they were all in one room engaged in a discussion as to their hunting expedition.

"Och, 'tis m' misfortune that I am nae a tracker," Duff said. "If I were, we could have followed their tracks from the site of the train wreck. As it is, we are nae closer to finding them now than we were on the day we started."

"Maybe we could hire a tracker," Ina Claire suggested.

"There's no need to hire one," Meagan said. "All we have to do is send a telegram."

"Send a telegram?" Ina Claire asked. "To who?"

"Duff knows where to send it."

"Aye," Duff said, nodding his head. " 'Twas my mistake in not bringin' him with me in the first place."

415

"You know he won't come by himself," Meagan said.

Ina Claire flashed a big smile. "You're talking about Mr. Gleason and Mr. Wang, aren't you?"

"Aye, lass, that I am."

"And they are good at tracking?" Ina Claire asked.

"I've heard it said that Elmer could track a bird," Duff said.

"Really?" Ina Claire asked, amazed by the statement. "Why, that's impossible, isn't it? How can you track something through the air? Who told you Mr. Gleason could track a bird?"

"Let me see," Duff replied as he stroked his chin. "I'm trying to remember now who it was that told me Elmer could track a bird. Aye, I remember now. 'Twas Elmer his own self."

Meagan and Ina Claire laughed.

"I'll send him a telegram and ask him to meet us here," Duff said.

"What will we do until he gets here?"

"We'll do a few more of our medicine shows 'n see if we can pick up any information on the brigands."

Rawlins, Wyoming Territory
Callahan was in the Bucket of Blood Saloon

when he saw a familiar looking red-haired man sitting at a table with two other men.

Five years earlier, Callahan, Red O'Leary, and three others had held up a stagecoach. Their information that the coach was carrying a money transfer was accurate, and they came away with a total of fifteen thousand dollars. That was still the most successful robbery Callahan had ever committed, but it was small change compared to the possible reward of a successful robbery of the First Federal Bank in Cheyenne.

Callahan went over to speak to him.

"Hello, Red."

O'Leary had not seen him approach, and when he first looked up the expression on his face reflected some irritation at being interrupted. When he saw who it was, though, the irritated look was replaced by a smile.

"Well, I'll be damn," he said. "If it ain't my old friend . . . uh . . . what moniker are you using right now?"

Callahan glanced at the two men who were sharing the table with O'Leary, and not knowing whether or not he could trust them came up with a name.

"Smith is good enough," he said.

O'Leary laughed. "If you two fellas will excuse me, I think me 'n my old friend, uh . . . Smith . . . here, need to catch up on what's been goin' on since we last seen each other."

The other two got up to leave, and Callahan took one of their chairs.

"I seen in the paper where you escaped from jail," O'Leary said when they were alone. "Fact is, they's a reward out on you, 'n I could make five hunnert dollars just by turnin' you into the sheriff."

"I suppose you could turn in an old friend 'n make five hundred dollars," Callahan said. "Or you could throw in with me 'n make yourself anywhere from ten to fifty thousand dollars. And when I say fifty thousand, I'm talkin' about your cut."

O'Leary drummed his fingers on the table for a moment before he responded. "You got somethin' in mind?" he asked.

"Yeah, I got somethin' in mind."

"I hope it works out better'n than that train holdup you just tried the other day."

Callahan blinked in surprise. "How do you know about that?"

"This is a railroad town," O'Leary replied. "Ever'body all up 'n down the track knows about the four men who wrecked the train, kilt some people, 'n didn't get away with any of the money. 'N the leader of the group, they say, was a big man with a broken nose 'n a scrunched-up ear. I figured that was you."

"We didn't kill nobody," Callahan said.

"They was kilt in the wreck, so you same as kilt 'em."

"Yeah, well, that didn't work out all that well, I admit, but what I got in mind now will."

"Why are you askin' me to join you? I don't remember us bein' all such good friends that you just want to give me fifty thousand dollars."

"I'm askin' because I'm goin' to need you in order to make it work. Seein' as you are the one that first come up with the idea. 'N I know you've studied on it some."

"I'll be damn!" O'Leary said with a broad smile. "You're talkin' 'bout the First Federal Bank of Cheyenne, ain't you?"

"Like you said, that's where all the money is."

"Railroad money," O'Leary replied. "Ha! Wait, there ain't no way me and you could do this by ourselves, though. Let me ask you this. Them men that was with you for the train robbery, have they run off on you? Or do you still have 'em?"

"I've still got 'em."

"That makes five of us then," O'Leary said. "Yeah, that should be enough to do the job."

"I'll also be wantin' you to scout the bank out for us." Callahan put his hand to his nose. "They's been enough descriptions of me writ up in newspapers lately that if I was to go into a bank 'n just start lookin' aroun', could be that someone could get a little suspicious."

"I've already checked it out half a dozen times," O'Leary said. "But now that I know it's actual goin' to happen, I'll be glad to scout it out again."

Rock Creek

Duff, Meagan, and Ina Claire were waiting at the Rock Creek depot when the train pulled into the station. They watched as the passengers stepped down. Elmer and Wang were not among them.

"Oh," Ina Claire said. "Do you think they missed the train?"

Duff pointed to the stock car, which was located just before the baggage car. An inclined access had been lowered from the car to the platform, and Elmer and Wang were leading their horses down the ramp.

"Oh, there they are!" Ina Claire said happily. "Mr. Gleason! Mr. Wang!" she called loudly.

Elmer looked over toward her and smiled.

A moment later he and Wang joined Duff and the others.

"Hello, darlin'," Elmer said.

"Elmer, I know we are friends, but you dinnae need to be callin' me darlin'," Duff said.

For just a moment Elmer looked surprised, then they all laughed.

"I was hoping you would send for me," Elmer said. "And after those three came lookin' for you, me 'n Wang made up our minds that we would come find you whether you sent for us or not."

"I'm a little surprised that it was only three men who came after me," Duff said. "It could have been seven."

"Yeah. Well it was three, 'n we tried to tell 'em you wasn't there, but the sons of bitches wouldn't take no for an answer." Elmer slapped his hand over his mouth. "Oh, damn, I cussed in front of you ladies again, didn't I? I'm sorry as hell. I won't do it again."

Duff laughed. "Elmer, dinnae be making promises ye can't keep."

"I'll damn well try 'n keep that promise. Son of a bitch, I just done it again, didn't I?"

This time everyone, including Wang, laughed.

"A medicine wagon?" Elmer asked, looking at the bright red and gold vehicle. "Are you tellin' me you three has been travelin' around in somethin' like this, lookin' for Callahan 'n his bunch?"

"Indeed we have."

"Ha! I reckon you didn't want him to see you comin'."

"Aye, that was my intention."

"Duff MacCallister, that don't make no sense at all. Hell, they could see this comin' from a mile away."

"The eye that sees large will not see small," Wang said.

"Now there you go again, sayin' somethin' that there don't nobody understand," Elmer said.

"I understand what he is saying," Ina Claire said.

"Well then, darlin', I wish you would explain it to me."

Ina Claire smiled. "It means that someone will see the medicine wagon, and because it is gaudy, and different from any other wagon, the wagon and the show become the whole thing and the people of the wagon are overlooked."

Wang smiled. "*Xiaojie* Ina Claire has the beauty of a new bloom and the wisdom of an ancient sage."

"What you are sayin' is, this little girl is smarter'n me?" Elmer asked.

Duff laughed. "Elmer, I dinnae believe for a minute he is saying that. I told you before that I consider you one of the smartest people I know."

"Now how can you say that when I got near-'bout no book-learnin' at all? Oh, wait, what was that word you used? You said I ate knowledge, or somethin' like that."

"The word that I used was innate. Knowledge is preserved in books. Intelligence is inherent," Duff said.

"Now if you ain't beginnin' to sound just like Wang, talkin' in riddles like that."

Meagan put her hand on Elmer's shoulder. "It means that you are far smarter than the mere words you can find in a book."

Elmer looked at the others, then he smiled. Making a fist, he raised it so that his thumb was pointing back toward his chest. "Well, this here smart feller thanks all of you for your kind words."

"Duff, now that Elmer and Wang are here, do we continue to travel with the medicine wagon?" Meagan asked.

"Aye, I think for a while longer anyway, at

least until Callahan and the others do something else so we can follow up on their action."

That night the little group camped by the medicine wagon just outside of Medicine Bow. Wang had prepared their supper for them, and everyone enjoyed the meal, especially the wontons and the egg rolls. After the meal all gathered around the campfire, which they kept burning by occasionally feeding it another small log. The fire put out a golden bubble of light and snapped and popped anytime the little trapped gas bubbles in the firewood were ignited.

"Meagan, how did you and Duff meet?" Ina Claire asked.

"We met because of a mirror," Meagan replied.

"A mirror?"

Duff chuckled. "Aye, lass, 'twas a mirror she was holding that caused us to meet. And 'tis a good thing, too, because without the mirror, I might have been killed."

Ina Claire got a confused look on her face. "How did holding a mirror save his life?"

"A lot of men had come to town," Meagan replied. "They were evil men, bound on killing Duff, but they didn't care who else they killed. So the town, as much as Duff, was being held in siege that day."

"One o' the men who came to town that day was a brigand by the name o' Rab Malcolm," Duff said. "He had killed someone close to me back in Scotland, 'n came to America with the Somerled brothers to kill me here. I killed the two brothers in New York, 'n then I got away from Malcolm, thinking he would go back to Scotland. But he didn't. He came all the way to Chugwater to finish what he had started, and he hired some killers to come with him."

"What does that have to do with a mirror?"

"Hold your horses, Ina Claire, I'm getting to it," Meagan said. "Anyway Duff MacCallister knew the men were in town waiting for him, so he came in playing 'Scotland the Brave' on his pipes; a lone knight, you might say, standing up against the dragons of evil. There were evil men hiding behind the corners of the buildings, one up on top of Fiddler's Green hiding behind the false front, and two more inside the saloon itself.

"Then I saw two more men lying on the ground behind the watering trough, just in front of my shop. They cocked their pistols and started toward the edge of the trough. I didn't really know Duff then, I just knew that he was one of the bravest men I had ever seen, taking on all of these men by himself. If he had no idea these men were here, they would have an advantage over him, and I couldn't let that happen."

"I know what happened," Ina Claire said. "You yelled at him, you warned him."

Meagan smiled. "Now, who is telling this story? You or me?"

"You are," Ina Claire agreed.

"I had a customer in the store at the time. It was Mrs. Riley, and before the shooting started, she had been standing for a fitting in front of a full-length mirror. That's when I got my idea, so I told her to move into the back of the shop until all the excitement was over. Then I unscrewed the knobs that held the dressing mirror on the frame and carried it to the front. Standing in the front of my shop, I turned that mirror on its side so that it had a lengthwise projection. I held it there, praying that Duff would see it."

"Here now, woman, 'n would ye be for letting me finish the story, seeing as what happened next happened to me?"

"You've got the floor," Meagan said, making a little sweep with her hand.

"What Meagan didn't tell you is that I was behind a watering trough myself," Duff said. "But my trough was on the opposite side of the street. I slithered on my stomach to the edge, then peered around it. The first place I looked was toward Fiddler's Green to see if I was going to have any trouble there, but the saloon was quiet. Then, looking across the street, I saw a woman in the window of the dress shop. I'd never met the lass, but I had seen her before. She was the same pretty woman I had seen step down from the stagecoach the first day I came into town. I wanted to yell at her, to tell her to get down, that she was being foolish exposing herself as she was.

"Then I saw exactly what she was doing. She was holding a mirror, and looking in the mirror I could see that there were two men lying on the ground behind the watering trough that was directly across the street from me. I had no idea they had been there, and had Meagan not held up the mirror so I could see them, 'twould have been easy enough for them to shoot me.

"I watched as one started moving toward the end of the trough in order to take a look, and I aimed my pistol at the edge of the trough and waited.

" 'MacCallister!' Malcolm called from the darkness of the saloon. Malcolm, ye see, was the evil black heart who had come all the way from Scotland to kill me.

'MacCallister!' he called again. 'Why don't you come back out into the street, and I will as well? We can face each other down, just as Western men do. Oh, yes, I know all about the Western gunfighters, I have read of them in dime novels. What do you say? Just the two of us, alone in the street?'

" 'You don't expect me to believe that, do you?' I called back.

" 'Believe what?'

" 'That it would just be the two of us.'

"Malcolm laughed. 'Ye think that because I have friends with me, that I would be for taking unfair advantage of ye, MacCallister? Alas, that is probably true. Tell me, what does it feel like to know that you won't live long enough to see the sun set tonight?'

"All the while Malcolm was talking, I was keeping one eye on the mirror and the other on the corner of the watering trough. Then my vigil was rewarded. When I saw the brim of a hat appear, I cocked my pistol and waited.

"That was when I saw the man's eye appear, I aimed, and touched the trigger. Looking in the mirror I saw the man's face fall into the dirt and the gun slip from his hand."

"What about Malcolm?" Ina Claire asked, enthralled by the story. "Did Duff kill 'im?"

428

"No, darlin', I'm the one that killed 'im," Elmer said.

"You killed him? Then you were in town with Duff?"

"No, ma'am, I kilt the son of a bitch when he come out to Sky Meadow to kill Duff."

Duff smiled. "Elmer's telling the truth. Malcolm was about to kill me, 'n Elmer it was that saved my life."

"Oh, my, that's a story you and Meagan can tell your grandchildren!" Ina Claire said.

Duff and Meagan smiled at each other.

CHAPTER THIRTY-FOUR

Centennial, Wyoming Territory

Callahan and his men were camped about three miles outside of the small town of Centennial. One hour earlier the sun had set to be replaced by a vault of stars, from bright pin points of light that seemed close enough to reach up and pluck from the night sky, all the way down to a light blue dusting so faint that individual stars could not be seen. The moon was a brilliant silver orb, bright enough so that the Medicine Bow Mountains were quite visible. Within the campsite itself, the small fire projected a tiny bubble of wavering orange light.

There were five men squatting around the fire, drinking coffee and eating hardtack that had been fried in bacon grease. Near the encampment an owl hooted his displeasure at having his space invaded. Farther away they could hear the howl of a coyote.

They had come to Centennial to rob a bank.

"There ain't all that much money here," Callahan explained. "But we're down to practically no money at all, and we're goin' to need some money to get us by 'til we hit the big bank in Cheyenne."

"If there ain't that much money in this bank, why is it we're a-robbin' it?" Morris asked. "Why ain't we a-robbin' a bank that has a lot more money?"

"They's lots of reasons why it is that we're robbin' this bank," Callahan said. "First of all, like I said, we need the money. And second, on account of this bank is real little 'n all, it ain't never been robbed 'cause there ain't never been no one who thought it was worth robbin'. What that means is, there won't be nobody expectin' it to get robbed.

"But the third reason, 'n this is a good one, the man that built this bank is the same man that built the First Federal Bank in Cheyenne. This is a lot smaller bank than the one in Cheyenne, but they are both laid out just the same, so robbin' this one will give us a good practice," Callahan said.

"Why do we need to practice? Robbin' a bank is robbin' a bank, ain't it?" Cooper asked. "What I'm sayin' is, why waste time with a little bank, when we could just rob the one in Cheyenne 'n be done with it?"

"Have you ever seen a football game, Cooper?" O'Leary asked.

"A football game? No, I've heard of football, but I ain't never seen me no game," Cooper replied. "Why did you ask me that? What the hell does a football game have to do with robbin' a bank?"

"Well, football games is most played by colleges 'n such back in the East, but I've seen me a couple of 'em. It has a lot to do with robbin' a bank. You see, here's the thing about football. You have a team, and that team has to do everything together, sort of have it worked out in advance so as they know what ever'one is goin' to do.

"That's what we'll have to do when we hold up that bank in Cheyenne, 'n it's what we'll be doin' when we hold up the bank here in Centennial. We'll be practicin' so that when we hit the bank in Cheyenne, we'll know exactly what ever'one is to do."

"Yeah, well, I say let's hold up this here bank," Manning said. "I'm kinda anxious to have some money again."

"First thing we need to do is scout it out," Callahan said.

In the small town of Centennial, the bank, made of brick, stood out on a street that was lined on both sides with somewhat flimsy looking buildings, thrown together from rip-sawed lumber. Some of them were leaning so that it looked as if a good stiff wind would knock them over. The sound of the hoof falls of so many horses echoed back from the buildings.

The fact that there were five men riding together didn't attract all that much attention, as cowboys from the nearby ranches often came into town in similar sized groups. The few citizens who were out on the board sidewalks, strolling from store to store, paid the riders no mind.

"Let's do it and be gone," Manning suggested.

"Wait a minute, wait a minute," Callahan said, holding up his hand. "Remember, we're goin' to do this one just the same way as iffen it was the bank in Cheyenne we was robbin'. So that means that the first thing we're goin' to do is take a ride up and down the street first, just to take a look around at ever'thing."

"Yes, that's a very good idea," O'Leary said.

"Cooper, while we're ridin' down the street, I want you 'n Morris to be lookin' out at ever'one you see on the left side. Pay particular attention to anyone you see carryin' a gun 'n make a count of 'em. Manning, you 'n O'Leary will be doin' the same thing on the right side o' the street."

"What'll you be doin'?" Cooper asked.

"I'll be keepin' my eyes on the middle of the street, just in case anyone comes ridin' up."

The five men rode slowly down the entire length of the street, then they turned their horses and rode back.

"All right, what did you see?" Callahan asked.

"Me 'n Manning seen three that was wearin' guns on this side of the street," Cooper said.

"We only seen one on this side," O'Leary added.

"Any of them look like they knew how to use them?"

"The old fart on my side looked like he didn't even have the strength to pull his gun out of the holster, let alone use it," O'Leary said.

"Cooper?"

"No," Cooper answered. "They didn't none of 'em look like they knew much more'n which end of the gun the bullet come out."

"Hell, I coulda tole you soon as we come into town that we wasn't goin' to find nobody on the street to worry about," Morris said.

"That's prob'ly true," Callahan agreed. "But remember, we're doin' this as practice. When we get to Cheyenne, we'll need to do the same thing as we just done, only Cheyenne bein' bigger, they's goin' to be lots more people that's not only wearin' guns but that also knows how to use 'em."

"Yeah," Cooper said, nodding. "Yeah, I see what you mean."

"Well, then, boys, what do you say we go into the bank here 'n get us a little travelin' money?" Callahan suggested. "Manning, you stay out with the horses."

Stopping in front of the bank, Callahan, Cooper, O'Leary, and Morris swung down from their horses and handed the reins over to Manning, who remained mounted. He held the reins of all the horses with his left hand while in his right he held his pistol, though he kept it low and out of sight.

When the four men went into the bank, Morris and Cooper went to either side, taking a position in the corner where the guards would be in the First Federal Bank. O'Leary stepped to the end of the counter and glanced toward the vault.

The teller was the only other person in the bank, and he looked up at the strange actions of the four men with an expression on his face that reflected as much fear as curiosity.

"Gentlemen, I'm the only one here now, so if you'll just line up in front of my window, I'll take care of all of you."

"You'll take care of all of us now," Callahan said. He pulled his pistol, which was the signal for the others to pull their guns as well. It really wasn't necessary for them to draw their weapons, but this was a practice run for the bigger bank with its bigger reward, later.

"What? What is this?" the teller asked, his voice quavering with fright.

"Well, now, you seem like an intelligent enough man to me. I'm sure that you have figured by now, haven't you, that this is a holdup?" Callahan asked. He handed a cloth bag to the teller. "Empty out your bank drawer and put all the money in this here bag!"

Nervously, the teller began to reply, emptying his drawer in just a few seconds.

"This is all there is," the teller said, holding the bag back toward Callahan.

"That's all you have in the cash drawer," Callahan said with a smile. "And you did that very well. Now, I'll be asking you to give us everything you have in the vault."

"I can't do that," the teller said.

"I can see the vault," O'Leary called over from his position at the end of the counter. "The vault door is open."

"Oh, well, that means you can do it," Callahan said.

"No, you don't understand. I'm just the teller, I don't have the authorization to take any money from the vault. Only Mr. Matthews can do that."

"That's all right," Callahan replied easily. "We don't really need you. Since the door to the vault is open, we can just kill you and help ourselves."

"No!" the teller shouted quickly. He reached for the cloth sack. "Give me the sack, I'll fill it."

"I thought you might see things my way," Callahan replied with an evil smile.

The teller began taking bound packets of money from a shelf in the vault and dropping them into the sack. A moment later he returned with the sack full and handed it to Callahan.

"It's been a pleasure doing business with you," Callahan said with an evil smile.

"All right, men, let's go."

The teller, who now had his hands up, watched as the four men did a strange thing. They fired their guns into all four corners of the bank, though there was nothing there for them to shoot at. They also shot toward the vault, and the bullets whined as they ricocheted off the heavy steel door.

Leaving the bank, the four men mounted the horses Manning was holding for them, then they rode out of town, firing their pistols to either side of the street, forcing those who were outside to flee into or around the corners of the buildings.

The people were so shocked by the sight of five men galloping down the street and firing their pistols indiscriminately, that not one of the armed citizens of the town thought to shoot back.

"What ranch did them crazy cowboys come from?" someone asked angrily, as the five men, now beyond the town limits, galloped away. "Somebody needs to talk to the boss of those fools."

"Help!" someone shouted, running out to the street in front of the bank.

"See here, ain't that Rick Adams?" someone asked.

"Help!" Adams shouted again.

"What is it he's a-yellin' about?"

"Help!" Adams shouted again. "The bank has been robbed!"

The five outlaws left Centennial with no

one in pursuit. Riding south, they reached the Little Laramie River, then turning west, they followed the river valley into the Medicine Bow Mountains. Once they were well into the valley, Callahan called for a stop.

The men dismounted, and the horses moved to the river for water.

"All right, let's see how we did," Callahan said, dumping the money from the cloth bag. As the others watched, eagerly, he began counting. It took less than a minute, but the results were rewarding, more rewarding than any previous job had been.

"Five thousand seven hundred and fifteen dollars," Callahan said with a wide smile.

"Hey, that's pretty good!" Cooper said. "That's more'n a thousand dollars apiece for each of us!"

"Yeah, well, you wait until we hit the bank in Cheyenne," Callahan said. "We'll be rich enough to open our own bank."

"No, I don't want to do that. What if somebody like us was to come along 'n rob us?" Manning asked.

The others laughed.

"When we goin' to do it?" Cooper asked.

"It's up to Red here, he's the one that's been studyin' it."

"Not the next Wednesday, but Wednesday

week from now," O'Leary replied.

"Why then?" Manning asked.

"On account of that's the second Wednesday of the month, 'n it's always the second Wednesday whenever the railroad brings in all the money that they need for paying folks and buyin' things. It ain't never less than a hunnert thousand, 'n lots of times it's over two hunnert thousand."

"Damn!" Cooper said. "I can't hardly wait!"

CHAPTER THIRTY-FIVE

Medicine Bow

Duff finished playing the pipes, as Ina Claire drummed, and they both acknowledged the crowd's applause.

"And now, ladies 'n gentlemen, ye are about to see an act so dangerous that ye will marvel at the courage of the young lady who will be putting her life on the line, 'n the steadiness of the young man who will be demonstrating his skill. Ladies, if ye be a bit frightened by the sight of danger, it might be best for ye to shut your eyes until the demonstration is completed."

Elmer brought out a large, wooden square, about seven feet high and four feet wide. The two-by-six boards that made up the square were painted gray, but there was a red outline drawn onto the board, the outline done in the curves of a woman's body.

When the board was in place, beside the

wagon, Meagan, Ina Claire, and Wang Chow stepped out. With a smile toward the audience, whose faces reflected their curiosity, Meagan backed up against the board, positioning herself inside the red outline.

Meagan and Ina Claire were both wearing their "show dresses," which were cut and designed to show off their svelte figures. Wang was wearing wide, white silk trousers, and a white silk blouse with a long tail.

Ina Claire was holding a golden bucket and she and Wang stepped off a distance of about forty feet from Meagan. Ina Claire reached into the bucket, pulled out a knife, and handed it to Wang.

"What's he a-plannin' on doin' with that Arkansas toothpick?" someone asked.

With a quick flip of his wrist, the knife flew from Wang's hand and stuck in the board, very close to Meagan.

The audience gasped as they witnessed the first throw, and a few shouted out loud.

Wang tossed a second knife.

"I can't watch this!" a woman in the crowd said. "He can't miss her every time!"

Wang continued to throw the knives, and the crowd eventually stopped gasping and just watched in fascinated silence until the last knife was thrown.

"Now, Miss Meagan, 'n would ye be for

steppin' away from the board and take your bow, now?" Duff called down from the lowered tailgate.

Meagan stepped away, and when she did so the people in the crowd gasped again, but this time in wonder. The red outline on the board was now augmented with the addition of fourteen knives, each knife perfectly placed, not only on the outline but within the red line itself.

"Ladies and gentlemen, I present to you the honorable Wang Chow, who as priest of the Shaolin temple was a personal bodyguard to the Quing emperor."

Wang made a perfunctory bow to the crowd, who returned a generous applause.

As a result of the new addition to the show the crowds grew much larger, and in a town like Medicine Bow, which was one of the larger of the railroad towns, they drew two hundred people, the biggest crowd since they had begun doing the shows.

"Aren't you scared when Mr. Wang throws all those knives at you?" Ina Claire asked Meagan. It was night, and they were camped halfway between Medicine Bow and Carbon, which would be their next stop.

"No," Meagan said. "I know how skilled Wang is, and I know if he had to err, he would err on the side of my safety."

"Err?" Elmer asked. "Does that mean make a mistake?"

"Yes."

Elmer chuckled. "You don't have to worry none about that," he said. "Wang don't make no mistakes, never."

Meagan smiled at Elmer's grammar. "Well, that's good to know," she said.

"I oncet knowed me a feller, an able-bodied seaman he was, on board the *Sara Sue*. He fancied hisself to be real good at throwin' a knife. And he was right good with a knife, too, but he warn't nowhere near as good as Wang is."

"What's the *Sara Sue*?" Ina Claire asked.

"The *Sara Sue* was a ship, darlin', a clipper ship, and the finest ever to sail the seven seas. Why, I was on board her when she sailed from San Francisco to Singapore in only forty-two days."

"My, that must have been fun."

"Tyin' yourself to the mizzen mast so's that you don't blow over in a typhoon ain't exactly what I would call fun, but it was interestin'."

"And it has given you stories to tell," Meagan said. "Vi says you have told her a lot of the most wonderful stories."

Vi Winslow was a widow who owned Vi's

Pies, and she and Elmer often "kept company."

"Ahh, don't listen to ever'thing Vi tells you," Elmer said. "Sometimes she kinda stretches the stories out some."

"Ha, that's funny," Meagan said. "That's exactly what I told her about you."

The others laughed.

"Say, Duff, how long are we goin' to stick with this medicine show thing before we start out after Callahan 'n his bunch?" Elmer asked.

Duff was holding a long stick that he used to poke into the fire.

"I don't know," he replied. "I have to confess that it's nae working out like I hoped it would. I'm about ready to drop this whole idea 'n try something else."

When they rolled into Carbon the next day Duff went to see the deputy sheriff as soon as they arrived in town.

"Yeah? What can I do for you?" the deputy asked.

" 'Tis hoping I am that ye can do a lot for me, Deputy," Duff said. This time, rather than using the ruse of acquiring a permit to put on a show, Duff was straight with him.

"The name is MacCallister," he started, but before he could get any further, the deputy interrupted him.

"MacCallister? Would you be Falcon MacCallister? What are you doing in Wyoming? I thought your territory was Colorado."

"Och, so ye've heard of my cousin, Falcon, have ye?"

"Your cousin, is it? Well, Mr. MacCallister, from all I've heard, your cousin, Falcon MacCallister, is one hell of a man. If you're one-half of the man he is, you'll be somethin' to behold. Stiles is the name, Deputy Morgan Stiles. So, I'll ask you again, what can I do for you?"

Duff took the governor's commission papers from his pocket. "As ye can see by this document, Deputy, Governor Hoyt has commissioned me 'n four o' my friends as special state officers."

Duff didn't tell the deputy that two of his group were female, nor did he say that, technically, Elmer and Wang had not actually been commissioned by the governor. Duff had just assumed the right to deputize them, figuring he could take it up with the governor later if it ever became a question.

"We're looking for four men; Clay Callahan, Zeke Manning, Dooley Cooper, and Pogue Morris."

Stiles nodded. "Yes, I can see why the

governor is after them, seeing as two of them, Callahan and Manning, escaped hanging. And of course, from all the information I've been getting, they've been running roughshod ever since. They even picked up three more men recently. It was seven of 'em that held up a stagecoach not too long ago."

"Aye, but three of the seven have since been killed," Duff said. "There's only the original four again, and they wrecked a train, killing the engineer and some of the passengers."

"That was them, huh? Well, I heard about the train robbery, only it turned out not to be a robbery. From ever'thing I have heard, they didn't get nothin' from the holdup."

"That's correct."

"I reckon you'll be wantin' to know what the latest information I've got on 'em is," Stiles said, "but you already know that, bein' as it is about the train robbery. I ain't heard nothin' else on 'em since."

"All right, Deputy, I do thank you for your time," Duff said.

After doing their show in Carbon, Duff decided to head back east. To that end he booked passage on the train, not only for them and their horses, but also for the mules and the medicine wagon. Several days earlier, Duff, Meagan, and Ina Claire had done a show in Laramie, but when they returned to Laramie today, they were neither in the wagon nor in costume, and as a result, nobody made the connection between those who rode into town today and the people who had presented the show. It also helped that Elmer and Wang were with them now, and they had not been with them before.

Off-loading the wagon, they stored it on the depot grounds and boarded the mules in the livery.

"Have we given up the medicine show?" Meagan asked.

"Aye, for now at least," Duff said. "I think we can cover more ground on horseback than driving the wagon."

"I liked the wagon," Ina Claire said. "I thought it was fun."

"I did, too," Meagan said. "But what I really liked was seeing Duff in his costume."

"Och, woman, dinnae ye be bedeviling me so," Duff said, but his smile softened his words.

"Well now, 'n would ye be for looking at this paper?" Duff suggested, holding up a copy of the *Laramie Boomerang*.

"What is it?"

"I believe it may be a story about the brigands we are chasing," Duff replied. "If it is, they did a little better this time."

BANK ROBBERY IN CENTENNIAL

Word has come to the *Boomerang* that on six days previous, the Centennial Bank was robbed. The exact amount hasn't been disclosed, but it is believed that the five outlaws got away with a little over six thousand dollars.

No one was killed or wounded in the robbery, but it is reported that the robbers did a very strange thing before they departed.

Though there were no security guards in the bank, and indeed only the teller, Rick Adams, was present, the robbers fired their guns into every corner of the bank before they departed with their ill-gotten gains.

"This can't be them," Meagan said. "According to this newspaper article, there were five of them."

"They picked up another man," Duff said.

"What makes you think it's them? There are no descriptions of any of them," Ina Claire asked.

"Because I feel it," Duff replied.

Meagan chuckled. "You feel it?"

"Aye. 'Tis hoping I am that ye be ready for a bit of a ride, for I think we should go to Centennial and visit with Mr. Adams, and anyone else who can give some useful information."

"I'm ready!" Ina Claire said enthusiastically.

"Child, I think you were born ready," Meagan said with a little laugh.

That night they camped on the Little Laramie River.

"Duff, before it gets dark, I would like to take a bath," Meagan said.

"Yes," Ina Claire said. "Me too!"

"All right," Duff agreed. "Elmer, Wang, and I will act as sentinels to ensure your privacy."

Half an hour later the two came back from the river, scrubbed and in clean clothes. They had also washed the clothes they had been wearing.

"I don't know how we are going to dry these," Meagan said, "but they were getting so dirty they just had to be washed."

"I can dry them," Wang said.

"How?"

Wang walked away from the others and began moving among the trees and low-lying shrubs, occasionally leaning over to cut something with his knife. A few minutes later he returned and constructed a wooden frame alongside the campfire. Then he took the trousers and shirts Meagan and Ina Claire had washed, and spread them out on the frame.

"They will be dry by tomorrow," he said.

As Wang had promised, the clothes were dry the next morning.

CHAPTER THIRTY-SIX

When the five of them rode into Centennial the next morning, there was a noticeable unease at their presence.

"Damn, here they are again!" someone said.

"Now it ain't. One of these is a China-man, 'n two of 'em is women."

For a moment Duff was confused by the comment, then he remembered that it was five riders who had come into town to rob the bank, and in a town this small it was probably rare for as many as five riders to come in at the same time. It was just a co-incidence that the numbers matched.

It was nearly lunchtime, so they stopped in front of a red-painted building that had a sign in front reading LITTLE MAN'S RES-TAURANT.

There weren't more than half a dozen customers in the restaurant, and they looked up as Duff and the others entered. Their faces reflected the same curiosity and concern that Duff had seen out on the street.

A man wearing an apron approached them. He was somewhat rotund and quite short, shorter even than Ina Claire. Duff was sure this must be Little Man.

Little Man's approach was cautious, and his face reflected his disquiet until he was close enough to ascertain that two of his new customers were women, then a smile spread across his face. It was also then that he noticed one of his new customers was Chinese, and he blinked in surprise but the smile didn't fade.

" 'Tis my hope that ye'll be having nae trouble in serving us," Duff said.

"Trouble?" Little Man replied. "Oh, you mean because one of you is a celestial? No, if he can eat American food, I got no trouble."

Wang, who very rarely showed a change of expression, smiled.

"I can eat American food," he said.

"How come you didn't ask Duff if he can eat American food? He ain't no American, neither, bein' as he's Scotsman, which you'll figger out if you listen to him talk some. I'm the only one who is American," Elmer said.

"You are the only one who is American?" Meagan asked. "So tell me, Elmer, is it your belief that Ina Claire and I are French?"

"No, you ain't French 'n there ain't nobody a-said that you was, only the thing is, you 'n Ina Claire is both women," Elmer replied.

"See there, Ina Claire, that's the second time someone has said that we are women. I'm beginning to believe that perhaps we really are women."

Ina Claire chuckled.

Little Man followed the dialogue with a confused expression on his face, then he smiled. "Well, just so's that you know, you're all mighty welcome. I made up a big pot of chicken and dumplin's today. You take a bowl o' that 'n a biscuit, 'n you got yourself one fine meal and I got me no problem a-tall in a-tellin' you that, even if I did make it myself."

"Then chicken and dumplings it will be," Duff said.

Because the chicken and dumplings had already been cooked, it took very little time for Little Man to deliver the food to the table. The food was good, and the conversation among them was quiet, mostly pertaining to the food. But as they were eating, Duff noticed that one of the men sitting at another table seemed to be paying them an inordinate amount of attention. When the man stood up and started toward them, Duff wasn't surprised.

Duff was buttering a biscuit when the man reached his table.

"How do ye do, sir," Duff asked.

"I know you folks ain't just passin' through Centennial," the man said. "I know that 'cause folks don't just pass through here, seein' as we ain't on the way to nowhere. That means if you are in Centennial, you come here of a pure purpose."

"Aye, that would be correct," Duff replied.

"So my question to you is, who are you, and what are you doin' here?"

"Here now," Duff replied. "I ask your forgiveness if I am misinterpreting your question, but it sounded to me as if there was a bit more of a demand than curiosity in the query."

"What kind of accent is that?"

"Ain't you never been nowhere, Sonny, that you don't recognize a Scotsman when you hear one?" Elmer asked. He topped off his question with a bite from his own biscuit.

"Scotch, are you?"

"Nae, scotch would be the drink," Duff replied. "If 'tis someone from Scotland, the proper word would be Scotsman."

"Yeah? Well I've no need to be taught English by a Scotchman and a Chinaman. And you didn't answer my question, so I'll ask again. Who are you, 'n what are you doing in town?"

"Rawlins, what are you doin' harassin' those folks?" a stern voice called from the door. The man who called out was a fairly good-sized man with broad shoulders and a square jaw.

"Ain't you none a-tall curious about it, Marshal Cummins?" Rawlins replied. "I mean, the last time five people come ridin' into town, look what happened. They held up the bank, 'n ever'one in town lost money."

The marshal pointed to Duff's table.

"I seen 'em when they come in," he said. "They's two women and a Chinaman with 'em. These damn sure ain't the same five. Now you get back to your table 'n quit botherin' these folks."

"I'm just lookin' out for the town is all," Rawlins replied.

"Lookin' out for the town is my job," Marshal Cummins said.

"Yeah? Well you didn't do so damn well last time, did you?"

"One more word out of you, Rawlins, and

I'll put you in jail for disturbin' the peace," the marshal said.

With a shrug of his shoulders, Rawlins returned to his table, and the marshal approached Duff.

"I'm Marshal Cummins," he said. "I'm sorry 'bout Rawlins, there, but I guess you can understand it, knowin' that he 'n a lot of folks lost some considerable money when the bank was held up."

"Marshal, if ye don't mind," Duff said, "we'd like to be for comin' by your office soon as we finish our meal and discuss that bank robbery with ye."

"Oh? Any particular reason you want to discuss a bank robbery?"

"Aye," Duff replied. "We are special law enforcement agents for the governor. I have our commission, which I'll be glad to show ye."

Marshal Cummins looked at the two women. "You all have appointments from the governor?"

"Aye, that we do."

"You'll pardon my askin', but why would the governor appoint a couple of women to such a position?"

"I'll explain it all when we visit with you," Duff said.

The marshal stroked his chin for a mo-

457

ment. "All right. My office is about four buildings down from here, just on the other side of the street. Come along when you've finished eating."

Half an hour later Duff and the others were in the marshal's office. The marshal had found chairs for Meagan and Ina Claire. He, Duff, Elmer, and Wang were standing.

"Excuse me, miss," Cummins said to Ina Claire. "It's strange enough to me to think that the governor would appoint women as special law officers, but you? How old are you, anyway?"

Duff showed the marshal Ina Claire's commission.

"As ye can see, she is old enough," Duff said without being more specific.

"All right, all right, I was just curious is all. And you did say that you would tell me why the governor would appoint a couple of women as state law officers."

"He appointed them because they can identify the bank robbers on sight."

"Oh? You know who they are, do you?"

"Aye. Their names are Clay Callahan, Zeke Manning, Dooley Cooper, and Pogue Morris."

"There were five of them," Marshal Cummins said. "You didn't name the fifth one."

"We don't know who the fifth one was."

"How is it that you know four of them? When I sent out word of the bank robbery, I didn't name any of 'em 'cause I didn't have no idea."

"Are ye for tellin' me, Marshal, that ye have no wanted posters on the men I just named? 'Tis for a fact that I know that they have been distributed all over the territory."

"Well now, could be that I do, but to tell you the truth, mister, I don't pay much attention to any dodgers that might come in here. You see, we are so cut off from everywhere else that we don't hardly ever get no strangers come into town, so postin' 'em, or even studyin' 'em seems like a waste of time. Plus which, we ain't got no telegraph service a-tall, and the stagecoach only comes about twice a month."

"Then let me ask ye this. Do ye have a description of the bank robbers?"

"Yeah, that we do have. Rick Adams, he's the teller, 'n seein' as how there didn't none of them robbers wear no kind of mask or anythin', why he got a real good look at all of 'em. Well actually he only got a good look at four of 'em. One of 'em stayed out front o' the bank, holdin' on to the horses, whilest the others was all inside the bank a-robbin' it."

"Do ye suppose we could talk to Mr. Adams?" Duff asked.

"Yes, sure, I'll be glad to take you down there 'n introduce you to him. Rick Adams is a fine man, as fine as any man in Centennial. He'll be glad to tell you anything you need to know."

"I didn't know there were five of them until later," Rick Adams said. "There were four who came into the bank. One was a big man with a flat nose, and sort of a scrunched-up ear. One had a real bad scar down his face, and one had red hair. To be honest I didn't see anything that was particular about the fourth one inside, and I didn't see the one that waited outside at all."

Duff nodded. "It's them, all right."

"Except for the one with red hair," Ina Claire said. "I don't remember anyone with red hair."

"That has to be the new man they picked up," Duff said.

As Duff, Meagan, Ina Claire, and Marshal Cummins were talking with Adams, Elmer and Wang were looking at the four corners of the bank. There were bullet holes in every corner. Wang used his knife, then dug one of the bullets out of the wall and brought it back to Duff.

"It looks like a .44," Duff said, taking the bullet from Wang.

"Yeah, that's what I'd say as well," Elmer added, examining the bullet that lay in Duff's hand.

"Tell me, Mr. Adams, did I read in the newspaper article that before they left the bank they shot into every corner?"

"Yes, sir, that's what they did, all right."

"And why would they be for doing such a thing?"

Rick Adams shook his head. "I don't have the slightest idea unless maybe it was to intimidate me. But I tell you truthfully, sir, I was already intimidated. I was more than intimidated. I was downright frightened."

Duff looked around at the layout of the bank.

"I don't believe I have ever been in here before," he said.

"No, sir, I don't think you have. At least, not since I have worked here, and I've been here for ten years."

Duff stroked his chin as he continued to look around the bank, then he shook his head. "I've nae been here before that's for sure. But 'tis like sometimes you get the notion that you have seen something or been to a place 'n you know it's not possible."

"Yeah," Elmer said. "I've done that before."

"I'm feeling that now," Duff said. "I know I've been in this bank before, but I also know that I haven't been."

"Now, don't you go gettin' all strange on me, Duff. It's bad enough I have to listen to Wang say things like that. How can you know that you've been in the bank before, 'n also know that you ain't never been here?"

"I don't know," Duff answered. "I just know that I have been here, even though I've never been here before."

"Duff, I'm with Elmer on this one," Meagan said, the tone of her voice indicating her confusion. "I don't have any idea what you are talking about."

"I don't, either," Duff said.

Wang cooked again and as they sat around the campfire enjoying their supper that night, Wang showed Ina Claire how to use chopsticks.

"Oh!" she said when she managed to pick up a won ton. "I did it! I did it!"

"There you go, girlie," Elmer said. "Next time you go into a Chinese restaurant, why you'll be usin' them things as good as any celestial."

"I've never been in a Chinese restaurant," Ina Claire said. "I would love to go some day."

"They's a real good one in Cheyenne," Elmer said. "Me 'n Wang have been there lots of times. We'll take you there next time we're in town. We'll take all of you there."

"Can we, Duff?" Ina Claire asked.

"Sure, I don't see any reason why not. Next time we're in Cheyenne we can . . ." Duff paused in mid-sentence. "Cheyenne!" he said aloud. "Cheyenne! That's it!"

"What's it?"

"Cheyenne is where I was in that bank in Centennial before!"

"What do you mean, Cheyenne is where you were in the bank in Centennial before? Duff, you want to take that back to the starting line and run that by me again?"

"The bank in Centennial is smaller than the First Federal Bank of Cheyenne, but it is laid out exactly the same. That's why when I was here I had the feeling I had been there before."

Meagan smiled. "Well, I'm glad you finally figured that out. It's good to see you weren't actually losing your mind."

"That's where Callahan and the others will go next," Duff said.

"What?" Elmer asked. "What makes you

say that?"

"Why do you think they robbed the Centennial Bank?"

"My guess would be because it is a small bank, out of the way of ever'thing, which made it an easy target to rob."

"There are a lot of small, out-of-the-way banks that would be easy to rob," Duff said, "but they chose this one. Why?"

"You got me there, pard, I got no idea why," Elmer replied.

"They were rehearsing," Duff explained. "Mr. Adams said they shot into every corner of the bank, didn't he?" Duff asked.

"Well yeah. Me 'n Wang dug out one of the bullets, remember?"

"Why do you think they did that?"

"Mr. Adams said it was to intimidate him," Meagan said.

Duff shook his head. "No, it was to practice. At the First Federal, there are guards in every corner. I think Callahan intends to kill them."

CHAPTER THIRTY-SEVEN

"You actually think that Callahan plans to rob the First Federal Bank?" Sheriff Sharpies asked.

"Aye, 'tis as sure I am that he'll do it as I am of my own name."

"What makes you think this?"

"I think this because they robbed the bank in Centennial."

The expression on Sheriff Sharpies was one of total confusion.

"I don't understand," he said. "How is it that because he robbed a bank in Centennial that you feel he is going to rob the First Federal?"

"I believe the Centennial robbery was naught but a rehearsal," Duff said. He explained how the layout of the Centennial Bank was a smaller but exact copy of the First Federal Bank. He also told the sheriff how Callahan and the others had shot into the corners of the bank.

"Damn! You may be right!" Sheriff Sharpies said.

"I believe he will be coming here, and when he does, my friends and I will be ready for him."

"If he does come here, and you see him, what do you plan to do?" Sheriff Sharpies asked.

"I'll give him the opportunity to give himself up."

"He and Manning have already been tried, convicted, and sentenced. If we arrest him now, there won't be any need for another trial. We can take him right to the gallows, and he knows it."

"Aye."

"Don't you see what I'm saying? If he knows he is going to hang as soon as we catch him, he isn't going to give himself up."

"I don't expect he will."

"So what you are really saying is, when you see him, you'll kill him."

"It may come to that," Duff agreed.

"When do you think he'll come?"

"It depends upon whether or not we can get cooperation from the railroad, the bank, and the newspaper."

"What do you have in mind?"

"I intend to set a trap for him. But any trap needs bait. And if I can get the railroad, the bank, and the newspaper to go along with my idea, we can not only bait the trap we can establish the time."

Bristol, Colorado
For almost a week now, Callahan and the others had been waiting in the small town of Bristol, just south of the Colorado-Wyoming line. They had taken all their meals in the finest restaurant in town, they had taken rooms in the Colorado Queen Hotel, and they had spent their spare time and no small amount of money on drinks, women, and gambling at the Silver Dollar Saloon.

Callahan had explained their relative wealth by saying that the five of them had brought a herd of their own cattle up from Texas.

"One hundred head at thirty dollars a head," he told the curious patron. "That's three thousand dollars, split five ways, and that comes to six hundred dollars apiece. There ain't none of us ever had that much money at one time before." Callahan laughed. "And the way these boys is spendin' the money here, we ain't likely to have none of it at all left by the time we get back down to Texas."

"Well you just don't worry none about

467

that, cowboy," Sally said. Sally was one of the bar girls who worked at the Silver Dollar. "There's no need for you to be goin' back down to Texas anyway. Me 'n the other girls can give you everything you need right here. Right girls?"

"Right!" the others shouted, each of them making a personal claim on one of the "Texas cowboys" who had money to spend.

It was over supper that night that Callahan saw the newspaper article.

"Damn!" he said. "Look at this article, Red! This is better than we hoped!"

LARGE CASH TRANSFER

The Union Pacific announced today that it will be building a spur line railroad north to Chugwater.

"There are some fine cattle ranches in that area, and we plan to build a rail head closer to the source," C. L. Crawford said. Crawford is in charge of expanding the UP. "I believe such a facility would be mutually beneficial to the cattle ranchers, and to the railroad."

Crawford said that building the new railroad will require an immediate outlay of funds, both for the material needed and for the right-of-way. To that end the railroad is bringing three hundred thousand dollars in cash, which will be held in their account at the First Federal Bank of Cheyenne. The money, which will arrive by special armored rail car Wednesday morning, will remain in the bank for that day only.

"What is today?" Callahan asked.

"Monday."

"Good. That gives us time to get the others out of the saloon and sobered up in time to hit the bank on Wednesday. Sixty thousand dollars apiece!"

"Once we get that, you know every sheriff and marshal in the entire West will be looking for us, don't you?" O'Leary asked.

"Yeah, well, we'll go east. I figure our best bet will be to break up as soon as we have made the cut, then go our separate ways. There are some fine saloons in St. Louis. I figure to buy me one. Hell, this will set me up for the rest of my life."

"I'll be goin' to Ireland," O'Leary said.

"Ireland? Why the hell would you want to go there?"

"I was born there," O'Leary said as if that were explanation enough.

Cheyenne

"I don't know," Robert Dorland said. Dor-

469

land was president of the First Federal Bank.

"What is it you don't know?" Duff asked.

"I don't know if it was a good idea, putting a story in the newspaper that said we had three hundred thousand dollars in cash. Seems to me that is setting up the bank as bait."

"Aye, that is exactly what we are doing."

"It could be dangerous."

"It could be," Duff agreed. "But if all goes well, they won't set foot inside your bank."

"How will that be?"

"The other state marshals and I will stop them on the street as soon as they come into town."

"You can promise me that, can you?"

"That is our plan, but, as they say, the best laid plans of mice and men often go awry."

"What does that mean?" Dorland asked.

"It means we will do our best to stop them before they ever reach the bank," Duff said.

Shortly after leaving the bank, Duff returned to the medicine wagon. He had arranged to have the wagon and team of mules shipped to Cheyenne by rail, and now it was set up on Central Avenue, no more than twenty yards from the front of the bank. Meagan and Ina Claire were already in costume, and Duff stepped into the wagon to get into costume as well.

Elmer was on top of the leather goods store, which was right across the street from the bank, standing behind the false front so he wouldn't be noticed. That position allowed him a good observation, not only of the street but of the entrance into town, from both north and south.

Wang, dressed in Chinese garb, was standing on the porch in front of the apothecary, which was but two buildings down from the bank. Because he wasn't wearing a gun, and he had his arms folded across his chest, he didn't represent a threat to anyone.

There was a sign mounted on a tripod in front of the medicine wagon.

Malcolm Campbell's
Scottish Heather Extract
SHOW BEGINS AT FIVE P.M.
~ *Come one, come all* ~

"When do you think they'll come into town?" Meagan asked.

"I don't expect it'll be too long," Duff said. "If I am right, I think they'll be in town is less than an hour."

"What if you're wrong?" Meagan asked.

Duff smiled. "Then I will be quite embarrassed."

Even as Duff was talking to Meagan, his attention was drawn to a lone rider coming from the south. He rode slowly into town, stopped for a moment in front of the bank, then twisted in his saddle to have a look all around. He was wearing a hat, but the sun fell on a bit of hair that hung from beneath the hat. The hair was bright red.

"As a matter of fact," Duff continued, "I think we will only have to wait another few minutes."

"Why? What makes you think that?" Meagan asked.

Duff nodded toward the red-haired man, who was now leaving town the same way he arrived, toward the south.

"I think they have just sent in their scout," Duff said. "And since I doubt that he saw anything that was suspicious, he will report to the others that all is well."

One mile south of Cheyenne

"What does it look like?" Callahan asked.

"Very quiet," O'Leary said. "You was right to say we should hit it first thing in the mornin'. I rode all the way up 'n down Central Street 'n didn't see hardly nobody at all. 'Bout the only thing I did see was a medicine show."

"A medicine show?"

"Well, it was just the wagon really. Warn't no show goin' on, 'n the sign says there ain't goin' to be one 'til five o'clock this evenin'.'"

"Ha!" Cooper said. "By that time we'll be scattered all to hell 'n gone, 'n ever'one of us will be rich men!"

"How much is it we're a-gettin' again?" Manning asked.

"Sixty thousand dollars apiece," Callahan said.

"I ain't never even knowed nobody that's got that much money," Manning said. "Come on, let's get this done."

"All right, boys," Callahan said. "When we first ride into town, we'll do it same way as we did when we robbed the bank in Centennial. We'll ride from one end of town to the other, and two of you will check ever'thing out on the right, the other two ever'thing on the left, 'n I'll look up 'n down the street. Are you ready?"

"Hell yes, we're ready!" Morris shouted. "Let's go!"

The five riders started to town, and though they wanted to keep their horses calm so they wouldn't be too tired out if they had to run later, the horses seemed to sense the riders' excitement and nervousness. The horses were rather skittish for the first few minutes. Finally, they got them all calmed down.

Cheyenne

"Here they come," Duff said. He said the words quietly, almost conversationally. He turned to look up onto the top of the leather goods store and saw that Elmer had seen them as well. Elmer and Duff exchanged nods.

A glance toward Wang showed that he, too, had seen the men coming into town.

"It's them!" Ina Claire said with a little gasp.

"Wait, lass," Duff said. "Don't spring the trap too quickly."

The five men rode by, continuing on beyond the bank to the far end of the street.

"They aren't going to do anything," Ina Claire said, disappointed.

"Hold on," Duff said. "I believe they are just looking things over. They'll be back."

True to Duff's prediction, when the riders reached the other end of the street they turned and started back toward the bank.

Duff snapped the reins over the team of mules, and the wagon started forward. Then, just on the other side of the bank, he turned the wagon so that it blocked off the approaching riders.

"Ladies, get down on the opposite side of the wagon," Duff said.

"Callahan, what the hell is that damn medicine wagon doing, parking in the street like that?" Cooper asked.

"I don't know," Callahan replied. "You!" he shouted. "Get that damn wagon out of the street!"

"I dinnae think so," Duff said, climbing down from the driver's seat. He was holding a pistol in his hand.

"What the hell do you think you're doin', mister?" Callahan demanded.

"I'm stopping you from robbing the bank," Duff replied.

"Callahan, that's the same son of a bitch that sent us to jail!" Manning yelled.

"Five to one? I don't think so, mister," Callahan said.

"He isn't by himself," Ina Claire said, stepping out from behind the wagon, brandishing the sawed-off shotgun.

"Damn!" Cooper shouted. "That's the cap'n's daughter."

"I'm glad you remember me," Ina Claire said. "I want that to be the last thing on your mind before you die."

"Ha!" Callahan said. "Five of us against one man and a girl?"

"And a woman," Meagan said, stepping out then.

"And a Shaolin priest," Wang said, having walked up from the apothecary so that he was now standing beside Duff.

"Hell, Callahan, the Chinaman don't even have a gun," Morris said.

"He don't need a gun, sonny," Elmer said. "I know Wang, 'n without a gun he's better than any two men with a gun."

Elmer had dropped down from the roof of the leather goods store and now stood in line with Duff, Wang, Meagan, and Ina Claire. Less than ten yards separated the two groups. The difference was, Callahan and his gang were still mounted, Duff and the others were on foot.

"I'll be for asking ye men to dismount, now, and drop your gunbelts," Duff said.

"The hell we will!" Callahan shouted, pulling his pistol. The others, taking their cue from Callahan, drew their guns as well.

For the next thirty seconds, Central Street could have been a battlefield in Tel-el-Kebir, or Shiloh, or Little Big Horn. Guns roared and billowing smoke clouds obscured the action.

Then the guns grew silent, the only sound remaining being the hoofbeats of the retreating horses.

All five men of the Callahan gang lay on the street, dead or dying from their wounds. Morris, who had pointed out that "the Chinaman don't even have a gun," was dead, a throwing star having severed his jugular vein.

Cautiously Duff approached them. Ina Claire started forward as well, but Duff held out his hand.

"Wait," he said.

Callahan was still alive, though barely.

"Three hundred thousand dollars," Callahan said.

"What?"

"I damn near got my hands on three hundred thousand dollars," Callahan said, a smile on his face. "That's a lot of money."

Duff started to tell him that it had all been a ruse, that the bank didn't actually have three hundred thousand dollars, but he held his tongue.

"Aye," he said. " 'Tis a lot of money."

"Damn," Callahan said. "I coulda . . ." he gasped a couple of times, then died.

A crowd began gathering in the street.

"Did you see that? That girl shot 'em!" someone said. "Who woulda thought a little girl woulda done somethin' like that?"

Ina Claire stepped up to the bodies and

looked down at them.

"Don't let this bother you, darlin'," Elmer said, walking over to stand by her. "These are the same sons of bitches that kilt your ma and pa. If ever there was anyone who needed killin', it's these five sorry bastards that's lyin' here."

"It's not bothering me," Ina Claire said. She broke down the shotgun and pulled the empty paper casings from each barrel. Then, bending down, she lay one of the expended shells on Cooper's body and the other on Manning.

"It's not bothering me at all," she said as she straightened back up. "I feel like Mama and Papa can rest in peace now."

"Aye, you're right, lass. And they'd be proud of you, the way I'm proud of you," Duff said.

"Thank you," Ina Claire said. "Thank all of you for helping me."

"Aye. Ye couldn't have stopped us, lass," Duff answered. "Now we should be going home. This day of reckoning is over."

ABOUT THE AUTHOR

William W. Johnstone is the *USA Today* and *New York Times* bestselling author of over 300 books, including *Preacher, The Last Mountain Man; Luke Jensen Bounty Hunter; Flintlock; Savage Texas; Matt Jensen, The Last Mountain Man; The Family Jensen; Sidewinders;* and *Shawn O'Brien Town Tamer.* His thrillers include *Phoenix Rising, Home Invasion, The Blood of Patriots, The Bleeding Edge,* and *Suicide Mission.* Visit his website at www.williamjohnstone.net.

Being the all-around assistant, typist, researcher, and fact checker to one of the most popular western authors of all time, **J. A. Johnstone** learned from the master, Uncle William W. Johnstone.

He began tutoring J.A. at an early age. After-school hours were often spent retyping manuscripts or researching his massive American Western History library as well as

the more modern wars and conflicts. J.A.
worked hard — and learned.

The employees of Thorndike Press hope you have enjoyed this Large Print book. All our Thorndike, Wheeler, and Kennebec Large Print titles are designed for easy reading, and all our books are made to last. Other Thorndike Press Large Print books are available at your library, through selected bookstores, or directly from us.

For information about titles, please call:
  (800) 223-1244

or visit our website at:
  gale.com/thorndike

To share your comments, please write:
  Publisher
  Thorndike Press
  10 Water St., Suite 310
  Waterville, ME 04901